The Tell-Tale Treasure

Diane Sawyer

Published by:
Southern Yellow Pine (SYP) Publishing
4351 Natural Bridge Rd.
Tallahassee, FL 32305

www.syppublishing.com

This is a work of fiction. Names, characters, places, and events that occur either are the products of the author's imagination or are used fictitiously. Any resemblance to actual persons, places, or events is purely coincidental.

The contents and opinions expressed in this book do not necessarily reflect the views and opinions of Southern Yellow Pine Publishing, nor does the mention of brands or trade names constitute endorsement.

ISBN-10: 1-940869-84-6
ISBN-13: 978-1-940869-84-1
ISBN-13: ePub 978-1-940869-85-8
ISBN-13: Adobe eBook 978-1-940869-86-5
Library of Congress Control Number: 2016952016

Printed in the United States of America
First Edition
August 2016

Dedication

As always, for my husband, Robert

Acknowledgments

Many thanks to the following:

My son Kirk, his wife, Lin, and their sons, Colin and Cael; my daughter, Barrie Sawyer Buenaventura, her husband, Lou, and their daughter, Sonia, for all their love and support

Peggy Nolan and Elenora Sabin, gracious and talented St. Petersburg writers and exceptional friends, for their advice and continued interest in my writing from the first draft to the last. With a heavy heart, I mourn the passing of Grace Murdock, incredible writer and longtime friend, who influenced this novel and all my previous writings.

My friends, family members, classmates, travel companions, and neighbors for their encouragement through the years.

My indispensable readers, Cindy Hanks, Polly Higgins, and Claire A. Stiles, for their generous time and effort with the manuscript.

The librarians and staff at the South Community Library in St. Petersburg, for their help and friendship.

Everyone at Southern Yellow Pine Publishing (SYP), from the enthusiastic publisher, Terri Gerrell, to her dedicated staff of editors, cover designer, production crew, and author-coordinator, for their assistance every step of the way. Last but not least, a special thank-you to the numerous SYP authors for their encouragement.

1
Frank Brandt

Sunday, October 12, 2008, 8:00 P.M.

I sat perfectly still in my seat. I didn't talk to anyone or look them in the eye. That kept my thoughts from racing like a team of wild horses through my head.

The applause exploded from everywhere! I gripped my binoculars and watched my beautiful Ivy walk with tiny steps to the center of the stage. Her gown and fancy high-heeled shoes sparkled. The conductor and orchestra didn't amount to squat. She smiled at me, only me.

"Rescue me, Frank. Take me home," she said through her musical instrument. Stupid people call it a Chinese fiddle, but I'm a super brain. I knew it was an erhu.

Monday, October 13, 2008

Ivy finally finished saying goodbye to her so-called friends at the ritzy Vinoy Hotel. I set my binoculars aside, revved up my tow truck, and headed to the circular drive. A parking guy signaled me forward. "Get out of my way," I told him. He said to give him the keys and he would park my vehicle. Vehicle? Big word from that little twerp. I hit the gas pedal and drove right past him like a tornado. He jumped back, tripped over his own feet, and shook his fist at me. "Too bad, loser," I shouted and laughed loudly.

Just in time, I saw Ivy driving away in a black Lincoln Town car. Raindrops splattered my windshield as I followed her to downtown St. Pete. She was such a tease. Wait, wait, and wait. All I could do was watch her while she visited shops and unloaded packages. Finally, she left. I trailed her to the Dalí Museum where I parked on the roadside, far from sneaky cameras and nosy security.

When Ivy returned to her car, I transmitted my thought, "It's time." She obediently drove to a Quick-Mart. I parked nearby and cut through the shrubs on foot, carrying my trusty wrench. She'd be so proud that I adjusted her car engine and beat my best time, two minutes four seconds. Nobody noticed me or my wrench. We were doing our job.

She left the Quick-Mart carrying a bottle of water and drove south. She wore the pretty black skirt, pink blouse, and little black shoes with embroidered designs. That's what she wore for the farewell breakfast at the Vinoy Hotel, but this time she dressed up just for me. It was our first date, and she wanted to impress me. Did she forget my transmitted thoughts? "Stay in St. Pete. Find a deserted area. I'll meet you there." We were approaching the Sunshine Skyway Bridge. I never expected her car to get this far.

Following at a distance, I paid the toll and headed over the bridge toward Sarasota. Off the bridge, the traffic thinned out. The sky was getting darker by the minute. At long last, her car stalled and jerked. I was super ready, with my cap tugged down and my nametag on my shirt pocket. She pulled onto the stretch of grass alongside the road. Trees and bushes grew everywhere and the road curved. This was great! We weren't so visible. She got out of the car and hurried to pull up the hood. It was dark, and she was probably frightened. She didn't know I was nearby, ready to rescue her. I posted the sign "Road Service" in my window and pulled in front of her.

I hurried out of my truck. When I saw a lake down a one-lane dirt road, a plan flew into my mind like a jet plane. This new plan would be difficult, but I couldn't risk towing a car across the bridge. There would be too many questions, too many suspicious minds.

I walked over to Ivy. She was surprised and then relieved to see a tow truck and me coming to help her. She smiled. I shone my flashlight up to my face, so she'd know it was me.

"Ivy, it's me, Frank. It's time to begin our life together," I said, blinking through the light. A look of fear spread across her face. "We have waited so long, my love," I said.

"Stay away from me," she shouted and her eyes went wild. "Help! Someone help me!"

I covered her mouth with one hand and took the syringe I'd hoped I wouldn't need from my pocket. I injected her with it. "Sleep, my darling," I told her.

She went limp in my arms. No cars passed by. I quickly set her on the floor of my truck by the passenger seat. Oh my. The touch of her little black velvet shoes made my fingers tingle. In two minutes flat, I opened the trunk of her car with her key, placed her suitcase in my truck's storage area, and set the erhu case at her feet. Unable to resist, I removed the erhu from the case and rested it on the seat so I could stroke it as I drove.

While she slept, I hooked her car to my truck and hauled it toward the lake. Electrified, I released her car, jumped out, placed my hands on the trunk of the car, and pushed hard. Once the car started down the incline, it built up speed and sunk beneath the surface.

I was delirious with joy. What was that? Bushes rustled behind me. I turned my flashlight toward my truck. It was Ivy, walking on unsteady legs toward the road. "Come back!" I cried.

"Leave me alone!" she shouted over her shoulder and struggled on through the vines and leaves. "Someone please help me!" She fell but got back on her feet. She was limping. She had lost a shoe, giving me a glimpse of her bare foot in the moonlight. The excitement of the moment thrilled me.

I caught up, encircled her with my hands, and pinned her arms to her sides. "Don't cry, little one," I whispered to her. "We're together now."

2
Rosie Renard

Rosie tossed her Rays baseball cap onto the table and dropped to her knees in front of the metal footlocker she'd set aside. What a busy morning. She, her cousin Jack, and her crew had already unloaded two truckloads of merchandise into the holding area of her popular second-hand shop, Rosie's Treasures. Now, came the fun part. Alone in the workroom, she briskly rubbed her hands together, anticipating—well, she didn't know what. Beneath the spider webs and dust, she just might discover a rare book, or a hand-carved toy, or a flowery love letter from long ago. It could be anything at all, and there was only one way to find out.

She began emptying the contents of the footlocker. A china tea set with an ivy-leaf pattern rested near the top. She gently pulled back the newspaper pages tucked around objects near the cups. What beauties! A sugar bowl and creamer with the same ivy design. Well, how about that? Two pillowcases with a chain of ivy leaves stitched along the edge.

She set all those items on a worktable and continued toward the bottom of the footlocker. She came across a man's tacky suit, shirt, and tie along with rumpled and stained gray work clothes. What were they doing here with all these fine things? She moved them aside and found exquisite hand-tailored silk blouses and a cream-colored gown. She held up the beaded beauty, and it slithered from her fingers toward the floor.

Her breath caught in her throat. The gown looked hauntingly familiar, like the one worn by world-renowned musician, Ivy Chen. But how could that be? Ivy Chen had disappeared from St. Petersburg several years ago, after playing a series of concerts with the Florida Orchestra. She had never been found. Curious, Rosie grasped the only remaining item, a large envelope, and tapped out the contents. Her heart beat wildly. A program from the Florida Orchestra fell at her feet and so did a large color photo of an erhu, a two-stringed musical instrument shaped something like a fiddle. It had python skin near the bottom, a typical feature of an erhu, and a carved dragon at the top. That wasn't typical at all.

"Oh my God!" Rosie exclaimed. That dragon. It was definitely Ivy Chen's erhu and that had to be her dress. Professional photos of Ivy Chen wearing that very dress and holding that unmistakable erhu had flooded the media, immediately after her disappearance.

Rosie backed away from the footlocker and squeezed her eyes shut. This was so familiar and so painful, it triggered heartbreaking memories of her cousin Tess, Jack's younger sister. Rosie took several deep breaths and tried to calm down. The police needed to know about the contents of this footlocker, but first she wanted to talk to Jack to lessen the shock. She pulled out her cell phone and pressed #1.

"Jack. It's Rosie." Her heart pounded. "I'm calling you before I call the police."

"What's wrong?" Jack's voice rose.

"I went through the footlocker. I found clothing and a photo, and I'm sure they belong to Ivy Chen. You remember her, the musician who disappeared." She blinked away her tears. "All I can think of is Tess."

"It's not the same, Rosie."

"But I keep replaying that day." A missing-person story always opened old wounds, especially if the person didn't survive. "If only we had waited for Tess after we got off the school bus. If we had, Tess wouldn't have been kidnapped and—"

5

"I know," Jack cut in. "I've told myself that so many times. And our parents never let us forget it."

Their words echoed through Rosie's mind. *"You abandoned Tess. You should have protected her."* Rosie sniffled. "I know we can't go back and change anything, but maybe there's something we can do for Ivy Chen."

"It's worth a try," Jack said.

"Yes it is," Rosie said defiantly.

"I hope Ivy Chen's family doesn't have to go through what we did." His voice cracked.

"I was thinking the same thing. I need to call the police."

"Get a detective who handles cold cases."

"Okay. We'll talk later. I'll let the police know we'd like to help find this missing woman."

"Maybe she's still alive," Jack said.

Chills swept through Rosie. Maybe this time, with Ivy Chen, the news would be good.

"Call me," Jack said quietly, and she knew what was going through his mind.

Rosie shuddered. Guilt about what had happened to Tess had clouded her life and Jack's too. She knew what Ivy's disappearance must have done to Ivy's family and what it must still be doing even now. She wanted to help bring them closure—and offer hope, slight as it might be, that Ivy could be found alive.

Rosie drew a deep breath and tapped #10, the St. Petersburg Police Department. "May I speak to a detective?" she asked.

"I'm Officer Jones. Maybe I could help."

"My name is Rosie Renard. I need a detective. It's about an old unsolved case."

"Just a minute. I'll transfer you to Detective DeLuca. He's in charge of cold cases."

"Miss Renard, this is Detective DeLuca." His deep voice had a pleasant lyrical quality. "I hear you may know something about a cold case. Talk to me."

"I just opened a footlocker I bought along with lots of old furniture and other things. I'm quite sure a dress and other items belong to Ivy Chen. A photo—"

"Ivy Chen, the musician? Hold on while I speak to my partner." His eagerness traveled through the phone.

Rosie heard Detective DeLuca muffled words: "Hank, could you pull up the file on Ivy Chen? Yeah, three years and three months ago. And let the tech team know we may be looking into her DNA. Thanks."

"Sorry about that, Miss Renard." His voice now came through clearly. "Where did you get this footlocker?"

"At an estate sale in Allendale."

"When?"

"Very early this morning. My cousin Jack Renard is in charge of the sale. I bought everything in the storage area over the garage, including the footlocker, more or less sight unseen." She gasped. "I'm wrong. I didn't buy everything. I left behind an old mattress, blanket, and pillow stashed in the corner. I was only looking for trunks and boxes that might hold collections. I didn't—"

"Where are you now, Miss Renard? What's the address of the house where you bought the foot locker? And what time did the estate sale begin?" His words rushed out.

"I'm at my shop, Rosie's Treasures, on Central Avenue. The estate's about fifteen minutes away in the Allendale neighborhood." She rattled off both addresses. "The sale began a few minutes ago at eight o'clock. I predict a mob scene."

"I'll meet you at your shop in ten minutes. The tech team will be coming along too. Please don't touch anything until I get there. I'd like your cousin Jack's cell phone number. I need to speak to him right away."

"Of course." She recited it from memory. "Detective, I'm confused about something."

"About what?"

"Newspaper pages in the footlocker were wrapped around a creamer and sugar bowl. Those pages are recent. They date from only two years ago."

"Forget about ten minutes. I'll be there in five!"

3
Ivy Chen

Monday, October 13, 2008

When I got out of bed and took several steps, I felt woozy and sat back down. I burst into tears as I realized that the man who stopped to fix my car had drugged me and brought me here while I was unconscious. He said his name was Frank. He said we would spend our lives together. He had me mixed up with someone else. I had to get out of here.

Holding onto the wall for support, I walked slowly through the dimly lit bedroom. The casual clothes I'd brought with me to Florida were piled on top of the bureau. My erhu rested against a chair, but my suitcase and concert clothes were nowhere in sight. I entered a small living room and headed for the door. I wanted to leave and call Mama. She was waiting for me in Sarasota. She must be worried sick about me.

A key rattled in the lock on the other side of the door.

The door whipped open and slammed against the wall.

I screamed as the man who called himself Frank stomped into the apartment. He was more muscular and stocky than I remembered, and his face was badly scarred with pock marks.

"I want to go home," I said. "My mother—"

He slapped me so hard I fell to the floor. My shoulder burned with pain.

"Please stop," I cried out.

"There are rules in my home," he said. "You'll learn them soon enough. Today's rule is don't talk back to Frank." He balled his hands into fists. "Say after me, I will not talk back to Frank."

"Please—" I tried to get up. He kicked me. Black spots jumped up and down before my eyes. My rib cage was on fire.

He raised his fists. "Say it."

"I will not talk back to Frank." Sobs burst from my mouth.

"That wasn't so difficult was it?" He asked.

"No," I said and gasped for breath.

His beady eyes bore through me. "I am providing this home for us. In return, I expect your obedience. Do you understand me?"

"Yes," I said and held back my tears. I didn't know what to do or say. This couldn't be happening to me. At any moment, I would surely wake up from this nightmare.

He pulled me to my feet, shook me, and threw me onto the floor. The last thing I heard was the door slamming. When I came to, my entire body ached. I didn't know how long I'd been lying there.

Despair came over me. I pulled myself up and stumbled to the bed. I sat down gingerly and cried until I had no more tears to shed. I turned on the lamp switch, but nothing happened. The darkness terrified me. I curled in a ball, closed my eyes, and tried to fall asleep, but a horrible thought overwhelmed me.

This wasn't a nightmare. This was my world. This was happening right now.

Tuesday, October 14, 2008

After only one day in this prison, I knew all too well the brutality Frank was capable of and that my life or death would be decided by him. During the following days, as I recuperated, Frank barged into my apartment three times a day to bring me fast-food meals. He wore work clothes covered with grease and stains. He barely spoke and stayed only long enough to slap or kick me or push me into the wall. As he left, he slammed the door behind him. The walls trembled, and so did I.

Painfully and slowly, during my recuperation, I searched every inch of these three small windowless rooms where my life took place. There was a bedroom, bath, a small area next to the bath with a refrigerator and sink, and a sitting area that also served as my music room where I played my erhu. My search turned up a dozen sheets of lined paper and two pens, tucked underneath the mattress as if hidden. But who would have hidden them there? I had no idea, but I planned to put them to good use so I could keep track of the days and record my thoughts and maintain my sanity. My first written words were:

> "This place is soundproof. The only natural light comes from a tiny skylight, but it's so high I would need a very tall ladder to reach it. I've tried throwing things at the glass to capture someone's attention in the outside world, but so far, no one has come to rescue me."

Other words followed later. After five days of this routine, I stopped feeling sorry for myself. There had to be skills I could put to good use. Most of all, I needed a plan of escape. The first beating left me too weak to walk, let alone escape, so I had to avoid another beating by any means possible. I clung to my erhu and played for short periods of time until the pain overwhelmed me. Then I stopped, cried myself to sleep, and hoped that tomorrow I would be stronger.

4
Rosie Renard

"Miss Renard?" the man asked as he strode into Rosie's workroom. Tall, with dark curly hair and craggy features, he wore a wrinkled gray T-shirt and black jeans. They looked like he'd slept in them for days. "I'm Detective DeLuca. Tony DeLuca."

"Call me Rosie."

"You bet. First off, Rosie, thanks for your call. I haven't had any good leads since I took over the case a year ago. I've read the file many times hoping to find one loose detail, something missed, anything, but nothing ever popped. All the way here, I kept wishing this would be the lead that would rev up the case. My tech team feels the same way. They'll be here very soon." He raked his fingers through his hair. "Now let's see that footlocker you mentioned."

"Here it is." She stepped past the two wooden trunks she'd also set aside. "And everything I found in it is over there on the table and workbench."

He whistled long and low as he stared at the formal gown draped over the table. "This could be the real thing," he said. He snapped on a pair of latex gloves and moved quickly from one item to the next. "In my twenty years on the force, I've never seen this much evidence turn up so many years after a disappearance."

He jotted a few things in his notepad. "Are you sure that's everything?"

"Not quite. Something in the footlocker struck me as odd."

"Talk to me."

"Everything I found in there is elegant. I'm talking about the women's clothing and even the two pillowcases, which are of designer quality. But the men's clothing is tacky."

"Men's?" His jaw dropped.

"Over here," she said and pointed out the men's inexpensive dressy clothes and the stained and tattered work clothes, lying in a heap next to the work bench. "I didn't want them touching the glamorous concert dress and nice things."

Before Rosie could say more, the tech team, three men and two women, arrived. They said a quick hello to her and conferred with Detective DeLuca. He quickly ran through the pertinent information and said, "Give Rosie a few minutes to fill me in about the men's clothes. Yeah, you heard right. Men's clothes. Meanwhile, you know what to do." The camaraderie between the tech team and the detective shone through the grim nature of their job.

Several minutes later, after discussing with Rosie the footlocker and the items in it, DeLuca called out to the tech-team guy wearing a Rays baseball cap. "Hey, Mack, I need you over here!" Mack hustled over and DeLuca said, "I'd like you to take the men's clothes back to the lab ASAP. Check for everything. And I mean everything."

DeLuca turned to Rosie. "The work clothes could be a turning point in the investigation. Think, Rosie. Did you happen to notice a brown leather suitcase in the storage area where you found the footlocker?"

"No."

"When Ivy disappeared, that we know of, she didn't have a footlocker. According to her mother and friends, she had a brown leather suitcase with her, filled with her clothes and personal items, stored in the trunk of her car. She was taking it with her to Sarasota to visit her aunts and her mother. Did you happen to see a suitcase at the estate?"

13

"No, but I never went inside the house. I only saw the storage area over the garage. I can say for certain there was no suitcase there. My cousin Jack would know about the contents of the house. He would know if a suitcase was there."

"Excuse me for one minute, Rosie. Don't touch anything, and don't leave. I need to call my partner, Detective Hernandez, and relay all this to him."

When Detective DeLuca finished his call, Rosie asked, "Do all these items belong to Ivy Chen?"

"I'm almost certain," DeLuca said as he came over to the table and stood near Rosie. "The day Ivy disappeared, she called her mother who was visiting friends in Sarasota, and said she'd be there later that day. She mentioned that she'd visited shops on Central Avenue and bought ivy-trimmed pillowcases and a tea set with an ivy design. So that accounts for those items."

He narrowed his eyes and studied the photo of the erhu. "Yes, indeed, it sure looks like Ivy Chen's musical instrument." He shook his head as if he still couldn't believe what he was seeing.

"I think so too," Ivy said. "Wood is my specialty. Ivy's erhu is made of China's prized, red sandalwood, a favorite wood of the Ming and Qing dynasties. When Ivy went missing, the newspapers had lots of information about the erhu, and her erhu in particular, including the wood. I added that information to my files."

"Thanks," DeLuca said and set down the photo. "If there's anything else you notice, just speak up. I'm open to anything that could help with the investigation." He glanced around the shop. "With your knowledge of merchandise, you might spot something significant."

"I'll be on the lookout for anything and everything," Rosie said, eager to help.

"Good. Let me jar your memory with the timeline when Ivy Chen disappeared. It was all over the media at the time, but it happened more than three years ago."

"Thanks. I'm sure I've forgotten many of the details."

DeLuca studied the workroom as he talked. "Ivy was at the Vinoy late morning. As I mentioned, she called her mother who was visiting friends in Sarasota to say she'd been shopping along Central Avenue and would arrive in Sarasota at dinnertime. She called again to say she'd visited the Dalí Museum. Back then, the detectives questioned employees and checked surveillance tapes in all those places. No one bothered Ivy in the shops or appeared to be following her. The Dalí Museum security tapes show her going through the galleries alone. No one pestered her. She left alone, and no one followed her car out of the parking lot. The tapes at the Sunshine Skyway Bridge show her crossing toward Sarasota around six. Again, no one appeared to be following her." He drew a deep breath. "Now, are those recent newspaper pages here?"

"Yes. Over there by the cups and saucers."

"Good," he said with a look of relief. "I'll wait for the tech team on that."

He waved his hand across the two wooden trunks. "Did they come from that house in Allendale too?"

"Yes."

He glanced around the workroom, the size of a one-car garage. Bins and shelves wrapped around the walls and overflowed with tools and supplies—varnish, hammers and nails, paint and brushes, sandpaper, glue, and a staple gun. Next to a washer and dryer stood a coat rack holding a hard hat, protective goggles, and paint-spattered shirts.

DeLuca took a second glance. "You said on the phone that you bought two truckloads of items. Where'd you store the rest?"

"There's a large holding area through those doors." She pointed at the double doors on the side wall. "It's twice the size of this room and jam-packed with stuff from this morning's estate sale and other sales too."

"There could be something belonging to Ivy Chen in a drawer, behind a cabinet door, somewhere like that. Have you checked through any of it yet?"

"No. I went right for the trunks, my specialty, and the footlocker too, often a gold mine of marketable items. My helpers, Rocco and

Alonso, unloaded the trunks and footlocker for me right here in the workroom."

"Okay. We'll want to look at everything in the holding area later." He pulled a pen and notepad from his pocket. "Right now, I need to confirm a few things. I have a few questions to help us identify and eliminate fingerprints."

"Sure. Go ahead."

"Who else, besides you, touched the footlocker and other items from the estate?"

"It's a short list. My helpers, the father and son team, Rocco and Alonso Conti. They've been with me all eight years since my shop opened. Jack Renard, my cousin—as you know, he's running the estate sale—helped us move things too." She paused for several seconds. "That's it. That's everybody."

"Thanks. When we're done, I'll need their phone numbers and addresses. We'll need to fingerprint them and you too. Meanwhile, could you fill me in on a few things?"

"I'll try."

"I'm not clear about how Jack ended up in charge of the estate sale and why you were there at five in the morning carting away stuff. I know about that early-morning drive-away because of an anonymous caller, probably a neighbor. She called the station to report that she saw flashlight beams crisscrossing the yard and driveway. Minutes later, she saw two trucks drive away loaded down with items from the estate. Officers went to investigate, but the neighbors had no additional information. None of them owned up to making the call, but we can trace it."

"I can clear all that up," Rosie said. "Jack was hired by the realtor who's selling the estate. It was owned by an elderly couple, the Cassells. They lived there for fifty years, but they'd been in failing health and passed away about a month ago, just days apart. They left the estate to their son and daughter. Jack can give you the names. All I know is they live out of state. They wanted the estate sold quickly, as is, without having to spend money on repairs. They asked the realtor to find someone to take care of the grounds, clean up the house, and sell off all the contents."

Rosie caught the detective's impatient expression and his fingers fidgeting with his pen. "Here it comes, Detective, the reason why I was there so early in the morning."

He brought his pen to a standstill. "Ready."

"The son and daughter didn't want lawsuits coming from crowds trekking up and down the steep stairs to the storage area over the garage. They asked Jack to find one buyer to buy out the entire upstairs contents before the sale inside the home began. Jack and I are close. We grew up a few houses apart in New York and moved here after college, looking for an exciting life. We weren't expecting it would involve the police."

"We get that a lot," the detective said. "So you're best friends."

Rosie nodded. "Jack called me about buying everything in the garage storage area. When my helpers and I finished clearing it out, Jack posted a sign declaring the stairs off limits and roped off the area. A smart move, considering that staircase. What a nightmare. I hope Rocco and Alonso are still speaking to me. Usually, I sort through and take what I want. But there wasn't time or enough light to inspect the two truckloads of treasures before driving them to my shop. We worked fast to load and unload everything so Jack could return to the estate before the crowds of bargain-hunters arrived."

"Okay. That explains that," DeLuca said and jotted a few words in his notepad. "I appreciate your extremely detailed explanation."

"That comes with my line of work," she said. "Customers love details. Sometimes it's what makes the sale happen." She noticed the hint of a smile at the corners of his mouth. "I talk when I'm nervous. Don't worry. I'll shrink my answers."

"Don't hold back. Your insights could help, so keep those details coming."

"Okay."

"Moving on, I'd like to bring you up to speed. Half the tech team is working the scene here, and the other half is at the Allendale estate. My partner, Detective Hank Hernandez, is in charge of that end of the investigation, and he'll be working with your cousin Jack. The estate sale will be postponed. Officers have been sent there to control the crowd and make sure nothing leaves the premises. Any questions so far?"

"No."

"Okay. I'm going to open the trunks and see if there's anything else of Ivy Chen's stored in them." He flexed his fingers in the latex gloves.

Tentatively, he opened the first lid and peered into the trunk. "Wow!" he exclaimed and quickly opened the other trunk. "They're both full. I'm looking at a possible fortune in bling, cash, bonds, coins, and watches. There must be at least thirty or forty watches. With this many, we're not looking at a collection of old family heirlooms...and all this silverware with lots of different monograms. You don't have to be Sherlock Holmes to figure out the contents came from several sources. Most likely, they were stolen. "

Rosie leaned closer. Her eyes popped at the sight. "Detective DeLuca, do you think this treasure has anything to do with Ivy Chen?"

"It's too soon to say. This is all light stuff you can pick up and run with. My best guess? A burglar gathered this stuff from different places and stored it here. I don't know how Ivy Chen fits into that, but the tech team should clear it up. Meanwhile, don't touch anything.

"Okay, Rosie," DeLuca said. "While the tech team does their work, let's get back to those trunks. Were they ever left alone here, say while you, your crew, and your cousin went back and forth to the estate?"

"No. We drove here from the estate in two trucks and unloaded everything into the holding area, except for the trunks and foot locker. I left my truck in the parking lot out back. Rocco and Alonso drove Jack back to the estate in their truck. I was here the whole time. Nothing in this workroom was ever out of my sight."

Detective DeLuca pursed his lips. "Nobody happened to drop by, say a friend or a regular customer?"

"No." She frowned. "What are you getting at?"

His eyes narrowed in determination, lending a steely look to his handsome face. "We're not sure what crime, if any, has been committed. Probably a robbery, given what's in the trunks. A possible abduction or even the murder of Ivy Chen, based on what the tech team discovers. I want to be thorough about who's been here since you brought in all this."

He checked his notepad. "And let's not forget that an anonymous someone called the station around five o'clock to report that two trucks were driving away with goods from the Cassell estate. Whoever called could have followed you. You could have something they want or something they don't want you to see. They might hurt you or maybe worse. The bottom line, Rosie, as part of this investigation, my job is to protect you, your helpers, and your cousin."

"Thank you, detective, and your team too," she said and glanced at them. They were working hard, poking through everything in the trunks and the contents of the footlocker.

"We'll get to the bottom of all this," DeLuca said. "After you removed everything from the footlocker, did the contents stay in this room or did you move a few things somewhere else? Don't rush your answer. This is important. Close your eyes and try to recall every move you made."

Rosie did as he asked and thought for several moments. Her eyes sprang open. "Everything's right here." She pointed toward the clothing and jewelry, the pillowcases, the tea set, and the photo of the erhu the tech team was examining with special flashlights.

"Do you have any questions?" he asked.

"Just one." She gnawed at the side of her lip. "I've been praying that Ivy Chen's alive." Her breath caught in her throat. "What are the odds of finding someone alive after more than three years?"

"Statistically, not good. But those two-year-old newspaper pages you mentioned are promising. If there are fingerprints and clues on those pages, our tech team will find them. Someone wrapped things in that newspaper two years ago. That's more than a year after Ivy went missing. It could be Ivy herself. It could be someone else, and that someone might know where she is. There's also the possibility that

19

someone saved those newspaper pages and only recently wrapped the tea cups with them."

"You think of everything," she said.

"That's how we approach every criminal investigation. Keep in mind, Ivy could be alive. My partner, Detective Hernandez, and our entire team will make every effort to find her. We're committed to that."

"So am I, and so is Jack." She choked up.

"What's wrong? You seem on the verge of tears."

"There's something I haven't told you," Rosie said. "It's painful to discuss. It's even harder for Jack, but I don't feel right keeping it from you any longer."

Detective DeLuca's eyes flashed concern. "If it's in any way related to this investigation, you need to tell me."

Rosie shifted from one foot to the other. "Years ago, my cousin Tess, that's Jack's sister, was abducted on her way home from school. Jack and I were with her minutes before she disappeared. A neighbor took her. She was only ten years old. He raped and murdered her and hid her body in his basement. She was found several days later."

The color drained from DeLuca's face. "I'm so sorry," he said.

"The neighbor, the killer, was caught. He was tried and convicted and sentenced to death. He's still on death row. I try not to think about him and what he did, but—" She took a deep breath. "I think maybe Jack figured by moving away from New York where it happened, to Florida, he could make a fresh start. He thought in new surroundings the loss of his sister wouldn't hurt as much. But we both know that's not the way the mind works."

She took several deep breaths to compose herself. "Jack's a private person. He won't want to discuss it, but I can tell you this. Our helping you find Ivy Chen alive would mean so much to both of us." She took one more deep breath. "Am I crazy, thinking Ivy Chen could help us find peace in some way?"

"It's not a crazy thought. And I'm glad you told me about Tess. The outcome in a missing person case can turn completely around in a heartbeat. Happy endings are possible. We wish they happened more often, but we don't give up."

"Have you seen many of these cases?" Rosie asked.

He nodded.

"And how do they usually turn out?"

"Bad."

"I've only seen one...and it turned out really bad. Maybe this time it will be different."

DeLuca's eyes clouded over. "I'm sorry about Tess," he said. "We see so much suffering in this line of work, but we never get used to it, especially when it involves children."

Rosie blinked away her tears. "Tess was a great kid, with a real funny sense of humor. Jack and I miss her so much. Sometimes I think Jack and I are close because we see reminders of Tess in each other. Jack wouldn't admit it, but it's true. Our parents see Tess in us and often remind us of that. Too often, maybe. We were twelve when Tess disappeared."

Tears pooled again in Rosie's eyes. "I'm not looking for sympathy. I just want you to know that Jack and I are rooting for you. Jack called me just before you arrived. He'd like more than anything to be there when Ivy Chen is found alive. He's counting hard on seeing one family reunited. It's too late for our families but maybe not for Ivy's family. We're willing to help you in any way. Please remember that."

"Thank you, Rosie. I'll pass along to Detective Hernandez what you shared with me. We'll keep it in mind. You never know about cold cases. New leads can give us a good outcome."

"I'm with you on that," Rosie said and brushed away her tears.

"You've been here eight years you said?"

"Right."

"So you've seen lots of changes in the area."

She nodded. "Back then, the Grand Central District wasn't a vibrant place like it is today. This was a run-down, two-story rambling building, but I fell in love with the possibilities."

"You bought it."

21

"Me and the bank. I took out a loan, plunked down several months' rent, and refinanced a mountain of college debt. Luck was on my side. The area caught on and expanded with restaurants and bars, art galleries and craft shops. Next thing you know, the Central Avenue Trolley was bringing people to the area. The stars must have been aligned because the first trolley stop is smack-dab in front of my shop, another bit of good luck. I live in an apartment upstairs, so I save commuting costs and rent too."

He frowned. "Do you live alone?"

"Yes. Why do you want to know?"

"Your shop is part of an investigation. Curiosity seekers and sometimes troublemakers come by. Maybe you shouldn't be here alone for a while. Is there anyone who could stay with you?"

"No. My boyfriend and I are taking a break from each other. It may stay that way permanently."

"So it would be accurate to say he's out of your life."

"Yes." She shrugged. "Well, it's more like a definite maybe."

"In that case I'd like his name, what he does for a living, and where he lives and works. Give me all the details."

"Why?"

"I need to check him out. If he comes back into your life, he'll be here. He may overhear things that are police business, and we'll want to give him the same protection we're giving you, your helpers, and your cousin Jack."

Rosie nodded. "Okay. I understand. His name's Ted Romero, and he manages an organic produce business. He lives near Boyd Hill Nature Preserve in South St. Pete. "As you can guess, he loves the outdoors and Mother Nature."

DeLuca cocked an eyebrow. "If there was an emergency, he could be here in about twenty minutes?"

"Right. And the farm area where he works is in Hillsborough County, near Tampa. That's maybe forty-five minutes away."

DeLuca's phone rang. He checked caller ID. "I have to take this," he said and stepped away.

Thoughts of Ted filled Rosie's mind. He brought fun into her life. He believed in balance, a time for work and a time for play, or as he said, "Time to sort produce and time to make love." She missed Ted. He was such a great guy. Why had she driven him away? What was she thinking?

DeLuca slid his phone into his jeans' pocket. "Okay, Rosie. Tell me what else I should know about Ted Romero."

Rosie snapped back to the present. "You mean like is he a good guy? Does he have good values?"

"We're on the same page," DeLuca said. "But I'll need a few facts."

"Okay. Besides managing an organic food co-op, he writes an online newsletter about nutrition. He's passionate about the earth. He grew up on his grandfather's farm in the Midwest and fell in love with planting and harvesting. During summer vacations from college, he worked as a landscaper's helper. He moved to Florida so he could fish and swim when he wasn't farming. And he dances a lot."

She caught the smile crossing DeLuca's face. "You told me not to hold back on details."

DeLuca smiled again. "I think you'll be glad to have him back in your life."

"I think you've been reading too many Dear Abby columns, but you could be right. I sort of miss him."

"You could call him and see if he'd come over and stay with you for a while. With all that's going on here, it might be a good idea."

The detective's phone rang. "Sorry again, Rosie," he said and stepped away. "Hey, Hank. How's it going there?" After several minutes and a mixture of frowns and smiles, DeLuca finished the call.

"Some good news?" she asked.

"Police business, which I can't discuss," he said. "But I can tell you this. Detective Hernandez is on his way here with your cousin Jack. Like you predicted, the Cassell estate turned into a mob scene—trucks and vans everywhere—angry people wanting to peek in windows. The officers are doing their best to keep everything under control. The estate sale is postponed for a few days, maybe longer, depending on what we find. And I think you've already figured out what's going to happen here at Rosie's Treasures."

She nodded. "Examining a new load of goods is like an addiction for me. I can't wait to get started, but I know that nothing can be touched until you're finished here."

"It's not all bad news, Rosie. You can go about your business in the front of your shop but not here in the workroom or holding area."

"I understand," she said.

"One more thing. The fewer people who know about what's going on here, the better. Crowds of curious people can slow things down. They can even contaminate evidence."

"I'd better call Rocco and Alonso."

"Thanks to Detective Hernandez, that's already been taken care of."

A knock at the back door startled Rosie, but then she sighed with relief. "Come on in," she said, and stood on tiptoes to give her cousin Jack a peck on the cheek. He gave her a big bear hug, lifting her off her feet.

"Rosie, this is Detective Hernandez," Jack said, introducing the tall slender man with a winning smile. "He gave me a ride here."

After introductions all around, Detective Hernandez peered into the trunks. "Looks like the pirates stopped here on the way to the Caribbean."

Rosie picked up on his soft melodic speech. Possibly he could be Jamaican or Bahamian, but she held her natural curiosity in check and didn't discuss it with him. Right now everyone needed to concentrate on Ivy Chen.

5
Ivy Chen

Tuesday, October 28, 2008

I have been here one whole week. I'm certain because I've been keeping track on the composition paper I found. I figured out it was still Monday when I woke up because Frank was wearing the identical shirt with a ripped collar and the same pants with grease on the pocket. Today, I worked up the courage to ask Frank if I might step outside and breathe the fresh air. He deprived me of food and water for an entire day. In case I didn't take him seriously, he threw me on the floor and kicked me. Black and blue marks soon covered my body, and I felt very weak. There was so much I wanted to write, but the beating sapped my energy. Instead of writing, all I could do was try to organize my thoughts.

Another week has gone by since Frank Brandt kidnapped me. The two pens and twelve sheets of paper have nearly run out. I needed a notebook and more pens, but I knew better than to ask Frank for anything because he interpreted requests as an insult to his generosity. I already learned that the hard way when I asked to go outside.

From my first moments here, the sound of a key fumbling at the lock to my door, knowing that Frank was about to enter my room, gave me a feeling of terror. My heart would beat loudly. A sick feeling of uncertainty would come over me. What would be expected of me? What would happen to me? I was terrified that Frank was going to insist on sex and resort to rape if I didn't agree. But Frank didn't demand or expect sex. He wanted, he claimed, "his right to be my only audience." Civilizing him with my music was my best chance of avoiding beatings and staying alive. I couldn't eliminate his ingrained brutality, but with effort, maybe I could curb it.

Although many people say the distinctive sound produced by the erhu resembles a woman's voice, Frank maintained it *was* a woman's voice—not just *any* woman's voice. He insisted it was *my* voice. This obsessive fascination offered me hope. If I found a way to take advantage of the erhu's power over Frank, I would be one step closer to leaving this three-room windowless prison.

Every day after work, Frank came to my apartment, sat down on the couch, and waited for me to play the erhu. I sat across from him and took my time as if I were performing at a great concert hall. I balanced my erhu on my left thigh and held the bow in my right hand, which was upturned. I passed the bow back and forth across the erhu's two strings with my right hand while my left hand stopped the strings. My right arm worked hard, and glorious sounds rose and filled the room. I was hoping the age-old rituals of classical music would chip away at Frank's brutal nature. It seemed to be working, although not consistently, but any little bit of progress was extending my life on earth.

To help me clarify my thinking and come up with ideas that might help me escape, I picked up a pen and paper and began writing:

> "The only escape from my apartment is through the doorway that connects to Frank's 'principal residence.' That's what he calls his part of the house, keeping with his habit of making up fancy expressions for anything about himself. I have never seen his quarters because he doesn't allow me to leave my apartment. I miss the sunshine, taking long walks, talking to friends, everything about my old life. One thing I know for certain. If I am ever going to escape from this prison, I must find a way into Frank's quarters. But how is it

26

possible? I am frustrated and disappointed that I can't come up with a solution.

"He insists that I call him Frank. My other names for him, like delusional psychotic, I keep to myself. Once, in a moment of complete despair, I shouted, 'You crazy psycho,' to his face. He knocked me to the floor and threatened to storm out of this house and never return, leaving me to die a long, slow death alone. He told me that in his home, he was in charge, and he wanted respect. At work, the guys called him Pock-Face and Pit-Face. He had no control over them because they had seniority, but he had complete control over me. He often said that if I knew what was good for me, I'd call him Frank. I have decided that as part of my escape plan, I must always address him as Frank. I can't risk being abandoned here and left to die from starvation and dehydration. That's how Frank threatens me. He tops it off with a slap, a kick, or a punch, and sometimes all three."

I set aside my pen and paper and tried to put things in perspective. The hardest part of my life was seeing and talking to only one person, Frank Brandt. I had lived my first eighteen years without ever leaving China, and later because of my career, I became a citizen of the world. I'd had contact with so many people and enjoyed our conversations. In all those years, I had never experienced such evil. Frank was a crude, punitive, volatile man, the opposite of every trait a good person possesses. He knew nothing about compassion, gentleness, or tolerance. He had no concept of balance or harmony. He didn't understand we must give people respect or that in Chinese tradition, respect equaled face, and face, meaning one's sense of dignity or prestige, equaled a sense of worth and honor. Face held more importance than truth or justice. I wished he comprehended the basic truths that, as human beings, we must maintain dignity, avoid conflict, and strive for elegance.

My beloved Baba taught me the ways of the Chinese, the honorable values by which we should live. Mama reinforced what Baba said, giving examples from her American world where she was born and lived until she met Baba in Shanghai at a language school, and they married. I must not forget my parents' teachings or begin to doubt them. To do so, would mean I was giving in to Frank's evil way of thinking and acting. In the end, I would adopt all his despicable ways.

Baba used to say if you threw a dirty shirt in the laundry with a clean shirt, the clean one would get dirty. Then he added, the story didn't end there. If you separated the two shirts, and washed each one by itself, the shirt that had been clean but was now dirty would become brighter with each washing until it was like its old self. Remembering his words, I wiped away the tears running down my cheeks. I would never become like Frank. I had two powerful weapons, my upbringing and my heritage. They would help me stay strong and positive and focused. I would set aside my sadness and put all my energies into finding a way to escape.

If I allowed myself time to dream, my thoughts turned to Vincent Ivanov, my sweet Vince. I hadn't known him very long, but we loved talking to each other about everything and nothing. He had such a tender heart. I feared that he had already forgotten me. Our time together was brief, but I would never forget him. He loved the violin the way I loved the erhu. I grew up in a home where my parents and I spoke Chinese and English. Because of his parents' heritage, he spoke Italian and Russian at home, and in school he learned English. His accent was beautiful.

Closing my eyes, I thought about what might have been. I now knew the sweet regret of a budding love that would never have a chance to blossom. Whenever I was overwhelmed by Frank's cruelty, I thought of Vince, the complete opposite of Frank. I hoped when I was free and back in my familiar beautiful world, Vince and I would take a long walk in the moonlight. We would talk until the moon and the stars faded away and the sun came up.

Tuesday, November 4, 2008

To enjoy some measure of happiness, I chose the music for each day with great care, making selections that lifted my spirits and allowed me to briefly escape this horrible existence. How I loved *The Garden Field in Spring*. It filled my mind with pictures of the gardens of my childhood. *Flying a Kite* brought a smile to my lips as I pictured the wind encouraging the kite to soar in a clear blue sky. My favorite at the moment was *Small Flower Drum*, a delicate piece that reminded me of the beauty in the world beyond this prison. I used to love *The Flickering Candle Light*, but I no longer played it. Flickering, about to be extinguished, the loss of light, these concepts were heartbreaking to contemplate. I promised myself that when I returned to the bright world where I used to live, I would play *The Flickering Candle Light* every day and enjoy its sad beauty.

Sunday, December 28, 2008

Even expressing myself in as few words as possible and on rare occasions, I used up all my paper. I was desperate to record my thoughts in a freer more expressive style so that it sounded like me, not some robot. Frank never saw my pages, and he never saw me write a single word. I was afraid he would destroy everything, but I could not continue that way. I was ashamed then and now to admit I relied on deceit. I told Frank I was running out of ideas about how to make the erhu speak to him. I said a notebook would allow me to write down my thoughts about what the erhu would be able to express to him. That sent him into a frenzy of shouting and stomping around. He turned his anger on me and shoved me with tremendous force. I hit the floor hard and cried out in pain. My knee, already the victim of a previous beating, felt like it was going to explode.

Frank ignored me. He punched the walls until his knuckles bled. He stomped back and forth in front of me, shouting frantically about the unfairness of facing life without the erhu's voice. He looked at me like he was seeing me for the very first time. He stared for several long seconds at my hands, arms, and shoulders. His stare shifted to the erhu. Without a word, he stormed out of the room. I worried he would return and beat me unconscious.

The very next day, December 29th, he flung a stack of brand-new notebooks and several pens at my feet. I couldn't believe this was actually happening. My deceit worked. He believed I needed, that the erhu needed, the notebooks. My knee was very sore. It was turning black and blue, but it wasn't broken, and I have been babying it to encourage the healing process. If I suffered a broken bone or life-threatening injury, I would never see a doctor or a hospital. I was terrified I would die here, but I tried to remain positive. The notebook allowed me to stay in touch with reality and clarify my thoughts about finding a means of escape. Maybe, with luck, I could come up with behaviors and strategies that would stop Frank from beating me. Weakness and achiness became my daily companion. That must change or escape would not be possible.

Saturday, January 17, 2009

I thumbed through the pages of my notebook, overflowing with my thoughts expressed with Chinese characters, until I came to the first blank page. After taking several deep breaths to calm myself, I began recording my thoughts:

> "I feel so defeated today. I have been Frank's prisoner for more than three months, since Monday, October 13th, 2008. Is this what my life is going to be forever, trapped here, at the mercy of a vindictive man who punches and kicks me, knocks me around, deprives me of light, and keeps me locked up? That thought goes through my mind over and over again. But I must not squander paper and ink with defeatist words. I must continue to record the facts so that I can review them often. They will allow me to see opportunities to defeat

Frank, gain control of him and my surroundings, and plan my escape.

"For now, I am still catching up with a more detailed account of all that happened since Frank drugged me and brought me here. The very first day I began writing in my notebook, Frank asked to read it. He was furious because I was writing in Chinese. I told him that's what the erhu wanted, that's what the erhu understood. Sometimes I wonder who's crazier, Frank or me. Then a crazy boldness came over me, and I told him he must never touch the notebook or let anyone else touch it. If that happened, the erhu would lose its power of speech. He said I was bossing him around, and he kicked me in the shin. Before his anger intensified, I picked up my erhu and bow and sat down on the chair, ready to play.

"I told him calmly that if anyone touched my notebook, the erhu would remain silent. The notes would still be heard, the music would continue, but the erhu's voice would be silenced. I told him I could demonstrate how that would sound. But he yelled at me to stop and not to even think about such 'blast-phony.' I didn't laugh at his mispronunciation of blasphemy. He brags about his intellect and likes to impress me. I was just thinking about my little moment of triumph, regarding the erhu's voice remaining silent, when Frank slapped me hard across the face.

"'Don't forget your fate is in my hands,' he said. 'Life or death, it's up to me.'"

I set down my pen and notebook. Before he turned on me, I actually thought the erhu and I might talk our way out of here by threatening silence. How could I be so naïve, so rational, so hopeful with an insane and cruel person in charge of my life?

Unwilling to even think about an answer to that question, I burst into tears.

6
Frank Brandt

Tuesday, January 20, 2009

I pulled into the same parking place at work, next to the rusted-out car corpses, third space from the end. The dogs snarled. They stood on their hind legs and clawed the chain link fence, trying to get to me and rip out my throat.

Here we go again. Same old yapping and baring their teeth like they thought they could scare me. They didn't get it. They were prisoners in a pen. I was free to come and go as I pleased.

Grabbing my lunchbox, I slid out of my truck and picked up a handful of gravel. "Get lost, you stupid ugly mutts," I shouted and threw the gravel at them through the openings in the fence. Good for me for scoring some mighty fine hits. They skulked away. I won. They lost.

I knew what my day would be like. No surprises. Remove the parts, chop the cars, flatten the cars, pull another wreck off the highway, and start all over again.

It was terrible having to work with these jerks. They were taller and tougher than me, and they liked to taunt me and throw insults in my face. I wasn't pathetic. They were. If they knew what my life was like, they'd want to be me.

Ivy waited for me at the end of every day. She and her sweet erhu talked to me about pretty things. They never criticized me. They loved me. What's that big word everybody on TV talked about? Un-condition-only. Ivy and her erhu—they were almost one and the same—they loved me un-condition-only. Not quite, but I was working on it. And I knew how to get results.

I opened the door to the shop and braced myself for the guys' nasty comments. Here came the boss followed by his adoring squad of thugs. They wouldn't get the better of me. I'd make it through this day. Ivy was waiting. Soon I'd be home with Ivy. All I had to do was teach her to love, honor, and obey me. Any day now, she'd wise up. If not, there were other pickings out there.

7
Rosie Renard

Saturday, January 7, 2012, 12:15 P.M.

Detective Hernandez opened the door and came into Rosie's workroom with Jack following right behind him.

"Jack has some information about the Cassell estate I'd like you both to hear," Detective Hernandez greeted Detective DeLuca and Rosie. "He found out something very interesting. Go for it, Jack!"

Jack eased his tall, lanky body past Detective Hernandez into the center of Rosie's workroom. "Hey, Cuz," he said and gave Rosie a quick smile as he leaned against the workbench. "When I started cleaning up the estate for the owners a few days ago, several neighbors, about ten I'd say, came over to thank me. They lived close by. They were glad to see the Cassell house being spruced up. They were afraid in its present condition it would hurt the values of the homes on their street, but they saw tremendous possibilities."

"How about giving me some examples. I haven't seen the house yet," DeLuca said.

"If you overlook the neglect, you'll see a fantastic home. Large, two-story, stone façade. It's a real gem."

He cleared his throat. "But here's the part Detective Hernandez wants me to tell you. I asked them who'd been living in the garage. They said no one as far as they knew."

"Get to the good stuff," Detective Hernandez encouraged.

"I'm just laying some groundwork. A little landscaping humor," he said good-naturedly. "One of the neighbors, Ben Andrews, hung around. You know the type. He lets you know he's got the inside track on what's going on. So I raked while Ben talked. He said a local handyman had done a lot of work for the Cassells. They allowed him to use the garage. He kept it locked because that's where he stored tools, paint, and other supplies."

Jack removed his Rays baseball cap, wiped his brow with his sleeve, and plunked his cap back on his head. "I told Ben I wanted to get in touch with the handyman to have him remove his stuff from the garage. Ben said, 'Lots of luck.' According to Ben, the guy never stayed too long in one place, and he went everywhere by bike. To Ben that meant no car, no license, no forwarding address, no way of tracking him down."

Jack shrugged. "I called the realtor and got the handyman's name from Gary Cassell, the owner. I tried to locate this handyman guy. You know, Google him, Facebook, Craig's List, Angie's List, the usual ways, but no luck. I even tried Old School. You know, posted a sign on the garage door asking him to call me in case he turned up. Anyway, I never got through to him."

He swiped the perspiration from his brow again. "Sorry. I've been working non-stop at the estate, but getting back to the handyman. I had no reason to go to the police or suspect foul play, so I stopped looking. I was consumed with the Cassell estate. This was a rush job to get the house, yard, and garage in good enough condition to sell the place for a decent price. Then I had to dispose of all the furniture, clothing, everything. Even with all my helpers and contact people, we've put in long, hard days for two weeks. We were pressed for time. It wasn't possible to give locating the handyman another minute."

"Tell Detective DeLuca the handyman's name." Hernandez rolled his hands forward, urging Jack along.

"Ron Hemmings."

"You're kidding me." Detective DeLuca rocked back on his heels. "Hemmings involved in this? He left clues? Finally, he's getting careless!"

36

"Detective Hernandez had the same reaction. Now you?" Jack asked. "Can anyone tell me what the heck is going on here?"

"Hey, I'd like to hear it too," Rosie said. "And we can sit down. There are chairs—"

"No. We're fine," Hernandez said.

DeLuca picked up the story. "Hemmings is as slippery as wet tile. He's in and out of a house in minutes and doesn't leave a trace. He can pick a lock and crack a safe in record time. Neighbors see shadows. They hear cats meowing. Several people once thought they saw someone in a wetsuit. Others said the guy wore black clothes and a ski mask and carried a black backpack, but no one ever saw his face."

"Snorkel Man and Backpack Man were his nicknames for a while," Hernandez added.

"How did you find out his real name?" Rosie asked, eager to hear any bit of information that might open up the case.

"Luck was with us," Hernandez said. "Two years ago when Hemmings was robbing a house, the family returned. As they approached the house, they saw the beam of a flashlight moving across the living room. They hid behind the bushes, and the owner called the police on his cell phone. Officers arrived. Either Hemmings had all the loot he was able to carry, or something spooked him. He escaped through a window into an alley. He broke the glass to get out. Part of his pants and a bit of skin caught on a nail on the windowsill. The tech team got his DNA off that nail. Let me back up. Before the tech team arrived, the officers caught him in the alley and arrested him. He got off on a technicality, but having his DNA in the system cuts his chances of remaining a free man."

"You got that right," DeLuca said. "We've been saying it's just a matter of time. Well, it seems time has run out for Ron Hemmings. Where are we with this, Detective Hernandez?"

As hope sprang up that the detectives were making progress, Rosie grabbed Jack's hand and squeezed it. Perhaps this man named Hemmings might be found, and he would lead them to Ivy.

"I already called the station," Detective Hernandez said. "I told them we need to know Hemmings' last known address because he might be involved in the Ivy Chen case. Two officers are working it. As soon as they find out where Hemmings lives, we'll pay him a visit. I can't wait to see the look on his face when we show up."

Hernandez' phone rang. He listened for a few seconds, and Rosie figured that Hemmings had been located, and maybe he was on his way to the police station.

"Crap!" Hernandez bellowed. "How long ago?" He slammed his free hand against the wall. A few seconds passed, and he slammed the wall even harder. "Get back to me." He closed his phone. "Hemmings died a month ago. No one claimed the body."

DeLuca gritted his teeth. "Just when we were making progress!"

Rosie looked back and forth from one to the other trying to digest all that was being said.

"A charitable organization buried him," Hernandez said. "Anything he might have known about Ivy Chen died with him. Damn!"

Disappointment overwhelmed Rosie. Hemmings, the possible link to Ivy had just been severed.

Hernandez's phone rang again. He talked briefly, finished the call, and turned to DeLuca. "That was the tech team at the garage site. They're finished going over the mattress, blanket, and pillow. Now they're checking out the food wrappers and junk left on the ground floor of the garage along with the tools and equipment. Let's hope they find something that will give us Hemmings' DNA and maybe someone else's too. Maybe Ivy Chen's. Someone who can tell us what went on in that garage."

"I'll say a prayer to make those words come true," Jack said.

"I'll second that," Rosie said.

"Jack," DeLuca said, "we'd like the names and addresses of all the neighbors who spoke to you about Ron Hemmings. The sooner the better."

"Sure thing," Jack replied. "I added their names to my iPhone. You know; they might be future customers. I can have that for you in a few minutes." He stepped aside, worked quickly, and handed the detective the information.

38

"Thanks," Deluca said. "We'll eventually canvass the entire neighborhood, but we'll begin with these names."

Rosie jumped in. "I may know something about the Kinters. They live on the block behind the Cassell estate. I should have thought of this sooner and made a connection. I'm sorry. I was upset. All kinds of stuff was going through my mind. I wasn't thinking straight; I goofed."

"I understand," DeLuca said. "Talk to me about the neighbors, the Kinters."

Rosie swallowed hard. "This is about pillowcases with an ivy leaf on a vine embroidered along the edge, just like Ivy Chen's pillowcases. I'm sure more than two sets of them were manufactured, but—"

"Tell us what you know," DeLuca said, reaching for his notepad and pen.

"Mrs. Kinter called me at my shop about three months ago. They had furniture and other items they wanted to sell. I went there and bought everything. You know how it goes. Empty-nest syndrome, time to downsize, let's start living, honey."

She sensed DeLuca's rapidly clicking pen signaled his impatience. "Among the treasures I bought was a pair of ivy-trimmed pillowcases." They were luxurious, much better quality than anything else the Kinters were selling. I mentioned that tactfully to the couple. I have to be careful, Detective. I don't want to end up dealing in stolen merchandise."

"Good to know," DeLuca said.

Rosie shot him a deliberate look. "I finally came right out and asked Mrs. Kinter where the pillowcases came from. She said they'd bought everything at a flea market. They were thinking of refinishing furniture as a hobby. They hoped to renew the old spark of togetherness. They tried one small nightstand, but the Florida heat beat down. Tempers flared. She ripped the sander from the socket and flung it into the bushes, and her husband threw the glue gun in the trash. She told him 'it's me or this hobby from Hell.' You get the picture."

DeLuca nodded. "It happens in the best of marriages," he said, and Rosie wondered if he was speaking from experience. "Tell me,

Rosie, did the Kinters mention the seller's name or the name of the flea market or anything about the pillowcases?"

"No. And they moved. I don't know where."

"Are any of those items still in your shop?" DeLuca asked.

"I think they were all sold, but I'll check my records. I keep a complete list of buyers and goods and dates. I often contact previous customers to let them know something similar to what they bought just came in."

"Thanks. We'd like that information as soon as possible."

"Sure."

Jack piped up, "Maybe I should have pressed Ben Andrews for more information about Ron Hemmings' activities in the neighborhood. He might know something."

"Don't second-guess yourself," DeLuca said. "You couldn't have known where this investigation was headed."

"And don't worry, Jack," Detective Hernandez added. "We'll take it from here. We'll track down Mr. and Mrs. Kinter and see what they can tell us."

"Maybe I can speed up your search for the Kinters," Rosie said. "I made a notation about the property on Lake Michigan where they owned a vacation home. I thought maybe they'd like to pop into my shop and see if there was anything that would look good up north."

"Great!" DeLuca exclaimed. "Can you get that address right now?"

"Sure. And I wish I'd thought of those pillowcases sooner." She left and was back in a flash with the address and phone number scribbled on a slip of paper.

"I'll get to this in a minute," DeLuca said. "Now Rosie and Jack, there's something you can do for us."

"Name it," Jack said.

"I'd like you and Rosie to walk through the holding area and make two lists—the items from the estate on one list, and the items that were already here on the other list."

DeLuca stroked his chin. "Be very careful and very precise. If the two of you don't agree, stop and think again. This is important. We don't need to concern ourselves with stuff that didn't come from the

Cassell estate. Rosie, definitely check your records to see if everything from the Kinters was sold, especially the pillowcases. And I'd like you to double-check everywhere for those pillowcases. What do you say?"

"I can handle that," Rosie said.

"Me too," Jack agreed.

DeLuca smiled. "Rosie and Jack, cousins, huh? You look somewhat alike, and you seem to think alike."

"We hear that all the time," Rosie said. "People mistake us for brother and sister. Some even think we're twins."

"You're not gonna believe this," Jack said and shook his head. "We've been asked if we're identical twins. I say, 'go take an anatomy class.'"

"Good one," DeLuca said. "Now before you get started in the holding area, do you mind telling me in a sentence or two about the business you're in?"

"No problem," Jack said. "You've got a case to solve. I can fly the facts past you in two minutes. Eight years ago, I set up my own computer repair business. I had several companies that kept me busy full-time keeping their electronics in good running condition. When the economy tanked, I farmed out that work and jumped at what I saw as a great opportunity in the housing market. I clean out and rejuvenate foreclosures, abandoned houses, and 'as is' properties for owners and investors. I have steady customers like Rosie who buy up entire contents, and that gives my fix-up crew room to work. I have other steady customers who buy collectibles and resell them on eBay. And, of course, several antique dealers. That's it."

DeLuca clicked his pen closed. "Okay. Glad I asked. Before you get busy in the holding area, we'd like a list of those steady customers. And the names, addresses, and phone numbers of your fix-up crew too."

"They're not in any trouble are they?"

"No. This is our way of gathering names of everyone who might have noticed something that might help us. It's routine."

"No problem." Jack held up his iPad. "I can make a copy and drop it off at the police station."

"Good," DeLuca said. "If other names come up, let us know. We need to make sure that nothing slips through the cracks."

"Then, I'd better get started," Rosie said. "Jack, catch up with me as soon as you finish the lists." Filled with a sense of purpose, she took off toward the holding area.

8
Ivy Chen

Monday, February 2, 2009

I slipped into my favorite cotton slacks and T-shirt and put on my sandals. I didn't want to spend the day in my pajamas and robe. I wanted to distinguish between day and night and maintain a routine, a sense of normalcy, a belief that I had some control over my life. I picked up my pen and began recording my worries in my notebook. Seeing them on paper often pointed me in a good direction:

> "I am so alone and so frightened. Being locked up with this monster, Frank Brandt, is unbearable. What terrifies me most is this imprisonment may go on forever. I pray every night that someone will find me soon. But as days and weeks have passed, I wonder if anyone will ever come to my rescue. The only person who knows I am here is a mysterious woman who arrives, usually every other Saturday, but sometimes another day instead. I can tell from the sound of her voice as she hums off-key with a wailing tone and her high-pitched hacking that the person is definitely a woman. She doesn't speak, and she makes little noise."

I set down my pen and thought about this mysterious woman and Frank's behavior. At first, Frank taped my mouth shut, blindfolded me, and tied me to a chair while she was in the apartment. Later when I agreed not to resist, he gave up the blindfold, the tape, and the ropes, but he locked me in the closet so I'd never see her. He threatened to kill me on the spot if I tried any funny business. In case I doubted him, he knocked me to the floor and kicked me hard in the thigh. I recovered in time for her next visit. I wanted to talk to her through the crack between the closet door and the wall. I was quite sure she'd be able to hear me, but was she trustworthy? She might tell Frank I broke his rule and talked to her. I couldn't risk it. He would keep his promise and kill me right then and there. But could she be helpful to me in some other way? I needed to write some more.

I opened my notebook and began writing:

> "The mysterious woman was here two days ago. I remained silent in the closet. After she left and Frank released me, I paid careful attention to what she does during the hour she spends in my apartment. She brings in supplies and food that doesn't require cooking, like fruits. She cleans, changes the sheets, does my laundry, replaces underwear as needed, and buys anything in short supply. Frank isn't trying to spoil me. It's self-preservation. He doesn't allow food that needs to be cooked because he doesn't want me to have a stove and set the house on fire. He doesn't want me to have cleaning supplies because I might make a bomb with them. That's what he said, and I acted like this was a normal thinking pattern from a normal person. It's one of my survival techniques.
>
> "I have started calling this woman 'Hope' because she may be my salvation. I must find a way to talk to her and convince her to let me go. There must be a way. There has to be. Something tells me this plan is filled with danger and possible violence, but right now, it's

my best possible route to freedom. As I think through the risks, my practical nature takes over. I tell myself that relying on Hope is a route, but not the only route. I have learned from life's lessons and music too that more than one way to achieve a goal is often possible."

I set down the pen and notebook and felt a small ray of hope that, with effort and determination, it might be possible to gain my freedom. But was I fooling myself?

9
Rosie Renard

Saturday, January 7, 2012, 4:00 P.M.

"Hi, Jane," Rosie said, leaning over the counter in the front room of her shop. "I hope you can stay an hour or so beyond closing. For now, I need you to run the shop while I help the detectives in the workroom."

"What's going on?" Jane asked.

"A cold case is about to be re-opened," Rosie said. She quickly filled in Jane about what had been going on since early that morning. Jane's eyes grew bigger and bigger as Rosie talked about Ivy Chen's disappearance, the estate sale, and the treasures which might belong to Ivy. "Right now the detectives and tech team are investigating all that."

"Wow! What a day! What a story!" Jane, a journalism major at USF, exclaimed. "I hope Ivy Chen finds her way home." Within seconds, Jane's serious expression brightened. "Hey, here's an idea. How about you work in the store, and I'll watch the action in the workroom. Just think of the report I'd end up with for my newspaper journalism class."

"Nice try, Jane, but no. Helping with this case is personal with me."

"You mean this is like what happened to your cousin Tess."

"That's right." Several months ago when she and Jane were enjoying a popcorn and movie evening, the movie stirred old memories about Tess. She had a terrible crying jag and told Jane everything about Tess's death. She immediately regretted it because Jane had enough problems of her own.

"No problem," Jane said. "Go back to the workroom. You're a smart lady, Rosie, and you probably don't need my advice. But here it comes anyway." She plunked her hands on her hips and stood tall. "Shake those old demons out of your head."

"Thank you, Jane, but tell me, how can I make that happen?"

"Go dancing with Ted. Rock the night away at some little club until your problems are shaken loose. Works for me…not with Ted of course. He only has eyes for you, but I've got friends who can shake up a place until it practically falls down around us."

"Thanks, Jane." Rosie opened the connecting door to the workroom. "I'll be back here if you need me."

"I've needed you since the day we met," Jane said. "But I don't like to admit it." She cocked an eyebrow. "Pretend you didn't hear me say it."

Rosie smiled and went into her workroom. Jane's advice sounded so helpful, dancing with Ted. Why hadn't she thought of that? Even if it didn't shake away her problems, it would be nice to be in Ted's arms. If only—

"Rosie, the tech team is finished with their preliminary work here," Detective DeLuca said, looking up from his notepad. "They'll be taking everything they need back to the lab for more thorough testing, but first, they'll photograph everything."

"So what's next?" Rosie asked.

"I called Ivy's mother, Anna Chen, in Chicago, to tell her what's happening here," DeLuca began. "I wanted her to hear it from me before this story hits the news. You can imagine her shock, her joy, her fears, all of that, and more. She wants to help, and she's arriving at the Tampa airport the day after tomorrow. That's the earliest she can get away because of medical complications. She didn't explain, and I didn't ask. By then, our team will be finished with the photos, and they'll be available to Mrs. Chen."

"How do you think it will go?" Rosie asked.

"She might be able to shed new light on the two trunks filled with bling. They're at the lab. We're checking the goods against robbery reports. I'm sure Mrs. Chen will be tired, and she should rest, but she wants to become involved as soon as she arrives. We'll want her to see those trunks plus anything else at the station and everything here too. We'd like all the help she can offer, but I'm sure you see the problems."

"I do. This will be emotional for her, but you don't want to delay."

"Right. She could easily see something all of us missed, something added, something taken away. She knows her daughter better than any of us do. We have to go with every possibility, and we have to be careful about offering her false hope that Ivy is alive. Let's think possibilities, not certainty."

"I'd like to be involved," Rosie said, absorbing his advice. "I have some idea what Mrs. Chen is going through, and maybe I can even help her." She took a deep breath. "My part-time helper, Jane Wheaton, is great. She's first year at Saint Petersburg College. She gives me as many hours as she can to free me up so I can work back here."

"Hey, I know her, and I agree. She's a great kid," Detective DeLuca said.

"How do you know her?" Rosie asked.

"She's been victimized in the park on several occasions by some tough guys who tried to steal her bike and her backpack. She fought back each time. She's got some good defensive moves going for her. She doesn't have a police record. What she does have is a strong belief in what's right. She can be her own worst enemy, but I like her."

"I see she's won you over too," Rosie said with a smile. "Anyway, Jane can wait on customers out front, and I'll stay back here with Mrs. Chen, if that's what she wants. If not, I'll get out of her way and help Jane."

"That's great," DeLuca said. "I was just going to ask you to do that."

Rosie opened the door to the front room and called out, "Jane, do you have a minute?"

Jane—all elbows and knees and over-sized glasses that magnified her freckles and brown eyes—strode into the workroom. Her ankle-top sneakers squeaked across the floor. Her straight brown hair swung across her scrawny shoulders.

"I'd like you to meet Detective DeLuca," Rosie said.

Jane shrugged. "We know each other."

"We do," DeLuca said, "and the pleasure's all mine."

"You got that right," Jane said. "Just kidding." She poked him with her elbow. "How are the mean streets out there?"

"Not so mean while you're in here," he said. "I was going to e-mail you. We found your skateboard and backpack tied to your bike in the park. You can pick up everything at the station. I would have delivered them, but I didn't have a current address for you."

"I'm in an apartment with three roommates near the college. It's cool. I'll come get my stuff. Thanks. Those same punks who've been harassing me chased me out of the park like they owned it. One of my sources told me who they are. Revenge is sweet," she said, rubbing her hands briskly together, "and you know what a sweetheart I can be."

DeLuca grimaced. "Don't do anything illegal."

"Where's the fun in that?" she asked.

The bell at the front door rang. "I'd better get back to work," Jane said. "And Detective, I'll come by the station later for my stuff. Don't even think about shining a bright light in my eyes or jabbing bamboo shoots under my fingernails to find out the names of my sources."

"Of course not." He waved off her comments. "That's old school. We're high-tech."

"Sure you are." She held out her hands, fingers splayed, completely rigid. "See me shaking like a leaf?" She breezed out the connecting door to the front room.

"If you don't reach Jane at her apartment, feel free to try her at my address and phone number," Rosie said, and passed him her business card. "She stays here when she needs to blow off steam. I keep a bed made up for her and special treats in the freezer. I enjoy her observations about the world around her. Her take on schedules and grocery lists is hilarious. Don't get me started about credit cards."

"You know her well," he said.

"I'm not the only one. The customers enjoy her sassiness. Lots of them drop by just to chat with her. I call them 'Jane's Groupies.' Jane likes that. It gives her a sense of importance and belonging. She deserves every bit of it."

"Good kid, bad breaks," DeLuca said.

"And unbelievable street smarts," Rosie said. "You know her story, don't you?"

"Most of it. She aged out of the foster care system. She's on her own, trying hard to make her way in this world. Her tough-girl ways and cynical attitude don't fool you or me. Am I right?"

"Absolutely," Rosie said. "Jane wants to believe that goodness wins out, that goodness conquers evil. Like us and so many others, Jane wants Ivy Chen to be found alive."

DeLuca's expression turned somber. "I understand your hopefulness and optimism, but the odds are not in Ivy's favor. False hope can be devastating when the investigation comes to an end and the victim isn't found alive. Let's soft-pedal everything."

Rosie knew that Detective DeLuca was right, but the reality was more than she could accept right now...or ever. Once had been more than enough.

10
Ivy Chen

Wednesday, March 18, 2009

I chose a blank page in my journal and began writing.

"I have now been in captivity for five months, but I still don't know for certain where this house is located, but it must be St. Petersburg. Frank mentioned his work at a chop shop, which he calls 'a vehicle reconstruction business.' While bragging about his important career there, he let it slip that the shop is near warehouses and some place called Tropicana Field. I don't know what or where that is, but this house must be in that same area because he admitted how pleased he was to drive home in five minutes to enjoy all three meals, or 'gustatory experiences, in the comfort of his own home, away from losers,' as he likes to say.

"He pronounces the word gustatory as 'goo-state-story.' I didn't catch on to what he meant the first time, but then I realized he was talking about food and contorting the word 'gustatory.' I take delight in his mangling of words because this tells me he isn't as smart as he thinks he is. Any miscalculations about himself might possibly help me escape from this dreadful place."

I finished writing today's entry in my journal, and I just tried something new. I read it aloud. This allowed me to hear myself speaking calmly without fear of Frank infiltrating my voice. I wrote in Chinese so that if he ever found my journal, he would not understand a single word. However, I read aloud in English since that's the language I will rely on to defeat him. My words rang out:

"Many nights I can't wait to lie down on my bed, pull up the covers, and pretend I never met Frank Brandt. My dreams offer me an escape to a better world than this nightmare where I am trapped. Fits of depression sometimes catch me off guard, but I know they come from the unrelenting solitary confinement. It's almost worse than the mistreatment that Frank metes out whenever his volatile personality goes haywire. Being alone crushes my spirit. I wish I had someone to share confidences with, someone to admit my fears to, someone to count on, and someone to shore up my courage.

"The best solution I've found for keeping depression at bay is to keep my mind busy. The first memory game I chose was listing every course I took at the university, year by year, with the names of the texts and the professors. I soon grew weary of that dull list. I chose instead recalling the proverbs Baba told me when I was a child. For an added challenge, I recited them in alphabetical order. If I skipped one by accident, I started all over. I translated them into English. After several weeks, my list reached twenty. I went back and determined how each proverb might help free me from this prison. I finished the exercise by meditating on each one. Of the twenty, my five favorites are:

- Reading 10,000 books is not as useful as traveling 10,000 miles.

My application is that I am stuck in this prison with Frank. My daily experience, observing what he does and thinks, what his routines are, and so on, not book learning, will set me free.

- When the wind of change blows, some build walls while others build windmills.

I remind myself that I must not let anger, frustration, and short-sightedness block my escape route. I must think positively and creatively.

- If one does not plow, there will be no harvest.

This tells me that preparation is the key to success, so I must devise a successful plan of escape followed by a successful run to freedom.

- Not only can water float a boat, it can sink it also.

This message about preparation and planning, that it's best to consider all possibilities before rashly deciding on one, could save my life.

- Misfortune does not come alone.

I must be prepared for many obstacles that might block my escape. Try, try, and try again will be my mantra."

I set aside my pen and notebook and went to bed. Sad thoughts came to me in the darkness. I hated the long dark nights. I didn't have control of the lights. They had to be on a timer located somewhere in Frank's quarters. At night, my apartment went dark automatically, and my sole source of light came from the moon through the skylight. For the first few moments of darkness, I was afraid. I prayed that in the morning the door to my apartment would be wide open, and I would walk out of this prison.

Light and darkness gave me an idea. If I had a flashlight, and if I were very creative, I could flash dots and dashes of light into the darkness, like an SOS signal in Morse Code. Maybe someone in the area who knew the Code would see the series of three dots, three dashes, and three dots, and he would barge in here and set me free. I soon came to my senses. This plan required a stranger's help. That person would come to the house to tell Frank he saw a message for help coming from here. Frank would make up an explanation to convince the stranger nothing was wrong. Once the stranger left, Frank would snap into a rage and punish me. His brutal kicks and punches might leave me maimed and unable to escape or even play my beloved erhu again.

No, I must forget about a stranger rescuing me. I had to rely on myself while I remained locked in this place, but the days of imprisonment dragged on. I hated every moment that Frank was anywhere near me, especially when he had a bad day at work. He called his job "a repression of his personality." I don't know why since his job was crushing cars and yanking out parts. That's how he treated me. He crushed my spirit and battered different parts of my body. When he came into my apartment and ranted about work, he always beat me as if his rotten job was somehow my fault.

The cleaning woman whom I have named "Hope" was the one other person in my life besides Frank. Crazy as it seemed, I looked forward to her visits to my apartment even though I was locked in the closet and had a very limited view of what she did. There was a predictable and comforting routine to her visits, like knowing the sun would come up tomorrow, and every new day offered new hope of escape.

I guessed Hope did the laundry at the nearby establishment Frank frequented. Apparently, there were no laundry facilities in this house. That information could help too. Was there any way to leave some trace of my identity in the laundry? No. That was too dangerous. Hope might show it to Frank.

One thought plagued me. Why would she work for Frank? If I knew the answer, I might be able to take advantage of Hope, and she could help me escape. That sounded like a daydream even as I contemplated it.

Frank was lonely, and I might be able to turn that to my advantage. He often barged into my apartment and took his meals with me when he delivered the greasy fast-food take-out items. Unknowingly, he revealed useful information as he chomped away at his food. I learned he stopped at a new sandwich shop within walking distance of this house and did his laundry nearby, exactly two minutes away by car. Every little bit of information was like a marker on a roadmap that would help me reach a safe place where people would call the police on my behalf.

He was especially lonely when he came home from work at the end of the day. He insisted I wear my concert dresses for our evening concerts. That's when I learned the clout and power of bargaining. I agreed but on the condition that he served wine with the dinner he brought for after the concerts. I figure he'd fall asleep, I'd steal the key, leave, lock him in, and run away. It just meant waiting for the right moment. I decided to take bargaining a step further. I would refuse to play the erhu unless Frank let me go outside every day for some fresh air.

This bargaining process went against everything Baba ever taught me. Mutual dependence was an admired trait in Chinese culture. I shook my head. If Baba knew how I was interpreting that concept to gain an advantage over Frank, he would be disappointed, but my life in captivity depended on making adjustments in thinking and behaving. I was certain that if Baba could see with his own eyes what my life was like, he would encourage me. He would want me to survive.

Refusing to play the erhu was a terrible mistake. Frank deprived me of food and water. I held out. He hit me so hard he knocked me off a chair and kicked me in the ankle when I was down and helpless. It took three days before I was able to eat. I still refused to play. He threatened to take away my erhu, my only companion in this isolated world. Regretfully, I caved in. I knew then that I could not refuse to play the erhu again. That was the equivalent of a death sentence. If the erhu went silent, Frank would get rid of me because I no longer served any purpose. Maybe I gave up too quickly on an escape plan that depended on help from someone I didn't know. What if the person were known to me? That might succeed.

The next morning, my purpose became clear: Find someone I knew to help me. As I worked out the details in my mind, I was both afraid and hopeful. After much thinking, I set my plan in motion. I wrote a note to my friend, Mr. Woo, who once lived near my parents and me in Chicago. He was kind to me and listened to me practice the erhu for hours. He now owns the Music House in Clearwater, about forty-five minutes north of St. Petersburg. I never visited him there, but he corresponded with my parents and always asked about me. I sent him a note when I came to this area for my three concerts with the Florida Orchestra. I had planned to visit him, but I never had the opportunity.

I wrote a message in Chinese at the bottom of a blank page: "Help me, Mr. Woo, my revered friend. Do you remember me, Ivy Chen? We lived near each other in Chicago. I was kidnapped here in Florida in 2008 by an evil man named Frank Brandt. He is standing before you now. Please don't show any fear, and don't let on what I have written in Chinese. This man has me imprisoned at his house or possibly a warehouse. I think it is near Tropicana Field, a laundry, and a lunch place, or maybe a fast-food place. Please help me. Call the police. Tell my parents and my friend Vincent Ivanov that I'm alive. "

Above that note, I wrote in English the names of four supplies that I needed for my erhu: strings, rosin, lint-free cloths, and sandpaper. I filled up the page in English with precise details about the supplies so Frank wouldn't be suspicious about why there was so much Chinese. If he asked, I would tell him it was a detailed translation to make sure we ended up with exactly what we wanted.

I pushed aside the paper and pen. I closed my eyes and prayed that Frank's crude mannerisms and butchery of the language would raise suspicions by the cultured soft-spoken Mr. Woo. I prayed, "Please let Mr. Woo read my note, follow my suggestions, and alert the police. "

Sometime after I finished the note, Frank whipped my door open and barged into my apartment.

"Frank, I need your help. The erhu needs your help. This is an emergency," I said. I talked very fast and this was the first time I had ever used the word "emergency," and he listened. I continued, "The erhu strings are wearing out, and they'll break very soon. They must be replaced. Without these two special strings, the erhu won't speak to you." Frank dropped down on the couch in a heap. I continued, "Usually the erhu strings are made of steel, just steel, but that is too plain and not good enough for our erhu." The more confusing and important I made this sound, the greater the chance he would take me with him to explain what was needed. If he didn't fall for it, he would at least take the note with him to explain exactly what he wanted.

I tapped my fingers on the note. "I want—the erhu needs—an inner string made of steel that is wound with 99.9 per cent silver. That will give a full and lasting tone. You will love the beautiful shiny appearance of such a string." I smiled and told myself, Frank Brandt, you will be hypnotized and fall into a dream state and carry out my bidding.

"And Frank, the outer string must be enhanced with gold alloy to increase the volume and give a gorgeous tone," I said. "The sounds from the new strings will be wonderful, and how bright and shiny they will appear! It's magical." I smiled again. They will hold your attention. Frank Brandt, you will not get rid of me if the erhu delights you more than ever with its glistening new strings.

"There's something else," I continued. "To speak properly, the bow hair needs to be treated with rosin. The erhu needs a cake of dark amber rosin, made from pine sap. The lint-free cloth is to remove the rosin dust that builds up on the erhu. The sandpaper is to rough up the rosin cake."

Frank pummeled the couch pillows. "I don't know where to find these oddball things."

"You can buy them online," I said, knowing from previous nasty remarks and suspicions he would never agree.

"Not me." He sneered. "I'm not taking chances and giving out my address. That would be playing right into their game."

"That's fine with me. I know of a store in Clearwater. Take me there, and I'll buy what our erhu needs." I doubted he would take such a chance, but I had to try.

"You're not going anywhere. I'll go myself."

I hid my disappointment with a forced smile and tried again. "Fine, but it can't be fiddle or banjo strings. It has to be strings meant specifically for an erhu." I compelled myself to remain determined. "We need rosin too. The bow's hair has to be rosined so it will grip the string and pull it."

"Big deal," Frank said.

"It is a big deal," I insisted. "If there's no grip, then the hair merely slides over the string, and there will be no sound. You, above all people, know the erhu is no ordinary instrument." I held out the note for Mr. Woo and Frank stood up and grabbed it. "This explains exactly what our erhu needs," I said. "And here is the address where they have the supplies."

I maintained my frozen smile while Frank read the note. His face turned bright red. He ripped off the part of the note written in Chinese, crushed it into a ball, and threw it in the corner.

"You think I'd fall for that old trick?" He sputtered. "This is Frank Brandt, super brain, you're dealing with."

I clenched my hands into tight fists. I wanted to hit Frank for ripping up that note. He had dashed my hopes that Mr. Woo would call the police and I'd be rescued, but I didn't hit him. Frank punishes me for "challenging his supremacy." So far I have endured cracked ribs, a broken toe, a twisted ankle, knee injuries, bruises, and cuts. Often, the pain is so horrible I can barely move. If his cruelty escalates, I won't survive.

He folded what was left of the note and put it in his pocket. "What's this stuff going to cost?"

I put forth a blank expression and checked my anger. "Four sets of strings, maybe fifty dollars. One cake of rosin, about ten dollars. Sandpaper and cloths, three or four dollars. I can't say for sure because I haven't been to a store recently."

Frank slapped his hand against his forehead. "I'm not made of money."

"Without new strings and rosin, the erhu will go silent," I said. "We have no choice."

Frank's anger consumed him for several minutes.

My mind was made up. If he backed off, I would find another way to take advantage of the erhu. I didn't like the idea of "taking advantage," for something so intuitive and sensitive, but it was my best hope of leaving here alive.

Frank opened his wallet and counted his folding money. Muttering something unintelligible, he slammed the door shut behind him. I stood there alone in the room, trying to imagine the scene in Mr. Woo's shop where Frank's rough ways and Mr. Woo's good manners would collide. I was convinced Frank's nastiness would alert Mr. Woo that this man was trouble. Frank would barge out of the shop with the supplies. Mr. Woo would think fast and catch Frank's license plate and call the police. Mr. Woo would tell the police he was worried that this man who just left his shop might be buying supplies for his family friend Ivy Chen, who had been missing for a long time, and the police would now be on their way to wherever this place is where I am being held prisoner.

But I wouldn't know whether Frank would actually go to Mr. Wong's shop and buy the supplies until he returned with them. Meanwhile, I worried and hoped. What seemed like hours later, Frank returned and stormed into my room. Before I uttered a word, Frank dumped the bag of supplies on my couch.

"I kept us safe," Frank said. "I said as little as possible to Mr. Woo. I didn't want my super intelligence and vocabulary to make him suspicious. You know, get him wondering about why a man in stained working clothes would be shopping here for these weird items. I said very little, just presented the note, paid cash, and left without slamming the door. Frank the super brain at work. That's me."

Disappointment and anger overwhelmed me. No police sirens. No help on the way. No possibility of freedom. Nothing. I wanted to slap him, kick him, run my fingernails down his face, and tear his flesh, but

I couldn't win that kind of battle. There would have to be other ways. The erhu was my best weapon, although I hated to use a warrior's term for the sweetest sounds this side of Heaven. So I asked, "Would you like to see how all these supplies you bought will improve the erhu's voice?"

"Yeah," he said and flopped on the couch next to the supplies.

I unwrapped everything and put my plan to the test. "Frank, see how the cake of rosin is smooth and polished?"

"Yeah. I'm not blind."

"It has to be roughed up with the sandpaper so it will stick to the bow hair. Just rub the sandpaper across the rosin several times. If you'll do that while I replace the strings, we can save time and get to the music."

Soon I was pressing the bow gently against the cake of rosin he had roughed up and taking long slow strokes to gather rosin dust on the up-bow and down-bow strokes.

"That's it," I finally said. "The erhu is ready."

I played *Praising Song*, as a way of showing my gratitude to the erhu which had helped me send Frank on a mission. He didn't take the note I had written in Chinese for my friend Mr. Woo, but possibly he slipped and mentioned my name or some detail about me. If that happened, and I prayed it did, Mr. Woo would have contacted the police by now. Frank was crazy, but he wasn't stupid. He would have guarded his words and not aroused any suspicions. My next plan would have to be better.

While I played *Praising Song*, Frank sat quietly and listened. Much of his usual anger dissipated. He seemed entranced by the cloud of rosin dust that floated above the erhu like mist over the lakes of China in the early morning. When I finished the song, I wiped off the rosin dust from the bow and strings with the lint-free cloth.

"All this takes a lot of time," he said.

"But ask yourself, Frank, is it worth it? Is the sound of the erhu's voice better?"

"Yeah. It's better. I guess I can wait every day while you mess with that dusty stuff."

When he left, I flopped onto the couch and raised my fists in triumph. The erhu's need for rosin, cloth, and sandpaper appealed to Frank. I didn't know if he noticed an improvement in the sound. Maybe at work he polished cars. Possibly, he related his work to my music and liked that feeling of belonging. Hooray! His fascination with the erhu would keep me alive. Hooray! The erhu was capable of creating a subtle shift in power away from him toward me. Hooray!

11

Detectives Tony DeLuca and Hank Hernandez

Saturday, January 7, 2012, 6:30 P.M.

Tony pulled out his phone, checked the number on the slip of paper from Rosie, and called the Kinter residence. He pressed the speaker button to allow his partner to hear the conversation. They were sitting at their desks at the police station.

"Mr. Kinter? Glad you're home. This is Detective DeLuca in St. Petersburg, Florida. Is Mrs. Kinter there with you?"

"Yes," he said. "May I ask what this is about?"

"We're working a cold case dating back several years ago. We have some routine questions, and we'd appreciate your help. It's about ivy-trimmed pillowcases."

"Here's my wife. She would know more about pillowcases than I would."

After some small talk, Tony said, "What can you tell me about a set of ivy-trimmed pillowcases you sold to Rosie Renard? She's the owner of Rosie's Treasures on Central Avenue. Do you remember where they came from?"

"Of course. My mind's like a steel trap. We bought them from Lou's Linens at the Wagon Wheel Flea Market."

"How many sets did you buy?"

"Just one."

"How many were there to pick from?"

"Just that one."

"What can you tell me about Lou's Linens?"

"Well, Lou's a nice man. He's been there for years, same table, same sales pitch: Why buy new at full price when you can scoop up almost new at half price? He has sheets, blankets, comforters, and shams. Some are matching. Some are just odds and ends. There might be a smudge or a tiny hole, but rehabilitation is possible, as Lou would say."

Tony frowned. "I'm lost. What did he mean by rehabilitation?"

"Many customers bought them and cut them up, using the good parts to make blankets, bedspreads, and comforters for dolls. Craft people flocked to Lou's booth."

"This is a whole new world to me," Tony said. "Any special reason you bought the ivy-trimmed pillowcases?"

"The best reason. They were a bargain. There were no matching sheets, so the price was rock bottom."

"You've been very helpful, Mrs. Kinter. Thanks again," he said. He dropped his phone into his pocket and turned toward Hank. "What are you thinking?"

"We need to talk to Lou at the Flea Market. He might remember who sold him the pillowcases. He might be able to describe the person. It's time to bring in Gretchen."

Tony cocked an eyebrow. "You find so many reasons to bring in that particular sketch artist. Does it have anything to do with her looks and personality and pretty smile?"

"Hey, give me some credit. I'm a professional."

"A professional who is sadly lacking a private life."

"Got any suggestions, oh man of the world?"

"Yeah," Tony said. "I'll talk to Lou from the Flea Market. If he remembers anything, one of us should call Gretchen."

"Good plan. Just in case, I'll call Gretchen now and see what her schedule is like."

♫♫

Two hours later, Tony called Hank. "Mystery of the pillowcases solved," he said. "No one sold Lou those ivy pillowcases."

"Are you saying Lou stole them? That Lou is somehow involved in this?"

"No. I'm saying Lou found them. His wife and two friends vouched for him. Get this. The pillowcases were laying near a dumpster at a convenience store. Lou spotted them as he left the store. They were in good condition. He kept them, 'recycled them,' to quote him. So guess where the convenience store is located."

"I'm going out on a limb here," Hank said. "Would it be near Allendale? Maybe close to the Cassell estate? You know where Rosie bought the footlocker with the pillowcases packed inside?"

"You're good at this." Tony chuckled. "Guess what? There's more. I asked Lou if he remembered selling the pillowcases to anyone. He said yes, a couple from Allendale. He didn't remember their names, but it was something with a K. I asked if that would be a Mr. and Mrs. Kinter. Yeah, he said, that's it. Kinter. Now for the bad news—"

"I don't get to call Gretchen and request a sketch."

"Right...but here's the good news. You don't need a crime to be committed to call her."

"I'll keep that in mind."

12

Detectives Tony DeLuca and Hank Hernandez

Sunday, January 8, 2012

"Sure is a beautiful morning," DeLuca said to Rocco and Alonso Conti, the father and son team who had helped Rosie move everything from the Allendale estate to her shop. "I appreciate your coming in."

"We work Sundays, just like you. We had to pass right by here on our way to a job," Rocco said.

"Good. This conference room is reserved for us," DeLuca said, ushering them into the room. "We have coffee, but several visitors claim it tastes worse than turpentine."

"We know all about turpentine," Rocco said. "I'll pass on that."

"If you got donuts that taste like wallpaper paste, we'll pass on that too," Alonso said.

"Don't mind us. We work with Rosie," Rocco added. "We make jokes all the time. She's got a slew of them. But you didn't call us in to hear our jokes. What's cooking?"

DeLuca sat down across from Rocco and Alonso. "For starters, tell me what type of work you do for Rosie."

"I'm Rosie's right-hand man, not just the muscle," Rocco said. "It goes like this. She appreciates my opinion about a piece of merchandise she's considering. Heck, she asks for my opinion. Not Alonso's opinion, not yet anyway."

Rocco reached over and ruffled Alonso's hair. "He's still green behind the ears."

"Green, huh?" Alonso laughed. "Are we talking mold or the color of money rubbing off?"

"As I was saying," Rocco gave DeLuca a knowing look. "We arrive at an estate sale or maybe a neighborhood sale. I touch. I can tell solid from veneer, cotton from silk. I smell. Musty? Okay, it can be cleaned. But then along comes a situation like this Allendale estate. It was a nighttime run, and the light was too poor to really see the merchandise. That's when it becomes a matter of gut instinct."

"That's my father's specialty, and he has the gut to prove it," Alonso said, pointing at Rocco's stomach which rolled over the top of his belt.

Rocco leaned close and confided in DeLuca, "Rosie and I are opposites. Rosie's more the thinker, the philosopher. Who owned this? How was it important in that person's life?" He rolled his eyes. "That's fine if we have all day, but this was more a grab and go kind of situation."

His hands were going like dueling windmill blades to help tell his story. "Bargains go fast. We can't stand around spouting Socrates and Plato. We need to be Rocco and Rosie, two people with a keen eye for what brings in a high profit. Sometimes Rosie gets all dreamy-eyed and wants to buy something that reminds her of a happy time or somebody special, and at that point she's willing to pay top dollar. That's just plain crazy."

"Does Rosie get her way, or do you?" DeLuca asked with a sly smile.

Rocco plastered his hand against his forehead. "I point out the foolishness of her thinking, but when the chips are down, Rosie gets what Rosie wants."

Rocco laughed. "I'm just her sounding board. When she bounces ideas off me, she's just convincing herself about what she's already

66

decided. Don't give me logic. I've just got to have it, she says, and the discussion is over."

"You're a good judge of character, Rocco," DeLuca said. "I appreciate your insights."

DeLuca turned to the son. "What do you have to say about all this, Alonso?"

"With all that philosophizing going on, somebody needs to flex some muscle and start lifting the heavy stuff. That would be me." Alonso tapped his chest.

"He's right." Rocco nodded. "My Alonso is as strong as a shot-put athlete, but let me be the proud father here. He's not just muscle. He's smart. Graduated in the top ten percent of his class at St. Pete High. That's no easy task with that crowd of egg-heads."

"Just a few more questions," DeLuca said, "and then I'll let you go. I see here in your work record from Rosie that you freelance. Did you notice any stuff in the storage area besides the trunks or the footlocker?"

"Just an old blanket," Rocco says.

"Could you describe it?" DeLuca asked.

"Not very well. We were working in the dark with just flashlights."

"Come on, now. With those eyes and instincts, I'll bet you noticed a detail or two."

"Okay. Nothing much gets past me." Rocco spread out his hands like an open book. "The blanket was messy, like somebody had been sleeping on it. I stay away from stuff like that. You wouldn't believe what we find in areas like that where people sleep. You get my meaning?"

"Unfortunately I do," DeLuca said. "In my line of work, I see it all."

"Well, stay away from it." Rocco wagged his finger at the detective. "Let me give you some advice from my father. He said, 'you lay down with dogs, you wake up with fleas.'"

"Good one," DeLuca said. "Still I need to ask. Did you see anything unusual, something that struck you as odd, maybe out of place?"

"Like I said, my son's the smart one. He called my attention to something, just an ordinary old mattress."

"I did," Alonso chimed in. "I asked myself, why would someone be sleeping on the hard floor on a blanket when there was a nice soft mattress over by the wall?"

"Smart thinking," DeLuca said. "Do you have any ideas on that?"

"No," Alonso said. "It just made me wonder. But I don't get paid to be curious."

DeLuca's eyes glistened as he pushed himself away from the table. "Thanks for your help." He walked over to the door and opened it wide. "I'll call you if I think of any more questions."

"Sure," Rocco said. "Keep us in mind if you need anything moved. Or if you need some insights into an investigation."

"You got it," DeLuca said and closed the door behind them. In one smooth movement, he pulled his phone out of his pocket and called his partner.

"Hank, where are you?"

"I'm at the Cassell estate in the living room."

"Are you doing your final walk-through?"

"Yeah. The tech team just left. Everyone's gone from our team, except Steve. He's re-checking the stairs to the storage area, thinking we might have missed something, like a piece of torn fabric on the splintery wood. You know Steve. Where there's a splinter or a jagged piece of glass, there's a clue. And he's got a photo collection to prove it."

"Everybody's a specialist these days." Tony chuckled. "Who else is around?"

"Jack and his crew are still here too. They're working outdoors. It's just me inside the house, seeing the big picture, looking for the little details."

"Good, Hank. I don't want to rush you or pull you from what you're doing—you've cracked many a case with that technique."

"You didn't call me to tell me that. What's up?"

"I may have a lead. I need you and Steve to go the storage area over the garage."

68

"Okay. Give us a few minutes."

A long pause.

"Geeze, Hank, you're wheezing like an old man."

"Rickety stairs." Hernandez gasped for air. "Okay. Steve and I are there. Now what are we looking for?"

"An old mattress."

"Got it. It's already been checked for DNA, fluids, the usual."

"I know, but this may not be the usual. Look along the edges of the mattress. See if there's an opening of some sort, maybe even pinned closed."

"You're thinking there's something inside the mattress."

"Yeah. Go easy, Hank. There's a chance it's a skeleton."

"You're psychic, Tony. There's a slit along one side, sewn shut with very crude stitches. The next sound you hear will be me ripping out those stitches."

Another long pause.

"Wow!" Steve's shout came through the phone to Tony.

"Whoa, Nelly!" Hank hooted. "There's no skeleton. And no rat crap this time."

"My curiosity's on overload," Deluca said.

"You want to know who Nelly is. That's my grandfather's donkey."

"Quit horsing around, Hank."

"Donkey, not horse," Hank said.

"Okay. Let's get down to business. Make sure Steve is a witness before you move anything, and make sure you put in your report whatever it is you find. Ask Steve to whip out his camera and take a few shots. Now, what's in the mattress?"

"Bills. Dollar bills. Hundred dollar bills. We're looking at a fortune." Hank laughed heartily. "Nice twist. Whoever did this? He didn't store his money under the mattress. He stored it in the mattress."

"Thanks, Hank. I'll send in some reinforcements. They'll be there soon."

13
Ivy Chen

Tuesday, April 14, 2009

I lay in bed, planning and hoping. As always, I assessed my situation and then tried to come up with a new and better plan of escape. Frank has held me captive here for six months. That was a sad realization, but I convinced myself the erhu would help me gain every step toward the freedom waiting beyond these walls. Maybe there was a perfect song that would lull Frank to sleep while I played. Listening to *Pine Song* was probably the best choice. If that didn't work, I would create my own songs, but I needed to do more. To get out of here, I desperately needed Frank's key to my apartment.

Every day, when Frank unlocked the door, he held the key to this room in his hands. He caressed it endlessly while I played the erhu. If he were to fall asleep and the key were to drop on the floor, I could pick it up, lock him in this room, and find a way out of this forced isolation. That plan needed fine-tuning because if the rest of the house was like my apartment, there were probably no windows within my reach, except skylights. Maybe the doors needed special knowledge or tools or keys to open. I had to find out.

My new plan began to form. I must bargain with Frank to gain access to the rest of the house and then observe how he came and went. Once I had that information, I'd make my escape. I must be patient. Mama and Baba always told me patience solved most problems, but this was more than a problem. This was the shriveling of my life, my hopes, and my dreams. An extraordinary amount of patience would be required.

With each passing day, I tried harder to hold on to the sweet memories of all the glorious days before I was abducted. I relived them often. They made me feel like myself, a lucky person with a wonderful life, blessed with a family, friends, and a joyful musical career. My last day of freedom was so special. I saw so many friends at the Vinoy, especially Vince, my wonderful Vince. I visited antique stores along Central Avenue, and after I spoke to Mama on the phone, I spent hours at the Dalí Museum. A guidebook helped me interpret the fantastic works by Salvador Dalí.

I closed my eyes and remembered the experience. In the very first gallery, the painting *Daddy Longlegs of the Evening….Hope* captured my attention. The soft cello, elongated and unable to make music, might be portraying how the arts suffer during wartime. The possibility gave me so much to think about, especially that a musical instrument could symbolize a complex idea. Eager to see more, I toured all the galleries, saving for last the three spectacular Dalí paintings of cellos on loan from the Spanish National Collection.

Now, as I languished here in captivity, my thoughts turned to those enigmatic cello paintings. Dalí painted *Bed and Two Bedside Tables Ferociously Attacking a Cello* shortly after the death of his wife Gala. His swaths of yellow, chartreuse, and orange revealed the chaos that dominated his world without his beloved Gala. Recalling that painting, I saw in my mind's eye the bedside table kicking or possibly stomping on the cello. But now I realized that the cello threw herself into the brawl and broke the nightstand's leg. There was a lesson for me in this painting. Fight back, if not physically since in my case Frank is incredibly strong and I am weakened by my injuries, then I must fight a psychological battle with him. That was the only possible way for me to manipulate Frank and ultimately defeat him. Thank you, pugilistic cello!

That day at the Dalí Museum remained so clear in my mind. I saw myself turn away from *Bed and Two Bedside Tables* to focus on the painting which was hanging on the opposite wall, *Topological Contortion of a Female Figure Becoming a Cello*. It too was painted by Dalí shortly after Gala's death. Here, the colors were gray, white, and beige, the colors of bones. Dominating the painting was the female hip structure which in its contorted form resembled a cello. A human hand and foot were receding into the skeleton, and soon the metamorphosis would be complete. The woman would leave behind all traces of her human form and become a cello. That wasn't so surprising since many musicians saw their instruments as an extension of themselves. They identified with them, but I now knew such an idea extended beyond musicians and artists and other creative people. In his sick mind, Frank believed he had the right to own a woman's voice, her heart, and her soul.

I got out of bed and began pacing my apartment. I thought about Frank's obsession with the erhu. He believed that it was me and that I had commanded him to obey me, capture me, and take me to his home. It depressed me to think about Frank. I pushed aside all thoughts of him and thought instead about Vince, my loveable Vince. He and a cello player in the Florida Orchestra seemed attracted to each other. A tinge of jealousy halted my pacing, but I worked at convincing myself his interest might not be the cellist. It could be the cello itself. The cello is often said to resemble the hourglass figure of a woman. Come to think of it, the cellist flirting with Vince was shapely.

I looked at myself. I was slender with slight curves but nothing that would be considered remotely similar to the hourglass figure with a tiny waist and voluptuous rounded hips. And now that I didn't have access to good nutritious food, I had lost weight, and my curves were disappearing. This depressed me. I should just concentrate on Vince. Vince, Vince, how I missed him. Was it Vince's fascination with a cellist that compelled me to see the paintings at the Dalí in the first place? It was possible. I hoped that one day I would have the chance to see again the violin paintings by Picasso and Braque. They would remind me of Vince. I wondered if some day an artist would feature the erhu. If Dalí were alive and learned of the erhu's powers, he would paint furiously until he had it all captured on canvas. And it would turn out just as dramatic as the cello or violin! Maybe more dramatic, but, of course, I was prejudiced in favor of the cello.

The sad reality intruded. I couldn't afford to get lost in the past, focused on my last day of freedom. Now, I must think about my next day of freedom, the day I find a way to get out of this prison–and the key, my inspiration, was my erhu and the captivating music it produced.

I stretched out on my bed again, relaxed for a while, and then began writing in my journal to hone my thoughts:

> "There's something Frank doesn't know about the erhu. It has the power of an enchantress. It can make sounds that evoke the chirping of a bird and the neighing of a horse, and maybe some others too. I must practice those sounds during the hours when Frank is away. They take great concentration. Those sounds will help me. But Frank is skeptical and fights new ideas. I must build up his listening skills so he will want to hear the erhu's specialties more than once. Somehow, I must convince him that he needs to hear those enchanting sounds in his quarters not mine. They will provide me with bargaining power. I must work out the details. This plan is better than all the others put together. This is a moment I have been waiting for...praying for with all my heart and soul."

I set down my pen and my hope waned. There was a stumbling block. The erhu's winning ways might allow me into Frank's quarters, but when I played the erhu, I had to remain seated to keep the erhu upright. How then could I move about and see all of Frank's quarters? There had to be a solution. If not, I was doomed.

14
Rosie Renard

Rosie answered her phone.

"Rosie? This is Detective DeLuca. Mrs. Chen just arrived at the station. Before she looks at the items we took to the lab, she'd like to meet you and thank you in person for bringing Ivy to our attention."

"That's so sweet of her," Rosie said. "I'll be here all afternoon. Come on over."

"Thanks. Mrs. Chen is tired. She may need to go to her hotel before coming back with us to the station."

"My place is comfortable. If you'd like, she could at least look at the photos while she's here."

"That might work," DeLuca said. "Many of the items have already been returned to you. Mrs. Chen can see them at your shop if that's okay with you."

♫♫

Rosie greeted Detective DeLuca and Mrs. Chen at the rear door of her shop. Rosie was stunned by Mrs. Chen's appearance. An online family biography that included photos stated that a vigorous-looking Mrs. Anna Chen was in her mid-sixties. One comment from the biography—that Ivy was a blend of her American mother's delicate beauty and her Chinese father's striking appearance—popped into Rosie's mind. But now, only three years later, Mrs. Chen appeared frail and exhausted. Grief seemed permanently etched into the pale pinched face that in photos had radiated happiness and good health. Her thick lustrous hair seen in the photos was now pulled back in a straggly loose bun at the nape of her neck.

"Come into my workroom," Rosie said cheerfully.

Mrs. Chen hugged Rosie. "I know we've just met, and here I am hugging you, but I'm so grateful. Thank you for calling in the detectives as quickly as you did. You can't imagine how much that means to me."

Just then the door opened.

"Rosie, this is Officer Betty Randall," DeLuca said, holding the door open as the officer, a tall, slender, bright-eyed woman probably mid-thirties, stepped into the room. "I asked her to meet us here. She's an invaluable part of our team. Her specialty is working with family members who are having a tough time—"

"Please don't take this the wrong way, Detective, or you either, Officer Randall," Mrs. Chen said. Her voice was surprisingly firm given the strain of a long flight from Chicago and the uncertainty of her daughter's fate. "I don't need emotional support if that's what you're thinking. I'm not going to break down and cry. I don't have time for that. I'm seriously ill. I don't have that long, and I don't want to go to my grave never knowing what happened to my daughter. I want her found. That's what matters. I'd rather have Officer Randall forget about me and go look for Ivy."

"Let's compromise," DeLuca said. "We can cut back on the emotional support, but Officer Randall needs to stay in the room in case police matters arise. That's a way of helping find Ivy too."

"We're a team, Mrs. Chen," Officer Randall said soothingly. "All of us here at Rosie's Treasures, the station, the crime lab, and the home where several items we believe belong to your daughter were found—all of us are working together to find Ivy."

Rosie was meeting Mrs. Chen for the first time, but she wanted to wrap her arms around her and tell her everything would be all right, that not every missing person stayed missing. That's how she had comforted her Aunt Jessica before they received the terrible news about Tess. Rosie knew all too well the heartache of being overly reassuring as she had been for those long heart-wrenching days when young Tess didn't come home. There needed to be room for doubt so the family can, if necessary, come to terms with the sad news that their beloved one was gone forever. She needed to be somewhat cautious with Mrs. Chen about Ivy, especially since three years and three months had gone by, not just a few days as was the case with Tess.

Rosie sent those memories to a far corner of her mind and concentrated on the present. "Mrs. Chen, if you'll follow me, we're all going to sit down together." She motioned to Officer Randall and Detective DeLuca to follow too. "Come on everyone," she said. A pot of steaming tea sat on a warmer in the middle of the table, surrounded by teacups and saucers and a plate of teacakes.

"I don't want to keep you from your work," Mrs. Chen said, tucking wayward tendrils behind her ears. "I know you have a business to run. My husband Yi and I ran an import-export business in Chicago and Shanghai, so I know how quickly work piles up when you can't get to it every day."

Rosie held up her hand. "Please. You're not keeping me from my work." She helped Mrs. Chen take off her jacket, gently easing out first one arm and then the other. She smoothed the jacket and rested it on the back of the chair.

"Thank you, Rosie. You're very kind," Mrs. Chen said, before turning to Detective DeLuca with sad eyes. "I want my Ivy back. I miss her so much."

"We're counting heavily on you," DeLuca said, as Mrs. Chen settled into the chair next to Rosie. "We photographed items that we believe belong to Ivy. They were found at an estate sale here in St. Pete's Allendale neighborhood." He pulled a local map from his pocket and ran his fingers along Central Avenue and then shifted them a short distance to the northeast. "Here's Allendale." He moved his fingers back to Central Avenue. "And here's Rosie's Treasures, where we are right now." He paused while Mrs. Chen studied the map. "Did your daughter happen to mention that she'd visited the Allendale neighborhood?"

"No. Is it a dangerous area? A bad area?"

"No, not at all," the detective said. "It's a residential area, known for its oak trees, brick streets, and charm." He leaned toward Mrs. Chen. "Maybe she had a friend who lived there?"

"No. And I would know because she confided in me about her friends. She's an only child. From her early years, she came home and chattered away to me about school, friends, everything. Yi was at work. Ivy and I never ran out of things to say to each other." Her eyes misted over. "We shared everything, usually in Chinese. That was Ivy's first language and the one she always turned to if she was upset or had a problem." She raised her hands, palms facing up. "People often assume I am Chinese."

That very thought was going through Rosie's mind.

"Please let me explain," Mrs. Chen said. "There were only a few Americans in our neighborhood, and we spoke English to them, but bit by bit, I adopted the ways of my Chinese neighbors, and Yi and I spoke Chinese to them and at home too. Yi's English was formal and a bit stilted, so from the very beginning, I preferred sharing our thoughts in Chinese. It was more intimate."

Her voice turned wistful. "Our meals were cooked in the Chinese way. Holidays were a mix of both cultures, and Yi and I enjoyed the traditions and stories of our youth. We spoke English of course, but Chinese was our principal language. It was natural for Ivy to do as we did."

Rosie studied Mrs. Chen, an American woman who had lived in America until she graduated college, moved to China to study, married Mr. Chen, and lived for many years in China. Maybe her extensive time spent in China helped explain why she had traits often associated with Chinese women. She was demure, reserved, and shy. Possibly the strain of being tired and ill and reliving Ivy's disappearance was making her seem even more reserved than she typically was. Maybe she already had those traits when she studied in China, married Yi, and raised Ivy there.

Detective DeLuca's words to Mrs. Chen, something about photos, pulled Rosie back to the moment. "We'd like you to look at the photos. The actual items are still being tested, and you'll have the chance to see them soon. The photos will show you everything in the footlocker that was brought here from the estate. We think some of it, maybe all of it, belonged to Ivy. If you—"

"A footlocker?" Mrs. Chen interrupted.

DeLuca shuffled through the photos and set out those that showed the footlocker from every angle. "Here it is."

Mrs. Chen peered at the photos. "I never saw this before. I'm sure Ivy didn't own a footlocker."

"We're not saying it's hers. It could have belonged to someone at the Allendale home or someone else. For now, all we know is that some of Ivy's belongings were in it when Rosie bought it."

Mrs. Chen sniffled. "She has a beautiful hickory-brown leather suitcase. Ivy's father and I gave it to her as a present. That suitcase went everywhere with her. It has special meaning to our family. Ivy's grandfather, Yi's father, was born in Shanghai in the year of the dragon. There's a dragon imprinted in the leather on the lid of her suitcase. Ivy's initials are imprinted beneath the dragon. Is that here too?"

"No," DeLuca said. "We're aware of the suitcase with the dramatic dragon imprint. You mentioned it during the original investigation. So did her friends. Two of them said Ivy had packed several concert dresses to show her aunts. Several friends remarked she had the suitcase and her erhu in its case in the trunk of her car when she headed to Sarasota to meet up with you and her aunts. That dragon stuck in everyone's mind.

Rosie piped up, "In the photos there's a dragon image carved into Ivy's erhu."

Detective DeLuca flipped through the photos and pulled out several shots of the erhu.

"You have her erhu?" Mrs. Chen asked. Her voice trembled. "Please let me see it right now. It's so much a part of Ivy. If her erhu is here, she must be somewhere nearby."

"I'm so sorry, Mrs. Chen," DeLuca said. "We don't have the erhu. All we have are the photos that were in the footlocker. Is this Ivy's erhu? Please look again. Can you be certain?"

Mrs. Chen tapped her finger on the dragon in the photo. "There are many different dragons in Chinese art. But this one? It's the exact dragon we had embossed on her leather suitcase. It's the same shape, the same size, the same fierce expression. It was the dragon image that Ivy's grandfather favored. It was the exact same image that was carved on her erhu."

Mrs. Chen peered again at the photo of Ivy's erhu. "Ivy's erhu came from Suzhou, an esteemed center of erhu making. It's located in the Jiangsu Province, Ivy's favorite place in the whole world. Because of its beauty and lakes, Suzhou is called 'Paradise on Earth.' We had planned to go back there and visit when her series of concerts ended."

A slight smile crossed her face. "Ivy's erhu was handmade by specialists, and it's of the highest quality. It's made of red sandalwood. See the strings?" she asked. "They're made of steel. Sometimes they are enhanced with 99.9 percent pure silver and gold alloy. Long ago, erhu strings were made of silk, but steel is more durable and practical. They give the player confidence they will last throughout the song. Ivy had a confidence that matched the depth of her interpretation."

"Excuse me, Mrs. Chen," Detective DeLuca said. "I need to call my team at the estate. I'll ask them to search again for Ivy's suitcase. If it's there, in the house or garage or on the grounds, they'll find it." He stepped aside and made the call. His enthusiasm came through as he gave explicit details about the suitcase and its importance. "No," he said. "Don't go to the station. Come here to Rosie's Treasures instead. All of you." He continued talking for several minutes and then said, "See you soon." He called Rosie to his side and confided to her, "Your cousin and others are on their way here. I'd appreciate your staying to hear what they have to say."

"Any special reason?" Rosie asked, wondering if there was a break in the investigation.

"I think Mrs. Chen needs a confidante. My experience tells me the personal touch will help all of us. "

Mrs. Chen studied the programs from Ivy's concert with the Florida Orchestra. DeLuca had pulled them out of one of his folders and left them on the table. The write-up from inside the program featuring guest soloist Ivy Chen filled one entire photo. Mrs. Chen's lips trembled. "This information about Ivy's background is familiar, but I never grow tired of reading it."

Rosie read silently over Mrs. Chen's shoulder: Ivy Chen's parents introduced their only child to music at an early age. Ivy Chen studied at the prestigious Shanghai Conservatory of Music and went on to become an erhu virtuoso. Her public debut as an erhu soloist took place with the Shanghai National Orchestra. She has been a guest soloist with well-known orchestras in the United States, Europe, and Asia.

Mrs. Chen had just finished reading the program and discussing it with Rosie when Detective Hernandez and Rosie's cousin Jack arrived. A wiry man with a buzz cut, who was wearing jeans and a pale blue buttoned shirt, came in with them. Rosie didn't recognize him.

"Everyone, this is Gary Cassell," Detective Hernandez said and made hurried introductions. "We're fortunate to have Gary here with us. He and his sister Beverly own the house in Allendale where the belongings were found. They inherited it from their parents."

Gary rotated his shoulders and stretched his neck. "Sorry. I'm still trying to dislodge the kinks. I left home in a hurry, just arrived at the airport, and went straight to my parents' house. I still call it that. I can't even begin to think of it as belonging to my sister and me. Anyway, time is important, so I'll come right to the point."

He opened an iPad. "I have photos of the interior of my parents' home, room by room, including all the furniture and all their collections of knickknacks, paintings on the wall, what was in the china cabinet. Everything, and I mean everything, like years and years of everything. When I visited my parents two months ago, they asked me to take the photos for insurance purposes. The hurricane scares made them want proof of what they owned."

"Here's the part I like," Detective Hernandez said. "His parents wanted a complete inventory, so Gary also took photos of the garage and storage area."

"I can't take credit for that," Gary said with a shrug. "It was my sister Beverly's idea. She was fussing about fire regulations because so much stuff was stored there. She's a worrywart. When we were kids, I used to tease her. I told her if she kept on, she'd end up like a witch with warts on her nose. You know how it is."

He gave a wry smile. "The older brother is supposed to tease his younger sister. Sorry, I jumped off the track with this family stuff. Without parents, a sibling becomes more important than ever. That kind of sounds like something from a greeting card." He shrugged. "Anyway, now it turns out that worrying can be a good thing. Maybe"—he crossed his fingers—"it will help you find your daughter."

"Thank you, Gary," Mrs. Chen said. "I appreciate the family history. I had an older brother. They can be annoying, but they can be wonderful too, when they set their mind to it. I miss my brother. I wouldn't mind his teasing one little bit. Sorry, now I'm the one going off the track."

"You and my sister Beverly would have a lot to talk about," Gary said. "Too bad she couldn't be here. It's a long story, so I won't go into it. I dropped what I was doing when Detective DeLuca called and told me what was stored in the garage."

Detective Hernandez nodded at his partner. "Here's a plan that Gary and Jack talked about on the way over here. I think it could work. They want to go through everything in the holding area here and then go to the estate and check out everything in the house. This will take the guesswork out of whether anything left the house and garage that we don't know about, and it will show us if anything was added in the two months since Gary took these photos. For me, the most important question is this: If anything was added or taken, is there any connection between those items and Ivy Chen?"

"It's a good, thorough plan," DeLuca said.

"I could have sent the photos electronically," Gary said, "but that might miss something dropped on the floor, fallen behind a dresser. You know how it is. There's stuff you see in person that you don't see in photos. Who knows? Maybe this is the time for me to take over my sister's job as the family worrywart."

81

Mrs. Chen chimed in, "My husband, who was a very smart man, used to say 'a worrywart is someone who defends against regret.'"

Gary smiled. "My sister would love to hear those flattering words."

"I'll pitch in and help you guys," DeLuca said. He turned to Officer Randall. "Why don't you stay here with Rosie and Mrs. Chen while they sort through the photos? Come get me if something unexpected turns up."

Officer Randall pointed at her iPhone. "Hold on a second. The news media has picked up on the story. Details about Ivy Chen, the estate sale, and Rosie's Treasures are all over the place."

"All the more reason to act quickly," DeLuca said. "The reporters are bound to show up here."

"I know what that's like," Mrs. Chen said. "But their reporting may encourage someone to come forward with new leads. Don't you agree?"

"You're right," DeLuca said. "Oh, there's one more thing, Mrs. Chen. I'd like to ask a favor." He waved the others toward the holding area.

"No favor is too much to ask," Mrs. Chen said. "You're the best hope I have of finding my Ivy."

"Would you mind taking a look at the rest of these photos? We want to make sure these items belonged to Ivy." He set them in front of her.

Mrs. Chen studied each one. "All of these are familiar. They are Ivy's," she said and set the photos of jade jewelry and clothing aside. "But these, the teacup set and pillowcases." Her breath caught in her throat, and her lips formed a tight straight line. "Ivy telephoned me shortly after she bought them in downtown St. Petersburg. She described them, but I never saw them."

"I know this is difficult for you, but every detail you remember helps us," DeLuca said. "Something else turned up in the footlocker. I've set the photos aside until now because these other items seem out of place."

"Photos of what?" Mrs. Chen asked and her frown lines deepened.

82

"Men's clothing." DeLuca reached into a folder containing a duplicate set of the photos and held up a large color photo of a man's blue suit, shirt, and tie, along with a set of grey work clothes. "Have you ever seen these items? Do you know anything about them?"

Mrs. Chen slowly shook her head from side to side. Sadness, mirrored in her eyes, aged her. "No. What do these clothes have to do with my Ivy?"

"They were found in the footlocker along with Ivy's personal items. The tech team is making them a priority. If you recall, you gave us Ivy's hairbrush after she first went missing. We have her DNA on file. We're testing every inch of the man's clothing for his DNA and Ivy's DNA."

Mrs. Chen shuddered. "Do you have any idea who he is?"

"Not yet."

"Do you have any suspects?"

"We're working on it," DeLuca said. "Do you remember the names of any of her men friends here in town? Any man she might have been meeting the Monday she disappeared on her way to see you in Sarasota?"

"Not from memory, but my address book might help. Most of her local friends were going to be at the Vinoy Hotel for that Monday morning breakfast. Their names are easy to spot. I put the letters SP for St. Petersburg next to them. All of her friends, men and women, were interviewed at the time of her disappearance. But, of course, nobody knew about these men's clothes back then."

"You're right," DeLuca said. "This is a new lead. We have a saying about that."

"I'd like to hear it," Mrs. Chen said, and a slight smile lifted the corners of her mouth.

"The cold case is heating up."

Her eyes shone with determination as she reached into her purse and withdrew a leather book with a dragon embossed on the cover. She passed the book to DeLuca. "Please, I beg you, turn up the heat, get a roaring blaze going, and find Ivy."

"We'll do our best. Your address book and anything else you can think of can help this investigation."

He held up the address book for Rosie to see. "It's not the same dragon that's on the suitcase and the erhu. Let's keep our eyes peeled for anything else with a dragon on it. Any dragon. It could be important. At this point, we don't know."

"Wait a minute," Mrs. Chen said, passing her fingers back and forth across her forehead. "I gave Ivy a pair of cute, black shoes. They were so dainty, just like her, and they had a dragon embroidered across the toes of each foot. She always wore those shoes when she visited me. Where are those shoes now? She would have been wearing them the day she was coming to see me and her Aunties. They loved her like a daughter. She called them Aunties. They longed to spoil her with cakes and tea." Her hands began to tremble. "This is a bad sign." She cried softly.

"Maybe not," DeLuca said. "The shoes could be in the missing dragon suitcase. They could all turn up together. Isn't that possible?"

She blinked away her tears. "Yes," she said and straightened her shoulders. "Call me if you need help with the names in the address book. I'll be staying at the Vinoy Hotel. That's where Ivy stayed. I'll feel closer to her that way. Or you can call me on my cell. The number's on the first page. Some of Ivy's friends stayed in touch with me, but as time passed...well, you know what happens. I haven't heard from them in over a year...in a couple of years. "

"Thanks. I'll make a copy and get this back to you." He tapped the book against the palm of his hand. "Was Ivy particularly close to any of these people? Was one of them a best friend, maybe?" He pulled up a chair and sat down next to her. "I've read the report from the initial investigation several times. It was thorough. Her friends were very cooperative. They were all members of the Florida Orchestra. Everything checked out. None of them were considered suspects. But now with this new lead, the men's clothes, we need to question some of them again."

"Are you saying one of them might have hurt Ivy?"

"No I'm not, but if one of those men was especially fond of Ivy, he might have been too upset at the time to remember something crucial. I want to re-interview her closest friends and see if they can come up with details that could help us now."

"I see," Mrs. Chen said. "Ivy was only in town for a few days. She didn't say anything about a best friend." She grew quiet and appeared a bit lost in her thoughts. "But now I recall she did mention she knew one of the violinists."

"Do you recall his name?" DeLuca asked, grabbing his pen and notepad.

"I believe she called him Vince."

Deluca flipped through several pages of the address book. "Here he is. Vince Ivanov. He's local, or at least he was local then. I remember seeing his name among those interviewed in the original investigation. Vincent Ivanov. He was not considered a suspect."

He pulled out his cell phone and punched in numbers. After a few seconds, he smiled and nodded to Mrs. Chen and Rosie. "Mr. Ivanov, this is Detective Tony DeLuca with the St. Petersburg Police. We've reopened the Ivy Chen case. I need to speak to you. Here's my direct line." He rattled off the number. "Call me as soon as you receive this message. Thanks."

He looked at Mrs. Chen and crossed his fingers. "If luck is on our side, this might be another new lead. Good work, Mrs. Chen." He slid the address book into his pocket.

DeLuca's phone rang. He answered it immediately. "Mr. Ivanov. Thanks for getting right back to me. Yeah, I know what you mean. Calls can pile up faster than bills. I mentioned this was about the Ivy Chen case. I understand you were at the Vinoy at a breakfast for Ivy the day she went missing." He paused. "Do you mind if I put you on speaker phone? Ivy's mother is here with me. I have questions. She may have some too." He pressed a button.

"Hi, Mrs. Chen. This is Vince Ivanov, Ivy's friend. I'm so sorry for what happened."

"We feel the same way," Mrs. Chen replied softly. "Ivy talked about you. She liked you. She said you were a gifted violinist."

"Thank you, Mrs. Chen," he said. "I feel the same way about Ivy and her music. I play her recordings all the time. It keeps her in my mind and keeps me hoping that she'll return to us. In my mind, I see her on the stage playing that sweet music. She hypnotized the audience." He choked up. "And me too."

"Thank you, Mr. Ivanov," Mrs. Chen said with a trembling voice.

"Please, Mrs. Chen, call me Vince. You, too, Detective DeLuca."

"Okay. Vince it is," DeLuca said. "I'll talk to you more in person. I'd like to meet at the Vinoy and have you walk me through what happened that day. But in the meantime, here's something I want you to think about. It's a question I often ask to stir up memories. At the time, you might have been too upset to notice details, but now maybe they can resurface. Are we on the same page?"

"Yes."

"Did anything unusual happen that day at the Vinoy?"

"No. Not that I recall."

"You'd been there before?"

"Many times."

"Think hard. Did anything seem wrong, out of place, possibly something that hinted at trouble?"

"Trouble would be unusual. The Vinoy is a classy place."

"Right. Think back to that day. Retrace what you did, where you went, what you saw and heard."

"Nothing's coming through. I'd like to make a suggestion."

"Sure."

"Let me hang up and listen to Ivy's solo from the concert. I'd like to concentrate on Ivy first and then shift my thoughts to that day at the Vinoy, and see if anything comes to mind."

"I like it, Vince. Do it, and get back to me."

A half-hour later, DeLuca's phone rang. He set aside the list of items from the footlocker and pulled out his phone.

"Detective? It's Vince Ivanov."

"You're on speaker again. Did you remember something?"

"Maybe," Vince said, and a slight smile tugged at DeLuca's lips.

"That Monday I took a break from the group and wandered away to the verandah which overlooks the Vinoy's circular driveway. I was standing there, leaning against the railing, pulling my thoughts together."

Mrs. Chen folded her hands in prayer. "Please," she whispered. "Please remember something."

"I could see and hear the cars pulling up to the valet area. A typical day, typical sounds. This may not be much—"

"It could make all the difference in the world," DeLuca said encouragingly.

"There was some trouble. A guy was mouthing off to a parking attendant."

"Take your time," DeLuca said. "Tell me what you remember."

"The guy driving the truck was surly, a real trouble-maker. He might have been there to tow a car away."

"What makes you say that?" DeLuca asked.

"He was wearing work clothes, and he was driving a red tow truck."

"Hold it," DeLuca said. "This is important. Tell me about those work clothes."

"Ordinary. Gray. That's all I remember."

"Any logo or company name on those clothes?"

"Nothing I could see."

"Okay," DeLuca said. "You said he was driving a red tow truck. Go back to that. What else can you tell us?"

"You know the kind of tow truck I mean. There's an attachment in the back that slips under a car's tires. It can lift the car's front or back off the ground and tow it away."

Rosie hugged Mrs. Chen. "We have another lead," Rosie whispered, trying to control her excitement.

"Keep going," DeLuca said.

"The driver of the truck drove away in a huff and nearly hit the valet. It all happened so fast, but I remember one weird thing. The guy in the truck was laughing really loud as he drove away."

"What did the guy look like?"

"I didn't see his face, but he had dark hair."

"Vince, this is Ivy's mother," Mrs. Chen cut in. "You didn't remember any of this at the time?"

"No. I was too upset. I've been thinking about that day off and on for years. I think the memory has been there all that time. I'm sorry I didn't recall it sooner."

"But you remember it now, and I'm grateful," Mrs. Chen murmured.

"Do you remember if there was a name on that tow truck?" DeLuca asked.

"I don't think so. All I remember is the bright red paint."

"I'm curious about something. Why did you wander away from Ivy's party?"

"You're putting me on the spot," Vince said.

"I'm just trying to get the full picture of what was going on."

"Ivy and I had been enjoying an e-mail and telephone friendship for months. We have a lot in common, professional musicians, things like that. When she came to the area for the three concerts, we went somewhere each evening to unwind. You know, a coffee house, a midnight movie, a walk along the waterfront. We were happy just to spend time together and get to know each other better." He choked up.

"Take a deep breath," DeLuca said.

"Maybe you already figured this out. I had fallen in love with Ivy. I think she had feelings for me too. I was working up the courage to tell her. I lost my nerve, but—"

DeLuca broke the silence. "But what?"

"That Monday at the Vinoy when we said goodbye, she kissed me, not like a friend. It was much more than that. She said, "Call me. Even if it's not about music, promise you'll call me." He struggled to catch his breath. "I never had the chance. I've been carrying this torch for her ever since. Please find her."

"Vince, you may have helped us more than you know," he said. "If you think of anything else, get back to me. I'll be in touch. I'd still like to retrace everything at the Vinoy. Being back at the place where it happened may call up more details. By the way, I'm curious about something. In the original investigation, there was no mention that you and Ivy were, you know, more than friends."

"Ivy is a very private person," Vince said. "And I've been called reclusive. We were just getting to know each other. We hadn't expressed our feelings to each other or to anyone in the orchestra. No one would have said we were more than friends. Until that weekend, we didn't know it ourselves."

"Thank you, Vince. You've been very helpful." DeLuca snapped his fingers. "One more thing, Vince. Did you happen to notice a suitcase among Ivy's belongings when she was leaving?"

"I definitely noticed. There was a dragon imprinted on the leather. It was unusual and very exotic. It was so much like Ivy herself."

"How about a footlocker? Did she have a footlocker with her too? You know the ordinary type like a kid might take to summer camp or college."

"No. I didn't notice anything like that."

"Thanks. I'll get back to you," DeLuca said.

"I'm easy to get in touch with. I'm usually home practicing for a concert. Call me."

DeLuca called his partner, Detective Hernandez. "We have something to work with." He ran everything by him that he'd just learned from Vince. "Yeah. I do believe him. He's one heck of a love-sick puppy."

After DeLuca finished that phone call, he turned to Mrs. Chen. "How much of this did you know about Vince Ivanov?"

"Just that Ivy mentioned him several times. How nice he was. He was shy. He had a good sense of humor. He was a talented violinist. Now that I put it all together, it's possible she was falling for him." She shook her head. "So many possibilities were taken from her that day."

"Mrs. Chen, I think you've helped us enough for one day," DeLuca said. "We can continue tomorrow at the lab and police station. For now, we'll take you to your hotel."

"Thank you," Mrs. Chen said. "I am tired, but if it's no trouble for Rosie, I'd like to stay and chat for a while."

"I would like that," Rosie said.

"Okay, we'll work around it," DeLuca said. He spoke privately to Officer Randall and then turned to Rosie and Mrs. Chen. "Officer Randall will stay here for now. And let's everybody keep in mind that the media just released some details about Ivy. The estate sale and Rosie's Treasures were mentioned. This is when the curious start walking by, peeking in windows, and making wacko calls. Officer Randall will see to it that everything here stays under control."

DeLuca pulled a folder from a stack of files. "Mrs. Chen, there is something of a personal nature in the original file that didn't make it to the newspapers, and I thought you'd like to hear it. It has to do with your husband."

Mrs. Chen's eyes lit up. "Please. Go ahead."

"One of the tea cups Ivy bought at Mrs. Arnoff's shop was chipped," DeLuca said. "Mrs. Arnoff, who prides herself on being honest, pointed it out. Ivy said the chip wouldn't change her mind about buying the set. She said there was an ancient Chinese proverb her father taught her." He checked a page of notes. "According to Mrs. Arnoff, it goes, 'the wise man seeks perfection, but only the fool expects to find it.'"

Mrs. Chen took a deep breath. "That proverb was one of the favorites in our house. Yi quoted it often. Thanks to him, Ivy and I drew upon the philosophy of ancient Chinese thinkers. Yi was so wise." Her voice trembled. "That was very kind of you, Detective. Thank you. I wish you had known Yi. You would see that Ivy inherited so many of his admirable traits and philosophy."

After Detective DeLuca left, Mrs. Chen embraced Rosie. "I want to thank you again for contacting the police about Ivy. I have a good feeling about this investigation." She looked at the stack of photos Detective DeLuca had set on the table.

"Do you mind if I look at the photos of the items in the footlocker?"

"Go ahead," Rosie said. "But please be honest. Would you like me to leave? Jane, my helper, left for the day. I'd be happy to work on inventory."

"No. I'd like you to stay."

"Okay then," Rosie said. "Let's get cracking." A sense of purpose coursed through her body. But that old sense of foreboding followed swiftly. It was very possible that Ivy, like Tess, might not be found alive.

15

Ivy Chen

Saturday, May 9, 2009

This morning Frank locked me in my closet while the woman I call 'Hope' cleaned my apartment. I still haven't seen her. I'd like to speak to her. Contact with another human being has become so important to me—someone, anyone besides Frank Brandt! But now all my energies have been directed at keeping Frank interested in the erhu. He has grown weary of the same pieces. I've gone through most of my repertoire and even the exercise pieces I practiced while a student at the conservatory. I've begun composing songs, but he hasn't heard them yet. I have not given up hope that I can lull him to sleep and sneak the keys away from him.

So far, I have finished four pieces and transcribed them on paper, and I have one more partially composed in my mind. The title of each one bore Frank's name. He was such a conceited man, he would adore the titles, and he would believe what he perceived as the truth in each one. It made me nauseous to even recall the names, but I know they were meant to mock him, and ultimately that gave me perverse pleasure. The first, I called *Frank, the Master of his Universe*. The second, *Frank's Devotion to Music*. The third, *Frank, the Creative Thinker's Dance*. And the fourth, my most complicated, *Frank's Way with Words*.

That horrid, rattling key! Fear raced through me.

Frank bolted into my room with a noticeably bored expression on his face. I was taking the song I had composed in my head and transcribing it to paper, using numbers, letters, and native characters. As Frank stared at my efforts, disbelief and confusion distorted his features. He had no concept of the native characters which were the typical cipher notation system I had learned in China. This was the system I still preferred over the more modern staff system typically shown with five lines for the right hand and five lines for the left.

"What are all these weird little markings?" he asked.

"Symbols," I said.

He scowled. "But what are they for?"

"They tell me what bowing technique to use, like play the outside string or the inside string." To heighten his interest, I picked up the erhu and the bow and demonstrated each explanation as I mentioned it. "The symbols also tell me whether I should push or pull the bow."

"That's it?" he asked.

"No. They also show me the required left-hand fingering, such as press the string with the index finger." I continued demonstrating. "Or press the string with the middle finger, or the ring finger, or the small finger."

I adopted the kindly expression of Miss Li, my first music teacher. "See these?" I pointed at an area of the page. "They are musical interpretation symbols."

"You're trying to confuse me."

"No. I'm trying to tell you about the symbols. Maybe you'd like to explain them to the guys at work. It's very interesting. The symbols tell me to pluck the strings with the right hand, or play staccato, or slide down, or—"

"Quit babbling like some snooty teacher, and just play the music." Frank waved his hand at the symbols. "That stuff is pure baloney. I've seen real music with lines and notes. I know what real music looks like."

"That's the staff notation system," I explained. "I'm describing the cipher notation system. It's just another way of showing the musician what to play. Look here."

"Shut up," he said and slapped me across the face. "You're giving me a headache and getting me all mixed up." He stormed out of the room and locked me in using that hateful key he always carried with him.

My cheek throbbed from hitting the wall, but the pain didn't distract me from my anger. Every word Frank uttered was an insult to the musicians who had delighted audiences and themselves for centuries with the sweetest sounds in the world. But if Frank didn't want to know the difference between the cipher and staff notation systems, then too bad for him! Let him and his small mind stay trapped in his small world forever.

He would never know what he was missing. If he at least tried to learn something new, he might become more introspective, more in tune with his feelings, more sympathetic to the plight of others. He might even regret having imprisoned me in this dark dungeon, but now I knew for certain that dragging him into the sunny happiness of understanding music in different forms was never going to happen. His heart and soul were surely dead. Maybe he had been that way since birth. Maybe he would go to his grave that way. If I had a say in things, that would happen today. As soon as possible. Like right now.

Enough of such negative thoughts. I pressed a damp washcloth to my forehead and felt a slight bump. I tried to ignore it. Right now, my mission was to keep Frank interested in music while I planned my way out of this soul-crushing prison.

Frank rushed into my room about a half-hour later. He made excuses about why he had returned, but I knew he wanted to hear a song from the erhu. He regretted not hearing any music earlier. I regretted being shoved into the wall. I would find revenge through the music.

Frank was relatively calm so I asked, "Frank, can you guess the name of this song?" I began playing a piece with an occasional discordant sound reminiscent of Frank's mispronunciation of words as he flaunted his vocabulary of three and four syllables. When I finished, I set down my bow. "I wrote it myself, so I named it. What name do you think I chose?"

"I don't know. Something like, uh, *Summer in China*, I suppose." He curled his lip.

"Maybe I'll save that for the next one. This one is named *Frank's Way with Words*." Frank didn't catch on that each word contained one syllable, but it was a rewarding moment for me.

He pointed at himself. "Me? I'm the Frank in that song?"

"Yes. What do you think?"

He couldn't contain his smile. "Play it every day. I'll decide and let you know later."

Later. Future time. Just what I was hoping for, and so much more. Seeing Mama and Baba, the sunshine and rain and sky, and Vince, my sweet, sophisticated Vince. All those images rolled through my thoughts and brought a smile to my lips.

Frank probably thought the smile was for him. If he only knew.

All of this turned into a good learning experience for me. Now I knew how to gain future time. Five paths existed: *Frank, the Master of his Universe*, and *Frank's Devotion to Music*, and *Frank and the Creative Thinker's Dance*, and *Frank's Way With Words*, plus the fifth one, incomplete and nameless at the moment. While thinking of a name, I relished the power the erhu has given me to inflate Frank's ego, and ultimately, with luck on my side, cause him to slip up and make a mistake. Oh, now the name of the fifth song, the fifth path to freedom, came to me. *Frank's Awesome Brain Power* will be the name!

The erhu and I had our work cut out for us.

16
Frank Brandt

Wednesday, May 27, 2009

If the guys here at the shop knew my name would soon take its place in music history, they would finally get it. I was somebody important. I was the subject of a song called *Frank's Way With Words*. They would finally admit I had a wonderful vocabulary. No, not wonderful…awesome. An awesome vocabulary. But these guys were hopeless. They didn't know squat.

I laughed out loud as I parked my truck in designated spot number three. Maybe the boss would move me up a spot when the news about me landed in the daily newspapers. I didn't want the number one spot. It was reserved for his favorite. His go-fer. His goon for handing out the day's assignments, the bonuses, and the break-times. Butt-kisser, that's what he was.

What was the big deal anyway about the number of a parking spot? My name would live on forever in the title of Ivy's work. No, not work, composition; that's what she called it. *Frank's Way With Words*. I liked it. My tremendous vocabulary inspired the title. Music lovers throughout the world would soon know my name. They would hum my song. Musicians would play my song. It would be written out for them the real way, with notations, not some wacky weird-o way.

As I got out of the truck, a thought propelled itself into my mind. Ivy couldn't tell the world about my song. She was a prisoner. No problem. I'd make it work. When the time seemed right, I'd put my name on the composition and mail it to TV stations and radio shows. The big shots in charge would love the song. They'd make sure everyone heard it. After all, I had a way with words. Those words would make me famous throughout the world, maybe even the universe.

17
Ivy Chen

Wednesday, June 10, 2009

Weeks have gone by, and so far I haven't come up with a convincing plan that would encourage Frank to let me enter the main part of the house. I haven't managed to steal his keys either. He offered to bring wine for our dinners before our erhu concerts. I agreed reluctantly, so he would figure he was doing me a favor. Ha! The wine and my sleepy songs encouraged him to nod off, briefly, but that wasn't enough. I needed him to fall into a deep sleep, so I could steal the keys and manage to escape without him waking up, catching me, and overpowering me. I needed to devise a more effective plan. Would Hope, the cleaning woman, help me? Or was she a prisoner here too?

I didn't dare whisper to her through the crack in the door. If she was Frank's prisoner, she wouldn't risk responding. She could possibly gain an advantage with Frank by turning me in for breaking the rules and speaking. Questions ran through my thoughts. Why would Hope go along with Frank's imprisoning me? Was she crazy too? Was I crazy to think she would betray Frank and help me?

Today, a new question cropped up because I realized that crazy people like Frank and serial killers too, often created a repetitive pattern. Had Frank kept a woman captive before me? If so, there could be traces of her in the apartment. I decided to look everywhere when Frank was at work. In the back of my mind, a question lingered. If a woman had been held here, how did she get away? I didn't allow myself to think of the alternative. Instead, I intended to study the apartment with fresh eyes.

A thought came to me about the twelve sheets of paper and two pens I found under the mattress soon after I arrived. At the time, I considered the possibility they might have been hidden. Maybe they were. Maybe a prisoner before me had hidden them. Was I crazy to let a sudden burst of optimism give me hope I might actually escape and see my beloved Mama and Baba again?

More than anything, I wanted Mama and Baba to know I am alive. I didn't want them to worry. I missed them so much. I daydreamed about our reunion, adding new details each time about what we would say and do and what our future together would be. But mostly I imagined the happiness we would share when we strolled along in the sunlight, hearing the laughter of children playing, savoring the fragrance of blossoms, free to go where we pleased without even a hint of fear holding us back.

18
Rosie Renard

Monday, January 9, 2012, 4:30 P.M.

"Mrs. Chen, I'll be right back. I'm just going downstairs to my shop for a few minutes. Please, have another cup of tea and more cookies," Rosie said, and checked her watch. "I want to encourage Jane to leave early. She's worked a very long day."

Mrs. Chen frowned. "Are you sure my being here and talking about such sad events isn't a burden to you? I should probably go to my hotel."

"No. Please stay," Rosie said. "I have my reasons, but I'll save that for another time."

Rosie walked past Officer Randall, who was sitting near the workroom with a pile of folders spread out on her lap. "Catching up on paperwork?" Rosie asked.

"I'm reading through all the reports and info about the investigation." Officer Randall rubbed her eyes with the heels of her hands and sighed. "I wish something would jump out at me and crack this case wide open."

"I know. It's so difficult to accept that sometimes evil wins out," Rosie said.

"Detective DeLuca told me about your cousin who went missing and didn't survive. I'm sorry. If you ever want to talk about it, let me know." She gathered the folders. "I'm working with a support group to help the family members of victims. I could learn from your experience, and maybe you could learn something from me. You know, a mutual help thing."

"It's probably too late for Jack and me. We went through the loss of his sister years ago," Rosie said. Her voice cracked.

"It's never too late." Officer Randall shook her head. "That's one of the things I've learned so far, and I've met with families of both adult and child missing persons."

"I'm assuming this is personal with you?" Rosie asked.

"No, I never experienced it myself, but I'm aware of groups like Let's Bring Them Home and the National Center for Missing and Exploited Children. Many of us in law enforcement develop a special interest. For me, it's missing persons. If you ever want to find out about a support group, talk to me. I have names and numbers."

"Thank you," Rosie said. "I'll keep it in mind." She turned and walked into the front room. She waited while Jane finished a phone call about an upcoming sale.

"Jane, thanks for all your help today," Rosie said. "You should run along and catch up to your friends. Have some fun before the concert."

"Thanks, Rosie. I'll just grab my backpack. Oh, by the way, Ted called twice."

"Did he ask for me?" Rosie tried to squelch her excitement.

"No. He wanted to talk to me."

"About what?"

"He's worried about you. He asked how you were holding up about the missing-person investigation."

"What did you tell him?"

"I said he should ask you himself."

"What did he say?"

"He's working up to it. Do you want my advice, Rosie?"

"When did you start asking my permission?"

"Ha, Ha. Very funny." She peered at Rosie through her oversized glasses. "My advice is quit being a hard head. You've been wearing a hard hat for so long, it's taking over. Give Ted a chance. He's such a hottie. All the guys in my life right now are scrawny and pale, like they only come out at night. The Vampire Brigade, sort of." She slung her back pack over her shoulder. "Don't get me wrong. They're my friends, and I love them, but Ted is so different. He's buff, and he has an adorable farmer's tan. That's so sexy. Besides, he misses you. And you miss him."

"Says who?"

"Look in the mirror. That's who."

After Rosie served more tea and cookies, Mrs. Chen looked one more time at the photos that showed the contents of the footlocker. She cried softly as she set them out and stacked and restacked them. Finally, she sat back and sighed contentedly.

"My Ivy is alive, Rosie. I know it. I can sense her spirit here among her belongings."

She took Rosie's hand. "I wish Yi, her father, could be here in this moment of hope. We knew so much despair for so long, but now, a change is about to take place." She touched her heart. "My Ivy will soon come back to me."

Rosie squeezed Mrs. Chen's hand. She knew the odds were slim. She could be honest with herself, but she needed to give Mrs. Chen every hope possible. Yet she must not get caught up in Mrs. Chen's belief that Ivy was definitely alive. "The detectives will ferret out every clue in the footlocker and at the estate."

"Poor Yi. I know the detectives told you he passed away. I shouldn't burden you with this."

"I'm a good listener. Please tell me about Yi."

Mrs. Chen began pacing the floor. "After Ivy's disappearance, I called Yi, and he flew to Florida immediately. The police declared Ivy a missing person, and Yi nearly went crazy trying to find her. He was convinced he could have kept her safe. He and Ivy were so close, so drawn to each other. They looked so much alike...dark hair and eyes, Ivy's graceful beauty, Yi's noble face. They were like two elegant ceremonial robes fashioned from the same bolt of cloth."

Pausing, she wiped the tears from her eyes. "After many months went by and the case turned cold, we each lived in our own private world of fear believing the unthinkable, that our Ivy was gone forever.

If she was alive, why wouldn't she return to us? We had no answers. You cannot imagine our suffering and silence. We couldn't speak about the possibility that she might never return. Then we stopped speaking altogether. We would lie in silence in our bed, side by side, never finding the words to make the pain go away. I had nightmares. I kept seeing my Ivy's body, abandoned, alone, and cold, but not even a body of a woman resembling Ivy was found."

She shook her head in despair. "Yi had nightmares too. He imagined Ivy trapped some place, hearing her cry out to him to come find her and set her free. He was inconsolable. We gave up on each other. I remained in our condo in Chicago and went back to nursing at a nearby hospital. Yi tried to run his successful import-export business, but his heart wasn't in it. He eventually sold it and returned to Shanghai. He didn't fit into life in China any more than he fit into his life in America. My poor Yi. He became a shadow of himself, no longer present wherever he was. He blamed himself for being too busy with work to have attended Ivy's concert series in Florida. He died in China six months after he arrived there. A heart attack, that's what the doctors said, but they were wrong. A broken heart is what killed him."

"This is too painful for you," Rosie said. "I'm worried you'll make yourself sick."

Mrs. Chen looked out the large, second-story window. Monk parakeets squawked in the trees. The music from an ice-cream truck rang out. "Once the world was normal like that for me," she said, pointing toward the cars passing along the street and a group of joggers jogging in place at a traffic light, "but then uncertainty became the new normal. The phone rang during the day and all hours of the night. Each time I picked up the receiver, I expected to hear a police officer say, 'Mrs. Chen, I have good news. Your daughter is here with us at the station. Would you like to speak to her?' But then the officer would say something like, 'We followed up this lead or that lead, there were so many leads, and this one didn't pan out. We have other leads, other suspects. We'll call you again when there's a new development.'"

Mrs. Chen sat down in the rocker next to Rosie. "But now that the case is reopened and you're here with me, I'm having good thoughts.

The names Ivy and Rosie come from nature, from Mother Earth. They suggest harmony. You and I want the same thing, to bring Ivy home. Ivy is descended from a grandfather born in the Year of the Dragon. Ivy has strength, power, and luck on her side. That will make our job easier. Her grandmother, Yi's mother, was born in the Year of the Snake. A snake is compatible with a dragon and will enhance his powers. Ivy has all that luck on her side."

"I may have some luck of my own to add," Rosie said. "I'm half-French on my father's side, the Renard side of the family, and I was born on July fourteenth, the French day of Independence. Freedom. Freedom for Ivy. We're a team, a lucky team, Mrs. Chen. We'll help the detectives."

"Yes, we will." Mrs. Chen smiled. "And this year, 2012, is the Chinese Year of the Dragon. That's another bit of luck for us. Rosie, you believe Ivy is still alive, don't you?"

"We should be cautiously optimistic." Rosie weighed her words carefully. "It's possible that even after all this time Ivy is a survivor. There have been several famous kidnappings where the victims survived for months or even years and eventually returned to their families."

"Yes, I know about them," Mrs. Chen said as she rocked slowly back and forth. "I've read the newspaper accounts of several ordeals so many times the facts are lodged in my memory. I've never lost hope that Ivy is alive."

She drew a ragged breath. "The reporters talked about the strength it took to stay alive. That's the trait I pray will bring Ivy home. She's strong in mind. She practices the ancient arts that Yi taught her. She may not look it, but she's strong in body too. She and I ran and jogged together for years until my knees gave out."

Rosie closed her eyes, letting the rocking of the chair soothe her. "Let's imagine Ivy strong and determined, overcoming fear, and staying alive."

Mrs. Chen's eyes misted over. She reached across to Rosie and held her hand. "I wonder if you found the footlocker or if the footlocker found you."

Rosie wanted to comfort Mrs. Chen, but the words wouldn't come. Heartbreaking memories of her cousin Tess tore through her mind. She and Jack got off the school bus with their friends and started walking home. Tess and Tess's friend Abby hopped off the bus and walked behind them. The day was no different than any other. She and Jack walked ahead paying no attention to the younger girls, Tess and Abby, who lingered behind. She and Jack went to their homes. Abby went to her home. Tess walked the final two blocks alone, as she always did. A half-hour later, Jack's mother asked him where Tess was. Jack said she was probably talking to Abby and would be home soon.

Tears rolled down Rosie's cheeks. If only the clocks could be turned back to that moment when they got off the bus, she and Jack would have done things differently. They would have waved goodbye to Abby and stuck together until they were all safely home, and then Tess would have followed her usual routine, rushing into the house, laughing as she told her mom everything that had happened at school that day.

But the clocks didn't turn back. Tess was abducted in that short distance from Abby's house to her own house when she walked alone. The man lived nearby. He knew Tess and every child who got off that bus. It came out during the trial he had enticed Tess into his house with a made-up story about his cat giving birth to kittens and his needing her help. Tess went into the house. Two days later, he strangled her and hid her body in the cellar. He had silenced Tess's infectious laughter forever.

Another heartbreaking memory came to Rosie. She and her parents visited Jack, Uncle Jeff, and Aunt Jessica to help bolster their spirits. They were sitting in the living room reminding each other to be optimistic, that Tess might walk through the door at any moment. The doorbell clattered. Fear shot through the room. No one wanted to open the door and welcome in bad news, but Jack finally gave in. The detectives entered and stood in the living room, looking sad and uncomfortable. Their words came slowly and softly. Tess had been found. A neighbor admitted he had abducted her. Tess didn't survive.

"Did my baby suffer?" Aunt Jessica asked the detectives, wiping away the tears that streamed down her face.

Rosie didn't remember hearing the answer, but Aunt Jessica pounded her fists on the detective's chest and then ran screaming into the back yard. She dropped to her knees and hugged the pine tree she and Tess had planted just a week ago. Uncle Jeff tried to pry her away from the tree, but she hung on, crying uncontrollably. The tree uprooted, and Aunt Jessica flung it back into the hole in the ground. Uncle Jeff tried to calm her down, but she became frantic, screaming and crying until she collapsed into his arms. He carried her back into the house and called the family doctor who arrived by car minutes later.

That was a breaking point. From that moment on, Rosie remembered that she and Jack faced an emotional gulf that stranded them on one side and their parents on the other side. The gulf narrowed over the years, but it never disappeared. There was always an unspoken accusation circling around Jack and her and clinging to them. In the first few days, their parents said in many different ways but always with the same meaning, "If the two of you had walked home with Tess, she wouldn't have been alone, she wouldn't have been abducted. You should have looked out for her." They eventually took back those words. She and Jack longed to hear the word "forgiveness," but it was never mentioned.

"Hey, Rosie and Mrs. Chen," Officer Randall called up the stairs, pulling Rosie from the flashbacks that always left her feeling empty. "Detective DeLuca just called. It's been a long day, but this is important. They'd like Mrs. Chen at the station. I'm driving."

"What did the detectives find out?" Mrs. Chen called down the stairs, her tired voice now charged with energy.

"The biggest breakthrough so far, but I don't know any details," Officer Randall exclaimed.

"Don't let me drag down the investigation," Mrs. Chen said. "For Ivy's sake, let's go right now. Oh, and I want Rosie to be there with me. She's inherited good luck. We need all we can get."

"I'll run it by Detective DeLuca."

Several long minutes passed as Rosie helped Mrs. Chen down the stairs.

"Okay, Rosie. You're on board," Officer Randall said. "Detective DeLuca agreed. Let's go!"

"Start the engine!" Rosie exclaimed, willing herself to be hopeful and cheerful for Mrs. Chen's sake. And Ivy's sake too.

19
Rosie Renard

Monday, January 9, 2012, 7:45 P.M.

Rosie and Mrs. Chen held on to the armrests in the back seat of the squad car as Officer Randall floored the gas pedal. She zoomed east, turned north toward the police station, and whipped into the parking lot. Minutes later, Rosie and Mrs. Chen entered the conference room. Detective DeLuca, who was leaning over the table in the middle of the room, looked up from the countless pages of notes spread out before him from a folder labeled in bold type: Ivy Chen, Missing Person, 2008.

Detective DeLuca greeted Mrs. Chen and Rosie warmly. "Sit right here by me," he said to Mrs. Chen and Rosie, and pulled back two chairs. "Detective Hernandez is following up something at the Allendale home. He'll be back soon. Mrs. Chen, we need your help in identifying a piece of evidence that's blurred. Rosie, you're here because that's what Mrs. Chen would like, and Officer Randall thinks it's a good idea. It's not standard procedure, but we're going along with it because it could help the investigation."

"Thank you," Rosie said, grateful to help in any way possible.

"We've been running the tapes from that Monday, the day Ivy disappeared. Let's take a look." DeLuca tilted the screen toward Mrs. Chen and Rosie to give them a good view. "Are you sure you're prepared for this, Mrs. Chen?"

"Yes, but do you remember our little talk when I first arrived in town? As I said then, you need not waste precious time worrying about how I'll take whatever developments arise. I've steeled my nerves to what I might see or even imagine. I want the person who took my Ivy caught and punished. This tape could reveal who he is. There. I've said my piece. I rehearsed it all the way here. That ride in the squad car was good practice for steeling my nerves."

DeLuca cocked an eyebrow. "Okay." He pressed a button. "Here's Ivy's car crossing the Sunshine Skyway Bridge toward Sarasota at 6:12 that Monday evening. Luck is on our side because the rain had stopped, and visibility at the toll booth is clear. We can see Ivy's face."

A small gasp escaped from Mrs. Chen's mouth. "I'm sorry. Even having seen this before, it's the very last film anyone has of her. Please continue."

DeLuca nodded at Mrs. Chen. "And here's Ivy paying the toll, and we can see she's saying something to the toll taker. She's smiling, so we're assuming they had a pleasant chat."

"I saw this part of the tape during the original investigation," Mrs. Chen said.

"I know. It's all in the report. But to stay on track, Detective Hernandez and I want to put everything in the right order. We don't want to jump to conclusions and knock out theories that might prove true. We'll work up to the new information, like the red tow truck. And there's a blurry image where we definitely need your help. Okay?"

"Okay," Mrs. Chen said firmly.

DeLuca pushed the button. "Let's go."

"Good," Mrs. Chen said, rubbing her hands briskly together.

DeLuca pointed at the screen. "Here's a view of some of the interior of Ivy's car. There's no sign of any luggage, so she must have stored it in the trunk. That's in line with what the shop owner, Mrs. Arnoff said the day Ivy disappeared. She sold Ivy the tea set with the ivy design that ended up in the footlocker."

He glanced at a page of notes on the table. "During the initial investigation, Mrs. Arnoff reported that she walked with Ivy to Ivy's car. She held the box containing the tea set while Ivy opened the trunk.

She said she didn't look into the trunk. It was drizzling, and she was holding an umbrella and wanted to get back to her shop. We're trying to locate her. We hope to have her work with a court-appointed psychiatrist who could mentally take her back to that day, that car, that trunk, and possibly Ivy's leather suitcase."

"That sounds promising," Mrs. Chen said. "Please do your best."

"Fortunately, for us, these surveillance tapes are in color. Often we can't get a reading of the license plate, but the color of the vehicle is a big help. So, let's get to the red tow truck and driver. Our team has reviewed all the tapes for that entire Monday, both afternoon and evening. Afternoon because he might have been ahead of Ivy, lying in wait for her as she exited. Evening because he might have been following her. There were several red trucks, but only one tow truck."

"Bring it on!" Rosie exclaimed. She clamped her hand over her mouth. "Sorry. I lost control."

"I'll give you a pass on that," DeLuca said, glancing up from the fax. "Detective Hernandez and I shouted something similar when we saw the tapes."

"Here's the red tow truck, a 1998," DeLuca said and hit the pause button. "There's no logo and no name. Ivy's friend Vince was right about that. But hey, an anonymous tow truck?" He shook his head in disbelief. "That's suspicious. Why wouldn't he advertise his services?"

DeLuca pointed at the screen. "The driver's face is partially covered by the brim of his cap, but we can see he has dark hair, and he's wearing a gray work shirt. That fits with what Vince told us. He's traveling five minutes behind Ivy. There were several vehicles between them. It's possible he stayed back because he didn't want to attract her attention. We're quite sure he was at the Vinoy when Ivy was having breakfast, and we can see he was definitely on the bridge at the same time Ivy was. Coincidence? I don't think so."

He fast-forwarded the tape. "But here's what really grabbed us," he said. "Right here, two hours later, at eight-sixteen to be exact, that same red tow truck crossed the bridge heading back to St. Pete. Ivy's car didn't re-appear on any of the tapes from that day."

Mrs. Chen balled her hands into fists. "Ivy was coming to Sarasota to visit her aunties and me." Her voice cracked, but she quickly regained control and continued. "Who's driving that truck? Get him. Find out what he did to my Ivy."

"Let me give a quick review," DeLuca said. "Ivy's Lincoln town car wasn't returned to the car rental place. She didn't cross the bridge back to St. Petersburg. Her car was never seen again. To answer your question, Mrs. Chen, our best guess is the man in the truck followed Ivy over the bridge. It's possible he approached her someplace where she stopped, a gas station or restaurant maybe. We've seen that many times before, and we're checking that out right now."

He picked up several faxed pages from the table and waved them. "This fax is from the detectives in Sarasota County. Some buildings where Ivy might have stopped were bulldozed, but some are still there, and some even have the same owners. Ivy might have been abducted from one of them. But that leaves a question. What happened to her car?"

He neatly stacked the faxed pages. "There are some thick brush areas along the road near where Ivy would have exited from the bridge. Our police friends in Sarasota will do a thorough search of the area. It's been more than three years, and I must warn you the chances are slim we'll find her car, but we won't know until we try.

"That leaves at least two possibilities about what happened to Ivy," DeLuca said. "Did someone take her against her will, or did her car go off the road? The photo of the truck passing back and forth on the Sunshine Skyway Bridge could back up either possibility, but the footlocker with both Ivy's fancy concert clothes and a man's soiled work clothes? That has the investigation leaning more toward abduction."

DeLuca held up a memo. "Here's something else we just learned. The license plates on that red tow truck are phony. I'm guessing the driver of that truck had the capability of making a license plate. This didn't come up in the original investigation because the red tow truck hadn't been mentioned by Vince Ivanov, and it wasn't directly following Ivy on the Sunshine Skyway Bridge. It had no logical connection to the investigation. Anyway, DMV has no record of the plates. That goes more with the planned-abduction theory. He'd have been looking for a way to escape detection."

"He's going to get away with this?" Mrs. Chen asked in a shaky voice.

"We have sources that can help us."

"You mean 'snitches,'" Mrs. Chen said and gritted her teeth. "I watch TV crime shows. I know about snitches. Drag them in here and slap them around."

"Calm down, Mrs. Chen," DeLuca said gently and patted her shoulder. "We're at the point where we can use your help. Here's that blurred image on the tape I mentioned earlier."

He hit the pause button and the interior of the tow truck filled the screen. "We can't see anyone in the passenger seat, but Ivy's petite, and maybe she's out of our line of vision. Look right there." He pointed to the passenger side. "Something's sticking up from the seat, near the window. See that blurred image?"

"Yes," Mrs. Chen said, leaning closer to the fuzzy image on the screen.

"The tow truck must have lurched forward." DeLuca dramatically pushed both hands toward the screen.

He slid a magnifying glass toward Mrs. Chen. "We don't know what we're looking at. See if you can tell what it is."

She checked the blurred image, squinting, trying first with the magnifying glass and then without it. "Oh dear." She grasped the edge of the table and held on as if it were a life preserver. "Is it possible?"

DeLuca crouched next to Mrs. Chen, their shoulders nearly touching.

"What do you see?" he asked.

"Please, please, let there be something that will help us," Rosie murmured.

"Oh, dear God." Mrs. Chen closed her eyes and folded her hands in prayer. "It's a dragon's head. It's Ivy's erhu."

"Are you sure?" DeLuca asked, peering at the blurred image.

"Yes. It's part of the dragon carved into the neck of her erhu. That's Ivy's instrument. She wouldn't leave it in a truck where it would bounce around. She wouldn't take such a risk. That could damage the erhu beyond repair. She would never have taken it out of the case and left it vulnerable."

Mrs. Chen stabbed her finger toward the screen. "Someone else did that. Not my Ivy. Not the devoted musician who loved her erhu as much as she loved the flowers in bloom and—" She sobbed. "The erhu is in the truck. We know that, but where is Ivy?"

Rosie held Mrs. Chen's hand and whispered soothing words to calm her. Detective DeLuca stepped away and made several calls on his cell. The words "cars," "tow trucks," and "license plates" were sprinkled through his conversations. His last three words came across loud and strong: "Ivy Chen's erhu."

DeLuca's phone rang and he picked up immediately. "Hank, what have you got?" He listened for several seconds without saying a word, and his face lit up. "Tell you what, Hank. Mrs. Chen figured out the blurred image is Ivy's erhu. It's looking like abduction, and the owner of the red tow truck could be our guy." He listened again intently. "I'd like Mrs. Chen to hear your news. I'm putting you on speaker. Rosie's here too. I'm going to trust them to keep all this to themselves. Mrs. Chen may know something else that can help us. She may confide in Rosie. Let's not go by the book. Let's go by our gut and include them in this latest development. What do you say?"

DeLuca listened for a few seconds. "Good," he said and pressed the speaker button.

"Hello, Mrs. Chen and Rosie. This is Detective Hernandez. I can't go into great detail. I'll save all that for Detective DeLuca, but here's the gist. The tech guys at the Cassell estate were doing a final sweep of the garage. They found a toolbox in a locked area, stored along with all kinds of plumbing, carpentry, and electrical equipment. They assumed the toolbox belonged to Ron Hemmings, the handyman. Everything's as shiny clean as the chrome on a brand-new Harley, except for a lug wrench with minute traces of grime that showed up under close inspection. It's the only tool specifically for a car. Our guess is it doesn't belong to Hemmings."

"Cut to the chase," DeLuca said.

"I hear you. We know from Hemmings' robberies and lack of evidence left behind, Hemmings was neat. The traces of grime could mean the lug wrench didn't belong to him, and a lug wrench brings up the possibility that the guy works on his own car or maybe other people's cars."

DeLuca broke in. "I'm with you on this, Hank. The work clothes left in the footlocker with Ivy's clothes were stained with grease. You're guessing the lug wrench belongs to the guy who wore those work clothes."

"Yeah, and let's take it a step further," Hernandez said.

"I'm reading your mind," DeLuca said. "The lug wrench and the work clothes belong to the guy who's driving that red tow truck."

"The guys here figure our person of interest is a mechanic or has something to do with cars."

"Sounds right to me," DeLuca said. "Lug wrenches are for loosening and tightening lug nuts on automobile wheels. He knows his way around cars, and he's not obsessively neat like Hemmings." He turned toward Mrs. Chen and Rosie. "Excuse me for a few minutes," he said. "I need to speak to Detective Hernandez. I'll be in the next room."

When he returned, he spoke to Mrs. Chen. "An officer will drive you back to the Vinoy. Get a good night's sleep. Watching these tapes had to be very stressful. And Rosie, we'll have another officer drive you home."

"That's okay, Detective. I'll take a taxi. There's no need for another one of your officers to waste time chauffeuring me." She would have preferred a leisurely walk and the chance to clear her head, but it had been a long day, and she was exhausted.

DeLuca walked with Rosie to the sidewalk in front of the police station and checked out the taxi driver who pulled up. "Don't take on a second passenger," DeLuca said. "She's to ride alone."

"Yes, sir," the taxi driver said and yawned.

"Take a brief walk while I talk to your passenger," DeLuca said.

"No problem," the taxi driver said and got out.

DeLuca stepped closer to the taxi. "Rosie, keep your guard up. The news about Ivy has spread beyond the radio and TV and newspapers. It's everywhere. Rosie's Treasures is mentioned. Be careful. Lock your doors and windows. We're going to keep an eye on your place, but there's no guarantee we can be there around the clock. Here's my card." He pressed it into her hand. "Call any time, day or night, and listen to me, Rosie. You need to take this seriously. You shouldn't be alone until this investigation is wrapped up. Is there anyone who could stay with you?"

"I'll be all right," Rosie said.

"Why don't you give your boyfriend a call? What was his name again?"

"Ted Romero. He's my ex-boyfriend."

"Right. Jane told me he's a decent guy."

"Come on. Jane is hardly an expert on guys." She shook her head. "Sorry, I didn't mean to snap at you."

"It's okay. I'm just saying, watch out for trouble, call me for any reason, and think about having someone stay at your place. It doesn't have to be Ted."

DeLuca signaled the driver to come back to the car and sent them on their way.

♫♫

The taxi driver reached forward and turned up the volume on the radio. "Are you following the story about the missing musician? You know, the gorgeous Chinese woman?" he asked over his shoulder.

"Yes, I am," Rosie said.

"I hope they find out what happened to that music lady. Lots of people think she's alive. Me and my buddies have been talking. Do you want to hear our theory?"

"Sure." She leaned toward the front seat.

"A beautiful young woman, a music hall, a mystery. It's like *The Phantom of the Opera* all over again. You know what I'm saying? A guy obsessed with a woman and her music. My buddies and I think there's someone out there in love with the beautiful musician. We figure he's been captivated by her all these years. He'll want a souvenir. He'll come for her stuff found in that garage, like that fancy concert dress. It probably brought back memories of her and that mysterious snake-charmer instrument she plays. You know what I'm talking about. It's covered with python skin."

Rosie absorbed his theory and her mind exploded with ideas. It was just like when she opened a trunk or bureau for the first time and something left behind caught her eye, and unbelievable tales of intrigue jumped into her mind. "Please pull over for a minute," she said, unbuckling her seatbelt. "I need to make a private call. Let the meter run. It's okay."

She hopped out of the taxi, pulled out Detective DeLuca's card, and called him on her cell phone. She stepped away to keep the call private.

"DeLuca here."

"Detective, it's Rosie. The taxi driver said something about the kidnapper that I think could help the Ivy Chen investigation."

"Okay. Let me hear it."

"He and his buddies think someone, they're calling him The Phantom of the Opera, will try to get his hands on Ivy's clothes and other things. The taxi driver said the Phantom will come back for souvenirs, like her concert dress. That gave me a new slant on the investigation."

"What did you come up with?"

"If Ivy was abducted, it's possible she was stalked first. You know, by some guy who has fantasies about her. I read about that in the newspapers all the time. I see it in movies too."

"What are you thinking?"

"Maybe the stalker attended her concert the weekend just before she disappeared."

"I like the way you think," he said.

"I'm guessing the stalker would go alone to the concert. Maybe the accounting records from the three concert halls would show how many single seats were sold."

"So maybe the Phantom went more than once to hear Ivy play," he said slowly, as if putting the pieces together. "She performed three times that weekend, am I right?"

"Yes. Friday, Saturday, and Sunday. Tampa, St. Pete, and Clearwater."

"This is good work, Rosie. We'll see if we can get a list of anyone who bought a single ticket for one, two, and possibly all three performances. All three would be the best place to start. I'm going to ask Detective Hernandez to check this out. He's a nut about patterns, repetitions, and so on. He'll jump all over this. Stay in touch, and stay safe."

"I will. I have to go. The taxi driver's giving me the evil eye."

Rosie got back into the taxi. "Turn left at the next corner onto Central," she said. All kinds of crazy ideas ran through her mind. She was concerned that such specific information, like Ivy's concert dress, had leaked to the press. What else was now common knowledge? She didn't want to tell the taxi driver to stop at Rosie's Treasures. She didn't want him to know who she was or where she lived. He could spread all kinds of information to the next person who hailed his taxi, and that person would pass it along, and on and on it would go.

When they were a block from her shop, Rosie said, "Just stop at the corner."

"This is near Rosie's Treasures, the shop that's involved in that missing musician's case," the driver said and pulled toward the curb. "Jeeze, Miss, someone just stepped out of the shadows a few doorways up the block." He slunk down in his seat and peered through the steering wheel. "Whoever he is, he's looking left and right like he's expecting someone. Do you know him?"

Rosie looked closely through the beam of light descending from the streetlamp. It was Ted, holding a bouquet of broccoli in each hand. That was so typical of Ted, and so appealing. He loved vegetables. Flowers were nice, but vegetables were better. That was his personal

117

view about Mother Nature's bounty. The first time he came to her apartment, he held out a paper bag and said, "Sweets for the sweet." She opened the bag, half-expecting chocolate and was surprised to find several sweet potatoes.

"Miss?" the taxi driver asked. "If you want, I'll chase him away, and you can slip inside without being mugged."

"It's okay. I know him." She sighed. The truth is she was glad to see him. She loved Ted Romero. Maybe it was because Vince Ivanov had made his love for Ivy sound so sweet and appealing, so darn right, or maybe it had nothing to do with Vince. Maybe it was just simply Ted, sweet and appealing Ted, and her undeniable love for him.

20
Rosie Renard

Monday, January 9, 2012, 10:30 P.M.

Rosie watched the taxi pull away and head down the street past Rosie's Treasures.

"Ted, what are you doing here?" she asked as he strode toward her.

"The Ivy Chen case, your name, and your shop were all over the news. I wanted to make sure you were okay."

They stood inches apart within the circle of lamplight. Everything beyond that sphere was inky black, and Rosie felt as though they were the only two people in this entire area.

"These are for you," he said and handed over the broccoli bouquets. "What do you say we go inside and talk about us?"

"Ted, there is no us."

"Give me another chance. Could we go inside and talk about broccoli?"

She rifled through her purse for her key as they walked toward her shop. "Okay," she said, "but broccoli, that's all. You're something, working every angle. You didn't bring carrots or cauliflower." She scowled and a smile escaped her lips. "No, you went straight for broccoli, my favorite." She unlocked the door and they stepped inside. "You did that on purpose, didn't you?" She fumbled for the light switch and found it, bathing them in light.

"I wanted to get your attention. I think I got it." He grinned.

Ted and his subtle humor were wearing down her resistance, but she refused to give in. Love was too complicated and too painful. "Come on up. I don't want any curiosity seekers coming by to peek in the windows."

"I'll follow you anywhere."

"Cut it out, Ted."

"You can't blame a guy for trying."

At the top of the stairs, she unlocked the door to her apartment. Her hand trembled. The key rattled. She didn't know if she was nervous because Ted was so close or that those old familiar longings clouded her judgment. Maybe it was the thought of curiosity seekers hanging around and pestering her or scaring away business. "I'll put the bouquets in the fridge."

"Let's sit down and talk this out." He patted the cushion beside him on the couch.

"We agreed to take a break from each other. You thought it was a good idea too."

"I did," he said. "But I miss you. I miss our Friday-night dancing and our talks about music. I miss everything. I wish things could be the way they were."

"I need room to breathe, Ted." She wouldn't give in to his charm. "I need a break from you. We've been through this."

"I'd like to say I'm running out of patience, but that's what you want me to say. That way, I'd be the one breaking things off. It's not going to happen that way, Rosie. If we break up for good, it's going to be because you say, 'I don't want to see you ever again.' Is that what you want?"

Tears pooled in her eyes. "No, it isn't. I want you to stay, but I'm so mixed up. I'm having those awful feelings about the past again. The flashbacks too. It's all so scary."

"Why don't you take a few days off? Come to the farm with me. Soak up the sunshine. Let the rain pour down on your face. Connect to what's real, not to the monsters that lurk in your mind, not to the guilt you've been holding on to for all these years. Does any of this make sense to you?"

"I guess so, but—"

"Your cousin Jack has the same problem. He talked to me about it. I get it. The two of you have been through the worst thing imaginable. Maybe your guilt feeds off his and vice versa. Like I said, I get it, but where does that leave me? We can't go on like this forever."

"I know that," Rosie said. "I know how unfair this is to you. I want to change. I think if Ivy Chen is found alive, I can accept that life can be good, not necessarily fair—it's never going to seem fair that Tess didn't make it—but I know that the only one to blame for what happened is the kidnapper. Not Jack. Not me. All the blame is on that heartless pervert, but I can't always be the carefree, happy person you want me to be. You'll get tired of this, of me."

"That's not going to happen. We have a good chance of living happily ever after." He leaned in and kissed her on the lips. He took her hand in his and raised it to his heart.

"Here's what we need to do," he said, kissing her fingertips. "We walk together to the bedroom. It's that easy. We've done it before. Being in bed together has always been great. We both said so. You're pushing me away because of the Ivy-Chen-missing-person case, aren't you?"

"No," she said. "We broke up weeks ago, before I knew anything about Ivy Chen."

"Okay, you're right, but I think she's going to keep us apart."

"What are you talking about?" Rosie asked.

"Ivy Chen has stirred up those painful memories for you, but nothing you do or say will bring back your cousin Tess. It wasn't your fault any more than the disappearance of Ivy Chen is your fault. You're not the guardian of the world. You're just you. I love you. You've told me you love me. We love each other. Let's go from there."

Rosie slumped back on the couch. "It sounds so nice and simple when you say it, like 'roses are red and violets are blue', but I'm a mess, Ted. As long as I'm helping someone, I think of myself as a valuable person, but once I'm just me, without a cause, those old feelings of worthlessness overwhelm me. I know it's all connected to Tess being abducted. At first, I was blamed for what happened to her

121

and later some of the blame was taken back, but I wasn't forgiven. That's a lot to live with."

She blinked back her tears. "Every holiday after her disappearance, Tess was an unseen presence at the table. It's like she was there opening gifts, passing the gravy and mashed potatoes, and blowing out the candles. Her presence overshadowed Jack and me. We became invisible. That's how we felt, and that's how we acted. We wanted to escape. We even wondered if anyone would notice or even care if we moved away. Was it so wrong for us to laugh? To enjoy ourselves?"

"Quit tormenting yourself about what happened. You can't go back and change things."

"I know, but I just can't wrap my brain around it."

"We can go forward together, Rosie. Let's give love a chance. What do you have to lose?"

She cupped her hands around his face. "You. That's what. I'm lucky to have you in my life. I know that, but I throw it all away when you start talking about making a fresh start, and commitment, and growing old together."

"Cut me some slack," Ted said. "I'm thirty-eight years old. As I told you from the very beginning, I escaped from a disastrous marriage. I told you it was a case of opposites attract but can't live together. Not harmoniously, that's for sure, but there's more to it than that."

"I'd like to hear about it."

"I didn't tell you that Maggie decided she didn't want children. That wasn't what she said when we got married. I wanted children and never made any secret of it. I still do. I want children with you, Rosie. Think about us and the future we could have. Every morning a little boy and girl running around in Rosie's Treasures, giggling, calling you Mommy, and you chasing after them, and in the afternoon, they'd run around the vegetable patches with me. They'd have fun. We'd have fun. Come on, Rosie. What do you say?"

"I'll think about it. You paint a wonderful picture of family life, but it scares me. Our children will depend on both of us. I don't know if I can handle that responsibility."

"You will. You're very determined. You handle tons of responsibilities at work." Ted yawned. "I'm tired. Let's talk about this tomorrow. It's been a long day. We were shorthanded. We hustled. We pushed ourselves to keep up."

"You need to get some sleep," she said and rolled back the comforter and smoothed the sheets.

"Good. My eyes are already closing." He pulled off his shirt and pants and dropped them on the chair. He slid between the sheets and rolled onto his back. "Funny thing," he said, reaching over his head and gripping the headboard of the antique walnut bed. "A bed can last forty or fifty years, but a couple, even a couple in love, can't seem to survive three or four years." He folded his hands and rested them on his chest. "Maybe we're the exception," he said sleepily.

She slipped out of her clothes and pulled her terry robe around her. She sat down across from Ted in her favorite chair, where she usually curled up with a good book. She studied his ruggedly handsome face in the moonlight sliding into the room between the slats in the blinds.

"Ted, I want you to know something," she said. "You've had my love for a long time, from that very first dance at Club ZaZi. I don't say it very often. I should, but I don't."

"That's because it scares you," he said sleepily.

"I'm working on it," she said. "I liked what I saw that night, the hint of uncertainty in your eyes about asking me to dance. That was so refreshing, such a change from anyone else I'd met recently. You know the type. They have all the moves down pat, but you were different, and I melted on the spot."

"It must have been catching," he said. "I fell for you right then and there. You were willing to take a chance."

He stifled a yawn. "Sorry. I'm having trouble staying awake."

"You can fall asleep so fast, like a baby," she said. "How do you do it?"

"Even my conscience is tired."

Silence crept into the room. Minutes later, soft breathing sounds came from Ted's open mouth.

"Don't give up on me," she whispered, as tears slid down her cheeks. "I'll get over these awful feelings. I'll make everything up to you. I will. I promise."

She closed her eyes. The memory of the night they met flowed slowly through her mind like a meandering brook taking its own sweet time to reach the ocean. Every detail came through as crisp and fresh as if it had happened yesterday.

She arrived at Club ZaZi in Ybor City to relax, have a mojito, and dance. ZaZi Club was just the right place. The vibrant colors. The heat of the day giving way to a cool evening breeze. The dance floor not overly crowded. It was still early, but soon the place would fill up, and many would stay on until the three o'clock closing. She didn't recognize anyone, but that wasn't a problem. She liked the possibility of meeting new people.

Across the room at a table for two, a man with light brown hair and a winning smile stood up. He waited by his chair for a few moments, tapping his fingers on the table, as if he were keeping time with the music or was about to make an important decision. He tugged down the sleeves of his white cotton shirt, which was tucked into his black jeans, and came across the dance floor toward her.

There was a casual way about him, a loose stride that she found appealing. His eyes never looked away as he strode toward her. His glance slid from her head to her toes, returning again to her mane of dark hair that tumbled over her shoulders. He took in her white shimmering blouse and a black and white print skirt that swirled above her knees. She and this stranger were wearing color-coordinated clothing, black and white, like they had somehow planned on adding a touch of drama to the evening. His long-sleeved shirt added appeal, as if a dance club called for a certain bit of formality, or maybe to him, dancing was special and worth dressing up for.

She remembered making snap judgments, one after the other, but that came with her line of work, where in a few seconds she assessed people as well as merchandise. Meeting someone was part of the reason people came to Club ZaZi. She hadn't met anyone special in a long time, but maybe things were about to change.

He approached her table. "Hi. My name is Ted. Ted Romero." He groaned. "That sounded like Bond, James Bond." He groaned again. "Forget I said that," he added sheepishly.

"Forgotten, Mr. Ted Romero," she said, and tossed him a saucy look. She was glad he had the courage to walk across the floor, uncertain if she would agree to dance or say, "I'm sorry, but I'm waiting for someone. He'll be here any minute." Sometimes a man heading her way looked like he was about to walk the plank. Men had it rough, having to do all the work. She was attracted to Ted Romero from the start. He was the independent type, but a bit shy too. A nice combo. Like her, he came alone.

"May I have this dance?" he asked.

"I was just about to ask you that," she said. "Shall we dance?"

"I know you. You were Anna in *The King and I*. Let me warn you; I'm not a good dancer."

"Let's give it a try," she said.

They walked to the dance floor. His hand grasped her firmly around the waist. He wore a gold ring on his right hand, no wedding ring on the left. She liked being held firmly, but his grip was almost fierce.

"You're easy to lead," he said. "You're light on your feet. As light as an oak leaf floating toward the grass." He laughed. "I didn't go for the old cliché, light as a feather. I work outdoors. I see lots of leaves but very few feathers." He had a way with words. Now she was hooked. As they relaxed and talked, his grip loosened slightly.

"Do you live here in Tampa?" he asked as they headed back to her table.

She shook her head. "St. Petersburg."

"Me too," he said.

"Do you come here often?" She couldn't resist asking.

"Maybe not often enough," he said.

The lights swirled around them. He had stars in his eyes. They talked for hours, and the conversation turned personal. His divorce, now almost a year old, had broken his heart. Dating had turned into a series of disasters. He didn't click with anyone he met from speed

125

dates, blind dates, dates with friends of friends, or dates with people who worked out at the gym.

Creaking noises pulled Rosie out of her dreaminess. Her eyes opened. She wasn't at Club ZaZi. She was in her bedroom, and Ted was turning onto his side. He sat up and peered into the darkness. "Rosie? What are you doing over there?"

"Watching you," she said. "Talk to me. There's something I've got to know. What do you think brought us together? I think it was destiny."

"That's not true," he said, rubbing his eyes. "It was the music. We knew the same music. We liked the same music. And we liked to dance to that music. Without that connection, we never would have gotten together."

"That's crazy. You're crazy," she said.

"Crazy about music," he said. "Crazy about dancing. And crazy about you." He patted the sheet by his side. "Come on to bed."

"I thought you wanted to sleep. This isn't what I had in mind," she said.

"Just let things happen. Let's not analyze and reassemble. This isn't one of your trunks that you're turning into a toy chest for someone's first-born."

"And this isn't one of your organic vegetables that you can perfect with mulch, water, coffee grinds, and whatever else you throw in."

"Tender loving care and lots of attention," he added. "Let's not forget that. Those are the secret ingredients in the mix of what works right. Relax. Come to bed."

Rosie left her worries in the chair and slipped in beside Ted. She snuggled next to him. He drew her close and kissed her tenderly on the lips.

"I love you so much, Ted."

"Those are the words I like to hear."

"I'll say them more often."

"This is a new beginning for us," he said and kissed her neck.

She kissed him back and promised herself to work on letting go of the past. She would concentrate on the present, on Ted, on their love, and she would begin right now. She wrapped her arms around him and kissed him with all the love she had in her heart. One kiss led to another. He untied the belt to her robe. She pulled his undershirt over his head and tossed it onto the chair. They made slow, sweet love and finally fell asleep wrapped in each other's arms.

21
Ivy Chen

Friday, August 28, 2009

Brush, brush, brush. With every stroke of my hairbrush, I worked on a way to get into Frank's quarters. Progress remained slow, but I was determined to come up with a new idea. When I finished styling my hair, I sneezed. My hairbrush fell from my hand and lodged between my bed and the floor. When I reached down to retrieve it, I noticed a water color sketch on the wall near the baseboard next to my bed, partially hidden by the bedspread. Curious, I moved the bed slightly and saw the complete sketch. My breath caught in my throat!

The sketch was of Frank. Faint, like someone had attempted to wash it away, but it was there. I looked closer and covered my mouth so I wouldn't scream. It was Frank, but a shocking horrific Frank, exaggerated to emphasize his sullen face, beady eyes, pockmarked face, and cruel mouth. The artist's repulsion matched my own, and I was more fearful than ever about my future here in Frank's house.

The shock of this sketch sent my thoughts in a new direction. I had wondered if I was Frank's first captive. I had searched and searched, but I'd found no clues, no indication that someone else had been imprisoned in this apartment. In my weakened condition, I hadn't been able to move the bed. Now, feeling somewhat stronger, I eased it away from the wall. Now I knew. A previous prisoner had been kept in this room, and I wanted to know everything about her. I assumed it was a woman. That was the usual pattern: a male captor, a female captive. For now, I called her "Artiste" because the only thing I knew about her was that she captured the very essence of a person, in this case Frank, with every stroke of her brush.

I paced restlessly, trapped in this small space, wondering about Artiste. Who was she? How did she end up here? Did she escape? The answer to that last question frightened me. If she had escaped, she would have gone to the police, and they would have arrested Frank… and I wouldn't be here, imprisoned by this sick monster.

The day passed by. I searched everywhere, but nothing turned up. And then, I asked myself where I would hide something that I hoped would be found, not by Frank, but by someone who wanted to know what happened to me? I went to sleep thinking about possible hiding places. When I woke up, the answer was right in front of my eyes. The bedroom closet, the only closet in my apartment, that's where it had to be. Whatever was hidden would be out of sight, out of reach, and in an area that was difficult to get to.

I ran my fingers along the walls, checking every crevice and crack. I tapped on each and every tile on the floor, thinking of a secret space. I ran the teeth of my comb along the baseboard, hoping for a hidden niche. Nothing. I needed to search higher. I immediately set a chair in the closet, piled couch pillows on the chair, and put books in between the cushions to keep them stable. I climbed up and stood on top of the pillows. I looked everywhere, reached as high as possible, but I didn't find anything. Discouraged, I considered giving up. Making one last effort, I stood on tiptoes and reached again.

There it was! A letter tucked into a crevice where the shelf met the wall.

The letter, written on the front and back of a single page, had been folded many times into a very small square. The writing was small with pretty flourishes decorating each capital letter. I sat down on the floor as if I were going to practice yoga, cleared my mind, and smoothed the page.

An incredible exhilaration swept through my body as I began reading. Immediately, from the first words, I learned that Artiste's real name was Ali Kent. That initial pleasant feeling of knowing who she was soon turned to terror.

I stopped for a few seconds to grab my notebook and pen.

I copied her letter here so that the knowledge she gained would sink in and give me hope and courage. It might be too late for her, but maybe it wasn't too late for me. She wrote in such a heartfelt way that tears ran down my cheeks as I copied it. I translated it into Chinese in case Frank found it. Ali's style was clear and direct, and I enjoyed translating her words. It was almost like she was talking directly to me, and I realized more than ever how lonely I was for normal companionship:

"My name is Ali Kent. I'm twenty-three years old. My parents are Evan and Marion Kent, and they live on Peachtree Road in Atlanta, Georgia. I'm a self-taught artist. Words aren't my thing, but color definitely is. As a kid, I had trouble with reading, so I sketched and drew and experimented with paint and water. Eventually, I won several awards. What a wonderful unexpected surprise came my way. I received an invitation to present my paintings at the Mainsail Art Festival in the Spring of 2001. I entered fifty-three watercolors, filled with scenes of beaches, gardens, and streets.

"When the festival ended, I was so happy about my sales and commissions, I didn't pay attention to anything or anybody around me. I walked to my parking spot at the rear of the lot and loaded up my van to head home to Atlanta. A man jumped out of a clump of trees and grabbed me. I tried to fight him off, but he held me down and stuck a needle in my arm. When I woke up, I was here, a prisoner in these three rooms. My paintings weren't here and neither was my suitcase. Some of my clothes were piled in the middle of the floor of the tiny living room. My basic watercolor supplies leaned against one wall.

130

"His name is Frank Brandt. He's a vicious psycho ready to explode at any minute for any reason. He's creepy too. Every evening, he chooses one of my paint brushes and strokes his face with it, especially his lips, and makes weird noises while I paint. I want to vomit, but I don't because the odor would linger in this small place. I'm getting better at not reacting to his paint-brush routine. I'm no expert, but I think this is sexual for Frank, and then there's his crazy fantasy. He says my paintings talk to him. He orders me to paint every day. I refuse. He beats me until I pass out. When I wake up, I agree to paint. Apparently, my paintings cooperate and continue to talk to him.

"If I slow down or take a day off, he beats me everywhere except my hands. He doesn't get it. My heart and soul, not just my hands, turn my thoughts into paintings. As soon as I finish a painting, he takes it away, and I never see it again. That's so unfair. Depression presses its hooks into me. It's messing with my head and destroying my creativity. Frank is tiring of me. That's bad because I know he'll kill me with those big, greasy hands without a second thought. He has already cracked two of my ribs. Sometimes when I paint, every bone in my body aches. He knows he's hurt me real bad. He likes to hurt me. He's always angry. That's what he's all about.

"By chance, I saw the woman who comes here to clean. She's a skinny older woman in poor health. I am stronger and faster than she is and could overwhelm her. She's Frank's sister, Marta. She told me so. She got mixed up and came on the wrong day or at the wrong time and let herself into my side of the house. She begged me not to tell Frank. I promised. She believed me. What planet does she live on? She set down her key. Big mistake!

131

"While she cleaned, I grabbed the key, locked her in, and got loose in the house. It turned out to be a warehouse with no windows. I tried to escape, but I couldn't open the front or back doors. They have a combination, and I don't know it. The numbers I tried didn't work.

"I looked everywhere for another way out of the house, but I didn't find anything. I panicked when I heard car breaks squeal outside. Frank burst into the warehouse, screaming and kicking and punching. Something in the house, probably a hidden camera, must have alerted him I was moving around.

"He and his sister fought. Frank gave me the worst beating ever. It was days before I was well enough to paint again. He didn't like my paintings after that. He called them 'revengeful and spiteful.' Him and his big words. He throws them around like peanuts to squirrels, and they don't always make sense. Since that last beating, he carries a big hunting knife strapped to his leg. I think he's planning to kill me. I'm afraid. Last night, while I painted, he sat on the couch in my living room for a long time and polished the knife.

"He said, 'I can rip the life right out of your thankless heart. Keep that in mind when you create these paintings. If I don't like them, what do I need you for? I can find somebody else, somebody better than you.' He stood up and threw the knife at the far wall. It stabbed the plaster and stuck there until he yanked it out and stormed out of the room. Plaster dust trickled down the wall from the knife cut to the floor. It was like my life was trickling away.

I pray every night to sweet Jesus. Please don't let me suffer a horrible death. Please let my family find out what happened to me. My parents must believe me. The fight we had my last night at home about borrowing money for a new van isn't the reason why I never returned. I was taken against my will. I loved my family then, I love them now, and I will love and cherish them forever. If you find this note, please give it to my parents and give them a big hug for me."

♫♫

That evening I re-read Ali's letter. I imagined her, a sweet country girl writing that note, freckles maybe, and possibly wavy hair tied back so it didn't dip into her paints. I cried again for the suffering she had endured and for what I feared might have happened to her. Having no one to turn to, I sat down and cradled my erhu in my lap. Tears and sorrow were not enough to express my sympathy to Ali and find consolation for myself. The erhu, my beloved erhu, could do both. I thought through all the pieces in my repertoire and came up with the most appropriate work for Ali, who suffered the same isolation and loneliness I now endure.

I chose *A Moon Image in Er-Spring*. She would appreciate that now, after so many long months without being free, so many months without the familiar moon and stars to help her through the long, lonely nights.

Just like me...

22
Ivy Chen

Tuesday, September 1, 2009

After reading Ali Kent's letter and knowing her fate, I was sick to my stomach and lost my appetite for several days, but I realized I must keep myself strong because I now had someone besides myself to think about, and I now had three reasons to escape: to reunite with my parents, to tell Ali's parents and the police about Ali, and to lead the police to Frank's warehouse where they would surely capture him. I was afraid to keep the letter where Frank or Frank's sister Marta, who cleaned this place, might find it. In case I didn't survive, I wanted Ali's letter kept in a safe place and eventually found. It would be a saving grace for her parents. The letter had survived all this time in that hiding place tucked behind the closet shelf. If it hadn't been found by now, that must be the best place of all. I folded it along its creases and put it back in the very spot where I'd found it.

For several days, Ali's letter never left my thoughts. Her information was a gift to me. Knowing that Marta was Frank's sister could help me bargain with her. Three other pieces of information might help me escape: this building was a warehouse; Frank had cameras or some other device to track movement in his quarters; and a certain combination was required to open the doors. I kept thinking about ways to bargain with Marta, and I now saw the folly of escaping into Frank's quarters all by myself. If I couldn't get the doors open, I would be trapped there just like Ali was. No. As much as I hated to admit this, Frank had to be with me.

I spent hours thinking of ways to convince Frank to let me go beyond these three rooms. I noticed he liked to learn things because he wanted to convince the people he worked with he's smart. I could offer to teach him Chinese, but that could be done here in my apartment when he came in for the evening erhu concert and dinner. No, I must teach him something that required a large open space, larger than my apartment. What would appeal to him? What would give me freedom of movement in Frank's quarters? That was my next project, my next step toward freedom and seeing my beloved Mama and Baba again, and maybe my sweetheart Vince, too.

23
Detective Tony DeLuca and Vince Ivanov

Tuesday, January 10, 2012

Detective DeLuca and Vince met at the entrance to the dining room of the Vinoy where the farewell breakfast for Ivy had been held. After pleasantries, DeLuca said, "Shall we get started?"

"Yes," Vince said. "I hope this time I can remember something important enough to help you find Ivy."

"Sometimes it's the little things that come out of nowhere that do the trick," DeLuca said. "Let's begin by retracing your steps from here to the porch. We want to take it real slow. Think of everything and everyone you saw along the way. Don't rush this."

"I'll give it my best," Vince said. "Andante sostenuto"—he rolled his hands slowly—"not prestissimo"—he rolled his hands quickly.

"Your hand motions are telling me slow, not fast. That's just what I'm looking for." DeLuca smiled. "My father spoke Italian at home when I was growing up."

Vince's handsome face lit up. "I grew up speaking Italian and Russian."

"You got me there," DeLuca said. "I don't speak a word of Russian."

"And Ivy grew up speaking Chinese," Vince countered. "We're like a little United Nations. Sorry. I'm talking too much. I'm nervous. I can't stop thinking about Ivy."

"I understand," DeLuca said. "Let's walk. I won't say a word while you take your time reconstructing what you saw and heard the day Ivy went missing."

DeLuca glanced at Vince. The worry lines between Vince's eyes hinted what he'd been going through, missing Ivy for more than three years and brooding about it. He'd admitted carrying the torch for Ivy all that time. This was too much for Vince or anyone else to bear. Something had to break in this investigation soon. Even a small glimmer of hope would ease some of the pain for everyone who loved Ivy.

"A family with two kids, a boy and a girl, were walking along in front of me," Vince said as they made their way to the porch that overlooked the semi-circular driveway. "When we got right here to the porch, they continued down the stairs and out to the street. Maybe they were going to lunch or sightseeing or anything. I heard the boy mention the yachts docked across the street. They were laughing, having a good time. A server brought drinks to two middle-aged couples sitting in wicker chairs around a low table on the porch. I don't remember much about them, but I can recall the sound of the ice cubes rattling around in the glasses. No one stands out in my mind."

"You're doing great, Vince. Now, at this point, you went over to the railing?"

"Yes."

"I'd like you to concentrate real hard and try to picture that red tow truck you saw that day."

Vince leaned against the porch railing and thought for several minutes. "I watched the cars arriving at the driveway and the valets greeting the drivers and parking the cars. That's when I saw the red tow truck. The driver had an argument with the valet and nearly ran him over. The driver laughed a hideous laugh and drove off. The valet was upset but not injured."

Vince turned to DeLuca, his sad brown eyes expressing his disappointment. "I know this is more or less what I told you before. I can't think of anything else to add to that. I wish I could. I'm sorry."

"Let's try something else," DeLuca said, hoping for the best. "Close your eyes. Don't talk, just think."

Vince rested his hands on the railing and closed his eyes. A gentle breeze passed by. The sweet fragrance of honeysuckle wafted through the air. Several minutes passed by in silence.

"Oh, wait a minute," Vince said, and his eyes popped open. "I never realized this at the time, but—"

"What are you remembering?" DeLuca's words flew from his mouth.

"Erhu music. Ivy's erhu music! It was coming from the red truck."

"Keep going. Talk to me."

"I think the guy must have been playing a tape or a CD of Ivy's music. Maybe he bought it at one of Ivy's concerts. Maybe he knew her or he knew of her because of her music. Maybe he even met her."

"You're thinking like a detective," DeLuca said.

"I'm thinking like a musician, too," Vince said, and his shoulders straightened a bit. "I love her music so much. I have all her albums at home. I play them all the time. The music coming from the truck was so familiar to me. It's in my head so much, it just seemed normal that day, a typical everyday part of my life. I didn't make anything of it then. But now, I know I heard Ivy's music coming from that truck. It was definitely Ivy who was playing. I've heard other musicians playing the erhu, even playing the very same composition, but I'd be able to pick out Ivy's hauntingly emotional style with my eyes closed."

"You just did," DeLuca said and shook Vince's hand enthusiastically. "And just possibly you've put a new slant on what happened that day. The driver didn't just pick up any woman. I'd say he targeted Ivy. By all indications, he knew her music. He wanted to meet her, or possibly he had already planned to abduct her and knew she would be at the Vinoy that day. Either way, I'm convinced it was Ivy he was after."

DeLuca looked into the distance beyond the Vinoy. "Where is he? Where did he take her? Where on earth are they?" He asked out loud and gritted his teeth. "Sorry for drifting off. Let's backup to the erhu music for a moment. Tell me; how popular is it?"

"More than you would think," Vince said. "The erhu's haunting sound is catching on in certain circles in the United States and abroad."

"What circles?"

"Well, there's erhu fusion, erhu rock, erhu jazz, and the soundtrack of the movie *Crouching Tiger, Hidden Dragon* featured the erhu. That added to its popularity. The acrobatics were great too, but for many of us, it was all about the music."

DeLuca narrowed his eyes. "So whoever was driving that truck might have bought a recording in any number of places. I was thinking maybe one leading online site or store."

"No. There are many choices." Disappointment tugged down the corners of Vince's mouth. "So that won't help you."

"But this new information about the driver of the truck could help this investigation." DeLuca crossed his arms firmly over his chest. "If what you're saying proves true, Ivy didn't disappear. Ivy was taken. We need more proof, something besides Ivy's music, but you've been a big help."

"Detective, I don't mean to tell you how to run your investigation, but—"

"Don't hold back," DeLuca said. "I get suggestions all the time, but that's a good story for another day. Tell me what's on your mind."

"Please move as fast as you can." Vince took a deep breath. "I saw with my own eyes that the tow truck driver has a violent temper. I have nightmares about how he might be treating Ivy. Promise me you'll find her."

"I'm doing my best," DeLuca said. "And so is my entire team."

"How do you think this is going to end?" Vince asked and his voice cracked.

"There's no way of knowing, but you should never give up hope."

Vince shook his head. "That creep was playing Ivy's music that day, right here. I wish he had crashed into a tree when he roared out of here and ended up in the hospital"…"or gotten into a fight with somebody bigger and stronger than he is. I hate to say this, but I wish he had died that day. If that had happened, Ivy would be here by my side. Now, I don't know if I'll ever see her again."

"Listen to me," DeLuca said. "I want you to stop thinking like that. Try to hope for the best so you can get through each day."

"Man to man," Vince said, "Is there anything worse than losing the love of your life?"

DeLuca took a long, deep breath. "No, there isn't."

Vince studied DeLuca long and hard. "Are you saying that because it's the answer you think I'm looking for?"

"No."

"Then why?" Vince asked.

"Because I know what you're going through."

"Someone you loved was kidnapped?"

"No, but I lost the only woman I ever loved. Let it go at that."

"I'm sorry. I didn't mean to pry. I just don't know where to turn and what to do."

"Come on, let's leave right now," DeLuca said. "Give me your keys. I'll drive you home and pick up my car later. You should rest."

"How do you and the other detectives stand it?" Vince asked as they got into his car.

"How do we stand what?"

"Dealing with monsters."

DeLuca turned the key in the ignition. "When we catch them, it stops them from hurting someone else." He gripped the steering wheel so hard his knuckles turned white. "That's what makes it bearable."

24
Ivy Chen

Wednesday, October 7, 2009

As I waited for Frank to arrive, I sat down, smoothed my yellow satin dress, placed the erhu on my lap, and gripped the bow. This preparation wasn't meant to please him, as he probably thought. Possibly it stopped him from hitting me. He wouldn't want to risk damaging the erhu or tearing my dress. He enjoyed these evening concerts. He demanded them.

The key rattled in the door, and I braced myself for my well-thought-out daring plan that would take Frank beyond his comfort zone and allow me to gain access to his part of the house. I was determined to try it but fearful of the probably violent outcome. If I could have made my words personal and showed him my concern for him, I might have gotten through to him. Such phoniness and deceit were repulsive to me, but I was running out of ideas.

"What are we waiting for?" Frank asked as he barged into the room and plunked down on the couch. "Start playing."

"Frank, your work leaves you angry and exhausted," I began pleasantly with a concerned look on my face and hugged the erhu even closer to me. "You need to relax and unwind before our concerts. You're short-changing yourself. If you practiced the ancient art of tai chi, your body, mind, and soul would calm down, and you would enjoy the music more."

"What's this tie cheap stuff you're talking about?" His expression turned sullen.

"Tai chi," I said sweetly.

"Whatever. You've been acting weird. I notice things, you know. For the last two concerts, the erhu's voice has been blah. What's wrong with her?"

"This tiny apartment cramps her. That's what's wrong." I was thrilled that my holding back the erhu's emotional range affected his enjoyment. "The erhu needs a larger room with better acoustics so that the music can float freely. Then it can approach you from all directions."

He curled his lip. "What are you blabbing about?"

"The connection between tai chi, the erhu, and happiness."

"What the hell does this have to do with me?"

"If we practiced tai chi in an area larger than my apartment, and if I played the erhu in that larger area, why, then life would be much better for the three of us—you, me, and the erhu. We would all be happy."

"What are you trying to tell me?"

"The music will be even more beautiful if you are relaxed. Tai chi will relax you."

"Cut the crap and play the damn music," he said.

I sighed and began playing the erhu softly and with no expression.

Frank jumped up and stamped his foot. "Okay, I'll try your stupid Chinese voodoo stuff."

"Good," I replied. "Let's move to an area beyond my apartment. There must be more space to move around out there."

He scowled. I sat perfectly still while his bad temper ran its course. After he punched a hole in the bathroom door and pushed his fist under my chin and held it there sending pain through my jaw, he said, "Okay, but I need time, a day should do it, to prepare the primary residence. Until then, our concerts remain here in your apartment and there will be no Chinese voodoo." I had expected much worse, worthless promises, delays, even more violent temper tantrums, and a punch from that awful fist of his, but the power of the erhu proved invincible.

Thursday, October 8, 2009

The next evening, Frank stormed into my room.

"Here's the deal. He slammed the door shut. "I'll practice this tie-cheap crap with you in the primary residence, but you have to do something for me. Fair's fair."

A chill shot up my spine. "What do you want?"

"Explore the dragon with me," he said, and my eyes popped wide open. Had I unleashed the beast inside him? No. I forced myself to think clearly. I was overreacting.

"Are you listening to me?" Frank asked angrily. "Tomorrow you must explore the dragon with me."

"Yes, I'm listening," I said, and shuddered at what he might mean by 'explore.' For once, I was glad to be in my apartment, not beyond these walls where the dragon, whatever that meant to him, waited.

Friday, October 9, 2009

The next afternoon at five-fifteen sharp, Frank unlocked the door to my apartment. "Get out here," he said, "and don't try anything funny." He glared at me with his bloodshot eyes. "Got it?"

"Yes, Frank," I said and took in the shabby room filled with scruffy, mismatched furniture, all gray, black, and brown. Windows didn't exist. As I feared, only skylights allowed in light. But the walls, alive with the joyful colors of spring, surprised me, dozens of paintings, maybe a hundred of them, all watercolors. Scenes of gardens, beaches, and villages covered the walls. I knew even though the paintings were unsigned that Ali Kent, whose place I had taken in the apartment, had painted them. Frank would never have allowed her to sign them. Someone might break in, see Ali's name, and report it to the police. Possibly, in his sick way, he considered the paintings his, not hers.

I had to hold back my tears. Frank would haul off and hit me hard if I cried in front of him. From the very first day, he had made it clear that I was meant to spend my life with him because I had expressed those thoughts to him through my erhu. Anything less than gratitude for his providing me with a home and concert arena sent him into a rage. Had I forgotten? I was merely the instrument that made the erhu speak to him. A tear slipped from my eye, and I brushed it away.

"Don't you dare cry," Frank shouted. "Do I have to remind you? Babies cry. They get punished for crying. If I see you crying again, I'll spank you until your bottom is red and send you to bed without any supper. Is that what you want?"

"No," I said, and reminded myself to put all my feelings on hold when Frank was in the house. Alone, I could be my true self. With Frank, I was someone else whom I hardly knew or recognized.

"Now you know the size of the area, and you can prepare accordingly," he said.

I clenched my teeth so I wouldn't laugh out loud at his mangling of the word "accordingly." At least he came up with something musical.

"Let's leave," he said. "Tomorrow night, we'll hold our concert here, and you will explore the dragon with me."

I prayed he would forget about exploring the dragon, whatever it meant, but this obsession ruled him. He mentioned it two more times all the while rubbing his hands together and licking his lips. Each time, I tried hard to think of beautiful gardens and a pretty blue sky, but trying to convince myself all would turn out well was very difficult.

Before heading back to my apartment, I glanced at Ali's paintings along the wall. The most recent ones, those at the end of the line, changed drastically, just as Frank had complained about to Ali. Dull bland neutrals replaced the joyful reds, yellows, blues as Ali's depression turned her world into a colorless existence. Blossoms appeared shriveled, rowboats were beached with holes in their sides, fruits and vegetables were riddled with beetles and worms.

I finished the third piece and set down my bow. Frank headed to the door. Before leaving, he turned abruptly toward me. "I am going to ask you one question. I want to hear your answer loud and clear." His eyes narrowed. "What are we doing tomorrow evening besides the tai foo crap and our concert?"

"Exploring the dragon," I said, and my stomach churned in fear of the unknown.

"Good." He turned and left, slamming the door behind him. The room shook.

I showered, hoping the soap and warm water would wash away the disgust I felt for Frank. As I toweled myself dry, I thought about poor Ali Kent and tears streamed down my face. By the time I crawled into bed, despair overcame me. My heart ached for Ali. The talent imbedded in her earlier watercolors radiated from the walls. This brute of a man, Frank Brandt, had probably killed her sometime after the horrible beating he gave her when she tried to escape. There was little doubt about that. If she had escaped, she would have brought the police here. No, she was gone. He had killed her.

So many people were deprived of the wonderful works Ali would have created throughout her lifetime. I vowed to never forget the viciousness Frank Brand unleashed on her. I renewed my plan to figure out how the doors opened, no matter how long it took. I told myself, "I will escape! I will run for my life!"

25
Ivy Chen

Saturday, October 10, 2009

During our evening concert in Frank's quarters, I played three pieces for Frank. Fear nearly paralyzed me. Fear of his demand that later tonight we would explore the dragon. I prayed the tai chi would somehow delight him and he would forget about this obsession with a dragon, but I knew I was fooling myself. Before Frank kidnapped me, I had always believed we should never give up hope. Now, I had doubts.

Balance every bad thing with a good thing, Baba would tell me if he were here. The bad thing was exploring the dragon. The good thing was it gave me the opportunity to observe Frank's primary residence and discover the location of the doors to the outside world. Freedom! My freedom depended on a doorway. I said a silent thank-you to Baba and moved the erhu out of the way, so it wouldn't get knocked into.

I stood across from Frank in his living room, in the area right outside my door. "You agreed that tonight we will begin our tai chi lessons, so—"

"I don't like new things," he cut in.

"Just take ten relaxing breaths," I said as calmly as possible and hoped for the best.

As we breathed, I mentally reviewed the tai chi movements I had chosen, called shibashi movements, but I didn't intend to teach Frank the typical smooth, controlled, grounded movements I had practiced since I was a young girl. They wouldn't work for me now. I had to move freely around the room, as freely as possible in my concert dress, seeing everything without making him suspicious. My invented routine would keep him so focused on his hands and feet he wouldn't notice my eyes searching everywhere. I felt like a traitor to my heritage, as if my big steps and leaps were mocking the age-old classical movements Baba had taught me and revered. At the same time, I felt a sense of pride that my heritage possibly had the ability to set me free.

"Just imitate me, and enjoy the moment," I told Frank as I moved across the room in great strides. "Let go of your worries." I repeated those words again and again. In a few days, I planned to encourage him to close his eyes during our tai chi sessions. Then I'd be able to see everything.

I threw myself into an exaggerated interpretation of a particular shibashi movement called "scooping of the sea."

Frank imitated every move but muttered under his breath, "This is stupid."

"That's very good, Frank," I encouraged him. As I moved about, I noticed a rickety desk in one corner, overflowing with a dictionary, a thesaurus, books of antonyms and synonyms, and index cards. I moved closer and saw five words and a date scrawled on each card. Frank must have worked for a long time at developing his vocabulary to make himself appear educated. His horrible pronunciation was a give-away that he had seen the words but probably not heard them.

"I think you'll like this movement, Frank," I said. A student of the art would never recognize my overstated interpretation of a movement called "pushing the waves." But it allowed me to observe the doors, the combination locks on them, and anything else that might prove useful in my escape.

Frank's robotic movements pained me to watch as we alternated scooping the sea and pushing the waves, but I forced myself to compliment him so I could take larger steps and see around corners into the kitchen, dining room, and bath. The bedroom lay beyond my line of vision. Moving onward with the shibashi movements, I caught several glimpses of the kitchen, but I didn't learn much because Frank needed constant encouragement and instruction.

It was no use. The power of tai chi wasn't working on Frank. The disgusted expression on his face told me he would soon call off this plan of mine, possibly even tonight. That would keep me out of the primary residence. I couldn't let that happen. I needed to come up with a better plan if I had any hope of seeing more of Frank's quarters. The erhu remained my best hope. Frank would fall under the spell of the erhu, but he would need a very large dose of the erhu's magical sounds.

"I've had enough," he said. "I don't like this crap."

"Frank, I agree with you. You don't need tai chi after all. I made a mistake. I apologize." His startled expression told me he rarely had anyone apologize to him. I continued, "You appreciate the erhu, and that is what you shall have from now on. We'll forget all about tai chi. If you can wait until tomorrow evening so that I have time to prepare, I'll show you what the erhu is capable of in an area the size of your primary residence. It goes beyond anything you can imagine."

He eyed me suspiciously. "You're up to some kind of trick. Tonight we were supposed to explore the dragon. You can't change things around like that."

"I think that by now there has to be a bond of trust between us," I said, praying he wouldn't turn on me and attack. "Trust me. I just need one day to prepare. You'll enjoy the erhu's special treat."

He raised his fists. "If it's not truly special, you won't survive another day. And neither will that erhu."

Sunday, October 11, 2009

The next evening, I wore my pretty pale green concert dress, carried the erhu close to my heart, and followed Frank into the primary residence.

"You remember my warning?"

"Yes, Frank," I said, and prayed the erhu and I would survive this evening.

"Good. Now what's this new thing with the erhu?" he asked warily.

"You must sit in the middle of the room to fully appreciate the secret," I said. He sat down on a chair, scowling, but he didn't make his usual surly remarks. I sat across from him with a partial view of the kitchen and bathroom. What a disgusting sight. Greasy streaks glistened on every wall and surface. The odor of mildew stung my nostrils.

How strange that he arranged to have my apartment kept so immaculately, and that I kept it that way too, while he lived in this filthy place. My explanation? He loathed himself and figured he deserved something so filthy.

"Are you ready, Frank?" I asked.

"Yes. Hurry up. I don't have all night. I have to get up for work in the morning." His voice was tight and high-pitched with excitement.

"If you close your eyes and concentrate, you'll hear the sounds of birds, horses, and dogs," I said, hoping he would be able to let his imagination take over. "It's like they're right here in this room with you."

"You're making this up. You're messing with my head."

"No, I'm not. Relax. Breathe deeply. The sounds will soon come to you." I gave my all to the exquisite composition, *Song of Birds in Desolate Mountain*.

Several long slow minutes passed, and then he said dreamily, "Birds are chirping," and my eyes roamed freely. I figured there must be another door in addition to the one in the living room. Ali had mentioned a front and back door. Did she mean a kitchen door? If each night I changed the position of my chair, I would see more and more of the house.

"Horses are neighing," Frank said and chuckled as I maneuvered the erhu's strings to create the dramatic sounds Mr. Zheng, my erhu teacher, had once taught me. Mr. Zheng would chide me, "I do not want to hear the snort of an ox nor the bray of a donkey." After several of my efforts, he said, "Now you're on the right path. The sound must be powerful and hypnotic."

Mr. Zheng taught me well. If he knew what I had just done with his meticulous instruction, he would exclaim, "Ai-ya!" I hoped to tell him one day in person. He would say, "Sit down right now and play for me those animal voices while they are so vibrant in your mind. Don't ever let a creative moment slip away. It might not come back." How I missed his philosophy about music and life.

As I studied what I could see of the kitchen, I prayed for help in finding my way out. I prayed to Mama's Christian God, the trinity of the Father, the Son, and the Holy Spirit. I prayed to Fu Lu Shou, the three personified deities Baba described to me when I was a child living in China: Fu Star is known as Good Fortune, Lu Star is Prosperity, and Shou Star is Longevity. Mama had a crucifix on her bureau, and Baba kept ivory carvings of the three lucky gods in his study. Seeing them in my mind's eye helped me realize the power of prayer that my parents and grandparents appreciated.

"Dogs are barking," Frank said and clapped his hands in delight. Good. I needed to see the rest of the kitchen to determine if there was a door.

When I finished playing, I said to Frank, "I need a glass of water. May I help myself?"

"No," he said firmly. "I'll get it for you."

When Frank returned with a glass of water, he said, "It will soon be time to explore the dragon."

I had worried about this dragon expression since he'd first mentioned it. I didn't know what he meant, and I didn't like the creepiness of his words, but I didn't show my fear. I was disappointed that I didn't get into the kitchen, but I'd try again tomorrow night. I watched as he gripped a knob on the wall of his living room. The knob was about two feet above the floor. It blended in with the random knobs that supported shelves that held loose coins, bottle caps, buttons, a belt buckle, and other dingy mismatched items. It was like a collection of junk that Frank set there because he was too lazy to throw it away.

I stood close to Frank but beyond his reach. I held my breath and watched intently as he tugged open a door which was about three feet high and not quite as wide. I couldn't imagine what this tiny space was for, other than storage. He reached inside. He pulled on a chain attached to a bare bulb, dropped to his hands and knees, and crawled in.

He grabbed hold of my suitcase and slid it toward him. I dared to take a step closer and peeked over his shoulder. A sour stale odor escaped from the alcove. I could see that the musty alcove served as a storage area. Frank backed my suitcase up against the wall next to the door to my apartment. "We'll keep it here from now on," he said. "This is the most convenient spot."

Frank knelt in front of the suitcase and closed his eyes as if he were praying. He rocked back and forth murmuring words I couldn't hear, but they kept him in a trance-like state. My gaze and interest shifted to my suitcase, a present from Mama and Baba to celebrate my first concert in Shanghai. Joy and fond memories overwhelmed me. That suitcase meant the world to me. The dragon embossed on the lid was special to me because my grandfather was born in the Year of the Dragon, 1916, and my grandmother was born the following year, the year of the Snake. Frank's attraction to the suitcase would have been immediate because the dragon matched the erhu's carved dragon which watched over me. All this time, I assumed he'd thrown my suitcase away when he captured me.

When he said we would explore the dragon, he must have been talking about the dragon embossed on the lid of my suitcase. It must be part of some kind of routine he practiced, an important routine because he had been so insistent. Suitcase. Suitcase. What was the significance of that word to Frank? It must have some special meaning. But what? I couldn't figure it out. Suitcase. Ali Kent's note jumped into my thoughts. She wrote that her suitcase was missing too. I was filled with sick apprehension.

Frank stopped rocking. He glanced at me with an ecstatic expression on his face and opened the lid slowly, as if it were a shrine. At first, his fascination with the contents puzzled me. Then as he lifted my silk negligee and rubbed it across his neck, chin, and cheeks, I became aware of what he was doing. Horror overwhelmed me, but I had to hide my disgust. His reaction to my disgust would be a beating I might not survive. He balked at criticism and rejection. Outright disgust would surely throw him over the edge. Earlier, when he mentioned exploring the dragon, I was afraid because I was afraid of the unknown. Now, I realized this was some kind of perverse pleasure for Frank. My whole body trembled. I tried to calm myself, but it was impossible.

"Let's take out the fancy stuff, slowly, one piece at a time," he said.

"You go first," I said, bewildered and terrified about what he might do next.

"Thank you," he said in a whispery voice. He touched my pale green silky blouse, caressed it, and kissed it.

I shuddered at the sight of his thick slobbering lips on the blouse my grandmother had created for me. I felt violated and dirty.

He returned my blouse to the suitcase. "Your turn," he said dreamily, and his glazed eyes held a far-away look.

I looked into the suitcase and was surprised to see the pillowcases with the ivy trim along the edge that I had bought in a shop in St. Petersburg the very day Frank abducted me. I had left them in their original packaging in a shopping bag. Yet here they were, unwrapped and in the suitcase. Frank put them there. But why?

He didn't wait for me to take my turn. He picked up the pillowcases and ran his fingers over them and buried his face in them. I was sickened at the thought of sleeping on them. Then it came to me. That was what he wanted, his touching them and then my sleeping on them. That was his way of getting closer to me, an intimacy he was not capable of, physically or emotionally. I avoided the pillowcases. Disgust—that he might be touching something destined for my pillow and so close to my face— took hold of me. I chose not to touch them, hoping to convince him they were not important to me. I had regular sheets and pillowcases on my bed in my clean living area in this filthy place.

The bitter taste of bile invaded my mouth. I realized he was blending our two lives. I resented this more than I could express with words, but I held back my thoughts and moved away from the pillowcases to something more impersonal. I saw he'd also added the cups and saucers I'd bought in St. Pete to the contents of the suitcase.

The suitcase was soft-sided, so maybe he figured they wouldn't break. I set them up as if preparing for afternoon tea.

He sneered, letting me know he wasn't interested in the tea service. Apparently, it wasn't intimate enough to please him. Turning up his nose at the tea cups and saucers, he removed the formal silk dress I wore for concerts. Mama had helped me pick it out. It was my favorite because of the elegant pale green silk embroidery on the neck and sleeves. He held it with one hand while he ran his other hand back and forth several times from the neckline to the hemline.

I saw men's clothing, a shiny blue suit, an inexpensive white shirt, and a necktie, stuck in between my belongings. "What's all this?" I asked, taken by surprise.

"My concert clothes, to show respect to the erhu, of course. Touch them," he ordered.

I clenched my teeth as I touched each item briefly and returned each of them quickly to the suitcase.

"Look under those concert clothes."

I did as he ordered even though I feared something disgusting might be lurking there. I came upon a worn-out set of grey work clothes. Stains and torn places were obvious. "Are these yours too?" I asked. I remembered them from the night he abducted me along the roadside, but I didn't want to attach any importance to them, to make him or those clothes special in any way in his mind.

"That's my daytime life," he said. "See how different they are from my concert clothes, my nighttime life?"

"Yes," I said, wishing this exploration would end. I tried rubbing away the tension in my neck, which was unbearably painful. I wasn't successful.

"That's enough for one night," he said with a far-away look in his eyes. "We'll do this again, tomorrow."

I nodded, forcing a smile, and fought the scream of "No!" that was eager to escape from my lips.

"We'll get better at this with practice," he said, and I shivered at the thought.

Monday, October 12, 2009

The next night we knelt in front of my suitcase again. Frank was in a trance, methodically running his fingers across the lingerie at the top of the pile. He removed my slip, my nightgown, and my panties one by one, caressing them, rubbing them against his chin and cheeks, and then returning them to the suitcase.

When it was my turn, I was startled to find my favorite black shoes resting side by side at the bottom of the suitcase. Mama had given them to me to wear when I relaxed. She called them "my good luck shoes" because they were embroidered across the toes with dragons, which were very special to our family. I wore those shoes with a casual outfit after concerts when I returned to my hotel by taxi. I wore them to breakfast at the Vinoy. How was it possible that both shoes were here? The afternoon Frank captured me and I tried to run away, one of them had fallen off and was left behind.

I blurted out, "How did both shoes end up here?"

"I returned to the lake and searched for the missing shoe until I found it lying there, waiting for me to rescue it," Frank said with obvious pride. "I don't like anything that's not perfect. Now you have both shoes, and everything is perfect." He grinned, exposing his large yellowish teeth. "I can look at two lucky dragons, one on each dainty foot."

Frank's creepy intimate words disgusted me, but I took hope from his returning to the scene of the crime. Maybe someone saw him. Maybe he left something of his behind and didn't realize it. If the police figured out the route I traveled to see Mama and my aunties, they might be able to track him down. With their technology, they might find their way to Frank's house and save me. That was a possibility. I must not give up hope of being found.

"Your turn," he said, and I focused on the tea cups, a choice which annoyed him. He pointed at his clothes. He wanted me to touch them. I did and made my mind go blank as I participated in this disgusting ritual, filled with sexual implications that fed his perverted fantasies.

During the next several evenings, hope endured even as I participated in that sickening routine with Frank's clothing and mine because Frank was growing tired of it. There were no new clothes, and I assumed that the novelty of acting out his perversion had worn off.

The next evening Frank didn't kneel in front of the dragon suitcase. He pushed it aside with his foot. "We aren't going to explore the dragon tonight," he said.

"Good, because the erhu wants your undivided attention," I said, thinking fast. "The erhu is probably jealous of the dragon suitcase. She has her own dragon design. The explorations should stop forever. If we continue, the effect on the erhu could be devastating."

"Slow down," Frank said. "Let me think about all this gibberish."

"There's nothing to think about. Tomorrow night I will prepare a special erhu concert to surpass all the others." I had set myself up for a difficult task, but I now had the opportunity to move on to something where taking control was possible. The erhu would be my friend, my ally, my escape from here. It always had been until Frank got sidetracked with his fascination for everything that touched my body, my panties, my negligees, even the sheets and pillowcases on which I slept, but that phase of his sick mind was drifting away...at least for now.

Friday, October 16, 2009

The following evening, in Frank's living room, after our concert of three erhu songs, I said, "Close your eyes, Frank. The magic is about to begin." The sounds of birds, dogs, and horses emerged from the erhu, but this time I didn't hold back anything. The sounds were more vibrant than before, more expressive, and Frank's happy expression told me he was thoroughly entertained. I sat where it was possible to see into the far side of the kitchen, hidden from my view the other nights. I was thrilled. There was a door with a combination lock on it. When I finished the concert, I repeated the same little speech I had given the previous nights. "Frank, I need a glass of water. May I go to the kitchen and help myself?"

"No," he said. "I'll get it for you."

I had my answer ready. "Please, let me. I'd like to see your kitchen."

"No. You want to run out the door," he said.

"That's not true, Frank," I said, thrilled to learn there was an outside door in the kitchen. "I'm not going anywhere."

"You're being sarcastic, like the guys at work," he said. "I don't like sarcastic people. They laugh at stuff that's not funny. The joke's always on me."

"I'm not being sarcastic, Frank. This is my home. No one remembers me out there beyond these walls. I have nowhere to go. This is my residence now."

"Stay put," he said. "I'll get the water."

He went into the kitchen, and this time, from where I had strategically placed the chair, I saw him clearly. His back was to me. He took a glass from the cabinet. Several dead roaches filled the bottom of the glass. He pulled a keychain from his pocket. He chose one of the two keys dangling from the key ring and opened the kitchen door with it. The door swung out. He tossed the roaches out the door. In that one split moment, I saw a darkening sky above the treetops and a dirt yard at the level of the door sill. A large garage loomed in the fenced-in yard.

The outside world and freedom were so close, just one room away. The very thought of that amazed me and gave me hope. My attention flew to the key in Frank's hand.

A key! Unbelievable! A regular, ordinary key opened the door. The combination was just camouflage. Frank had a key to the kitchen door and another key to my apartment. Marta must have both keys if she was able to open the door at the front or back of the house and then open my apartment door. The artist, Ali Kent, wrote that Marta had taken the key. The key...one key, not two. Marta must not have kept both keys on the same keychain.

The key Marta had taken was for my apartment only. Did Marta still keep the keys separate? I needed to know that if I was going to escape. I needed the key to an outside door, not just my apartment. My other choice would be to steal the keys from Frank. That was too dangerous, a desperate last resort, because he would overpower me in an instant.

Frank cut into my thoughts and shoved a glass of water at me. "Do you want the water or not?"

"Thank you," I said.

He headed back to the kitchen to turn off the dripping faucet. As he stood at the sink with his back to me, I dumped the roach-tainted water in a grimy pot that held a dead poinsettia plant.

Back in my room, as I thought through everything, I wept for Ali Kent until I had no more tears to shed. She had come so close to escaping from this monster. Would that be my fate too?

26
Detectives Tony DeLuca and Hank Hernandez

Tuesday, January 17, 2012, 7:15 P.M.

Tony and Hank approached the counter of Tijuana Flats and placed their orders for their usual Taco Tuesday specials. "I got it this time," Tony said as he pulled out several bills to pay the check.

After stopping to choose hot sauces, they seated themselves at their usual spot, the quiet corner table by the window, overlooking busy Fourth Street.

"Tony! Tony?" the blonde server with a pony tail and a big smile called out as she wove her way between the tables, gripping a tray that held two plastic baskets.

Tony waved. "Over here," and the server brought their order to the table. "Two blackened chicken tacos, no jalapenos, and two blackened chicken tacos, black beans, no jalapenos," the server said, setting down the baskets, and hurried back to the kitchen.

Tony finished off the first chicken taco. "Okay, Hank, you're the check-list guy. Let's run through it and see where we are we with all the details."

Hank pulled a small notepad from his pocket. "First up, Mrs. Arnoff. I just got word from the court-appointed psychiatrist. We've gotten all we're going to get from Mrs. Arnoff. No luck. She didn't recall anything she hadn't already told the detectives during the first investigation. She walked with Ivy to Ivy's car, held the umbrella while Ivy stored her purchases in the trunk of her car. There was no one suspicious near Ivy's car. No one bothered Ivy in her shop. She didn't recall seeing a leather suitcase, so that went nowhere. She was cooperative, eager to help, but nothing came of it."

"Okay. We'll drop that," DeLuca said and gulped his soda.

Hank checked off Mrs. Arnoff. "Next up, the Florida Orchestra," Hank said. "Did they come up with a list of people who bought single tickets for all three concerts?"

"Yeah, they did," Tony said. "But their records going back that far named only people who paid with credit card or check. There's no way to trace those who paid cash. If our guy was there, he's nameless and untraceable."

"And the people on the list who paid with credit card or check?"

"Those we located were willing to cooperate, nothing suspicious about them, no weird behavior that required an usher's intervention. It was a long shot. Too bad it didn't give us anything to go on."

Hank checked off the Florida Orchestra. "That brings us to the silverware, jewelry, and all the bling found in the trunk Rosie bought from the Allendale estate. Where are we with that?"

"We matched the merchandise with the pieces reported stolen. Bottom line? The jewelry is all accounted for and matched with the owners. It's safe to say Ron Hemmings held on to everything he stole during his Allendale spree until the heat was off, so we now know with certainty that none of the merchandise belonged to Ivy Chen."

Hank checked off the stolen jewelry. "That leaves Gary Cassell and the inventory photos for his parents' insurance company. That didn't give us anything either. There was nothing that Rosie bought that didn't belong to the Cassells, except the footlocker. Gary's photos saved us a lot of time. Nothing slipped by us. Another check mark?"

DeLuca nodded. "Good going, Hank. Just one loose end. What about the money in the mattress at the Cassell estate?"

"That's hard to account for with any accuracy," Hank said. "Cash was stolen during the robberies, and possibly he pawned stolen merchandise from previous robbery sprees not in the Allendale area. Either way there's no provable connection to Ivy Chen."

"So as far as our investigation goes," Tony made a 'clean-sweep' motion with his hands, "we can put all that to rest."

"Done and satisfied," Hank said. "But there's one detail that will probably never be nailed down."

"What's that?" DeLuca asked and gulped his soda.

"Ivy's suitcase. My theory is that Ron Hemmings was afraid it would be easily identifiable because of the dragon on the lid, so he destroyed it after he transferred the contents to an ordinary footlocker. He was afraid the dishes might break, so he wrapped them in ordinary newspaper. We'll never know. I hate unfinished business, but I guess I'll have to live with this."

"Maybe the suitcase will turn up some day when we least expect it," Tony said.

Hank nodded. "Stranger things have happened during our investigations." He slid his notepad back into his pocket and scooped up a handful of chips. He chewed them slowly, almost thoughtfully. "Something's been bothering me about that red tow truck."

"You wish you had one like it."

"Nah. I'm more a Corvette man." He dipped several chips in hot sauce and bit into them. "I think we may have overlooked something."

"Like what?" Tony asked.

Hank downed most of his soda to quench the flames in his mouth. "I don't think this is the tow-truck driver's first time to mess with a female driver alone on the road at night. He's experienced. I'd say he's done this before."

"Any facts to back that up?" Tony asked.

Hank wiped his mouth with a napkin. "A tow truck with fake plates and no advertising? You said yourself that showed "you-won't-catch-me" preparation. So we agree this was no spur of the moment thing. He seems like a sick-o with experience in tracking women on the highway. He probably started following Ivy Chen from the Vinoy. Possibly, he bided his time while she shopped and went to the Dalí. He gets his kicks from the anticipation. He's breathing hard. Then that

160

perfect moment came along. At long last, he followed her over the bridge."

"You're getting into this guy's head, and you're creeping me out. Where are you going with this?"

"If Ivy was abducted, maybe she wasn't the first. We could be looking at a serial kidnapper."

"Let's check the records," Tony said. "You thinking what I'm thinking?"

"You bet. If he's like most of these guys, he has a type."

Hank tossed his napkin on the table. "Petite like Ivy. Maybe long dark hair? Exotic-looking? Is that what turns him on?"

"We'll spread the net to see if other young women went missing." Tony waved to the staff as he headed toward the door.

Hank stepped outside into the humid evening. "Any information about previous disappearances could fire up this investigation."

"Let's start with ten years ago, work our way forward, and see what we find," Tony said.

Hank rubbed his hands briskly together. "At a time like this, my Jamaican grandfather would say, 'the bananas are ripe. What are you waiting for? Go pick 'em.'"

27
Ivy Chen

Filled with self-doubt, bordering on defeatism, I set aside today's journal and splashed water on my face. This has proven an effective way to invigorate myself so I can gather my thoughts and focus on strategies. I concentrated long and hard.

Even if I outsmarted Frank, I'm not sure I'd be able to escape without some degree of force. Violence went against every belief my family ever taught me, but I was running out of options. I have decided to find something that would be an effective weapon. I would keep it in my room in case an opportunity presented itself, and I could break free. It would have to be something that could knock out Frank. He was brawny and strong. I'd get one chance. If he fell but stood back up, I was done for. The choice of a weapon was crucial. It must be heavy, portable, and available. My eyes would be wide open for such an object.

When I find a way into his quarters, I'd look everywhere to figure out where he kept his tools. I hoped they weren't stored outside. I'd never seen his bedroom, and I doubted I'd ever get the chance. The kitchen would be my best bet. It was in view, and I saw it every day. I'd seen the inside of his cabinets above the sink when he got me a water glass, but the contents of the cabinets beneath the sink were unfamiliar to me. That would be the most logical place to store large, heavy objects.

What could I say or do to get the chance to look in those lower cabinets? I couldn't ask Frank point-blank. If I did, and if I managed to take something, he'd remember it and come looking for it. No, I must search the cabinets when he wasn't looking. This plan was filled with many 'ifs', but I must be prepared for any opportunity and grab it immediately.

I grew impatient as days turned into weeks, and Frank was always in the living room with me for our nightly erhu concert. Hope faded, and I wondered if I'd ever have the chance to search the cabinets.

Thursday, January 21, 2010

I just finished the final song of our little evening concert in Frank's quarters.

Frank jumped up from his chair and startled me. "I left my glasses in my truck," he said. "Stay right where you are. I'll be back in two minutes."

He left.

I dashed into the kitchen, a few feet from the couch where I had been sitting and quickly opened the cabinets under the sink. There, right before my eyes, was a black, wrought-iron skillet.

Perfect! That's it! If I hit him over the head, I could knock him out or at least stun him and give myself a chance to hit him again.

I heard Frank's truck door slam out there in the driveway or somewhere. He was coming back. There wasn't time now to get the pan and hide it in my room. But next time, yes next time, I'd grab it and run.

Monday, January 25, 2010

Today I was sitting on the couch writing in my journal about my plans for the heavy pan when keys rattled in the lock. I quickly shut my journal because Frank insisted on my full attention. He hated the notebook. He was jealous of it.

Frank yanked my door open and stormed into my room, wild-eyed, knocking over the furniture in his path. He shouted nasty words and charged into my bedroom. He knocked my hair ornaments off my bureau onto the floor. He ripped my bed pillows apart with his bare hands, sending feathers flying in every direction. I had never seen him this angry, and I wanted to know what had happened—maybe something bad for him but good for me, like police officers knocking on the door about some problem in the area—but I'd learned to let him speak first. Otherwise, he would haul off and knock me to the floor.

After he stomped his way back to my sitting room, he dropped onto the couch and hammered away at the cushions on either side of him. "Someone broke into this place, my home, and stole the dragon suitcase with everything in it."

"No, that can't be true," I cried. "All my formal clothes and—"

"You're upset?" he screamed. Anger flashed in his eyes. He smacked me hard across the shoulder. My skin felt like it was burning. "Someone stole my cash, my TV, my best watch—it was my grandfather's—and my tools that I need for work!" Spittle formed on his lips.

Ignoring the pain, I wondered why I hadn't heard anything. The wall between my apartment and Frank's quarters wasn't completely soundproof. Whoever did this must be a professional thief. "I'm sorry about all this, Frank," I said, but I was overjoyed and filled with hope when I realized if a thief could get in, surely I could get out. "Do you have any idea who did this?"

"No."

"Did you just discover it?"

"Yes. A few minutes ago when I got home from work. Did you hear anything?" he hollered into my face.

"No. I can't hear anything in my apartment."

His shoulders stiffened.

I spoke calmly. "May I see the living room?" I asked. "Whoever did this might have left clues. I'm good at searching for what isn't obvious at first sight. That's how I approach a piece of music with my erhu, always looking for the unexpected. It just might work for you too. Right now."

"Okay," he said hesitantly, frowning as he absorbed my words. "You got three minutes." He pulled me to the other room. I quickly glanced at the front door and moved to where I could see the kitchen door. I didn't see any sign that a lock had been broken or a door had been knocked off its hinges. "How do you think the thief got in?" I asked.

"What difference does that make?" he snapped. "They took my things."

My thoughts were spinning through my head. Concentrate, concentrate. Either the thief had a key, or there had to be a third door. Please, let there be a third door. What other options were there? Where could a third outside door be? In my two years here, I had never seen Frank's bedroom. The third door must be there, or was there another possibility that I hadn't noticed? Baba used to say many things are hidden in plain sight. Calmness came over me. Baba's words, 'hidden in plain sight,' would guide my search.

Frank jerked my arm. "Quit dragging your heels," he snarled and checked his watch. "Do you see one of those clues you were yammering about?"

"Not yet."

"This is bad." Frank's voice was high-pitched with fear as he shoved me toward my apartment. "If the police catch the thief, they'll trace my clothes back to me. They have their ways. They show no respect. They don't understand creative people."

He screwed up his face. "That thief, whoever he is, stole the dragon. I want that dragon back and our clothes too. Why did a thief choose my house? Why did he have to come here?" He stopped shoving me and stomped his foot on the floor, like a child in a tantrum. "I want my dragon back."

I thought hard. Without the dragon suitcase and its contents, Frank could grow tired of me and look for someone new. To stay alive, I needed to come up with an idea. The dragon, that's what he missed the most. The dragon was gaining as much importance as the erhu. I could work with that, but my first priority was finding that third door.

Frank was still so angry there was no way I could talk to him about anything. I picked up my erhu and played the sweet song *Small Flower Drum* to calm him. I saw his tense jaw grow slack and his fists relax. My sweet caring erhu had performed its magic.

"I'm going to track down the thief," Frank said. "I'll check the pawn shops right now. Tomorrow, I'll hit the second-hand shops. If any of our stuff was brought in, I'll find it. Strike while the iron's hot. You probably never heard that before, but that's what a smart man like me does. I'm going to strike." He shoved me into my room and locked the door.

Late that night, I climbed into bed and closed my eyes. I convinced myself his bedroom had no outside door. That's how most of the homes I'd seen were constructed. My work was now cut out for me. I imagined each room of Frank's living quarters, each wall. Could there be a door hidden in plain sight? My mind traveled, wall by wall, room by room, through the places I had seen. "Come on wall, come on door, and show yourself!" I said into the darkness.

I sat bolt-upright in the dark, pumped my fist, closed my hands in prayer and said, "If it's not in Frank's bedroom, it's in plain sight somewhere in Frank's quarters! There is no other possibility. That's where it has to be. If so, it's been right in front of my eyes all this time."

28
Ivy Chen

Tuesday, January 26, 2010

I woke up, startled by the memory of what had happened last night. Frank had locked me in my room and gone to check on pawn shops. He was intent on finding the dragon suitcase and everything belonging to the two of us that he'd stored in it. I kept busy all day writing, playing my beloved erhu, and imagining myself back home with Mama and Baba. Late in the day, I turned again to my journal to put my thoughts into words. The key rattled in my door, and I quickly set my journal aside.

Frank unlocked my door and pushed it open.

"Here's dinner," he growled and shoved a take-out box at me. "I had no luck with the pawn shops. I'm going to the second-hand places. I have an hour before they close. I'll hit a few shops every day. I'll find that dragon suitcase and bring it back. If not today, then tomorrow, or the next day." He was angry but too rushed to inflict his anger on me. He slammed the door and locked it.

The quiet unnerved me. As always, loneliness and depression set in because I had to face the sorrowful truth that after these two long years, no one was coming to find me, but I couldn't let that defeat me. I would keep my mind off this prison as I always did by playing my erhu. I could always count on the erhu and the music to console me. Today my choice was *Happy Songs of Xiangjian River*. I would allow it to stir up memories and relive those special moments Vince and I shared. I would think of life, of joy, of Vince, especially the correspondence, e-mails, and phone calls we enjoyed, and most of all, our three special evenings together just before Frank abducted me.

The music soared, and my spirits lifted. I finished the piece and set down my erhu. The memories floated back to me, and I welcomed them with all my heart. After the concert that first night in Tampa, Vince and I stopped at a bistro for a latte. We talked until closing time, caught up in each other's stories. Our hands touched. His beautiful hands that made music soar to the stars held my hands. He folded his hands around mine, and they appeared to be locked in a tender embrace. He kissed my fingertips, and I felt transported.

"The violin and the erhu are a perfect match," he said.

"Tell me what you mean," I said, hopeful that he would express his romantic feelings for me.

He gazed into my eyes. "You know what I'm going to say, but I'll say it anyway. The erhu has two strings. The inner string, the one nearest to you when you are playing, is tuned to D4. The outer string is tuned to A4."

"Yes. Tell me more," I said, hoping he would make some connection between those notes and us.

His dark exotic eyes held me in a trance. I could not tear myself away from his handsome face with those expressive eyes, those sensuous lips, and the dark hair that framed his face and moved when he was animated. We were shy with each other, but that added to his appeal and made me feel comfortable with him. We were inexperienced in matters of the heart, but we were finding our way. I'd read about taking things slowly. We didn't know any other way.

"Think about it," he said. "The erhu's two strings are tuned to the violin's two middle strings."

"Yes?" I framed the word more like a question so he would explain more precisely what he meant. I was imagining something like his arms encircling mine.

"So when I practice the violin, I think of the erhu and realize we have the same notes. What I mean to say is when I'm practicing, I often think of you, not the erhu, not the music, just you. Do you ever think of me when you practice?"

"Yes, during practice, but never during a performance."

A surprised expression crossed his face. "Why?" he asked.

"You know why," I said softly.

"I think so; I hope so, but tell me anyway."

"I would be too distracted and play the wrong notes or forget to play any notes at all."

His smile melted my heart. "I'll think of that whenever I hear your recordings," he said, and his eyes glistened. "I'll listen for a skipped note, and I'll convince myself you were thinking of me."

We were reserved, so caught up in our music for so many years that romance and romantic words had taken second place to our careers, but I sensed things were about to change. There was room for more in our lives than sharps and flats, major and minor keys, and concertos and symphonies.

I remembered every detail of those three glorious weekends and wished we could have spent many more evenings together. We were friends, but I knew deep in my heart that one day we would become much more.

I discovered so many things about him that evening. He liked old black and white movies, swimming, and reading novels set in foreign countries...so many things. I wish we could have shared some of those experiences, but it wasn't meant to be. By now, he was probably happily married with several children. My instincts told me he chose that pretty cellist who always brought a smile to his striking face. I couldn't remember her name, but Vince commented how talented she was. Sometimes instincts could be wrong. I was hoping Vince hadn't married the cellist and that he still thought of me, but if he did marry, I'd be glad he chose a musician, especially one who played the cello, one of the brightest jewels of the orchestra.

I picked up my erhu and began composing music. Every note was about Vince, my feelings for him, the hope that we would have gotten to know each other better if we had spent more time together, the happy future we might have planned.

Details enriched my every thought, where we would live, how many children we would have, the applause we would shower on each other after a solo performance.

Sometime mid-afternoon, the sound of keys clicking in the lock on my door stole away my happy thoughts.

Frank unlocked the door to my apartment and came into my room, without his usual stomping and shouting, but I knew better than to expect kindness. I'd seen this calm before the storm too many times. "No luck," he said, but he didn't raise his fist or lash out at me. "Whoever stole my stuff must be keeping it for himself. I'll try again tomorrow."

Saturday, January 30, 2010, 8:30 A.M.

Frank barged into my room and handed me a tray overloaded with take-out boxes. "Here's breakfast and lunch," he said. "I'm going to spend all day at the second-hand shops. I'm coming home with that dragon suitcase this time. You can bet on it." I didn't know what to think about Frank's lack of brutality, but I prayed it would last.

Saturday, January 30, 2010, 4:30 P.M.

Hours later Frank nearly ripped the door off its hinges as he stormed into my apartment. "They're hiding that suitcase from me. It should have turned up by now."

He slapped his forehead with his hand. "Oh Jeeze," he bellowed. "I forgot that whole other area of second-hand shops on Central. I heard about them wherever I went. They're trendy, whatever the hell that means. I better go there right now. I've put in so much work. I can't quit now. Thoroughness, that's what it takes."

He rushed out of my apartment toward the front door of his quarters. Out the door he went without saying another word.

I stood there and couldn't believe what had just happened. Frank forgot to lock me in my room!

Here, at long last, was my chance to explore his quarters. Here was my route to freedom. I rushed toward that freedom with laughter, my arms outstretched, my feet nearly dancing along the floor. Freedom!

29
Frank Brandt

What a long day. I'd been to so many second-hand stores in this stupid city; the gas in the truck was near empty. The Grand Central District was coming up on my right.

Jeeze, who named this area? There was nothing grand about it. I would check it out real fast. I didn't care a rat's ass about their junk but wanted to know if the dragon suitcase or any of my stuff was brought in.

Just in case somebody was watching me—you can't be too careful these days—I drove around to the back street and pulled into one of the parking spaces. My mission out here in the world was clear. Obtain that dragon and my lug wrench and all her pretty clothes, and I wouldn't quit until I had them. Nobody else would be looking for the stuff. I didn't report it missing, so the police don't know anything about this. I was too clever for them.

I walked into the first store, a big one near the trolley stop. The name, Rosie's Treasures, was painted across the front window. I hated this place. There was so much stuff there was hardly room to move. I wouldn't waste my time using big words. In, out, on to the next shop, that was my plan. Once inside, I picked up one of the owner's business cards and read it. "Rosie Renard," I said several times under my breath and slipped the card into my pocket.

Three customers, two women and a man, were talking to a plain-looking sales clerk. They called her Jane. Plain Jane. That made me laugh. Jane looked at me to see what was so funny. I didn't tell her. She wouldn't get the joke because the joke was on her.

"I'll be right with you," Jane said with a tight-lipped smile and waited on the three customers. She talked to them about a glass turtle on a shelf near the door. "I like turtles," Jane said. "They're so smart. They're never homeless because they carry their homes on their backs. We sure could learn a lot from turtles."

"That's a very nice thought," said the taller woman.

The shorter woman said, "I collect roosters. Do you have anything with painted roosters?"

"Right this way," Jane said.

I looked everywhere in the shop. I didn't see the suitcase or anything else that belonged to me. Finally, the shorter woman pulled out a credit card. What a fool. Credit cards could be traced. Cold cash. That was the way to go. Better yet, the old tried and true five-finger discount was even better.

The shorter woman bought dishes with roosters all over the place. I wanted to stand up tall, puff up my chest, and shout 'cock-a-doodle-doo,' but these people were very stern. They wouldn't find it funny. They watched me suspiciously from the corners of their eyes.

I waited while Jane wrapped the roosters and said goodbye to the people. Roosters weren't big and powerful like dragons. Why the heck would anyone collect roosters?

I glared at Jane. "So you finally have time for me?"

"I wait on people in the order they come into the store," Jane said, smiling at her sarcasm and enjoying every moment of it. "That's the fair way."

"What do you know about fair?" I asked.

She plastered a fake smile on her face. "Maybe I can help. Are you looking for anything in particular?"

I wasn't going to mention the word "dragon." She was into turtles and roosters. She'd make fun of dragons. She'd say something stupid like "dragons aren't real." She didn't know squat.

"I'm looking for a leather suitcase that came in recently," I said. I didn't want to be too specific and make her suspicious. "Is it here?"

"No," Jane said.

"How do you know? You didn't even look."

"I know what comes in every day." She mocked me with that fake smile. "No suitcase came in during the last few days or weeks."

I kicked the door on my way out to let her know I didn't like her attitude.

"Hey, Mister, cut that out," she hollered at me.

I showed her. Standing in the shop, I slammed the door shut and then opened it and slammed it shut again. The shelves near the door rattled and shook. I knocked my elbow against the glass turtle she liked. It fell off the shelf. It shattered into tiny pieces all over the floor near my feet. That stupid girl. It was her fault. She made me do it.

I looked over my shoulder.

Jane plunked her hands on her hips and shouted at me, "You owe me for that. Pay up, Mister."

Some nerve. "Make me," I said.

I waited to see if she called the police. If she reached for the phone, I'd kill her on the spot with my bare hands. She didn't. Instead, she called up the staircase, "Rosie. Take over. I'll be back soon. I'm gonna show this jerk he can't treat our treasures like that. Who does he think he is?"

"I'm just getting out of the shower," the person named Rosie called from somewhere upstairs. "Don't do anything crazy. I'll be down in a few minutes."

Jane hurried from the stairway toward me. I knew trouble when I saw it. I pushed my sunglasses onto the bridge of my nose and ran.

"You're messing with the wrong person," Jane said and chased after me.

I rushed to the corner, went around back, and hopped into my trusty, black pickup truck. I roared out of the parking spot, gasped for a breath, and looked in the rear mirror. What the heck? Jane was pedaling a bike down the street after me like a wild woman. She followed me at breakneck speed. What a fool! She thought she could outrun me. I left her behind, becoming smaller and smaller in my side mirror.

What the hell! Now what? She must have taken a short cut. She was pedaling behind me, legs pumping. She came closer and closer every time I stopped for the jerks in front of me. They slowed down at every stop sign. Now a red light stopped everyone in front of me. And me too! Jane weaved through the traffic. She stopped inches behind my truck and jumped off her bike. She tossed the bike into the back of my truck.

"Come on, you stupid light, go green," I shouted at the windshield.

Jane hoisted herself into my truck and crawled over her bike.

"Get out of my truck," I yelled out the window and pounded my fist on the door.

"Pay me for that glass turtle, you cheap-skate," she yelled back.

I slammed my foot on the gas pedal. My truck lurched ahead. I could see her in the mirror as I pulled away. She held on to the side of the truck with her left hand. With her right hand, she grabbed a key ring from her jeans pocket. Using the keys like knives, she scraped the cab of my truck. Back and forth, back and forth went her terrible keys. She was laughing at me. It was that 'I'll show you' laugh I hated. I hit the brakes, and then the gas, brakes and gas again and again. Jane bumped around in my truck. She would give up soon. She'd learn not to mess with super-driver Frank Brandt.

At the next red light, Jane hopped out of the truck and dragged her bike with her. She rode away like she was in one of those stupid bike races that tie up traffic. Was she going to call the police and show them the smashed turtle and blame me? I should scram right now. I would let things cool down for a day or so, and then I'd check out the rest of these shops.

I had a feeling my suitcase was in this area, maybe right there in Rosie's Treasures. That's what Jane was protecting. It wasn't a glass turtle. No. It was a suitcase. My dragon suitcase!

30
Ivy Chen

Frank forgot to lock me up! I couldn't believe it. Running toward freedom, I made quick decisions. I tried both outside doors, but they were locked tight. I rushed into Frank's room. It was a grungy, foul-smelling mess of clothes and junk-food wrappers thrown everywhere. Even with all that mess piled up, I could see there was no outside door. Charging from his room, I followed my hunch, my last hope, that a door was hidden in plain sight.

I checked my watch. Five fifteen.

It had to be here in the living area.

I looked at the tiny door about three feet high that led to the alcove where Frank had stored my suitcase. The alcove was right outside my apartment, so close to where Frank had set my suitcase, where we had explored the dragon. I stood there stunned. My thoughts raced. Could this really be it? Could it lead to the outside? I'd been looking at it every day. This was a third door, a third possibility of escape. All these years of looking and not seeing! But Baba used to say, "The crafty rabbit has three different entrances to its lair."

I crossed the room as if I were in a slow-motion dream. I ran my fingers along the door frame willing it to lead me to freedom. Moving quickly now, I did exactly what I had seen Frank do when he pulled the dragon suitcase out of this alcove, and we began our sick nightly ritual.

I opened the door, yanked on the chain to the light bulb, and dropped to my hands and knees. I peered ahead into the storage space, where Frank had kept my suitcase. The bulb flickered. The odor of the place stung my nostrils, but I crawled forward. I gagged but continued crawling, convinced I could endure anything to escape. A putrid smell stopped me for several seconds, but I wouldn't give in.

Frank's clothes, hanging from hooks, swatted my face. His shoes and boots, scattered across the floor, blocked my way. I picked my route across them, touching the floor as I went. My fingers slipped on something wet and sticky on the floor. I gagged. I ducked away from the source of the putrid smell. The light from the bare bulb illuminated what it was. Two traps. Each held a dead rat. A third trap held a rat that was barely alive, wriggling to set itself free. I gagged again. I couldn't throw up. That would leave a trace. I crawled onward toward the back wall of this alcove-closet.

A thin band of light about one inch wide illuminated the base of the back wall. Please let it be an outside door! Yet I couldn't imagine why there would be an outside door here. It was so difficult to get to, but the band of light wasn't my imagination. It was right there in front of me. Please let that light be coming from the world outside through a crack near the floor.

I looked again in the dim light. The door was normal height and width. This part of the alcove-closet was regular height too. I stood up tall and found plenty of headroom above me. The beam of my flashlight showed two different woods that came together in this full-size part of the closet. This large section was obviously an addition. Frank or a previous owner had added this larger part. Maybe the plan was to eventually enlarge the smaller area...but for what purpose? Maybe it had something to do with the place being a warehouse. A truck could pull up to the door, unload merchandise, and it could be stored in the closet. That could be it.

On closer inspection, I noticed the door to the outside was actually two half-doors chained together and fastened with a padlock, like what you might expect on a warehouse or at an industrial site–primitive but effective until some thief broke in and stole the dragon suitcase. I pushed hard against the door. It didn't budge. I pulled on the padlock, but that didn't work either. Metal filings glistened on the floor in the bit of light that crept into the closet. Either Frank had recently repaired the chains that held the padlock in place, or the thief had shattered them when he broke in.

This padlocked door, once opened, was my escape to freedom. I needed to smash that lock. I didn't see any tools in the alcove-closet, but the wrought-iron pan under Frank's kitchen sink would work! I needed to get to the kitchen and grab that pan. I lingered close to the door for a few seconds to breathe in the sweet smell of fresh air.

Noises came from beyond the door. Noises like tires skidding on gravel, like car brakes slamming. Frank must have returned! He might come in this way and catch me. He might come in the front door. There wasn't time to get the pan. I needed to get to my room before Frank entered the house. So close! I had been so close!

I hurried back as fast as I could go, dropped to my hands and knees when the ceiling sloped down, and crawled the rest of the way. It seemed to take hours to get out of that closet, but it was two minutes at most. I rushed back to my room. Quietly, I shut the door, and without a sound climbed into bed. My apartment was dark.

My heart pounded with fear. I squeezed my eyes tight. I didn't want to see Frank storm into my room, raise his fists, and beat me until I passed out. Minutes passed. Long, slow minutes. Then the door opened. It didn't fly open as it usually did. For the first time ever, it inched open.

"You in there?" Frank asked brusquely.

"Yes," I said with a yawn, faking a sleepy voice. "I decided to take a nap. I'm very tired."

"Go back to sleep, and keep quiet," he said. The beating I had feared didn't happen. But why?

"Somebody might have followed me here," he said. "I zigzagged all over the place, and I think I lost them."

"Who followed you?" I asked.

"Somebody who wants to cause trouble. Somebody who wants to see us separated. Your part of the house is soundproof, but silence is our best bet in emergencies like this. Do you hear me?"

"Yes," I whispered and clapped my hand over my mouth. I feared I would shout for joy that help might be on the way.

The door slowly creaked shut. His voice contained something new, a trembling he couldn't conceal, the unmistakable sound of fear. The strong smell of his sweat lingered in my room even though he had not crossed the threshold. What had he done that made someone decide to follow him home? I couldn't imagine what had happened at those Central Avenue shops where he went looking for my dragon suitcase, but one thing I knew for certain, it frightened him beyond reason.

I turned and faced the far wall. Beyond it lay the alcove-closet that led the way out of this prison. All I needed to do was get my hands on that wrought-iron pan and hide it here in my apartment. "Hooray!" I said to the pillow. "Hooray for me!" the next time Frank forgot to lock me in, I would charge into that closet with the pan and pound that padlock to smithereens.

My heart sang a new tune, a joyful tune that signified freedom. In my mind, the erhu accompanied me with a carefree sound that flew around the room like a kite propelled by an autumn breeze.

31
Frank Brandt

Tuesday, February 2, 2010, 7:30 P.M.

What a clever guy I was, especially on a misty night when the stars were playing hide and seek. It was a perfect night for my black shirt and pants, my trusty ski cap with eyeholes, and latex gloves. I was truly a pro! No one noticed me slink along the rear wall of Rosie's Treasures or stop at her back door. The lock was a joke.

Once inside the workroom, I stood perfectly still and listened hard as I peered into the darkness. Just as I deduced, that was one of Sherlock Holmes' favorite words, no one else was there. Rosie just left in her noisy, old truck. Her nasty helper Jane left more than an hour ago. If I ever saw Jane again, I'd carve a big deep scratch on her forehead, and maybe another on her back, and another on her stomach. She'd be sorry she messed with my truck. The vicious way she acted told me the real story. She was protecting something in this shop. Not a turtle. Not a rooster. No, it was my dragon suitcase. It was here, and I was going to find it. If Jane didn't know where it was, her boss, Rosie Renard, certainly did.

I turned on my flashlight. The fuse box was as easy to mess with as the lock on the door. I looked everywhere for the dragon suitcase. It wasn't here. I opened the door to the storage area and shone my flashlight into every corner and all around the place. It wasn't there. I made my way to the shop and looked top to bottom and everywhere in between, but there was no dragon suitcase. I was ticked off as I returned to the workroom.

Headlights flashed across the windows. I quickly turned off my flashlight and hid behind a large bureau far from that back door. The excitement of this moment was so deliciously unbearable that my mouth watered. Little Miss Rosie Renard would tell me where she hid that dragon suitcase. She'd tell or—

A key turned in the lock. Someone flicked on the light. Surprise! No lights. She must be scared. Would she skitter away like a little mouse? Let her try. I'd trap her before she even made it to the door.

"Darn," a female voice said.

It was Rosie. Who else could it be? She strode in like she owned the place. I stifled my laughter. She did own the place, but right now, she was my guest and, as she was about to find out, my prisoner. Same difference. I must stop thinking. The ski cap was so thin, she'd hear my thoughts.

32
Rosie Renard

Rosie set down her packages on the table by the back door of her workroom. She flicked the light switch. "Darn." No lights. She flicked the switch several times. "What bad timing," she muttered as she approached the fuse box. Taking advantage of the beam of light from the flashlight hanging from a cord in case of emergencies, she made several attempts to replace the main fuse.

Finally, success! The lights came on. She was looking forward to finishing Ted's birthday gift, two comfortable rugged chairs for his living room. She had already restored the oak arms, legs, and trim to their original patina. She had replaced the foam rubber on the backs and seats. Now she was ready to reupholster. That was the icing on the cake.

The chairs were a perfect choice for Ted's fieldstone cottage, a woodsy retreat nestled among pine trees, near Boyd Hill Nature Preserve. She couldn't wait to see his surprised expression when she pulled into his driveway and parked behind his custom-painted grass-green truck, and began unloading the treasures. "Happy Birthday," she'd holler and wave him over.

He'd say, "You shouldn't have. You work too hard." And she'd say, "But Ted, this was a labor of love." Ted would laugh. They would kiss and whisper sweet nothings and linger over every heartfelt moment of their deepening love. These little lovers' rituals had worked for so many couples for countless centuries. She smiled. They were working for Ted and her too. She'd been such a fool to try to drive him out of her life. Ted. She truly loved Ted. She couldn't get enough of Ted.

Enough daydreaming about Ted! Time was flying by. She carried the shopping bags to her worktable. Reupholstering was a long and exacting process. Creases and bunched fabric were tell-tale signs of an amateurish job. She would start one chair tonight and work on it tomorrow and several more days if necessary. She would give equal time to the second chair. She didn't want to rush and end up botching the job.

Rosie dumped the contents of the packages on her worktable, unloaded a carton of industrial staples, and inserted them into her staple gun. She set out a hammer and brass upholstery tacks and placed one of the chairs on her work table. She rolled out the durable eye-catching fabric she had discovered at the bottom of a hope chest at a garage sale. The soft browns with flecks of gold, avocado, and plum would be perfect. The chairs would go well with the cocoa brown sofa, the only comfortable piece of furniture he owned. The earth-friendly tones reminded her of Ted and his love for the land. Lately, everything reminded her of Ted.

They had become so close, so loving. She had never felt like this about anyone before. At Ted's urging, she had been seeing a therapist and was working through her fears and trauma about losing a loved one and being blamed for the loss. She could see that with more time and more sessions, she could possibly welcome a relationship based on trust and love. It was up to her to make it happen. No excuses. No blame. No back-sliding into old patterns of thinking. And no expectations that anyone could make it happen for her. She was in charge of her own life. She needed to call the shots.

Her flashbacks about her kidnapped cousin hadn't disappeared, but they had retreated. Little successes could add up, one day at a time. All that kind of positive thinking helped. Life was good. She loved Ted more with each passing day, and he loved her. She wasn't hearing wedding bells. It was way too soon for that, but it was so nice to see

Ted every day and fall under the spell of his smile and his positive outlook on life.

Rosie was picturing Ted's handsome face when a squeak of floorboards came from the other end of the workroom. She looked in that direction, toward the stairs to her apartment. Nothing unusual. Probably the natural settling of the floor. Turning back to the fabric, she smoothed the edges and picked up the shears. She snipped across the fold, leaving two identical pieces.

Another sound, this time a stifled cough. Her head shot up. Her body tensed. Quickly, she surveyed the room. Nothing amiss.

She eyed her numerous tools with sharp edges and pointy tips set along the walls. They took on the sinister appearance of weapons. The shirts on the coat rack looked like people, silent faceless unmoving people. The hard hat—

Was that labored breathing she heard? No, it had to be her imagination. Surely, it was her imagination.

"Who's there?" Rosie called out in a strangled voice.

In a heartbeat, total darkness.

Her thoughts ran together. The fuse box had been tampered with. Someone was definitely in the workroom. She wasn't alone.

She inched her way through the darkness toward the back door, the nearest way out. Noiselessly, she pulled her cell phone from her pocket.

The sudden odor of body sweat stung her nostrils.

She turned as a hulking figure lurched toward her. He knocked the phone from her hand.

She ran toward the door. Get out. Get away. Run. "Help! Help!"

The man charged from behind. Too late! He caught her in a choke hold. His hands were smooth and smelled of powder. He was wearing latex gloves!

"What did you do with my suitcase? Where is it?" he hissed in her ear. He yanked so hard on her neck that her feet lifted off the floor.

Rosie tried to punch, and kick, and scratch, but she couldn't fight him off.

Mustering all her strength, she slammed both her elbows into his stomach.

His arms loosened.

She burst free and rushed through the darkness, arms stretched out in front of her. Her worktable. She had to get to her worktable.

There. She made it. Her fingers quickly searched the top of the table. Scissors. Where were her scissors?

Frantically, she ran her hands across the table. The staple gun! That would work.

She gripped the handle. Her finger curled around the trigger.

Ready!

She heard the intruder stumbling noisily in the dark toward her. Closer. Closer. Again, that horrible smell of body odor.

Aim! She lifted the staple gun and pointed it in the direction of his breathing.

Fire! She squeezed the trigger. Again and again she squeezed.

"Owww! Damn you to Hell! I'll get you. Owww!" he screamed. "Stop!"

Rosie continued firing away. Her attacker kept threatening her and screaming in agony. Good! The staples found their mark.

She fired several more times.

"I'll kill you," he howled and lunged for her. The staple gun fell from her hand and skidded across the floor somewhere into the darkness.

Rosie reached out with her free arm. Her hand hit the table. The hammer! She grabbed it, lifted it over her head, swung it blindly this way and that.

He pushed her aside. She crept away from the work bench. In a series of lightning-fast movements, she tripped over a carton of foam rubber, lost her balance, fell onto her hands and knees, grabbed the hammer, and stood up. She gasped for breath.

The man grunted. "Tell me where my suitcase is!"

Rosie tried to make her way toward the back door. She couldn't mask the noise of her breathing or of her work boots on the concrete.

Wailing and cursing her name, the man threw the weight of his entire body at her.

She sidestepped before he gained momentum for a second attack. Gripping the hammer, she hauled off and hit him as hard as she could.

His croaking, gravelly groans echoed off the walls. Objects crashed to the floor. He staggered away, growling like a wild animal His heavy footfalls cut through the growls each time he took a breath.

The back door opened and slammed shut.

In the darkness, Rosie stumbled to the staircase that led to her apartment. Carefully and quietly, she made her way to the top, struggling to catch her breath, all the while listening for the man's return. Her fingertips gingerly found the key on the ledge over her door. If the intruder were already on the stairs behind her, dropping the key now in the darkness could leave her trapped on the stairs, easy pickings for him. Holding the key tightly, she unlocked the door, bolted the door shut behind her, and rushed into her bedroom. She grabbed the land phone from her nightstand and dialed 9-1-1.

Waiting for a police officer to pick up, Rosie shifted the curtain aside just an inch or two to avoid being seen.

Her heart raced. She peeked out the window overlooking the parking lot behind her shop. Her breath caught in her throat. Was he in the parking lot, or was he climbing the stairs to her apartment?

She exhaled her fear at the sight of a man wearing dark clothes stumbling toward a black pickup truck. He heaved himself into it and roared out of the parking lot. In the dim light, Rosie couldn't see the license plate, but the truck looked like it might be a Ford-F150. She couldn't be sure. There was nothing distinctive, no oversized tires, no stickers pasted anywhere.

Where are the officers? What's taking them so long? Her entire body trembled at the thought of what had happened and what could have happened next if she hadn't wounded the man.

"Thank God," Rosie said when a voice finally came on the line. "Hello, this is Officer Mulligan. How can I help you?"

Rosie's voice trembled as her words poured out, "Officer, please come to my shop, Rosie's Treasures. A man attacked me in my workroom. I locked myself in my upstairs apartment. Hurry. I'm afraid he might return." She rattled off the address.

The next five minutes seemed like a lifetime to Rosie as she stood near the door to her apartment. She gripped a heavy stone bookend in each hand, ready to strike the attacker if he returned.

♫♫

"Rosie, Rosie Renard. It's Officer Ed Mulligan." His deep voice traveled up the stairs to Rosie's apartment. "You can come out now. It's safe. The lights are on. Officer José Silva is here with me."

Rosie set down the bookends. She opened the door to her apartment and looked down the staircase. Two officers in uniform stood in the workroom, holding up their shields.

"Am I glad to see the two of you," she said and hurried down the stairs.

"I'm Officer Mulligan," the taller officer said, "and this is Officer Silva."

"Thanks for coming," Rosie said, still fearful from what she'd been through, but at the same time grateful that the officers had arrived so quickly.

"Tell me what happened," Officer Mulligan said.

"It was worse than my worst nightmare," she said.

"Are you hurt?"

"He tried."

"But he didn't succeed?"

"No. I hurt him."

He scrutinized her from head to toe. "You're on the small side. How did you manage that?"

"I shot staples at him and hit him with a hammer."

The two officers exchanged surprised glances.

"There's a trail of blood headed toward the door," Office Silva said. Now he scrutinized Rosie from head to toe. "There's no sign of blood on you. The blood must belong to your attacker. We'll call the tech team."

He nodded at Officer Mulligan, who pulled out his phone. "They'll get DNA off that blood. Now, tell me, did you know the person?"

"He was wearing a ski mask. There were no lights, so I didn't see his face," Rosie said. "I didn't recognize his voice."

"Do you think he intended to rob you?"

Rosie shook her head. "He said he wanted his suitcase."

Officer Silva scratched his head. "Suitcase? Does that mean anything special to you?"

"No. My treasures are mostly wooden pieces of furniture. That's my specialty. That's what customers come looking for, but suitcases, no. My guess is the intruder had too much to drink and got mixed up. If he wanted a suitcase, he would go to shops farther down the street, and I don't know what he meant by my suitcase. If he had sold me a suitcase and changed his mind and wanted it back, we could have reached an agreement. Uh... wait a minute."

"Did you think of someone?" Officer Mulligan asked.

"Maybe this is a coincidence," Rosie said, narrowing her eyes, "but someone came here to my shop on Saturday. I was upstairs in my apartment. I never saw him. My assistant Jane waited on him. He wanted a suitcase. We didn't have any. The man got real nasty. He broke Jane's favorite object, a pretty glass turtle. He said he didn't like her attitude. They had a little squabble. You could maybe call it a big squabble."

She shifted from one foot to the other. "Jane stood up for herself and didn't take any guff from him. She wasn't hurt. He never laid a hand on her. I didn't report it. He took off in his truck, a black pickup truck, old model, nothing fancy. She chased him on her bike. Words were exchanged."

"Okay," Officer Mulligan said. "I'd like you and Jane to come to the station and fill out a report. It's late. This can wait until tomorrow. Stay with a friend until things cool down. Do you have a friend nearby?"

"Yes. I'll call him."

"Do you have a last name, a telephone number, and an address on your assistant Jane?"

"Yes." She wrote everything down and handed it to Officer Mulligan.

"Make your call," Officer Mulligan said. "As soon as the tech team gets here, we'll follow you to your friend's place to make sure there's no more trouble. May I give you some advice?"

"Sure."

"You were lucky tonight. That guy could have killed you. At the first sign of trouble, you need to get away."

"I know."

"One more thing," Officer Mulligan said. "You could have called us when some guy gave your assistant a hard time and destroyed a piece of your merchandise. We could have driven by for a day or two to make sure everything was okay. Two incidents in four days could be a coincidence. Could be somebody's got a grudge against you. Is this getting through to you?"

"Yes," Rosie said. "Call the police when there's trouble."

"Let those words sink in," Officer Mulligan said.

Officer Silva stepped forward. "Officer Mulligan had his say. Now let me put in my two cents. Next time, and let's hope there is no next time, just work on escaping. No Superwoman stuff. Do you get what I'm saying?"

"Yes, Officer. No staples, and no hammers. Believe me I was just trying to stay alive, but maybe he'll think twice about coming back here."

Officer Silva shrugged off her comment. "And maybe he'll come back with a sledge hammer and a roofer's nail gun. Paybacks can be hell."

A flurry of thick extra-long staples flying at her face flashed through Rosie's mind. "You've made your point," she said as she shuddered, "and it's not pretty."

♫♫

Weeks later, Rosie received a call from Officer Silva regarding the attack in her workroom.

"I wanted you to know we got the DNA from the trail of blood left by the intruder in your workroom. The bad news is he's not in the system."

"Does that mean he never committed a crime before?" Rosie asked.

"Maybe, or it could mean he's never been caught. As you know, he was wearing latex gloves, so he left no fingerprints."

"He must be a professional thief. He planned this as part of a robbery or something. Maybe he didn't intend to come to my shop, but he was up to no good."

"We thought of that too," Officer Silva said. "However, there were no robberies in the immediate area the week before or after."

"That's good news for all my friends on the block."

"This disturbance at your shop could have been random," he said. "You may be right. Someone got mixed up and went to your shop instead of one that specializes in suitcases, so you may have seen the last of this guy, but be careful. There are crazies out there."

"Thank you, officer, and you're right about crazies. That guy might have killed me, all because of a suitcase."

"I believe it. We've seen it happen over a parking space. In case there's any further trouble, we have everything in a file with your name on it, including a notation that there's no name or photo or any other details about the attacker, other than that he drove a black pickup truck, possibly a Ford. We have the description of the man your helper chased. Unfortunately, the guy kept his hat pulled down low to make an ID difficult, and he was wearing sunglasses."

"So that's it?"

"Be cautious. Keep your eyes open for trouble. Try not to spend time alone in your shop. If you see a black pickup truck driving back and forth in front of your shop or parking in the lot behind your shop, call us. No staples, and no hammers this time. Just call!"

33
Ivy Chen

Tuesday, February 2, 2010, 10:15 P.M.

A gentle knocking at my door surprised me. Frank usually burst into my quarters, startling me with his brutish ways. Could it be someone else? Someone here to rescue me?

I jumped to my feet, eager to see a friendly face.

The lock turned. The door opened slowly.

"Turn away," Frank said in a strained voice, and my heart sank. It was Frank after all. "Don't look at me, and don't say anything until I say so."

I quickly turned my back to the door and pressed my lips together. After all this time in captivity, I knew if I disobeyed and looked at him or spoke, I would incur a beating. I heard his footsteps hesitate before he stepped into the room. He paused after taking several steps.

"I've been injured," he said. "There's blood all over my shirt. I'm wearing a ski cap for a mask, and I can't pull it off because it's stapled to my face. My shoulder took a real hard hit."

I couldn't believe what I was hearing.

He struggled to catch his breath. "I came home the back way. No one saw me, and no one followed me. I did all this to get back the dragon suitcase for us. It didn't work. I took a bad beating, and I know who did it. Rosie Renard. Smart me, I took her business card. I can find her place. I can find her any time I want. I memorized her name and address." He took her business card from his pocket, crumpled it, and tossed it on the floor.

A few more labored breaths. "I need to sit down. You'll have to be like a nurse and fix all this. Use your bathroom sink and counter like a medical area. Don't even think about running away or hurting me. I can still knock you down, and this time when you beg for mercy, I'll say no. Okay, you heard the gist of it. Don't scream, and don't speak until I give the word. You can turn around now."

I turned toward him and immediately covered my mouth with my hands to stifle my scream. Even with all he'd said to warn me, he frightened me. His mean eyes peered through holes in the blood-soaked ski cap that covered his entire head and face. Blood seeped through his shirt along his shoulder. I didn't care a whit about the blood or his injuries. He deserved everything horrible that happened to him. What pleased me was that he was disoriented, his movements slow and erratic, not enough so that I could overpower him, but he was definitely weakened. That gave me an advantage, and I planned to grab hold of it like a lioness on her prey.

"What do you have to say to me?" he asked.

"You frightened me," I said.

"What the hell do you know about being frightened? You're here safe in my home. I'm the one taking chances. I'm the one with staples cutting into my face and neck, my shoulder nearly broken by a hammer. Yeah, a hammer! I don't know how I'm going to explain this to the guys at work."

"Worry about that later. For now let's take care of the wounds. I'm not a nurse, but I'll do my best," I said, hoping to sound in charge as a means to get him under my control. At long last, it could be my turn to be the boss. "We'll need peroxide, cotton swabs to dab it on with, bacterial ointment and bandages," I commanded.

I needed to think of more items to keep him busy gathering them. "Also, scissors to cut away that ski mask, tweezers to pull out the staples, and tape to make sure the bandages don't fall off," I ordered. In his weakened condition, this was the best advantage I'd ever had…and probably the best I could ever hope for.

192

"I've got that kind of stuff in my bathroom," Frank said with a hint of gratitude. "I don't go to doctors. I'm my own doctor. They give you suspicious looks and ask too many questions, like what your parents died from. I don't get it. What's that got to do with staples clamped into my forehead?" He pumped his fists. "It's like daggers jabbing my brain. They've got to come out now."

He went to the door. "I'll be right back. Stay right where you are." In his single-minded quest to receive medical treatment for his wounds, he left without closing the door behind him. He was walking slowly, listing sideways instead of moving forward. Now and then, he leaned against the wall for support.

Overjoyed, I took several deep breaths to calm my nerves and waited until he was out of sight. I took off running. While he rummaged around in his bathroom and groaned with pain, I ducked into the kitchen. Quickly, I opened the cabinet door under the sink and grabbed the wrought-iron pan. It was so heavy; I had to hold it with both hands. If I dropped it, Frank would surely come to investigate. For several brief seconds, I imagined myself raising that pan over my head and crashing it down on Frank, knocking him out. This was the most vulnerable he'd ever been, but if I missed, or if the force of the pan didn't knock him out, he would beat me to death. No, I had to stick to my plan. That was the way to succeed. I couldn't let a last-minute idea ruin everything.

I rushed back to my bedroom and hid the pan under the mattress. I had imagined this so vividly, so many times, that now it seemed like I wasn't stealing the pan. It was like I was watching an actress in a play, and she was stealing it.

I figured Frank wouldn't come looking for the pan. The dead flies caught in the cobwebs on it told me he never used it. I had no choice but to leave the pan a disgusting, filthy mess for now. I couldn't risk Frank catching me with it while I took time to scrub it clean.

As I returned to the sitting area, I noticed the crumpled business card Frank had thrown on the floor. I picked it up, smoothed it out, and read every word. The person who had wounded Frank and made him suffer was Rosie Renard, and her shop was called Rosie's Treasures, on

Central Avenue. My breath caught in my throat. That was the very same Central Avenue where I had once walked and bought a tea set and pillowcases. Rosie's photo was on the card too.

I thanked God for this pretty, young woman whose smile radiated such joy. I hoped one day to meet Rosie and thank her for hurting Frank and weakening him and giving me an advantage in my psychological battle against him. I closed my eyes and imagined myself meeting Rosie Renard. I would say to her, "Rosie, please call my mother. Tell her I am alive. Call the police and tell them I was kidnapped, and I am a prisoner of a crazy and vicious man named Frank Brandt. I am imprisoned somewhere near a coin laundry."

I heard Frank's footsteps. I hid the card in my skirt pocket.

Frank returned with two shoeboxes filled with bandages and all kinds of medical supplies. I forgot about Rosie and concentrated on finding my own way of hurting Frank Brandt. I knew exactly what I wanted in return for nursing his injuries. I wanted to spend time outdoors so that I could figure out an escape route. I had suggested it once before and refused to play the erhu if he didn't agree to my request. He beat me, leaving me woozy, bruised, and unable to walk for two days, and I never asked again. But now, I had more bargaining power, and I planned to take every advantage.

"Sit down across from the mirror so I can see the front and back of your head," I said, standing behind him. I reached for the tiny manicure scissors, the only scissors he had brought. I cut away as much of the ski cap as possible, so I could see the wounds. As I checked the mirror, I saw the light glinting off those scissors that now were so close to his neck. I thought about stabbing him and letting him bleed to death, but I decided against it. I was certain I could get out of this room, but could I get out of the house? Ali Kent wasn't able to do it. No, I've been patient for so long. Now was not the time to grab at an opportunity that might not succeed.

"Quit daydreaming," Frank said, startling me.

I set down the scissors and picked up the tweezers. I pulled out the first staple. He yowled in pain but followed up quickly with, "Keep going. I can take it."

194

"Frank, put a dab of peroxide on a cotton swab. The staples have cut into your pockmark scars. I'll have to treat each one with care so you don't get a deep infection."

"Thank you," he said. That was the first time I'd ever heard him utter those words or any other polite or thoughtful words. No. What was I thinking? I must not allow any kind thoughts about Frank to invade my mind. Let my hatred and distrust of Frank Brandt keep me focused on a sure-fire plan of escape at the right moment. Success depended on my resolve.

Onward I went, removing a staple, dabbing the cut with peroxide, and cutting away more of the ski cap. "Frank, I have come up with a story you can tell the guys at work to explain about your face and shoulder. With this story, they won't laugh at you."

"Really?" he asked. "Tell me."

"I will, but I want something in return."

"Like what?"

I looked in the mirror and saw his jaw muscles tense. "I have to go outside for fresh air on a regular basis to keep up my strength."

"For what?"

"I need strength to play the erhu."

He growled his annoyance.

"We have to be fair with each other," I said.

"Okay, but on my terms," he said hesitantly. He thought for several long seconds. "You can go outside once. It has to be dark. You can stay ten minutes, and I have to go with you."

"Why can't I go alone?" I asked innocently.

"You'll run away."

"No. Where would I run? I don't know anybody anymore."

"I have to be with you to keep you safe," he said. "Now, what's this story you made up?"

One victory earned, but more could be eked out. I had one more bargaining chip I hadn't yet tried.

"Tell the guys you were cleaning out the garage," I said. "A beam fell on you, mainly on your shoulder. Nails poking out of the beam raked your face."

195

"Huh." He paused. "That's good."

"Practice it right now, so you don't forget. It will take your mind off these staples."

He recited his story three times and cried out in pain a few times. His pain made me so happy. I wished I could hurt him more.

"Good," I said and continued until I had removed the very last of the three dozen staples and the ski cap too. "That's the end of the staples. Now, I'll apply more peroxide, bacterial ointment, and then the bandages."

"Thank you," he said for only the second time in the two years I had been his prisoner.

"You owe me for this," I said, gritting my teeth to hold my anger inside me.

"What the hell are you talking about?"

"For what I've done so far, I want two visits to your yard, not one. And they will last fifteen minutes each, not ten."

He hesitated. "Okay," he said finally, "but no more deals."

"Tear the cotton into small pieces and put bacterial ointment on each piece," I said sternly.

It took great effort for me to finish cleaning and treating his facial wounds. I resented that what I was doing might save his life. He didn't deserve it, and I disliked my part in it.

"You owe me another favor for this treatment," I said and heard the anger in my voice.

"I told you no more deals."

Sarcasm got the better of me. "Shall I forget your shoulder wound? Is that what you want? Just say the word." For a brief moment, I felt the presence of Rosie Renard, encouraging me to do whatever it took to defeat this monster. She had attacked him with staples and turned his face into a bloody mess. I couldn't do that, but I could take advantage of his debilitated state and find my way out of this hell.

He frowned. "What favor do you want this time?"

"I need more fresh air to give me strength to play the erhu. You want to hear her sweet voice, her power that lifts you out of the cruelty and monotony of your daily work and gives you something to look forward to every day. This can happen if we work together. I need a third outdoor visit, and all three visits have to be twenty minutes each, not fifteen."

He shut his eyes and curled his lip. "Okay. Three visits, but fifteen minutes, that's all, and don't forget my shoulder."

"Thank you, Frank," I said and worked at bandaging his facial cuts.

As I cut away the part of his shirt that covered his shoulder wound, I said, "That's it. You're all patched up. We're done."

Finally, he left without a word and locked the door behind him. I immediately scoured and disinfected everything involving Frank's treatment to remove every trace of him. I hated myself for all the lies and deceit I had spoken. I hated Frank for keeping me locked up. I needed to get back to my world where good people did good things, and favors weren't bargaining chips to stay alive.

I flopped on my bed and stared at the skylight. Would I ever be free? I was like a song bird kept in a bamboo cage. I cried for several minutes, but tears did no good. I realized that birds sometimes escaped their cages and flew away. If they could, so could I.

I didn't even bother to undress. I just turned toward the wall and prayed for sleep. Doubts festered and crowded my mind. Could I have taken advantage of Frank's weak condition and stabbed him with those scissors and let him bleed to death? Could I have been less thorough with his cuts and let him die of an infection? On and on I second-guessed myself until I came right down to the basic question that I had been avoiding.

Was I capable of killing another human being? I didn't think so. Was I capable of plotting an escape and making a run for freedom? Absolutely yes!

Wednesday, February 3, 2010

The next evening, Frank made me wait in his living room while he opened the kitchen door that led to the outdoors. He didn't want me to see how he opened it, but I already knew.

"Come on," he said, "let's get this over with, and don't speak above a whisper once you're outdoors. Let's get something straight. Don't try anything stupid, or I'll have to kill you. You know it, and I know it. I don't want to do it, but if you give me any trouble, I will."

Although I longed to run past him and keep going, I forced myself to walk patiently through the kitchen. He had promised three outdoor visits, fifteen minutes each, and I wanted to take advantage of them to figure out how to overcome possible barriers like fences, barbed wire, and other nasty things Frank might have set in my way. Even though Frank would be with me, I would be in that yard, and I would be able to picture my escape route, step by step, minute by minute, until....

The door to the outside world opened.

The first thing I noticed was a foul odor, like decaying garbage, coming from the yard, but yard was not the appropriate word. There wasn't a blade of grass beneath my feet, only sand, rocks, weeds, tin cans, and plastic bags. Here and there a few gnarly, leafless trees had managed to survive near the ratty, old chain link fence that must enclose the property on all four sides. In a few places, bushes poked through the fence. I tried hard to see beyond the fence. I couldn't make out if there was a street or a sidewalk or another sandlot yard. In the shadows, dilapidated and seemingly abandoned industrial buildings jutted into the blackening sky. I looked up. The sky was filled with stars and a sliver of the moon.

This was the first time I had seen stars and the moon in two years. Even with a skylight in my room, I could never see much. The window was small and angled away from my view. But now, the big, heavenly sky extended over and around me, embracing me. The beautiful sight took my breath away. I saw the seven bright stars of the Big Dipper, the handle of three stars attached to a rectangular bowl of four stars. Baba told me the Big Dipper has several interpretations. His favorite was the seven stars, which formed a piece of basalt shaped like a snake. That comforted me because my father's mother was born in the year of the snake. Now, I knew she was watching over me. I wanted to stand there and wonder at the sky and its beauty, but I had to look away and study the yard, searching for a way to escape.

"Frank, look at the stars," I whispered. "Look how beautiful they are." While he studied the night sky, I peered in every direction. First, I noticed two side-by-side oversized doors on the side of Frank's house. Those had to be the doors in the alcove-closet. There were no steps from the door to the ground. I would have to jump down and run to freedom. I looked into the distance and saw dim lights. I heard traffic somewhere out there near the dim lights. That would be the direction to run. That's where I could find someone to help me.

Off to the left, I saw something raised above the ground, like a manhole cover. A ring of stones surrounded it. Curious, I walked toward the spot and moved closer for a better look.

"Stay away from there," Frank hissed and shoved me hard. "That well is sacred. That's Ali's well."

Ali was in that well? Shivers ran up my spine. Frank was capable of anything. The brave, talented, resourceful Ali Kent, the prisoner who lived here before me, had ended up in that well. What a horrible way to die.

"Time's up," Frank whispered, and I had to fight hard not to cry. The tears I held back were for Ali who didn't survive Frank's cruelty and for me, whose brief time under the beautiful heavens had ended so quickly.

♫♫

Later that night in bed, I awakened in a chilling sweat. Ali feared that Frank was going to kill her. The same fear now gripped me.

For hours, I couldn't fall back to sleep. When I finally drifted off, I woke up gasping for breath, dreaming that I was drowning in a black, slimy pit. My companions were the creepy creatures that suck the last breaths from those who struggle to survive and possibly call out for help.

Thursday, February 4, 2010

The next night, the same rancid smell of garbage permeated the area. An emaciated dog, sniffing around the yard, whimpered at us. "Go away," Frank hissed at the dog and threw a stone at him. He missed. The dog took off and leaped through a hole in the fence.

I couldn't believe what I had just seen. A hole in the fence!

Good doggie, I wanted to say. You didn't suffer from Frank's anger, and you showed me the way out of here. Gazing into the gathering darkness, I mentally mapped out that section of the fence in relationship to three misshapen trees nearby. That would help me find the hole in the fence even on a very dark night. The hole was small, but I was sure I could flatten myself and slither through like a snake, but not Frank. If he discovered that I was missing and came out here to look for me, he'd never fit through the opening. Good!

A torn T-shirt was stuck in a hole in one of the skeletal trees. Could be a drug drop, I thought, remembering several urban blight documentaries, part of a project for musicians to play concerts in poor, crumbling neighborhoods to help the children imagine the possibilities life offered. The T-shirt, if it were still there, could protect my hands as I tugged on the fence. Was I going crazy? I had T-shirts in my room. I just had to remember to take one with me when I escaped.

"Time's up," Frank said, and this time I didn't even think about crying. I had hope. Escape was possible!

Friday, February 5, 2010

The third and final night, I walked slowly in a circle peering in every direction. I wanted to make sure I had chosen the best route with the fewest problems and the greatest chance of success. I heard several dogs barking out there on the other side of the fence. They couldn't get to me in here, but if I escaped and got beyond the fence, then what? From the sound of their deep growls, they were big dogs. Would they chase me? Attack me? Suddenly, my hope plummeted and dragged down my courage right along with it.

My outdoor walks had come to an end. Frank locked me in my apartment. Disappointment set in, but I took a small measure of hope and courage knowing that the various parts of my escape plan were coming together. The third door, the door in plain sight, leads through the alcove-closet to the door that would set me free. I had that heavy frying pan to smash the lock on the alcove-closet door. That was a better plan than whacking Frank unconscious. I was squeamish about that from the very beginning and was glad I wouldn't have to do it, and I now knew the route from the yard to the hole in the fence and on to the dimly lit street and the traffic in the distance. I tingled with excitement. All I needed was the opportunity. Let it happen soon. I've waited so long.

In the back of my mind where doubts festered, I feared that I might be fooling myself. Was I convincing myself that courage and hope would sustain me until the day I was free? Or would they diminish as each day dragged by?

34
Detectives Tony DeLuca and Hank Hernandez

Tuesday, January 24, 2012, 7:15 P.M.

"I'm starving," Tony said, as he and Hank walked into Fortunato's on Central Avenue.

"Then this is a good place to be," Hank said.

The fragrance of fresh pizza dough, tomato sauce, and olive oil came from behind the glass where a variety of mouth-watering Italian dishes were on display.

"I'll have two slices of chicken barbecue," Hank said to the guy behind the counter.

"How's the calzone supreme tonight?" Tony asked.

"It's coming out of the oven as we speak. Large or small?"

"Large."

"We have a lot of agencies to thank for this information," Hank said as they paid at the counter.

"I know what's coming, Hank. I can tell from the smile on your face. You sorted through the information, found patterns, and you came up with something tied to this case."

"You got that right," Hank said, as they picked up their sodas and food. "But hey, I've been at this for quite a few years. As my Jamaican grandfather used to say, 'a new broom sweeps clean, but an old broom knows every corner.'"

"That's a surprise. I thought he'd say, 'Yeah, mahn. No worry.'"

"You've been watching too many Jamaican vacation commercials."

Tony chuckled. "Let's hear what you got," he said, heading for a table in the back.

They sat opposite each other. Hank set a folder stuffed with pages on the table and turned it sideways, so they could both read it. "We have sixty-eight young women who went missing in the past ten years. The good news? For the most part, they didn't disappear without a trace. They left. They came back."

"How does it play out?"

"About half, twenty-seven, were runaways. They came back on their own or with support and intervention by family members. Some moved in with their families, some went into rehab, and some took up life on the street. Several got hooked on drugs and were dragged into a life of prostitution. Two were beaten to death, and three died of an overdose. Many of the young women were victims of spousal abuse. Three died of their injuries, several returned to their partner and have been hospitalized off and on, but they are alive. Some moved away out of fear, but we have documentation they're alive. Several simply left St. Pete to start a new life somewhere else. There's documentation for them too. Others took up living on the street or in shelters somewhere within the state, but not in St. Pete."

Hank took a deep breath, folded the sheet of paper, and put it in his pocket. "We have three who were kidnapped, but it wasn't by a stranger. It was a family member, and it was a custodial issue. There were two others who didn't survive. The kidnappers were caught and are currently guests of the state."

He cleared his throat. "That leaves one missing woman. I'd say it's a possibility, so I saved her for last." He drained his cup of soda. "A young woman, a talented artist. Her name is Ali Kent."

"What do we know about her?" Tony asked.

"Our records show she went missing six years ago from the Mainsail Art Festival. We don't have much to go on. No one in St. Pete knew Ali Kent. At home, in Georgia, she had a small circle of friends but no real close friend she confided in. She traveled to St. Pete alone. She slept in her van near Straub Park, according to a maintenance crew member who saw her shaking out a sleeping bag early Sunday morning. That was the second and final day of the event. The van was noticed Monday morning, still parked near the Mainsail area, but Ali wasn't in the van, and she was never seen again. The detectives worked hard on that case, but it was like chasing a ghost. She didn't leave much of a trail."

Tony leaned back in his chair. "The Ivy Chen case is different. Ivy was seen by so many people in so many places, and she was well-known by a large circle of people involved in music."

"They didn't look alike either," Hank said. "But they were both talented. The connecting link could be that Ivy's a musician, and Ali's an artist. Art and music. Let's think of culture as the connecting link."

"That's a new one on me, but you're the one who always finds the missing link. Let's take another look at the women who went missing but later returned. Were any of them involved in the arts?"

Hank passed half the list to Tony. "You check those, and I'll check the rest."

Five minutes later Tony said, "No one in the arts in this batch. Not professionally anyway. As far as their having a hobby or interest in the arts, we can't tell from this information."

"Same here," Hank said, "so we've eliminated that possibility, given the information we have on hand. We're left with Ivy and Ali, linked by their ability in the arts."

He tapped his fingers on his chin. "There's something that doesn't sit well with me."

"Let's hear it," Tony said.

"There were many people who thought Ali was a runaway, but after reading the notes on file, I'd say she was an up-and-coming artist with a bright future. Several artists at Mainsail, even though they'd just met her, thought she couldn't have just up and disappeared. They doubted she would throw away a possibly budding career."

He pulled out several pages from the file. "Here are some comments about Ali's work from other artists who saw her watercolors at Mainsail. Pretty. Idealistic. Sweet." He returned the pages to the folder. "If those words about her style also describe Ali herself, an abductor might have been interested. We could say that Ivy Chen was also pretty, idealistic, and sweet."

Tony swiped a napkin across his mouth. "I think you're on to something, Hank. These missing-person cases could be linked. The same person could have abducted both women. Did anyone pursue that line of thinking back then? And what the heck did Ali Kent's family think happened to her?"

"I didn't see any info about the two cases being related," Hank said. "According to the report, the parents admitted they had a huge fight with Ali before she left for the art festival. There were bad feelings about money. Some of her relatives said she might have just decided a have a new life, a life without her parents."

Tony cocked an eyebrow. "There was a problem with the parents?"

"Sounds like they could be quite controlling," Hank said. "They didn't approve of their daughter pursuing a career as an artist. They said they didn't want people saying their Ali thought she was better than anyone else. I've begun checking out old newspaper articles online. Let's see if anything pops."

Tony nodded. "That's a good plan. The two cases may not be related, but, just in case, we should widen the investigation to cover both missing women."

Hank gulped the last of his soda. "If we're right about this, our serial kidnapper took Ali six years ago and Ivy two years later. That brings us to the scary part."

"I'm listening."

"If this guy has a pattern, and most of them do, he keeps a woman two years, and then—"

"He brings in a new one, meaning—"

Hank cut in, "Ivy's chances of being alive are slim."

205

"Hold on," Tony said. "I learned way back when, in some business class to beware a statistic of one. Maybe a statistic of two isn't so significant either."

"Using math to come up with a happy ending," Hank said. "I wonder what my Jamaican grandfather would say about that."

"Let's quit while we're ahead," Tony said.

35
Ivy Chen

Wednesday, March 16, 2011

I'm going to read aloud what I just recorded in my notebook. It comforts me since the only voice I hear other than Frank's voice is my own, and Frank is crazy:

> "During all these long months of imprisonment, I haven't had an opportunity to put my escape plan into action. This frightens and frustrates me. I'm beginning to question whether I will ever be free. I have the pan, my weapon. I've been outdoors and seen my surroundings. I'm ready to set my escape plan into action, but all the pieces have to fall into place. Everything hinges on Frank forgetting to lock me up so that I can roam freely through the house and get to the door that will lead me out of this prison.
>
> "When will that happen? Soon, I pray, but I've become accustomed to everything taking so much longer than I'd imagined. This existence isn't like the life I knew where I could make things happen if I worked hard. I took so much for granted back then."

Thursday, April 28, 2011

It's weird, but I've become somewhat jealous of my suitcase. Frank kidnapped it along with me in 2008. Then someone came along and stole it in January 2010, and Frank never found it in the shops he visited. I assumed the thief took the suitcase into the sunlight of the world of freedom. If only that could happen to me—but I must avoid the trap of letting fantasy rule my thoughts. My suitcase could have been thrown away by now. I'm still alive, and I must be thankful for that.

I needed to pay attention to Frank's escalating violence. The lull before the storm was long gone. Since the theft of the dragon suitcase, his temper has spiraled out of control. Besides punching holes in the walls, ripping my sheets and pillowcases to shreds, and kicking the table and chairs across the room, he has now turned on me for no apparent reason. The memory of last night has left me edgy. The scene has been popping into my head.

I was in bed drifting off to sleep, the only time when I could truly relax, knowing that many hours would pass before Frank charged into my room, but suddenly the door slammed open, and he rushed to my bed. He slapped me again and again from head to toe. I curled up in a ball to escape his fury. When he was finished, breathing hard from the effort he had put into the beating, he leaned over me and said, "That will give you something to think about. I'm in control of everything in this house, including you. Don't be getting any ideas about taking charge and running my life."

Frank managed to take away even that small measure of joy, the security of believing I was safe in bed at night. The beating wasn't because of any specific thing. It was about his power, and it was meant to keep me in line. The randomness and basic unfairness of the beating frightened me, but what did Frank know about fairness? He was beyond understanding. At times I thought he had no soul. Sometimes I thought he wasn't even human.

Tuesday, May 3, 2011

Frank became more paranoid with every passing day. The fear of another surprise attack hung over me and without warning propelled me into crying jags. Things were changing, and not for the better. Frank came crashing through the door.

"I want that dragon suitcase back," he shouted. "I miss the dragon. I'm sick and tired of you. There's other pickings out there. I've seen pretty women getting off the bus near work. They go to a canning factory. Any one of them would be nicer to me than you are. Without the dragon, you're ordinary. The erhu's music isn't as great as it used to be, and neither are you." He dropped onto the couch and kicked the table across the room.

I was desperate. The erhu was no longer enough to keep me alive. To make matters worse, I was weakening and losing weight, and my skin had turned sallow. I didn't know what to do. Baba's words came to me. "Only when there was no road left does one finally feel despair." But there was always hope. There could be many roads. I would try again and again for as long as it took.

Armed with Baba's words, I intended to give all the effort I was capable of to a backup plan. I'd been holding off using it until all other options ran out. That time was now here. My new weapon? The dragon.

"Frank, I know what's wrong, and I know how to fix it."

"What are you babbling about?"

"You miss the dragon, and so do I. You've seen the dragon on my suitcase and on my erhu, but there are many things you don't know about dragons…stories I learned as a child growing up in China, stories I could tell you. Amazing stories that will bring the dragon back into your life. Stories about how the dragon can help you."

His head jerked up. "Tell me a dragon story right now," he said. "A good one."

"Of course, Frank. Let's start out with a story about dragon fathers. They prepare food for their baby dragons so they will grow up strong, even stronger than the most famous Chinese warriors."

"Warriors?" Frank mumbled.

Here was the artful lie. "To leave their watery kingdoms and walk on earth, dragons often disguised themselves as warriors. We call them dragon warriors."

"Dragon warriors. Come on?" His questioning tone expressed doubt.

I must concoct the biggest lie I could imagine about a dragon. I must convince Frank that dragons have magical powers that can help him. Then he will want more stories, and that will assure that I get to live another day and another and....

"Yes, warriors wearing wondrous costumes!" I would make them resemble the superheroes of American comic books. I had the perfect choice, the excellent warrior Guan Yu.

"Not just any warrior," I said. "I am talking about Guan Yu. He is so fearsome and so gloriously colorful in his wondrous cape, robe, boots, and sword."

"What's this whoever's face look like?" Frank asked, and I figured he was buying this story.

I said, "Guan Yu has eyes like the phoenix, eyebrows like silkworms, a long beard, and many weapons."

"So what did he do to be so famous?"

"Try to imagine Guan Yu in action," I said. "Here's what you will see. Guan Yu races on horseback. Guan Yu brandishes his mighty weapon, his cloak flying behind him like a thunder cloud whipping across the sky. He will defeat all the forces of evil."

"Wow!" Frank exclaimed.

Another victory! Frank wouldn't kick me for some minor insult he'd gotten at work or give me a random beating just to show me he was the boss. He would want me well enough to tell him more warrior-dragon stories. I would create new episodes every day. First, I must encourage Frank to see in the dragon warrior a friend and protector.

"This dragon-warrior will help you, Frank. He keeps away evil forces. You've had so many evil forces in your life."

"What do you know about that?" he asked and jerked toward me.

"You've told me about the guys at work. The clerks in fast-food restaurants and stores who ask you too many questions. The bad person who scratched up your truck. The bad person who hammered your shoulder and shot staples into your face.

He sat there mesmerized, as if waiting for another story.

"That is all for now," I said. "I am too tired. The dragon is tired too. We'll continue this when I am well-rested and have endured no disturbances in my sleep."

He squinted at me, but neither of us mentioned the beating. We didn't have to. It was understood.

Wednesday, May 25, 2011

I decided to parcel out the dragon stories in bits and pieces so as not to delete my strength and, of course, to keep Frank interested for as long as possible. So far, I have mentioned dragon boats, but I never gave any details. They might intrigue him. I'd try and see how he reacted. In any case, the stories had the power to keep me alive, but I was not as strong as I would like to be, or needed to be, for an escape.

Friday, June 3, 2011

I told Frank a dragon story tonight, but he grabbed me by the shoulder. "You told me that one before. You think I'm stupid? I want a new story every time."

Thinking quickly, I said, "Of course, Frank. Whatever you want. However, some of the stories are very long. Half the story one night and the rest the next night is a good idea."

"Why?" he asked. His voice and manner were surly.

"The suspense will intensify the story. Taking a break from the story will give you time to figure out what's going to happen next. You're smart. Try it. You'll like it."

Grudgingly, he agreed. Good. I needed time. If I ran out of ancient Chinese fables, I would invent new ones even though they wouldn't be true to my heritage. Manipulating Frank to keep myself alive came at a great cost. I was losing the good principles that were so much a part of my upbringing. The best I could do now was convince myself that

211

when I gained my freedom, I would once again become the person I used to be.

Thursday, June 30, 2011

Tonight, in Frank's quarters, I played my latest creation which I named *Dragons on the Lake*.

"Nice song," Frank said, "but that's enough music. I want to hear a dragon story." He was so curious about the dragon, he could barely sit still.

"The dragon usually protects the people," I began. "He is their guardian. He brings rain, and that means our crops grow, and we have food. But—"

"Cut the crap about rain and food," Frank snapped. "Tell me an exciting dragon story."

"How about a story about dragon boats. I'm referring to boats that look like dragons. They are very popular in China."

"Skip the history." His eyes lit up. "Tell me about the dragon boats."

I had him now. He was on the edge of his seat. "Dragon boats are long and narrow, just like dragons. They have a head, a tail, and fish scales all over their bodies, just like dragons."

"Are they as big as a dragon?"

"Yes. They are wide enough to seat two people side by side. That's how wide a dragon is, and they're long like a dragon too, up to one hundred feet. The dragon boats race, and it is wonderful to watch. They are so fast, just like dragons."

He stamped his foot like a spoiled child. "I want to know why the dragon boats race."

"That will have to wait for another night. I'm tired. I must get a full night of uninterrupted sleep."

Frank scowled.

Friday, July 15, 2011

Tonight, as we sat in Frank's quarters, I forced myself to remain calm. I must not anger him. "I've told you the dragon boat festival is held every year to bring just the right amount of rain to the crops, but there is another reason."

Frank moved forward on his seat. "Probably something stupid," he said.

"The dragon boat races are to celebrate the memory of the poet, Qu Yuan."

"You're going to tell me about a poet?" He spat on the floor. "What good is that? The guys at work aren't going to be interested in a poet."

My eyes opened wide with surprise. He was talking about this at work. Maybe one of the workers would figure out that Frank was keeping someone at his house. Frank said they liked to tease him. To have something new to taunt him with, maybe they would follow him and check out where he lived, and see if anyone lived with him. Maybe they would find me and set me free. This storytelling could help me escape. I'd give this my all.

"Listen to the story, Frank. You'll like it. There's lots of excitement."

"Okay." He grumbled. "Make sure it's good."

"The poet either fell into the Mi Lo River, or he jumped in. No one knows for sure. The villagers ran as fast as they could to their boats. They hopped in and raced across the water hoping to reach him before he drowned. They kept their paddles moving in harmony, faster and faster, working together as a team, one for all and all for one, like when people are nice to each other, and there is peace in the world."

"Cut the peace crap," Frank griped. "What happened to the guy in the water?"

"The people banged on drums to scare the fish away so the fish wouldn't eat Qu Yuan's body." I banged my hands on the table to imitate the drums, faster and faster, louder and louder, hoping the noise might travel beyond these walls. Frank joined in banging on the table loud and fast, keeping up with me. He was even louder, but no one seemed to hear us or care about the noise. However, I was gaining time. Survival time.

"They splashed water on their oars, hoping to send the fish away." I acted that out, but Frank grumbled and didn't join in.

"Did it work?" he asked.

"No."

"I figured that," he said.

"But wait," I said. "The people did not give up. Some say the people paddled onto the river to scare the fish away. Some say they went to retrieve the body of Qu Yuan."

He curled his lip. "So who's right?"

"No one knows for certain, but they are still trying to save him. Those are the stories behind why we have a dragon boat festival. Now you know why the boats race. You have learned something today that very few people know. Tell those stories. Let people know how smart you are."

He didn't say a word, but I caught a sight so strange I gasped. A smile. Frank Brandt was smiling, flattered that I considered him intelligent, thrilled that I thought he knew more than the guys he worked with. What a great day! Frank was falling into my trap, like a heavy stone into water.

Monday, July 18, 2011

Frank liked our story-telling time. He wanted to know more about the dragon festival.

"The dragon boat festival has the longest history of all the festivals celebrated in China," I said. "Here in the United States, it is celebrated in various months and on no particular day. In China, it is always celebrated on the fifth day of the fifth month. That would be sometime in May."

"What's so special about May?" Frank pouted. "That's not when we have Christmas, Thanksgiving, the Fourth of July fireworks, or my birthday."

214

"There is more than one reason why that day was chosen," I said, trying not to show annoyance for his me-me-me attitude. "It's the sun's strongest day, near the time of the summer solstice. It's just before the summer rains fall. It's just after we plant the rice shoots." I took a deep breath. "It's all a matter of following tradition and doing what's best for everyone."

I folded my hands together. "It would be like your granting me time outdoors every day so that I am not always so tired."

Frank screwed up his face and glared at me. "Don't talk about outdoors."

"But Frank, the fresh air would give me more energy to play the erhu for you, energy to compose new works for the erhu, and energy to tell you more stories, but you're an intelligent man. You probably figured that out already."

I nearly choked on those flattering words. I made sure I didn't plead. I prayed that he grasped the concept of give and take, of doing what was best for everyone.

Frank exhaled a noisy, sputtering breath, and then several more, each one noisier than the last. He finally quit sputtering and glared at me for a long time. I found it hard to breathe. I was trembling inside with fear, but I forced myself to stay calm outwardly.

"I'll think about it," he said and locked me in my room.

I had escaped a beating by manipulating Frank and gaining the upper hand as my confidence rose. That was a triumph for me. Pretty images fluttered through my mind. The blue sky, the green grass, and flowers of every tint and design were blossoming out there beyond my apartment. If only I could escape. If only I were free. If only.

Monday, September 12, 2011

Tonight began with a huge surprise.

"I told the guys at work about the dragon boat races," Frank said. "They didn't believe me. I said you don't know nothing. They said, Oh yeah? Real snotty like. When the boss stepped out for a smoke, the guys Googled the dragon boat races on the office computer."

Frank scrunched up his face and laughed. "I was right. They were wrong. There are Chinese dragon boat races everywhere, not just China. They may even come to Florida, and they thought I was making up stuff about dragons. I saw dragons on the Internet."

"What did they look like?" I asked.

He shrugged. "There were different kinds."

"Frank, here's something you can tell the guys at work. All the dragons have something in common."

"Like what?"

"It's as easy as one, two, three," I said and counted off on my fingers. "One, bulging eyes. Two, flaring nostrils. And three, a wide open mouth."

"You sure?" he asked.

"I'm sure."

Frank was happy. Now was the time to gain an advantage. "Frank, think about this. We're a team, like the paddle teams in the dragon boat races."

He shrugged.

"You remember how we went outside those three times? Maybe we could go outside for a few minutes every day." I knew I was taking a chance bringing this up, but I had to.

"What's that got to do with the boat races?" He punched his fist into his open hand.

"Nothing. I just thought it would be nice."

"Quit thinking so much," he said. "It's time for you to go to your room."

I walked slowly and deliberately. He didn't push me, and he didn't say another word. He didn't slam my door behind me. He closed it like a normal civilized human being.

No! No! No! I absolutely must not think like that.

A normal human being wouldn't have captured me and brought me here. This terrible man Frank Brandt has condemned me to spend my days and nights with nothing to do but plot my escape, not knowing if that would ever be possible.

216

The last thing I heard before I burst into tears was the sound of the key turning in the lock, leaving me in this tiny dark world. That horrible despicable key. Had I gained anything from the dragon stories? I was so depressed, I couldn't think of an answer.

36
Rosie Renard

Friday, January 27, 2012, 11:30 A.M.

"Rosie, by any chance, is Jane there with you?" Detective DeLuca's voice crackled over the phone.

"Yes. Do you want to speak to her?"

"Both of you. We have a new development in the Ivy Chen case, and it involves you and Jane. Any chance you could both take a break now and come to the station?"

"I'll get my neighbor to cover for me. Her shop's just a few doors away. Is this good news or bad?"

"We're hoping it's good," DeLuca said.

Ten minutes later, Rosie and Jane sat in a conference room, whispering back and forth, wondering why they had been summoned to the police station.

Jane cupped her hand to Rosie's ear. "I've learned to always begin a conversation with four little words, 'I didn't do it.'"

"You have more life experiences than someone twice your age, and—"

Rosie cut off her sentence when Detective DeLuca strode into the room carrying several folders stuffed with sheets of paper.

"Thanks for coming," he said. "The DNA results from the contents of the footlocker came in. I want to share with you what turned up." He shuffled through one of the folders. "We have two matches to the DNA found on several pieces of clothing in that footlocker and on the footlocker itself."

"Two!" Rosie exclaimed.

"Who are they?" Jane asked.

"One set of DNA samples is from the thief Ron Hemmings, who stored the footlocker, clothing, and other items at the Allendale estate. As for the other DNA, we have a match, but there's no name to go with it."

"How's that possible?" Rosie asked.

"It's why we asked both of you to come here. We hope you can help us out. Rosie, the DNA matches the blood sample that came from your shop two years ago—"

"What?" Rosie sat straight up in her chair.

"Yes. Whoever the person is, he was in your shop. I know you called the police back then and gave a report, but I'd like to go over the details with you."

"Sure," Rosie said, and her stomach churned as the memory flashed through her mind. "It was at night. A man hiding in my workroom turned out the lights and attacked me. I escaped and called the police." She shuddered at the memory of that scary night.

DeLuca tapped another folder. "Saturday, three days before that attack, a man came to your shop. Jane, you waited on him, and Rosie, I know you told the officers who rushed to your shop everything that happened, but now we think this man may be the key to finding Ivy. My gut tells me the same man may have been involved in both incidents. Detective Hernandez and I are looking for anything that can help us. Let's start with you, Jane."

"I'll never forget him," Jane said. "He was the customer from hell. He broke a beautiful glass turtle right in front of me–on purpose."

"You saw the guy up close in the daylight. We'd like you to give us your description again. Possibly, you'll remember something that didn't seem important at the time."

"I don't know if I can be much help. He kept his head down, and his baseball cap was pulled low," Jane said. "He was wearing sunglasses too, so I didn't see much."

"Think. Is there anything else you remember?"

"I'm thinking," Jane said and tapped her chin repeatedly with her fingertips. She stopped tapping and snapped her fingers. "His hair is dark. I know because I saw his sideburns, and here's something I don't believe I mentioned."

"Now's the time." DeLuca pulled his pen and notepad from his pocket.

"He has pockmarks all over his face. Maybe he can't shave over them real close because he sure needed a shave."

"You're doing great. Anything else?"

"He has a thick neck, like a bull. Actually his whole body matches his neck. He's a burly dude, but not fat. Lots of muscle would be my guess."

"Yes, that part fits with the original report."

Jane exhaled loudly. "That's all I remember."

"Now did you happen to see him leave?"

"Yes."

"Did you see his vehicle?"

"Yes."

"Did you catch his license plate?"

"No. It was spattered with mud. I didn't think fast enough to squirt my water bottle at it. I just wanted to get even, so I went after him. I wanted to break something of his. Detective, it's a dog eat dog world out there, and I didn't want to leave hungry."

"And I want you to leave alive," DeLuca said sharply.

"As for you, Rosie, you're Jane's boss. You're in charge of what goes on in your shop and what happens to your employees. Why didn't you report that troublemaker immediately? You could have called the officers on Saturday when it happened, but you waited until Tuesday when you were attacked in your workroom. Then, you finally called. We know your shop is closed on Sunday and Monday, but still—"

"I wasn't thinking straight. I didn't want—"

"Don't blame Rosie," Jane cut in. "It's my fault. I have a confession to make."

"Let's hear it," DeLuca said.

"I chased that troublemaker on my bike. At a red light, he stopped. I caught up, I tossed my bike in the back of his truck, and I jumped in. He tried everything to bounce me out of his truck, but I showed him."

Rosie gasped. "Jane, you could have been killed."

"Two years have gone by, and now I'm hearing about this!" Detective DeLuca's eyes bored into Jane. "You were in that guy's truck?" His jaw muscles tensed. "You need to tell me exactly what you did."

"I got even. I should have told Rosie, but I kept it to myself."

"Why?" Rosie asked, and disappointment was written all over her face. "I thought we trusted each other."

"And what is it you didn't tell Rosie?" DeLuca asked, his face flushed with anger.

"When I was in the back of his truck, I grabbed my keys. I scratched the cab of his truck with them. I tried to get even. He had broken the glass turtle, so I tried to carve a turtle design. If he hadn't driven like a maniac, I could have done a bigger and better job, but I don't feel bad about what I did. He deserved it. When he stopped at a red light, he started shaking his fist at me. I thought he might hop out and grab me, so I jumped out of the truck, grabbed my bike, and took off. I got back to Rosie's shop all in one piece."

Rosie shook her head in disbelief. "Jane, you should have told me."

"You would have called the police. I would have gotten in trouble. I could forget any college loans or assistance. He was no sweetheart, and I let him know it."

"Okay, Jane," DeLuca said. "I understand your anger at the man. We can talk about that another time. Right now, I just need to know if there's anything else about him you can tell me, and let me back up one more step." He gritted his teeth. "Rosie, what the heck were you doing while all this was going on?"

"I was upstairs in my apartment getting dressed." Rosie gnawed at her lip. "Jane called up there was a troublemaker who was leaving. She hollered up to me to take over the shop, that she'd be right back.' I told her not to do anything foolish. By the time I got down the stairs, Jane was gone, and so was her bike. Panicked, I ran in all directions calling her name. Minutes later, Jane shot down the alleyway on her bike and pulled to a screeching stop right in front of me. She asked what I was doing out there in the alleyway. She thought I was minding the shop. I told her I was worried about her. I asked her point-blank if she went chasing after the guy. She told me to quit worrying, that everything was under control. I suggested we go inside and talk this out.

"Once we were inside, Jane insisted on cleaning up the mess the guy made. She grabbed a broom from the supply closet and quickly swept up the broken glass.

"Trying to calm down, I paced back and forth. As soon as Jane put the broom away, I told her to tell me everything from start to finish. Jane filled me in with her interpretation of what she did. I told her I could replace the turtle and order an extra one for her, for trying to protect my shop from that creep."

"Detective DeLuca," Jane cut in, "I knew that if I told Rosie exactly what I did, she'd report it to the police, and I'd get into trouble."

"I was wrong too," Rosie said. "I shouldn't have waited to tell the police about the guy breaking the turtle. I didn't think it was that serious. We've had other incidents before, and I haven't called in the police. I should have called them and told them the whole story right then and there, or at least what I knew of the whole story. That man could have come after Jane and hurt her."

"Let me tell this from my side." Jane plunked her hands down hard on the table. "It was a simple case of street justice. He got a scratched-up truck. I've got my pride."

"Help me out here, Jane," Detective DeLuca said. "Didn't Rosie call down from her apartment telling you not to do anything foolish?"

"Yes."

"What do you think she meant?"

"She sounded like my mother." Jane looked at Detective DeLuca. "Well, not my mother. I don't have a clue what she sounds like, but I've read about mothers like that. You know what I mean. A strict mother, the kind who's always telling you not to do this and not to do that."

Jane shrugged. "Rosie gave up the Strict Mom role and turned back into her usual fun Rosie self. After we cleaned up the broken glass, she said, 'What do you say we order takeout sandwiches from the Four Corners Deli? I can already taste that veggie special.'"

"Yuck," I said. "I was thinking pastrami on rye, oozing with butter, with a side of cheese fries."

"Okay, I get the full picture," DeLuca said through tight lips. "Rosie, you're the adult here. Maybe you had good intentions not reporting the part you did know, but it could have ended up with Jane being hurt."

"I know, and I'm sorry."

"Glad to hear it." He turned toward Jane. "Now, let's get back to the owner of the truck. Do you remember anything that could help us catch the guy who drove the truck back then?"

"Yeah," Jane said. "A foul smell."

"Go ahead," DeLuca said.

Jane twitched her nose. "I got a whiff of him in the shop. He smelled bad."

"Could you define 'bad'?"

"Have you eaten anything in the last hour?"

DeLuca tapped his stomach. "Cast iron. Go ahead and describe the smell."

Jane made a big show of pinching her nose shut. "I'd say it was a combination of gasoline, definitely a large dose of sweat and urine, and a stale musty smell like his clothes hadn't seen the inside of a washing machine since dinosaurs walked the earth."

"That bad," DeLuca said as he scribbled in his notepad. "Did he ever come back to the shop or follow you or in any way try to get even for what you did to his truck?"

"No. For a few days after that little encounter, I kept my eyes wide open for trouble. These eyes," she pointed at her big brown eyes, "and the eyes in the back of my head too. But with this guy, it's my nose that senses danger. Trust me, if he had come within ten feet of me, I'd have smelled him."

"Thank you for your vivid account," DeLuca said, calmer than he had been during the last ten minutes. "It's actually a big help. Rosie, can you add anything?"

"I'll try, but as you probably read in the file, it was dark, the lights were off, and he attacked me from behind. But I'd say he's several inches taller than me, maybe five-eight, five-nine, but not as tall as you, Detective."

"Okay, that narrows it down. I'm six feet. He's between five-eight and five-eleven."

Rosie nodded. "I saw him from my upstairs window when he left. The light was dim, but I agree with Jane. He's a stocky guy."

Jane cut in, "And unbelievably awkward."

"Talk to me," DeLuca said.

"When he ran from the shop, he was in slo-mo. If I hadn't gone to get my bike, I could have caught up to him. That's when a life of running away from trouble pays off. I couldn't have knocked him down, but caught up? Oh yeah. That big, old body slows him down. When he finally builds up some speed, he's out of breath. He's definitely not a tri-athlete. Don't waste your time looking for him in a gym or health club."

"He did seem uncoordinated," Rosie added, "but maybe that's because he'd been shot with staples and slammed with a hammer."

"Could be," DeLuca said and jotted down more notes. "Rosie, do you agree about the odor?"

"Yes. Sorry, I didn't mention it. I spend so much time around paint, stripper, and varnish that I tend to be oblivious to strong odors. But yes, in two words...he stinks."

"You said the truck was a black pickup, possibly a Ford. Anything else, like unusual hubcaps? Anything dangling from the inside mirror, like big Styrofoam dice? Anything?"

"No," Rosie said.

"Did you catch a partial license plate?"

"No. I couldn't see it. The light in the parking lot wasn't very bright."

"Thank you both for the extra details." DeLuca tapped the folder. "Now I have a more accurate picture of what happened." He narrowed his eyes. "I don't want to belabor the point, but Detective Hernandez and I are not the enemy. We're here to protect you from the enemy. Tell us what you know at all times. Are we clear?"

"Yes, we're clear," Jane said. "You definitely don't leave any room for doubt."

"Very clear," Rosie said. "I never imagined the man who came into my shop had anything to do with Ivy Chen, and now I realize two years ago when all this happened was 2010. That's the same year on the newspapers that wrapped the teacups in the footlocker." Her shoulders sagged. "I wish I had told you everything back then."

"I know you were trying to protect Jane, but in the future, just tell us what you know. Let me state the obvious. Every detail you give has the possibility of speeding up the investigation. Every detail that's omitted could slow it down."

Detective DeLuca opened the door and stepped into the hallway. "Detective Hernandez, we've got some new things to work on. I'll check back with you later and fill you in," he said and came back into the room.

"Let's talk about why the man came to Rosie's Treasures," DeLuca said. "Both times, first with you, Jane, and then with you, Rosie, the man said he'd come for a suitcase. Not just any old suitcase. His suitcase. Given what Mrs. Chen told us about Ivy having a very distinctive suitcase, I'd say his curiosity about a suitcase possibly links him to Ivy Chen. Possibly, not definitely. Did he happen to mention that he was looking for a suitcase with a dragon on it?"

"Not to me," Rosie said.

Jane shook her head. "Me neither."

"Maybe he was smart enough not to mention it," DeLuca said, "or maybe we're setting ourselves up for a wild goose chase."

"Yeah, I follow your thinking," Jane said. "He could have meant a beat-up, smelly, old suitcase covered with mold, and filled with—"

"Thank you, Jane. My cast iron stomach has its limits."

"Whatever you say," Jane said, and dramatically pretended to be buttoning her lip.

"Let's get serious," DeLuca said. "The DNA shows that he pawed through the contents of her suitcase, and Ivy's DNA was also found on the contents of her suitcase. We have her DNA, thanks to a hairbrush of Ivy's that Mrs. Chen gave us, but it's possible that the man and Ivy were not there at the same time. Somehow, the contents got moved from that suitcase to a footlocker that ended up in a garage in Allendale. We need to find this guy. He knows something. He could lead us to Ivy or to someone who knows her whereabouts or to a place where she was taken."

DeLuca tapped his fingers on the folder on the table. "We appreciate all your help, Jane. We have no more questions for you, so you're free to go. But Rosie, Mrs. Chen will be here soon. I asked her to come in, and she'd like you to be here with her. Her friends in Sarasota aren't well enough to travel. She's gotten attached to you, and she was insistent that you should be here."

He leaned across the table toward Rosie. "I don't want to disappoint her. She deserves every bit of help we can give. I hate to sound cynical, but she'll be more help to us if she feels comfortable. I know you have a business to run, but do you mind sitting in on this?"

"I'm okay with that," Rosie said, "and Jane, could you go back and run the shop until I'm done here?"

"Sure. I don't have a class until later. See you soon," she said and breezed out of the room.

Rosie looked up at DeLuca. "I know what you're going to say. I took protecting Jane too far."

"You did," he said sternly.

"I made a bad choice."

"That's right," he said.

"I should have realized Jane didn't tell me the whole story about what she did to the guy's truck. She was fidgety. I should have gotten her to confide in me." She sighed. "If Jane had told me about the scratches, and if I had told you about them, you might have been able to identify that truck by now."

"Even so, if he's got half a brain, he would have sanded down the scratches and repainted the truck, so let's not dwell on that. But—"

"I know. I know," Rosie said. "From now on, I need to tell you everything that could help the investigation. Well, you can count on it."

37
Rosie Renard and Detective Tony DeLuca

Friday, January 27, 2012 12:30 P.M.

Detective DeLuca strode into the conference room. "Mrs. Chen, I'm glad you're here, and Rosie, thanks for staying on and taking time away from your shop to help us out." He sat down at the conference table across from them. "Mrs. Chen, to save time, I'm going to come right out and say something has come to our attention, and we need your help."

"I'll do my best," Mrs. Chen said.

"We received the DNA reports from everything in the footlocker and also from the items in the storage area where the footlocker was kept. We'd like to share those results with you. This may be upsetting."

"I want to know every detail," Mrs. Chen said. "Not knowing is torture. Please, talk to me. What does the DNA tell you?"

"First off," DeLuca said, "the DNA on the mattress and blanket and in the storage area over the garage belongs to one person. That's Ron Hemmings. There's no trace of Ivy anywhere except on the objects in the footlocker, so we can assume she didn't sleep there and probably she was never there at all. The owner's son said Ron Hemmings didn't sleep there as far as he knew. There was no bathroom or AC, but he could have stored things there."

DeLuca cocked an eyebrow. "And that's what we figure Ron Hemmings did. He was a thief. He probably stored cash and stolen goods there, like jewelry, silverware, and other items we found in the wooden trunks. Rosie bought them along with the footlocker. We assume Hemmings kept what he stole there until the heat blew over, and then he probably fenced everything. Let's back up to the contents of the footlocker."

DeLuca fanned a handful of photos across the conference table. "Mrs. Chen, you saw these photos, so you already know a man's clothes were packed in the footlocker with Ivy's possessions."

"Yes," she said, leaning forward and peering at the photos.

"We now have vital information about those clothes."

"Tell me everything," Mrs. Chen said.

DeLuca nodded. "The tech team found samples of Ivy's DNA and Ron Hemmings' DNA. As you know, Hemmings was a handyman at the Allendale estate and stored tools and other things there, but there's more."

"Whatever it is, please tell me," Mrs. Chen said, wringing her hands.

"An unknown man's DNA turned up on the clothing and other items in the footlocker."

"What do you mean by an unknown man?" Mrs. Chen enunciated the last three words carefully.

"We have his DNA in the system, but we don't have his name or anything else about him."

"I don't understand," Mrs. Chen said.

"I'd like Rosie to tell you how we got this man's DNA and why we don't know who he is."

"This is too weird for words," Rosie said and fidgeted in her seat, "but two years ago a man came into my shop. This was around the same time as the dates on the newspapers that wrapped Ivy's teacups and saucers when I found them in the footlocker. My assistant Jane waited on the man. He wanted a suitcase. They had a terrible fight."

Rosie filled in everything that had happened to Jane and then to her when the man broke into her workroom and attacked her. "He was

229

driving a black pickup truck, not a red tow truck, and that's why I probably never made the connection. He wanted a suitcase, but he didn't say anything to Jane or me about a dragon on the suitcase, so I didn't make that connection either. I fought him off and wounded him real good with a hammer and a staple gun."

"Good for you," Mrs. Chen said, and a hint of a smile tugged at the corners of her mouth.

"I called the police," Rosie said. "They called in the tech team and got samples of his blood. He didn't leave any fingerprints because he wore latex gloves."

"I'm thankful you and Jane survived that man's fury," Mrs. Chen said, "and you give me a reason to remain hopeful. If you and Jane managed to survive, then maybe Ivy did too."

"For now, he's a mystery man," DeLuca said, "but we do know only a small percentage of the DNA on the clothing is from Ron Hemmings. Most of it is from the mystery man. However, Hemmings' fingerprints are all over the outside of the footlocker. It looks like he might have brought the footlocker to the garage at the Cassell estate in Allendale where he worked. The Cassells gave him access to the garage and the storage area above it."

"I'd like to hear more about this mystery man," Mrs. Chen said eagerly. "What have you learned from his clothes?"

"He's medium height, on the heavy side, and he has dark hair, and here's more information Rosie is hearing for the first time too."

Rosie's eyes opened wide. "More information?"

"The team found trace evidence on the man's handkerchief. They got a hair sample, dark hair, off the shirt collar. They found traces of lanolin and glycerin on the work clothes," DeLuca said. "Those are common ingredients in hand cleaners used by mechanics and other workers to remove grit and grime from their hands–first the tow truck, now the hand cleaner. This ups the ante that we might be looking at someone who has contact with cars."

DeLuca smiled. "Lucky for us, the DNA has given us even more precise clues to the mystery man."

"What did you learn?" Mrs. Chen asked.

"I can't wait to hear this," Rosie said.

"The gray work shirt had traces of motor oil and a blue cream which is filler putty. Mechanics use that kind of putty to repair or restore damaged car parts."

"But what does that putty tell us?" Mrs. Chen asked. She looked bewildered by all the news swirling around her.

"The key here is the damaged parts. The owner of that gray shirt and pants possibly owns a tow truck service or works in a place where damaged cars are restored," DeLuca said. "There's no name or contact info on the truck. More than likely, he's not the owner."

DeLuca's phone rang, and he took the call. "You're absolutely sure?" he asked, and his face lit up as if he had received good news. "Call me back with anything else."

He stood up. "Okay, let's all remain very calm." He rotated his shoulders several times as if to remove the kinks. "Mrs. Chen, please prepare yourself for some startling news."

"Go ahead," Mrs. Chen said, gripping the sides of the chair.

"A team of divers working with the Sarasota County detectives found Ivy's car." He paused as if to let the words sink in. "It was at the bottom of a lake near the exit of the Sunshine Skyway Bridge, but let me reassure you—"

"No, please, no," Mrs. Chen murmured, and Rosie steeled herself for bad news.

DeLuca held up his hand. "Let me reassure you; the detectives found nothing of Ivy's, not her luggage, not her clothing, and not her purse. Nothing."

"What about her body...her skeleton?" Mrs. Chen rasped the words.

"No. And I waited until all the facts came in before telling you any of this. The divers were thorough. Nothing pertaining to Ivy was found, not in the lake and not in the surrounding area. And we checked. No major work was done in the past four years to the lake or the surrounding areas."

Mrs. Chen wiped away the tears running down her cheeks. "My Ivy is alive."

"We can't guarantee that," Detective DeLuca said softly. "As we know, Ivy was on her way to Sarasota, but something happened after she crossed the bridge. We don't know what, but it sent her car into that lake."

Mrs. Chen blinked away her tears. "Do you think she lost control of her car? Is that what happened?"

"We're working on every angle," he said.

"Are you having any success?" Mrs. Chen asked as she folded her hands tightly in prayer.

"We're not out of leads. We still have the driver of the red tow truck. He crossed the bridge toward Sarasota and then returned an hour later with Ivy's erhu in his truck. We now have follow-up questions," he said. "You may be the one person who knows the answers."

Mrs. Chen's expression was rapt. "Please ask me anything that will help my Ivy." She placed her hand over her heart.

"Think hard, Mrs. Chen," DeLuca said, and his eyes narrowed. "When you spoke to Ivy the day she disappeared, did she say anything about having car problems? Maybe the engine stalling, anything like that?"

"No," she said immediately. "She wrapped one arm over the other and pressed them tightly to her chest as if to stop herself from falling apart. "But that's just like Ivy, not wanting to upset me. She was always trying to spare me bad news."

"Were any of her local friends involved in repairing or servicing cars?"

Mrs. Chen thought for several long moments. "None that I know of. Most of her friends were in music and the arts."

"One of our detectives just called the car rental place where Ivy rented the Lincoln Town Car. They checked their records. Ivy hadn't reported any car problems."

Rosie patted Mrs. Chen's arm. Clues were popping up all over the place about the man who had abducted Ivy. More clues meant more chances he could be identified and found, and if he were found, Ivy could still be with him. Or, if it was too late...she didn't like to think about that possibility.

Mrs. Chen rubbed her temples. "But even if Ivy's car went off the road, how did her clothes and other belongings end up in a footlocker in someone's garage?"

"That's one of the questions we're working on," DeLuca said. "But let's keep in mind that Ron Hemmings may not be our man. He was a thief. I'm not excusing what he did, but he never confronted or harmed anyone. He stayed below the radar. No one saw him until that time he got stuck in the house he was burglarizing and we got his DNA. As far as we know, Hemmings never worked with automobiles. In fact, he didn't own an automobile. From what we've pieced together, he usually committed the robberies at night, and he drove to and from the site on his bike. He had a large storage chest attached to the back of his bike. That's where he probably put the loot."

DeLuca moved gritty photos of the red tow truck to the center of the table. "Hemmings is dead, and we may never know his role, if any, in Ivy's disappearance. For now, we're focusing on the mystery man with the red tow truck and possibly a black pickup truck too."

He tapped his fingers on the photos. "Thanks to Ivy's friend Vince and his recollection of a tow truck driver, that theory is holding strong. At this point, our evidence is pointing at abduction. It's not a lock, and we don't want to exclude other possibilities, but it's shaping up. Once we find the mystery man, I believe this case will pull together. As it stands right now, he may be the only one who knows what happened to Ivy. "

"Please, dear God, make it happen," Mrs. Chen murmured.

38
Ivy Chen

Tuesday, September 13, 2011

I was waiting in the closet for Frank's sister Marta to finish cleaning when a sudden banging noise startled me. It was the familiar sound of Frank slamming open the door to my apartment. There was no way I could see through the crack between the door and the doorframe. I had tried it before, and it wasn't possible. The same was true with the sliver of space at the bottom of the door, but I could hear the conversation, especially what Frank said, because he was shouting.

"I hear you talking," he said to Marta, "and that's against the rules."

"I was talking to myself," Marta said.

"I heard two voices."

"You're hearing things again, Frank, but I'll give you an excuse. There are mice in the walls. You probably heard them squeaking."

"I know what I heard," Frank said. "When you come back to your senses, we'll talk, and maybe, that's a long-shot maybe, you can work here again. For now, you're fired."

"Come on, Frank. Don't be so mean. You need me to clean up. I need the money. It's a good deal for both of us."

"Shut up, get out of here now, and don't come back until I know I can trust you."

"Please, Frank."

"You're done until I invite you back. I'm in charge here. Got it?"

"Yeah, Frank. I got it. You'll be sorry when this place turns into a pigsty."

"You'll be sorry if you don't shut up and bug off now."

The door slammed. I panicked. Frank would know I had heard that conversation.

Thinking fast, I curled up on the floor and pretended to be asleep. The door to my apartment slammed open again. Frank had returned. I knew I'd get a beating, and sobs were already trapped in my throat. Frank jerked open the closet door. I sat up, stretching, and yawned.

"Wake up, and get out here," he shouted.

I stepped into the living area and held my shoulders tight to ward off the initial punches.

"There's been a change around here," Frank said. "The cleaning woman's not coming back for a while. Until then, you'll do your own cleaning and hand wash. Sheets, towels, and anything else, leave in the laundry basket. It will be taken care of."

He wagged his finger in my face. "No questions. Got it? Questions are like accusations. They get people into trouble."

He left, and I was relieved I had escaped a beating, but I had concerns. I began writing in my journal:

> "I look at my apartment with critical eyes and shudder. Marta hadn't finished cleaning the place when Frank kicked her out. I hope he'll leave me plenty of supplies to work with. I want my apartment to be spotless. If I become sick in this place, I won't have access to medicines, and Frank would never permit me to see a doctor.
>
> "Actually, I would prefer to do everything for myself, but at the same time, I hope Marta returns soon so I can approach her and see if there's a way to bargain with her for the key. I have no money to offer her because Frank took my purse and kept it. I'm ashamed to even consider bargaining with a poor, downtrodden

woman, who unfortunately is related to this horrible creature named Frank Brandt, and no doubt is completely under his control. I cannot imagine the terrible life she endured growing up with a monster like Frank living under the same roof, but there's a problem. Without Marta and Marta's keys, my chances of escape are reduced to one plan; the alcove-door would have to be my way out of the house.

"A very scary feeling about Marta's departure overwhelms me, but maybe my imagination is working overtime. Frank and Marta are brother and sister. He must have some concept of family loyalty. He may hate the outside world and harm anyone he comes into contact with at whim, but surely, Frank wouldn't harm his own sister!"

39
Detectives Tony DeLuca and Hank Hernandez

Monday, January 30, 2012

The detectives headed toward the parking lot at The Shrimp Store, after enjoying the fish and chips special.

Tony unlocked the car door with a click of his key. "We've run down every loose end and every lead and checked and re-checked what we know about the guy who kidnapped Ivy, so where does all this leave us?" he asked as he slid into the driver's seat.

"Stuck," Hank said. "We need our guy to show himself. We have to hold out some bait he can't resist."

"Like what?" Tony asked and backed out of the parking space.

"My Jamaican grandfather would say, 'Set out some ackee and salt fish and dumplings.'" Hank shrugged. "Who could resist that?"

Tony edged out of the lot and turned onto Ninth Avenue North. "I say we leak a little info to the press and see what pops."

"Something not too obvious. We don't want it to look like we planted info," Hank said.

Tony braked at the traffic light. "How about this? 'Hey, you sick-o bastard, you want your dragon suitcase? Come and get it at the Grand Central Saturday Night Art Walk. No offers refused. No questions asked.' What do you think, Hank?"

Hank sighed and shook his head. "Vague and understated. Keep working on it. Maybe Rosie can fine-tune it."

40
Rosie and Detective DeLuca

Wednesday, February 1, 2012, 10:00 A.M.

"Hey there, Detective," Rosie said as Detective DeLuca passed through her shop. She held up her hand as if she were stopping traffic. "You don't have to say a word. I know you by now. You're in a hurry. You want the notice I wrote for the newspapers. Hello, goodbye, thank you, later." She smiled. "Do I have everything right?"

"You do," he said with a smile. "Except I'd like to read the notice right now in front of you in case I have questions."

"No problem." She slid a sheet of paper out of a drawer near the cash register and moved it toward him. "Go for it."

Tony cleared his throat and began, "A new lead has surfaced in the cold case involving Ivy Chen, the classical musician who disappeared from St. Petersburg three years ago. A police spokesperson denies it, but sources close to the case say that a leather suitcase, with a dragon embossed on it, played an important role in the reopening of the investigation. The shopkeepers of the Grand Central District, who have their popular Second Saturday Art Walk this Saturday, wish to show their support for Ivy Chen. They will donate ten percent of all sales from that evening to anyone who comes to Rosie's Treasures with verifiable information about such a suitcase. Please come, one and all, this Saturday to support a worthy cause."

Tony folded the piece of paper and shoved it in his jeans pocket. "Nicely done, Rosie. I have no questions. Do you have anything to add that I should know?"

"Yes," Rosie said. "My cousin Jack poured his heart into helping me write it. He's counting on the guy being caught real soon. So am I. I just thought you should know."

"I'm glad you told me," Tony said. "The on-going help from you and Jack may be the turning point in this investigation."

41
Ivy Chen

Tuesday, November 22, 2011

I felt very weak. My health was deteriorating, and the stress of creating a story about dragons and telling it in an exciting manner has worn me down. I've tried to come up with a solution, but so far nothing has popped into my mind...until just a few minutes ago.

Frank stormed into my apartment ranting about how terribly he was treated at work and how difficult his work was. He looked me straight in the eye and said, "You sit around all day long and do nothing." He slapped me hard across my back, but I didn't cry. I knew better.

He continued ranting, "I work all day at the shop. Then I come home and fix things here and do more work. It's like I'm the worker, and you're the spoiled do-nothing brat." He huffed for a while and stomped around the apartment. "I'm the worker, and you're on vacation." He was quite pleased with those words. In a strange way he took pride in being the worker. I suppose that convinced him he was the boss. After I finished playing three songs on the erhu and telling him another made-up dragon story, he stomped out the door.

I collapsed on my bed and started thinking. Maybe I should put the burden of telling the dragon stories on Frank. Ideas flowed. If I were to come down with a sore throat or laryngitis, Frank would have to take on the burden of making up stories and telling them. With time off, my strength might return. I laughed out loud at my devious scheme.

Tonight, Frank briskly opened the door. "Let's do the dragon story first and then the erhu concert," he said and dropped onto the couch.

I pointed at my throat. "I'm losing my voice," I rasped. "You tell a story tonight."

His eyes went wild. "Which one?"

"Any one you like."

"I don't know all the facts or the twists and turns you're always bragging about."

"Just tell it in your own way. That's what storytellers do."

He shot me an ugly glance. "I don't like this."

"You keep telling me it's not work. Try it. I think you'll enjoy it."

"Okay," he said begrudgingly and sat on the couch. I sat across from him on the chair. He started with a weak voice but built up the volume. He mangled the details, told the story out of order, didn't remember the characters' names, and squirmed as he tried to speak and think at the same time.

I encouraged and complimented him, emphasizing that story-telling was harder than people thought. Soon he relaxed and threw himself into the story. He was quite proud of his efforts. He seemed to forget all about his work, his responsibilities, and his hatreds. All he had to do was repeat a story I had told him.

As he got up to leave, he said, "Even if your throat is better tomorrow, I'll be the storyteller."

"Good. You're better at it than I am," I said.

I looked forward to months of restful evenings. All I had to do was sit back, gain strength, and listen to Frank's awful interpretations of age-old stories. I could dream of escaping from this place, getting far away from Frank, and reading once again the real dragon stories with their subtle meanings and profound thoughts. A very small victory had come my way, but it came at a moment when I was losing hope and wondering what to do next. Now I knew. My job was to stay alive until that one magic moment arrived when Frank forgot to lock me in my apartment.

42
Rosie and Jack Renard

Thursday, February 2, 2012

Shielding her eyes from the sun, Rosie waved to Jack as he hopped out of his car at the St. Pete Beach parking lot. He cut through the sea grass and took the steps down to the beach two at a time. She looked at him and could easily see the tall gangly kid he was when they were carefree and naive, unaware that predators and murderers lurked even in neighborhoods where everyone knew each other and called each other by name.

"Thanks for meeting me here," he said.

"I've been looking forward to it ever since you called. We should do this more often," Rosie said, wiggling her toes in the sand and carrying her sandals. He hadn't said why he wanted to see her, and, as always, she would give him time to work up to what he wanted to say.

"Let's head toward the Don Cesar," he said, kicking off his sandals. "I'll treat you to one of those touristy drinks with a paper umbrella if we get that far." He squinted into the late afternoon sun.

"I won't be able to help out at the Saturday Art Walk," he blurted out. "Sorry. I know how important it is to you, and to me too, since the kidnapper may show up. With any luck, he might get caught, and in the best of all possible worlds, he might tell the detectives where Ivy is."

"I like that happy-ever-after world," Rosie said and linked arms with him.

"There's something else I have to do that night. I hope you're not disappointed."

She frowned. "It must be truly important."

"I'm meeting Lisa's parents. They're only in town for that one night."

"You and Lisa and her parents? This is getting serious."

"Yeah," he said. "But there's another reason I wanted to talk to you. I called my parents. We hadn't talked in a long time. It always turns into a disaster."

"I know," Rosie said and looked toward the waves rolling into shore as they continued walking. "How are your mom and dad?"

"Fine."

"And how are you?"

"Better." They walked along the water's edge in silence for several minutes. "Mom and I cleared the air on a few things. She wishes I lived closer. I told her that's not going to happen. She said I'm punishing her by staying here in Florida, and I'm using Lisa as an excuse. She said I never forgave her for blaming me for Tess's death. I told her that wasn't true, that it was a tough time for me, but I got through it. I told her she was crazy with grief over Tess and took it out on me. I had come to grips with that long ago. I explained that my staying in Florida was about the great weather and a life I hoped to share with Lisa. I said it had nothing to do with Tess. I told her we should let that stay in the past and not bring it up again. She cried. She said, 'I don't want to lose you too, Jack. You're the only child I have left.'"

"My God, that was an emotional roller-coaster ride. What about your dad? What did he have to say?"

Jack kicked a stone toward the water. "You know my dad. He's not like my mom. He doesn't get all emotional or even try to smooth things over. He doesn't know about forgive and forget. Why say something nice if you can cut someone to shreds with a razor-sharp zinger?"

"I remember." Rosie sighed with resignation. "So what did he say this time?"

244

"He said—let me quote him—'I heard from Rosie's parents that you and Rosie are helping out with that missing-musician investigation.' I told him that was true."

Jack kicked another stone, even further. "And Dad said, 'Hooray for you, helping a stranger, someone old enough to take care of herself, but tell me this, where were you when your own sister, who was just a kid, was taken from us?' He took a deep, ragged breath. "I couldn't find the words to tell him how sorry I was and how much I missed Tess."

Rosie wrapped her arm around Jack's waist and continued walking by his side. "I'm so sorry, Jack."

"The click of the phone was all I heard. I waited, I don't know how long, and then I turned off my phone." Jack's jaw muscles tightened. "Will this ever be over?"

Rosie thought for a while, knowing it was important to say the right thing. "Your father may never come around, but you and I have come a long way. Maybe that's going to have to be enough for us. We can't change what happened to Tess, and we can't change our parents. I talk to my mom and dad now and then, but there's no warmth, no love, no connection. It's like they're robots going through the motions of living, but Jack, you and I can stick together. You know how it used to be." She choked up. "The two of us against the world. As far as I'm concerned, that's how it's going to be for us, always. No matter what."

"Thanks, Rosie," Jack said. He leaned down and kissed the top of her head. "I needed to hear that. I can't keep waiting for my dad's forgiveness. It took me long enough to forgive myself."

"Let it go," Rosie said, but she knew better. A doctor had once told her the same thing, "Let it go." She had told the doctor, "I've tried, but it won't let go of me." She looked up at Jack. "Your dad has his demons, and we have ours. Not talking about it didn't help us. Talking about it didn't help either. Some things can't be fixed." She tightened her grip around his waist. "I'm glad you shared all this with me, Jack. It's haunted us for years that we couldn't save Tess."

Jack stopped abruptly and took both of Rosie's hands in his. "Let's not forget, no matter what my dad or mom or your parents or anyone else says, we didn't abandon Tess. We didn't do anything differently than we always did when we walked home from school. It was only a matter of a few minutes, and that creep took her."

"Thank you," she said softly. Jack's words meant more to her than he would ever know. They walked along the beach past the remnants of sandcastle villages. Finally, Rosie broke the silence. "Any particular reason you called your parents?"

"I'm trying to keep the lines of communication open. They say that's part of the healing process." He shrugged. "It's not exactly 'they.' It's Officer Randall. Because of her, I joined a group, a survivors' group, but it's much more than that. You and I have a lot of company out there, Rosie. There are many people who've been through what we have and much more. Why don't you come with me to the next meeting?"

"You've caught me off guard. I wasn't expecting this, but I'll think about it," Rosie said.

"Don't over-think it. That's one of the things I've already learned. Sometimes it's best to go with your gut."

"Like don't let your mind get in the way of your gut."

"Something like that," Jack said. "See you at the meeting?" He pressed a card into the palm of her hand.

"This is like old times," Rosie said, "our getting together and having a good talk."

"I miss those times," he said.

"So do I."

"See you. I got to go. Lisa's waiting for me."

"I should go, too. Ted's coming over at seven. She put the card in her pocket. "It's nice that we both have someone special in our lives, but let's not forget to stay close." She stood on tiptoes and kissed him on the cheek. "I'm always here for you."

"Same goes for me. Next time I'll make good on my promise and treat you to a touristy umbrella drink," he said and took off toward the parking lot. She watched him until he got into his car and drove away. She continued watching until his car was out of sight. Only then did she realize tears were streaming down her cheeks, but they didn't seem like tears of sadness. It was a teary farewell to Tess, the girl they couldn't save, but as both Jack and Ted had reminded her, the girl they hadn't abandoned either.

43
The Saturday Art Walk

Saturday, February 4, 2012

Late Saturday afternoon, Detective DeLuca met in Rosie's workroom with the thirty-some shopkeepers who were participating in the Second Saturday Art Walk.

"Thanks for helping us out," DeLuca said, looking out over the crowd. Some sat on chairs. Some stood. Some leaned against the walls. "And thanks to Rosie for offering her workroom for this meeting."

Rosie stomped her foot on the workroom floor. "I want this creep stopped right here, where he threatened Jane and tried to kill me. Poetic justice, that's what I want."

"Thank you, Rosie," De Luca said over the applause. "Now, let me come right to the point. As you know, the guy Rosie's talking about got away. We want him real bad. I can't go into the particulars right now, but we have good reason to believe he's coming back. He wants to buy or steal a particular suitcase he believes is his. Let's call him 'the guy' or 'our guy' until we discover his real name."

DeLuca looked from one person to the next. "I'm asking for your help, but under no circumstances, do I want you to put yourself in harm's way. Don't confront him. Don't provoke him. If he shows up, we'll use a signal. This one has worked before." He pulled several dollar bills from his jeans pocket and waved them over his head. "That will alert the detectives who will be mingling among the crowds. They will step in and flash their badges at the first sign of trouble. Let them do their job. Your job is to stay alert and remain cautious."

He returned the dollar bills to his pocket. "It's a fine line I'm asking you to walk. We want him, but we don't want to scare him off. We don't want him to overhear anything that would let him know we're waiting for him. It's your usual Saturday Night Art Walk. Act the way you usually do."

"That means weird," a tall man in the back piped up.

"Off the wall," said a woman with pink streaks in her hair.

Funny comments followed one after another, but fear and tension showed up in people's tight expressions.

"Here's the type of guy you should be looking for," DeLuca said. "A loner. Someone who seems interested primarily in Rosie's Treasures rather than someone going with the flow from one shop or gallery to another. Let me give you some specifics," DeLuca said. "The guy is burly. He has bad body odor. He has pockmarks on his face. He's about five-ten, give-or-take. He's strong. He has awkward movements. We're guessing he's in his forties. He has a bad temper."

"Sounds like my mother-in-law," said the man whose black T-shirt was painted with psychedelic designs.

"Rosie has something to say, so let's listen up," DeLuca said.

Rosie stepped closer to Detective DeLuca.

"Detective, I just want to say on behalf of all of us in the Grand Central District, thanks for your protection, and a big thank-you to all the detectives who will be here tonight. All of us in the Grand Central District appreciate your efforts. I'm sure I'm not the only one who wants this guy to show up. With such a police presence, he will surely be caught. Then, all of us can go back to what we do best—meet and greet the public and enjoy our Saturday Art Walk."

"We're on the same page," DeLuca said. "Again, I can't get into the guy's crimes, but we need him to give us information that only he knows. It's a matter of the sooner, the better."

DeLuca leaned close to Rosie and said in a low voice, "Thanks for not spilling the beans about the guy's connection to Ivy. If she's alive, that could compromise her life."

"And that's the last thing any of us would want," Rosie said.

He turned his attention back to the group. "I'll run along now so you can spend your time setting up for tonight. Thanks, and be safe."

There was a round of applause, a wave from Detective DeLuca, and a bustling of activity as everyone set out for their shops.

Later, as all the shopkeepers were finalizing their preparations, Ted wrapped his arms around Rosie. "Here's a kiss for good luck," he said and planted a warm one on her lips.

"One kiss? You're so stingy," Rosie said and grinned.

"We'll have to wait until later," Ted said, corralling spatulas, wooden spoons, hors d'oeuvre plates, and napkins, and moving them away from the woks. "Right now, you have visitors to talk to, and I have a stir-fry to prepare." He lowered his voice. "And we have to keep our eyes wide-open for our guy."

"I know." She looked left, then right, straight ahead, and behind her. "I'm wound so tight I feel like I'm going to burst open."

"We all are," Ted said. "And who could blame us?"

For the first time tonight, Rosie heard fear in Ted's voice, and he had good reason. This guy, this monster had caused so much trouble and created so much fear. She prayed this would soon be over and the guy would end up in jail.

As Rosie and Ted set to work, Vivien Ross, who owned the Vintage Shoppe two doors away, hurried over.

"Hellooooo, Hellooooo, Hellooooo," Vivien chirped as she paraded dramatically toward Rosie and Ted, swishing along in one of her skirts from another era, beige this time with lace everywhere, and her brown suede lace-up boots. "I just heard the news from the grapevine. It looks like we're attracting the biggest crowd ever. This is where it's happening."

"Let's hope so," Rosie said.

"I'll second that," Ted said.

Vivien tucked her stylish chin-length silver hair behind her ears and leaned close to Rosie. "Are you as nervous as I am?"

"Yes," Rosie said.

"Any signs of trouble so far?" Vivien asked.

"We're not supposed to talk about trouble or act scared. We're supposed to act normal. Remember?"

"Right," Vivien said, gnawing at the corner of her lip. "I got carried away in the moment. I'll see you later. Keep your eyes open."

As Vivien headed back to her shop, joyful sounds of laughter and animated conversations reverberated throughout the Grand Central District. People strolled along the sidewalk enjoying the cool evening breezes, unaware of the shopkeepers' worries.

As darkness descended, Rosie's nerves grew ragged. She peered at the faces in the crowd. Would a loner stand out in this hubbub? Earlier, when it was still light and merely a handful of people had shown up here and there, she had thought so, but now darkness lurked in alleys and around corners, and with so many people arriving all at once, pressing toward her, as part of a group or a couple, there were few, if any, loners.

Trying to remain calm, Rosie waved to people she knew. She winked at Ted. "Here's the bait I hope will reel in customers," she said, adding a few more pieces of furniture to the collection along the sidewalk. "If they stop to browse, I can size them up and see if our guy might be among them. I'll try to act normal and talk about furniture refinishing, paint removal, stuff like that."

"You have your methods, and I have mine," Ted said, playfully plunking a chef's pleated and starched white toque on his head. "This is me being normal," he whispered to her.

"You're sexy in that chef's hat," she said.

"Maybe I should wear it more often," he said and dropped several zucchini rounds into the wok. They sizzled in the hot oil.

"It's ready to go," he said and dumped a bowlful of cut-up veggies into one wok and pre-cooked seasoned rice into the other.

"You're making me so hungry," Rosie said breathing in the tantalizing aromas hovering over the table.

"I'll get people to stop and taste. You invite them inside your shop." He whispered, "Don't worry. Detective Hernandez has it staked out. I saw him earlier. He's making sure no one comes in the back door."

Ted juggled the containers of sea salt, ground pepper, and minced parsley.

Laughing at his antics, Rosie set out maps and brochures that listed all the shops participating. "Hey, Ted, check out the scene. We never had this much entertainment before." She pointed toward the street.

Crowds zigzagged past clowns, stilt walkers, face painters, and street performers who were creating balloon animals, playing harmonicas, juggling, leading Conga lines, and detailing chalk drawings. She wished she could relax and enjoy the activity, but she couldn't shake her fear that something terrible was going to happen before this night ended.

Keeping busy to calm her nerves, she handed out discount coupons to everyone who stopped by. "I have a sign-up sheet if you'd like to receive e-mails about sales," she told a young couple, "and this sign-up," she ran her fingers across a second sheet, "is advance notice of special demonstrations like chair caning and wood refinishing."

An hour or so passed peacefully, and Rosie began to wind down. She was talking to friends from her running group when angry shouts came from a short distance away.

"Wait your turn," a man's voice boomed.

"Go to the end of the line," blasted a woman's shrill words.

"Ted, what's going on?" Rosie asked with a trembling voice.

Ted looked in the direction where the commotion was coming from. For a better view, he moved closer, and so did Rosie.

"What's happening?" he asked several people. Everyone seemed to be talking at once, but the story finally came through. Ted turned to Rosie. "It was someone who jumped to the front of the line to buy a hand-made pretzel, and the crowd got belligerent, but it's over. Things have settled down." He lowered his voice. "If our guy is anywhere around, he won't be turned off by that little incident. He'll come forward."

"Good. I hope he gets here soon. I want all this to be over." Rosie whispered to Ted, "I have three wishes. I want him caught. I want him to confess where Ivy is, and I want her to be rescued and returned to her mom. So far, no one has come forward with any info about a dragon suitcase."

She looked at her shop. The lights glowed inside. She pressed her face to the window. There were no visitors, but she couldn't get rid of the scary feeling that the guy would show up and someone would be hurt.

The fun atmosphere quickly returned, but a short time later, Rosie thought she heard a child crying close by. The cries rose to hysterical screams. Panicky expressions distorted the faces of several shopkeepers. Rosie figured what they were thinking. This could be the guy stirring up trouble, maybe creating a diversion, while he checked around for information about a dragon suitcase.

Rosie moved to an opening in the crowd.

"I'm right beside you, Rosie," Ted said. "Stay close in case of trouble." His voice resonated with fear.

"Don't worry," she whispered. "I know how vicious our guy is."

Together they watched what was going on.

A toddler, a boy wearing jean shorts and striped shirt, screamed again and again. Several people tried to calm him down, but he tried to run away from them. A young mother struggled through the crowd, crying as much as the child.

"It's my fault," the mother said, picking up the child and hugging him. "I took my eyes off him for a moment." She fought back her tears. "Thank you, everyone."

She hugged her son again. "Let's go home," she said. By that time, he was smiling and reaching for a balloon that had slipped away from another child.

"Stop him!" a woman shouted.

"Now what?" Ted said sharply.

"Stop that skateboarder!" the woman cried out. "He stole my purse."

Rosie looked to her left and saw a skateboarder speed along the perimeter of the crowd. He was dressed in black head to toe, the peak of his baseball cap facing backwards.

"One thing I know for sure," Rosie said. "He's not the guy who attacked me in my shop. Our guy was older, heavier, and way too clumsy to be on a skateboard."

"I'd say the skateboarder's a thief, and he has a partner," Ted said. "He must have stuffed the purse in his backpack. I just saw him pass it to a young guy in the crowd, also dressed in black."

"There goes Officer Randall after the skateboarder," Rosie said, "and that other uniformed officer is chasing down the guy with the backpack." Several people were knocked to the ground. Passers-by helped them to their feet. Emotions ran high; the tension was palpable.

"Who would have thought all this would be going on tonight?" Ted commented.

"An absolutely crazy night, and no sign of our guy," Rosie said in a low voice.

After that, everything remained peaceful.

Eventually, people began to wander away.

"Rosie, you can relax now," Ted said.

"I know. I'm glad we didn't face a serious problem or real danger, but I'm disappointed our guy didn't show." She gathered her sign-up sheets and the business cards visitors had left. "It's been a long night. Let's close up." She waved to the other shopkeepers who were moving their merchandise and tables indoors.

"I'll load my stuff in my truck," Ted said. "Wait here. There are still plenty of people around. Promise me you won't go anywhere alone until I get back."

"I promise."

No sooner did Ted turn the corner than Rosie's cell phone rang. She picked up immediately.

"It's Detective DeLuca," he said. "I'm just letting you know we don't see any signs of trouble. We're scaling back some of our team unless you and Ted have concerns. I'll double-check with Detective Hernandez. If you don't hear from me, all's well."

"Thanks for being here," Rosie said. "I wish this evening had ended with the kidnapper in jail, Ivy back home with her Mom, and all of us experiencing trouble-free days ahead.

"That's a great plan," DeLuca said, "but—"

"But that's not how the real world works."

"No. Unfortunately, it doesn't. Good night, Rosie. Good night to Ted too. Tomorrow's another day, another chance to capture Ivy's abductor. In the meantime, think about your own safety. Keep your doors and windows locked."

♫♫

Rosie and Ted collected the leftover napkins and plates and placed them in a bag.

"Too bad there's no leftover food," Rosie said.

"Are you hungry?" Ted asked.

"Yes."

"Good." He held up the insulated bag he had brought back from his truck. "Because I just happen to have here a bottle of Merlot, a loaf of French bread, and your favorite Gouda cheese. I was thinking we could relax, listen to music, and enjoy a late-night picnic."

"Perfect," Rosie said and linked arms with him. "Let's go."

They entered her shop and closed the door behind them. A potent stale smell immediately stung Rosie's nose. She glanced around and up the stairs.

"Ted, someone's been here," she whispered and stepped back. "He's been here."

"How do you know?" Ted whispered back.

"That strong smell of sweat and unbelievably bad body odor."

"Let's leave now," Ted whispered, grasping her hand. He opened the door and they charged outside and down the sidewalk.

A short distance away, Rosie pulled out her phone and punched in Detective DeLuca's number. Ted's glance darted everywhere, on the alert for anyone who might rush toward them to attack.

"Come on, Detective. Pick up," Rosie said and turned to Ted. "I just remembered something." She frowned. "Where is Detective Hernandez? I thought he was in the workroom guarding the back door in case someone tried to get in."

"This is Detective DeLuca." His words were rushed.

"Detective, Ted and I are in front of my shop. Someone has been inside. It could be our guy, and I think he's still there. Is Detective Hernandez with you?"

"No. I can't reach him. I'm running down the alley behind your shop right now. Get down and stay down until—"

The phone went dead.

Rosie grabbed Ted's hand and pulled him behind an oversized wooden container filled with geraniums. They crouched there. "I think Detective Hernandez is in there with our guy," she said. "I think Detective DeLuca is going in to help Detective Hernandez."

Rosie peeked around the container of geraniums and peered at her shop window. In the dim light, she watched as Detective DeLuca and at least two other detectives, maybe three, rushed in with their guns drawn.

Silence.

Unrelenting silence.

Finally the front door opened and Detective DeLuca stood in the doorway. "Rosie? Ted? You'll be safer in here. Come on. Hurry." His words tumbled one after the other.

"Our guy's not here," DeLuca said as he ushered Rosie and Ted inside.

"We were worried about Detective Hernandez," Rosie said.

"So were we," DeLuca said. "He's okay, but he was knocked down and he's woozy. It was dark back there in your holding area. He didn't see who hit him."

Two detectives crouched by Detective Hernandez. "You're sure you don't want an ambulance," one of them said.

"Nah, no blood, nothing broken," Hernandez said, sitting up. "Just my feelings got hurt. He's like a ninja. Comes out of nowhere. Doesn't make a sound. Came up behind me. Caught me in a neck hold. I couldn't move."

"Everyone mentions that he stinks. Did you smell anything?" the other detective asked.

"No. My allergies are in overdrive."

"Did he say anything?" DeLuca asked.

"Yeah. 'Where the hell is my dragon suitcase? Where did you hide it?' That's what he wanted to know. I told him there's no such thing as a dragon. Big mistake. Next thing I know, I'm on the floor. The back door eased shut, silent as a whisper."

DeLuca turned to the detectives. "Let's check out the entire place, the apartment upstairs, everything. Then we need to go to the station and file a report. Ted and Rosie, we'll keep this place under surveillance, but don't let your guard down."

Detective Hernandez smiled. "My Jamaican grandfather used to say, 'A little axe can cut down a big tree.'"

"Hank, what are you jabbering about?" DeLuca asked.

Hernandez slowly opened his right hand. "I yanked this cheap-o watch off the guy's arm when he grabbed me. Maybe it can give us DNA or clues about him to make sure he's our guy."

"Good thinking, partner. Let's go downtown," DeLuca said. "The tech team will take a look at that watch." He answered his phone, said "Uh-huh" a few times, and turned to Rosie and Ted.

"Surveillance is on the way."

Ted put his arm protectively around Rosie. "We don't have to stay here tonight. Let's go to my place."

"What makes you think we'll be any safer there?" Rosie asked.

"My dog Wolf will chew this guy to pieces."

"Sounds good to me," Hernandez said.

Rosie left with Ted. Her mind filled with disturbing questions. When will this guy be caught? When will his reign of terror end? Will Ivy Chen come home, or will she remain lost forever? Will this guy break in and vandalize my shop while I'm gone?

She wrapped her arm around Ted's waist as they headed to his truck. As she closed the door and locked it, she decided there had to be a special place in Hell for this guy and people like him, evil people who kept loved ones apart and ruined lives.

44
Detective Tony DeLuca and Jack Renard

Monday, February 6, 2012

Tony flipped open his phone and punched in the numbers for Jack Renard. "Jack. It's Detective DeLuca. How's it going?"

"Okay, but I need to wrap up everything with the Cassell estate. I owe it to the owners, Gary, and his sister Beverly. I need to move forward with my new clients."

"I understand," Tony said. "That's why I'm calling. I'm double-checking that you want to go ahead with the estate sale."

"I sure do," Jack said.

"Sorry this took so long. Our chief just gave us the go-ahead. So, pick your date, and let us know in advance. Detective Hernandez and I would like to help you with the notice for the newspaper, and other details too."

"You figure Ivy's kidnapper will show up?" Jack asked.

"I'd bet on it," Tony said. "He took the bait and came to the Grand Central Art Walk. We'll come up with a newspaper ad for this too. We'll have the place swarming with plainclothes, but are you sure you're up to it? If you want to back out, we understand. We can switch gears and have someone else run it. That's not a problem."

"If it will help catch him, count me in," Jack said.

"You're in," DeLuca said.

45
Frank Brandt

Wednesday, February 8, 2012

I flipped open the newspaper at work to see what was happening in this cruel world. The paper kept me knowledgeable, my new word of the day, while I washed down my baloney sandwich and chips with a root beer. The guys were spread out at other tables, playing poker and shooting craps. They didn't give a rat's ass about learning and reading. Jerks.

To hell with them. I can't believe what I'm reading. I nearly spit up the root beer as the words sunk in. There's going to be a sale at the Cassell estate. Jade jewelry and one-of-a-kind formal clothing, size two, will be among the items this Saturday, the first day of the sale.

It's about time! It took two years.

I looked again at the announcement. Some guy named Jack Renard was supervising the sale. He had to be the thief who stole the dragon suitcase from my house. While he was at it, he helped himself to cash, my TV, my grandfather's watch, my lug wrench, and the list goes on. It didn't say there was a suitcase for sale. Maybe he was keeping it for himself.

I slammed my fist down on the lunch table. I was stronger than I gave myself credit for. The table caved in and collapsed on the floor. It took my root beer with it and splattered it everywhere. They don't make card tables like they used to.

The guys turned on me with their nasty faces just like the screws who bossed me around at reform school. "You made the mess, Frank. You clean it up!"

"Think you're better than us, sitting there reading a paper? Look where that got you!"

"Go outside and eat with the dogs, why don't ya?"

I cleaned up the soda, straightened the table and chair, and sat back down.

"Happy now?" I asked and looked down my nose at these clods. I continued reading.

Jack Renard was in charge of the estate sale. Renard. A familiar name. Renard? Renard! Oh yeah. Rosie Renard. She owned Rosie's Treasures. I took her business card when I paid a little visit to her shop. I'm so smart. I knew who she was. She was that little she-devil who stapled my face. She'd do anything not to admit she knew where the suitcase was. All the time, it was some relative of hers. She'll be sorry she didn't fess up.

I bought another root beer from the machine. Bought? Ha. I kicked it out of the machine with one well-placed jolt from my work boot.

One of the guys jumped to his feet. "You pay like everybody else, you stupid jerk," he shouted. "Now put your money in that machine, and quit messing up our lunch."

They made such a big deal out of everything I did. Who were they kidding? It's not like they were such honest citizens. They steal snacks from the machine in the hallway, and they keep loose change they find in the cars.

Ah, the hell with it! I put money in the machine and continued reading.

So somebody was finally admitting they had Ivy's stuff. I'd be at that estate sale and get back what was mine, and I'd find that Jack Renard alone and teach him a lesson or two. Maybe Rosie would be there. That would be perfect. I'd be ready for her with a super-duper, heavy-duty stapler. Fair's fair. Let's see her pretty face all bloody, on the way to some serious scarring. Oh yeah. This was turning out to be a great day after all. More fun than kicking tires, crunching cars, and scaring the crap out of the guard dogs.

Now wait one second. This was way too easy. I could be falling into a trap. The police might be looking for me. Maybe some hidden camera took my photo in Rosie's Treasures when that stupid glass turtle hit the floor and probably tripped a camera. Could be that vicious salesgirl eyeballed the license plate. Well, there was more than one way to skin a cat.

I knew what I was talking about. I hated all feline creatures. Great word, "feline." My sister Marta screeched like a cat, had sharp nails like a cat, and snuck around like a cat. She would do what I asked, like an obedient kitty. She's had years of training.

After work, I put a note in Marta's apartment mailbox. "Come see me Saturday morning before eight o'clock. I have a little business to conduct, and I think you'll like it." I don't phone, I don't e-mail, and I was a fan of the Old School can't-trace method, the basic note, with disguised handwriting. It was all about being creative to save your own skin.

Saturday, February 11, 2012

Bright and early in the morning, Marta and I had a little discussion about her working an hour or two for me. No cleaning, just snooping. She grabbed at the chance.

So here we were. I was driving Marta toward the Allendale neighborhood in a car I borrowed from work. I paid the car-lot jerk a nice wad of cash to keep his mouth shut and not tell our boss about our little private transaction. I looked at it as a rental. The boss, an ownership freak, would call it a theft. The car-lot jerk thanked me for the bonus.

"Let's go over the plan one more time," I said to Marta as I pulled up to a coffee shop, several blocks from the Cassell home, and parked.

Marta snorted a laugh. "I got it all up here," she said and pointed her bony finger at her forehead.

"Let me hear it one last time," I said.

"I look at everything that's for sale," she said. "I show no reaction if I see your dragon suitcase or lug wrench, or Grandpa's watch, or anything of Ivy's. Give me some credit, Frank. I won't do anything that would tip off the detectives who are probably there ready to pounce and haul me away. I don't speak to anyone. If I see what you want, I remember the price, and report back to you."

She coughed, and spittle sat on her chin. What a slob. She coughed again. The spittle dripped onto the ratty blouse she was wearing.

"Here's what I don't get, Frank. If they have what you want, are you sure you should go there? They might be looking for you. They might have a few details about you. Doesn't sound like the plan of a super brain like you, Frank." She clicked her teeth several times rapidly.

"I know that teeth-tic of yours. You're being sarcastic. You know I hate sarcasm."

"I'm not making fun of you, Frank. I have chocolate sprinkles from a donut caught in my teeth. So let's move on. How can you show up at this sale without being noticed?"

"Piece of cake. I have a diversion to fall back on. A fire at a neighbor's house should work wonders. I can pull that off. It's in my skill set."

"Good. Now, you said you'd tell me before I got out of the car. What's in this for me?"

"There's that bike you've been wanting. We could maybe work something out."

Her piercing eyes cut through my glare. "Maybe we'll work it out? I need to hear we'll definitely work it out."

"Okay already. We're wasting time. Go!"

While Marta took care of her end of the bargain, I sat in the car and waited. It was a bucket of bolts, but if the cops were on to me, they'd be looking for a truck. I was way ahead of those jerks.

Finally, Marta approached. Just like we practiced, she didn't look over her shoulder or show any fear. She waved like we were old friends and hopped into the car. Her disgruntled face, best new word of the day, told it all.

"Nothing?" I asked.

"Nothing," she said and made a sour face like she'd just bitten into a lemon.

"What monkey business is this?" I pounded my fist on the steering wheel. "There ought to be a law about false advertising."

I started the engine and backed onto the street.

Marta cracked her bony knuckles. It sounded like thunder in this tiny car.

"Now that your little snit is over, let's talk about that bike," Marta said.

"Not now." I didn't even try to hide my frustration and disappointment. "Have you noticed the whole world is filled with jerks? Present company excluded." I looked over at Marta.

Her face lit up with joy. "You talking 'bout me, Frank?" She cackled.

"Are you brain dead? I mean me!" I floored the gas pedal. No way was she getting a bike from me. What did I ever get from her? Some housework that I paid for and a promise to keep her mouth shut for a few extra bucks. I didn't get what I paid for, and she raided my fridge several times and helped herself to sodas and snacks.

This wasn't over. Not by a long shot.

"Come see me Monday morning before seven. You can start cleaning my place again."

"Thanks, Frank." She cackled. "How about a raise?"

"Don't press your luck."

46
Detective Tony Deluca and Jack Renard

Saturday, February 11, 2012, 10:30 A.M.

Detective DeLuca arrived at the estate sale and wandered over to the jewelry table where Jack was talking to customers. DeLuca picked up rings one by one, holding them up to the sunlight, pretending he was interested in rings, until he was alone with Jack.

"Anyone suspicious show up?" he asked. "Anything happening that tells you there could be trouble?"

"No," Jack said. "There was a big rush the first hour. Those are usually the best customers. They've read the ads and come for something specific, or they live nearby and see all the cars and signs and come by to browse and chit-chat."

"No one unusual?"

"No." He hesitated. "Well, maybe."

"Talk to me," DeLuca said.

"There was an elderly woman, all hunched over like her bones were about to break. The poor thing looked like she hadn't eaten a decent meal in months. She looked everywhere, but she didn't touch anything. She didn't buy anything either. When she came to this table, I tried to make conversation with her to make her feel welcome."

"How did that work out?"

Jack shook his head. "She didn't say a word to me or anyone else. I felt sorry for her. I doubt she had enough money to buy anything. She was alone, possibly disoriented. I figured she was out for a walk and stumbled upon the sale. Maybe she's just plain curious."

"Do you think she might have been stealing things?" DeLuca asked.

"I don't think so. She didn't have a bag or anything to put things in."

"Did you notice how she got here?"

"No."

"Give me a minute," DeLuca said and stepped away from the table. "This may not amount to anything, but I'm going to call this in and see if anything pops."

A few minutes later DeLuca returned. "No. Just a fluke, I guess. There have been no previous complaints about a woman who fits that description. How long ago did she leave?"

"Maybe an hour or more."

"Okay. I'm going to check with your helpers and see if anyone noticed anything else about her. Then I've got to get back to the station. If the woman returns, give me a call." He started to leave and turned back. "I saw you talking to a pretty blonde. When I came toward you, she hurried away. I didn't ruin anything for you, did I?"

Jack laughed. "No. I'll be seeing her tonight."

"Good. Does she know what's going on here?"

"Sort of."

"Tell me about her."

"What is this? Do you suspect her of something?"

"No." DeLuca chuckled. "You both looked happy. It's a nice change to arrive expecting trouble and end up finding happy faces."

"Her name is Lisa, and she teaches first grade. I've taken her class under my wing. The kids are great. I give her all the little treasures that turn up in the houses I fix up."

"Like what?"

"Colored pencils still in sealed boxes. Marbles that Lisa uses to teach her students how to count. Last week, it was boxes of Popsicle sticks they turned into a frontier fort, stuff like that."

"Sounds great. If you don't mind my asking, where did you two meet?"

"We just met a few months ago at a hardware store of all places. She had some questions. The salesperson was busy. I stepped in. We'll see where it goes. By any chance are you a married man?"

"No, but it wasn't my choice. It just happened that way." DeLuca cleared his throat. "Stop me if I'm overstepping," he said, "but I'm glad to see you reconnecting with the human race."

A startled expression crossed Jack's face. "What are you talking about?"

"Rosie told me about your sister Tess. I'm sorry for what happened. I have some idea of what you're going through because of the missing-persons investigations I've been involved with over the years. You know, trusting people again. Getting involved with people on a personal level."

"Wow! I know Rosie told you what we went through as kids," Jack said and shook his head, "but I never figured it would lead to talking about Lisa and trust issues."

"I just want you to know, Officer Randall is an excellent resource person in missing-person cases, adult cases like Ivy, and child cases like Tess. I know you went through this years ago, but guilt can linger for a very long time. Officer Randall is helping family members get in touch with support groups. Here's my card." He pulled his pen from his pocket and scribbled a name and number on the back of his card. "Here's how to get in touch with Officer Randall. She'd be glad to hear from you."

"Thanks," Jack said, taking the card, "but Officer Randall beat you to it. I'm already in a group she recommended. We'll see how it goes. It's helpful, but I'm not into that spill-your-guts style of problem solving."

"I understand, but there's more to it than that, and each group has its own style. Anyway, if you drop out of that group, consider trying another."

"Why are you doing this? Did Officer Randall twist your arm?"

"No, she didn't have to, but we can talk about this another time. Call me whenever you want, for any reason." He took off toward the parking lot and turned his head from side to side checking out the crowds with every step he took.

47
Frank Brandt

Monday, February 13, 2012

Where was that no-good sister of mine? Ten minutes late. She'd better hurry if she knows what's good for her. Loose lips was Marta's problem. She blabbed her big mouth to Ali, and I let that slide, but she spent too much time in Ivy's apartment all those times she was here. She wanted to talk to Ivy. She would do it just to defy me. Loose lips and that spelled trouble. Ivy was much smarter than Ali. Ivy would eventually have taken advantage of my sister and flown the coop, free as a bird. Oh sure, Marta denied talking to Ivy. She said I was hearing voices and that I was crazy, but she's been lying since the day she was born, and Mama always believed her. Well, now Mama's not here to stand up for Marta. Too bad for Marta!

Somebody was at the front door, coughing up a fit. It's got to be Marta. Nobody else coughed like that. I'd give her a good scare just for old time's sake. I waited out of sight in the kitchen.

Finally, the door opened, and there was Marta all bent over like she was going to fall forward on her face. She stepped inside. What a scrawny bag of bones. A real mess, as always, with her stringy hair and clothes that didn't match.

I walked toward her, eager to be done with this.

Marta looked up and saw me. Her eyes flew open. Fear, that's what I saw. Good.

"You startled me," she said and set down a laundry bag. "I thought you'd have left for work already."

"A friend is covering for me, and I could catch hell for this. How come you're late?"

"The bike path is a death trap. I had to ride on the sidewalk or risk getting sideswiped."

"Where's your bike?"

"Are you losing your marbles, Frank?" She had the nerve to grin as she threw that insult in my face. "It's by the front door where I always leave it." She jerked her thumb over her shoulder like I didn't know where the front door was.

"Well you shouldn't leave it out there. People steal bikes left and right around here. I'll bring it inside." Quick as a flash, I pulled the bike into the living room. Leave no evidence she was ever here. That was my goal.

"When am I getting that bike you promised?" she asked, with a defiance that shocked me. After everything I'd given her, now it all came down to that bike?

"Your note said you wanted me to start cleaning this place again. Is that part of the deal for me to get a bike?"

"You're just lucky I let you come back," I said. "You had to shoot your mouth off. I warned you not to talk to Ali, but you wouldn't listen. I can't trust you, especially with personal information, and I know you started talking to Ivy."

"I already told you I didn't speak a word to her. If you're so ticked off at me, why'd you ask me to come back?"

"Why do you think?" I asked and saw the fear flame again in her eyes as I grabbed the keys from her hand. "I could murder you right here. No one would miss you."

"My neighbors would," she said, narrowing her eyes.

"Don't talk back to me," I said and hit her hard.

She fell to the floor.

"Don't do this to me, Frank," she whined. "You're my brother. You're supposed to look out for me."

"See this?" I said, and rolled up my pant leg. Her eyes bulged at the sight of that big shiny knife strapped to my ankle. "I could kill you faster with a knife, but I don't want to waste my time cleaning up your blood."

"No, Frank, please," she cried.

"Scream your guts out begging for your life," I said. "I won't change my mind."

"What are you gonna do without me and my mailbox? Your mail comes care of me. If I disappear, so does your mail."

What a stupid woman. She didn't know squat. That mail was all addressed to Current Occupant. Nothing personal. Nothing important. "I don't need you or your mailbox. I have my own ways and a very cooperative boss who pays me off the books with cash."

I grabbed Marta under her arms and pulled her to her feet. Standing behind her, I wrapped my hands around her neck and squeezed. She kicked. I squeezed. She struggled to break free. I squeezed harder. She jabbed me with her elbows. I squeezed as hard as I could. "I beg you, don't do this," she rasped. Squeezing wasn't going so well. I clenched my hands together and snapped her neck. Finally, she went limp and slumped over. No more squeezing. No more clenching. I let go of her, and she fell like a sack of potatoes to the floor.

She didn't move. It was over. She lost. I won. Too bad Mama wasn't here to see it. "Be a man," she used to say. Well, now I was a man, the Dominator and the Terminator all rolled into one.

I spread out several large trash bags on the floor and taped them together to form one big sheet. I rolled her up and taped her nice and tight. There! No arms or legs poking out to slow me down.

Monday, February 13, 2012, 5:15 P.M.

I came home right after work to finish what I'd started. I could have made my job easier by throwing her down the well in the back yard. Fast and efficient, but that would be wrong. That well was sacred. It was Ali's last resting place. It may soon be Ivy's last resting place

271

too if she doesn't shape up and obey me at all times. It would be blasphemy to bury trash, like Marta, with treasures, like Ali and Ivy. If they just didn't fight me. If they could just accept the perfect life I gave them, but they forced me to make these life-and-death decisions.

Marta wasn't their equal. She didn't deserve that beautiful well. Ashes to ashes. I laughed out loud. First, it was trash to trash. Then it was ashes to ashes. It couldn't be dust to dust because Marta truly believed she was a magnificent housekeeper and good at dusting. What a crazy sister!

I carried Marta and her bike to my truck, put them in the back, and covered them with an old blanket. I drove to the town dump, the one that wasn't gated. Rules and regulations. They may run the world, but they didn't stop creative people like me, who thought outside the box.

There was no one at the dump but me. It was eerie here at night as the gravel crushed beneath my work shoes and the grating sound echoed off the pine trees. Rats ran around making little squeaking noises. Raccoons scavenged everything in sight. The only light was faint, and it came from houses in the distance. The moist air brushed my face and refreshed me, filling me with energy and determination.

I dropped Marta's bike on a pile of leaves and mulch near the center of a mound of debris. I set Marta's body on top of the bike. I tossed extra clippings across Marta's burial outfit, a plastic sack, and threw some branches and logs on top of that. More mulch came next and finally more leaves. Good enough.

I left quickly. You never know who might be lurking around a place like this at night. As I pulled away from the dump and turned onto the street, I looked in the rearview mirror.

"Good riddance, sister dear," I said, and headed home for a well-deserved night's sleep. A big belly laugh filled my truck. I was one shrewd guy. I just saved the cost of a bike!

48
Detective Tony DeLuca

Thursday, February 16, 2012

Officer Randall stood next to a large mound of leaves, underbrush, and branches sitting on top of a pyramid of trash. She pulled out her phone and made a call. "Tony, it's me, Betty. I got something for you. Actually I've got someone for you."

"What's all that noise? Where are you?"

"You're hearing the sounds of trucks, buzz saws, and huge flies. I'm at the town dump. It's not pretty. I was driving by, making the rounds, and decided to stop in and chat with Charlie. If anything is happening in that part of town, he knows about it. Anyway, before I could turn off the main road, Charlie came running down the path and flagged me down."

"He took you to meet someone? The noise is making it hard to hear. Is that what you're saying?"

"Yeah, but that someone is dead. My guess? She's been dead for several days."

"Charlie found her?"

"Charlie spotted a bike. The sun flashed off the metal. He grabbed a pitchfork to dig it out. You know him. He fixes old bikes, sells them, and makes a few bucks. Anyway, he said he nearly died of a heart attack when he saw several large plastic bags taped shut. He had a creepy feeling and looked closer. There was a rip in the bag. A woman's leg and sneaker poked out. It was a woman. Definitely a woman. She was lying next to the bike."

"I'll send help. Stay there until they arrive."

"Thanks."

"What kind of bike is it?" Tony asked.

"Old. Beat-up. Registration number's filed off."

"I'm getting a bad feeling. Please don't tell me she's another victim of our guy," Tony said. "Is she young and pretty like Ivy Chen?"

"No. Not at all. She's old. She has stringy gray hair, and I'd definitely say she was in poor health. She's as skinny as a broomstick. Maybe some violence took place. She has bruises on her arms and neck, and there's torn fingernails."

"What a world," Tony said. "How many times do we see a person's life end badly?"

"Too often," Officer Randall said.

"Yeah. See you soon. Meanwhile, think good thoughts."

49
Ivy Chen

Saturday, February 18, 2012

Frank stormed into my room as he always did, but his pale face and wounded expression were not how he typically looked. I couldn't tell if he was feeling pain or fear or possibly suffering from bad news.

He dropped down on my couch. "Everybody's ganging up on me," he blurted out. "I'd come to expect being teased and taunted at work, but then that snotty clerk in the used junk shop scratched my truck. Her boss shot my face full of staples. Now this." He rolled up the sleeve of his shirt.

I gasped. There on the bicep of his right arm was a tattoo of the tail and body of a— I looked closer. It was a dragon, an ugly, maimed dragon. The head, paws, claws, and talons were all missing. In their place, blood-red ink looked like blood was actually dripping, almost flowing.

"What happened?"

"I missed the dragon tattoo on our suitcase, and I missed having a dragon here in my house. I liked all those dragon stories you told me, but it wasn't enough. I wanted a dragon of my own, a dragon that could come and go with me, and be with me, keeping me company, right here on my own body."

"So you decided to get a tattoo," I said.

"Yeah. I checked online at work and found a tattoo artist who bragged about bargain rates. I went there. I met him. He's a big muscular guy about six feet tall, two hundred pounds, covered everywhere with tattoos. I told him I wanted a dragon tattoo on my arm, and he said okay, no problem."

Frank gulped. "He pricked my skin with needles. They hurt. He told me to quit moving around because I was messing up the dragon. He jabbed me hard with needles. I tried to get out of the seat. He told me he would be done soon for today, but this dragon would take several visits, and each visit would last several hours. I tried to stand up. He told me to sit still, and when I got home to take two aspirins and a glass of bourbon. I couldn't stand the pain. I said I'd come back for the rest of the sittings. He wanted me to pay right then and there. I told him no. Then he insisted on putting the finishing touches on what he'd done so far on my dragon."

Frank rolled up his sleeve several more inches. "Do you see this bloody mess? That nasty creep jabbed red ink all over the dragon where parts of its body were missing. I saw the massacre and screamed at him that he was a blood-sucking monster. He pushed me up against the wall and demanded his money. I shoved him to the floor and kicked him in the ribs. 'You're not getting any money from me, sucker,' I said and kicked him again."

"So you won?" I asked picturing this nasty fight between the two angry men, the tattoo artist demanding his money, and Frank refusing to pay.

"Yeah. I won," he said, but there was no joy in his expression or voice. The dragon was a disaster, and it would be with Frank for a long time, until he figured a way to get rid of it. That would mean enduring the pain all over again from needles.

"Did the tattoo artist call the police?" I asked, hiding my enthusiasm behind a solemn expression.

"He grabbed his phone and punched in three numbers. I'm super smart. I figured it was 9-1-1. I ran out of there and was on my way home when I heard sirens."

He huffed. "So here I am with a broken-down dragon on my arm. This dragon's not strong. He's not brave. He has no head or hands or feet. He can't protect himself, and he sure as hell can't protect me. You say dragons bring good luck." He pointed at his tattoo but turned his face away from it. "You call this good luck?"

Frank ranted on and on. I was so happy. From what Frank said, the tattoo artist had called the police, so the officers would now have a description of Frank. This was my lucky day. The dragon brought me very good luck. Praise the mighty dragon!

♫♫

Alone in my room, I danced back and forth and spread my arms toward the skylight. Soon, if good luck followed me, I'd enjoy more than a few hurried glances at the night sky from Frank's barren yard. Once I was free, I'd see the heavens above, the world beneath my feet, and my dreams coming true.

50
Detectives Tony DeLuca and Hank Hernandez

Saturday, February 18, 2012

The desk sergeant called out, "Hey, Tony, you'd better take this call."

"Go get 'em, partner," Hank called after him.

"What's it about?" Tony asked.

"A dragon tattoo."

"Are you kidding me?"

"You told me anything comes in about dragons, you wanted to know." He held out the phone.

"Detective DeLuca, here," he said into the phone. "How can I help you?"

He listened for a minute and smiled. "Did you get a good look at him?" There was a pause. "Great. I'll bring a sketch artist with me. Stay right there. We're on our way."

He hurried away from the phone and grabbed his jacket. "Hank, let's go. This could be it. A tattoo artist may have tattooed a dragon onto our kidnapper. Now we have a name. It's Frank."

"Does Frank have a last name?"

"No, but the day isn't over yet," Tony said.

They rushed out the door and down the steps.

Even with the siren blasting, the detectives lost time because of road construction and a delivery-truck breakdown along the way. Finally, they roared to a stop in front of the Tattoo Express and rushed inside. A man holding his bandaged ribs said, "I'm Gus. I called. Some nutcase named Frank made threats on my life. He said I tortured him with needles."

"Did you?" Hernandez asked.

"You ever had a tattoo?" Gus asked. He fumed and gritted his teeth. "It's done with needles. Was this guy Frank born yesterday? Under what rock has he been living? He should've expected needles."

"Calm down," DeLuca said. "How bad did he hurt you?"

"There's a walk-in clinic around the corner. I just got back here a few minutes ago. The doc fixed me up and said I'd live, but the money this jerk Frank owes me would let me live more comfortably."

"Gus, this is Gretchen, our sketch artist," DeLuca said, introducing the petite dark-eyed beauty who just arrived carrying a canvas bag that weighed more than she did. She shifted the bag overflowing with paper, pens, other art supplies, and a laptop computer to her other hand. She nodded at Gus and offered a saucy smile to Detective Hernandez.

"Let's get to it, Gus," Gretchen said. From those bow lips in that heart-shaped face, her voice roared like a drill sergeant. She asked several questions about the man's face, hair, and features. "I'm old-fashioned," she said and began sketching with pencil on paper. "Pencil sketches come out more natural looking and more accurate than a computer-only rendition."

In between Gretchen's pencil strokes and Gus's fine-tuned suggestions, DeLuca worked in questions. "Gus, did he give a last name or address or phone number?"

"All I know is his name is Frank. I saw him pull away in a black pickup truck."

DeLuca nodded at Hernandez and turned to Gus. "Did you see the plate number? Even a partial would help."

"No. Sorry. I was in pain. I wasn't thinking about plate numbers."

"We understand," Hernandez said. He stepped aside and confided to Tony, "We should have the valet from the Vinoy take a look at the sketch when it's done."

"This will just take a few more minutes," Gretchen said and smiled again at Detective Hernandez and added a wink. "Gus, here, has the eye of an artist." She smudged some of the harsh lines and the drawing took on personality. "Gus, if anyone else comes in here and beats the crap out of you again, I'd love to be the sketch artist that gets called in."

"I'll see what I can do to make that happen," Gus said with a sly grin. He winced with pain.

"I'm done," Gretchen said with a sigh of contentment and held up the sketch.

"Great," Gus said and gave the sketch a thumbs-up.

DeLuca leaned close to Hernandez and said in a low voice, "You've been talking about asking Gretchen out for drinks. What about right now?"

"Nah. I decided to take my grandfather's advice."

DeLuca rolled his eyes. "Now what's he got to say?"

"He says beautiful woman, beautiful trouble."

"You're making a mistake," DeLuca said. "I see how she looks at you. I see how you look at her."

"She's near-sighted, and I have astigmatism. That's what you're seeing."

"Got it. Maybe you should ask her to go to the eye doctor with you."

"Give it up, Tony," Hernandez said and chuckled.

Detectives DeLuca and Hernandez strode toward the Vinoy Hotel's valet parking station "Chet, thanks for seeing us on such short notice," DeLuca said to the valet who had been on duty the day Ivy Chen disappeared.

Chet looked at the sketch DeLuca held up. His eyes nearly popped out of his head. "That's the guy. That's him," Chet said pointing at the sketch.

"Is there anything else you remember about him?" Detective Hernandez asked. "Maybe something that isn't in this sketch?"

"Yeah, that stupid grin of his," Chet said. "He nearly ran me over, and he laughed like a hyena about it. I could never forget that grin. Is he an escapee from an asylum or what?"

"We hope to have the answer to that question and many others very soon," DeLuca said.

"Thanks again," Hernandez said. "We'll be going now."

As they walked toward their car, Tony said to Hank, "We need to make plans."

"For me and Gretchen?" Hank grinned.

"Do that on your own time. I'm talking about the sketch of this guy who called himself Frank."

"Let's distribute copies to every detective and officer."

"Good," Tony said. "For now, it's for police eyes only. We don't want this guy named Frank, if that is his real name, to find out we're closing in. As you know, guys like him are always cowards. If Ivy is alive, he might kill her, hide the body, and run."

51
Rosie and Ted

Saturday, February 25, 2012

Rosie and Ted found a parking spot on the street at the Event Parking Only area, close to where the main activities would take place. Eager to see the Dragon Boat Races that were about to begin, they walked toward Poynter Park overlooking Bayboro Harbor. Cheerful laughter and animated conversations swirled through the balmy air as crowds headed toward the area between the Poynter Library and the University of South Florida's Harbor Hall.

"This is going to be a fun day," Ted said and gave Rosie a quick kiss on the cheek. "My business is picking up. Things are going good with us, and a new sport has come to town. A good-news day all around."

"I like the sound of that," Rosie said with a smile. She shielded her eyes and looked down the sloping grassy area toward the bay. In the distance, yachts, sailboats, and rowboats bobbed in the calm waters as blue as the midday sky.

Rosie gasped with delight and pointed toward the water's edge several yards away. The unbelievably whimsical sight of colorful dragon boats lined up side by side had captured her attention. From the dragon's head at the prow, to the dragon's tail at the stern, the scales, painted vivid, crayon colors of red, yellow, and green, shone in the bright sunshine.

"Ted, look. Aren't those dragon boats something else? I can't wait to see them race."

"Neither can I. I was glad to hear they were coming to St. Pete. This should be a day of surprises." Ted checked his watch. "We have fifteen minutes before the races start. I need to check on my crew at my food truck and see if everything's okay."

They made their way through the growing crowds toward a dozen food trucks lined up on the grass parallel to the sidewalk and street. She immediately spotted Ted's Organic Foods banner fluttering in the gentle breeze. Lines were already forming in front of his truck decorated with painted fruits and vegetables.

"We adapt our menu for every event," Ted said with a hint of pride.

"Good, but I hope you've got your usual carrot fries, zucchini fritters, and veggie wraps."

"You bet, but for this festival, we've added a special treat with a tradition that goes back hundreds of years."

"What is it?"

"Rice dumplings. It's a spoonful of soft sticky rice wrapped in bamboo leaves and tied with string. What do you say we sample everything after the races?"

"My stomach's growling already," she said.

Ted talked to his crew and made sure they had enough supplies. They chatted with Rosie and promised to set aside some of her favorite treats. "Okay, everybody," Ted said, backing away, "I'll come back and check again. If there's anything you need, just call my cell. See you later."

Rosie linked arms with Ted. "Let's go find a good place to stand before the crowd grows larger."

Five minutes later, they stood in the spectator area not far from the water's edge. Rosie heard the applause of the crowd and looked to her right. About a dozen teams of paddlers, judging by the colors and logos on their shirts, made their way along the walkway toward the spectators.

The paddlers' enthusiasm was catching, and many people waved and cheered them on. Three teams came from St. Pete. Rosie rooted for the Grand Café team, friends and acquaintances of hers who owned cafés and shops near her shop. Ted, a graduate of USF, had stayed in touch with his college friends who enjoyed canoeing and paddle boarding. They had put together a dragon boat team, wearing the water colors of blue and green. Ted shouted, "Go blue and green," as they passed by.

After picking up leaflets entitled "Dragon Boating," Rosie and Ted moved further back to a shady area beneath the trees with a great view of the water.

A man holding a megaphone moved to the front of the crowd. "Welcome, everyone, to today's dragon boating race. Each team will compete in three races. The course is 350 meters long. Before the race begins, I'd like to tell you about the ancient ceremony of awakening the dragons. Legend has it that selected people dotted the dragon's eyes with red paint to awaken them. Once the dragons woke up, they came to the water's edge." He waved toward the four boats now lined along the shore closest to the spectators. "Earlier, our special guests performed that ceremony. All that's left to do is race!"

Rosie quickly read the leaflet and looked up to see everything mentioned happening right before her eyes. Twenty teammates climbed into each of the four boats. They sat two abreast the length of the forty-two foot long boat, each holding a paddle. A steersperson, using an oar as a rudder, stood in the stern. A drummer sat at the bow facing the paddlers. The twenty, aware that any movement would disqualify their team, dipped their paddles in the water and held them perfectly still. Muscles tensed, the paddlers waited expectantly for the honk of the starter's horn.

The silence filled Rosie and Ted and everyone with anticipation. They held their breaths and kept their eyes on the boats. And then....

"Honk!"

Without hesitation, the paddlers attacked their task, taking deep, powerful strokes in harmony with the pounding of the drum. The drummer, who created the sound of a dragon's heartbeat, inspired the teammates to paddle in unison.

The drumbeat went faster and faster. The paddlers kept the drummer's pace with their long commanding strokes. Then, all at the same moment, the paddlers switched to a sprint, a series of fast race strokes. They paddled in sync racing like the winds of an angry squall, then returned to the steady pace of long energetic strokes. Making a final frenzied push, the paddlers raced ahead and crossed the finish line. A blur of blue and white flashed toward the shore.

"Hooray for the Grand Café! The blue and white team won!" Rosie cried. She threw her arms around Ted, laughing. "Yeah!"

"Hooray for the blue and white," Ted cheered, keeping his arm around Rosie's waist, a big grin on his face.

The winning team raised their paddles over their heads. Laughing and shouting, the teammates splashed each other until they were drenched. ·

Everyone cheered as the winning team came ashore, followed by the other teams.

"What's that man doing?" Ted pointed at a guy wearing a navy blue baseball cap and gray work clothes. He was laughing and rushing toward the teams, now just a few yards from the spectators. A camera hung from a strap around the man's neck. Two oversized water bottles were strapped to his waist. He had a paintbrush in one hand, a can of red paint in the other, and he was waving them around.

The spectators stood riveted to the spot, uncertain if this was part of the program. Rosie peered at the man. He wore gray work clothes. His behavior was bizarre. He was here at an event with a Chinese theme. Could he be the man who had kidnapped Ivy? No. After all, what were the odds he would be here?

One of the paddlers hooted at the man, "What are you doing with that paint?" and Rosie's attention flew back to the man.

"I'm going to paint the dragon's eyes."

"No you're not. Don't spill that paint on this boat."

The man ignored the warning and waved the paintbrush joyfully from side to side as if it were a trophy.

"Set that paint can down," the paddler cried.

"Who died and made you boss?" the man asked and dipped the paint brush into the paint can.

"Get away from here."

"You can't tell me what to do."

"This is my boat. Now get lost."

Team members gathered around, shouting at the man, "Leave"..."Go away"..."Get lost!"

"Make me!" the man snapped back and lifted the paint can as if to throw it.

A team member knocked the paint can out of his hand. It landed on the grass, and red paint trickled like blood across the blades of grass.

The man threw down the paintbrush and splashed the paddlers with his water bottles. The paddler closest to the man yelled, "Beat it!"

The man started punching the paddler. A fierce fist fight ensued. The paddler was lithe and fast. The man was slow and clumsy but obviously very strong because he pummeled the paddler and knocked him to the ground for the second time.

"Ted, this can't be part of the event," Rosie said. "That guy's out of control."

"I'm calling the police," Ted said and pulled out his phone.

"I just reported it," a teenager near Ted and Rosie said and slid the phone into his pocket. "That same guy caused trouble earlier. He tried to push his way into a dragon boat. He's a nutcase. He thinks he's some ancient warrior who's going to save the universe or something."

"They're still at it," Rosie said, shifting her gaze toward the water.

The paddler's teammates tried to pull the man off their buddy, but the man was swinging his arms and kicking fiercely. He screamed, "It's a free country. I can paint and paddle if I want to."

Parents scooped up their children and backed away from the fight. Dogs on leashes growled and pulled their owners through the crowd.

Race officials rushed to restore order.

Security made their way forward threatening to escort the man away from the area.

Bedlam reigned!

52
Detectives Tony DeLuca and Hank Hernandez

Saturday, February 25, 2012

Hernandez rushed to DeLuca's desk. "Let's go. A call just came in," he said. "A teenager says some guy's causing trouble at Bayboro Harbor. The guy's ticked off because nobody let him paint the dragon's eyes."

"Dragon!" DeLuca exclaimed and jumped up from his chair. "Hank, are you thinking what I'm thinking?"

"Yeah. Dragons mean trouble. The kind of trouble that's connected to our investigation." Hernandez grabbed his keys. "My turn to drive."

"Geeze, who knew dragons would be taking over our cold case and leading us to Ivy Chen?" DeLuca scooped up a handful of the sketches of the guy they were calling Frank. "Come on!"

The two detectives sprinted toward the door.

Hernandez jumped into the car and roared the engine.

DeLuca turned on the siren and flashing lights. "Let's get the SOB," he said and clenched his jaw.

53
Rosie and Ted

Saturday, February 25, 2012

"This is turning crazy," Ted said and nodded toward the troublemaker.

"Looks like the security people will have to hustle him out of here," Rosie said, pointing toward the team that was approaching the troublemaker.

As Ted, Rosie, and the crowds took in what was happening, the man broke free from the paddlers and pushed past the security. With an awkward gait, he moved away from the water and headed toward the street. Everyone was so startled by this wild guy at such a peaceful event that no one tried to stop or subdue him.

"Go! Leave us alone!" shouted a young father cradling his toddler.

"Yeah! Beat it!" cried others.

One woman shook her fist and bellowed, "Don't come back, you big bully!"

A security guard, old and slow, lumbered after the wild man.

Sirens, growing louder, wailed in the distance. The man stopped briefly and looked toward downtown where the shrill sound was coming from. A terrified expression crossed his face. He took off running, pumping his arms and legs, gasping loudly from the effort and wiping the perspiration from his face onto his shirt. Ted and Rosie saw the man charging toward the street in the direction of the food trucks.

Ted speed-dialed his crew. "There's a crazy guy headed your way," he shouted into the phone. "Be careful. He packs a mean punch, and he's out of control. Don't let him near you or the truck."

"I'm going after him," Ted said.

"I'm going with you," Rosie said.

"I know better than to tell you what to do." Ted grabbed her hand, and they ran together toward the trucks.

As Ted and Rosie stopped to catch their breath, a tall woman with binoculars who was standing next to Rosie said, "That nutty guy just stopped at a black pickup truck."

A chill ran up Rosie's spine. "Ted, I'm calling Detective DeLuca." She grabbed her phone. "This guy's freaking me out. I think he might be the one who abducted Ivy Chen."

Ted's jaw dropped. "What makes you think so?"

"Women's intuition," Rosie said and pressed number ten. "That's how I know. And what about the dragons? Chinese dragons. The guy's wearing gray work clothes. Now he's getting into a black truck. It's him. I'm sure it's him."

Two rings and Detective DeLuca picked up.

"It's Rosie. You need to come to Poynter Park right away."

"We're already on our way. We got a call about a man causing trouble."

"I think he's the same guy who pestered Jane...who attacked me...who left his fingerprints on Ivy's clothes. He's got a black pickup truck. It's—"

"Stay away—" DeLuca's voice trailed off.

The sirens' wails grew louder.

Ted hopped onto the bumper of his food truck. He scanned the area and saw the man crouched by a black truck, poking around, reaching under the truck, as if looking for something.

"I think he lost his keys," Ted said and blinked his eyes. "He found them. He's opening the truck door. He's getting inside."

Ted jumped down from the bumper and took off toward the black truck. The man was now roaring the engine. The truck lurched forward and then backward as the man tried to get out of the tight parking space. All of a sudden, the truck came barreling toward Ted.

"Watch out!" Rosie shouted. "He's coming fast. Ted! He's going to run you over!"

The black pickup truck roared toward Ted.

Ted jumped out of the way.

The truck backed up and lurched forward for a second try.

Ted grabbed hold of a hanging branch, took a running jump, pulled his knees up to his chest, and swung across the road and sidewalk, hanging on to the branch for dear life. He landed in the grass and rolled over and over until he finally managed to bring himself to a stop and scramble to his feet.

"You stupid jerk!" The driver shouted. He shook his fist out the window and roared down the street.

Rosie caught a glimpse of his license plate just before the guy turned west on Sixth Avenue South.

"Detective DeLuca, are you still there?" she shouted into her phone.

"You bet. We're close. We're on Central Avenue, heading your way. We called in reinforcements."

"Don't come this far, Detective. The guy turned on Sixth Avenue South heading west. I got the first part of the license plate. It's F, M, and four. He tried to run down Ted, but Ted got away. The man is built like the man who attacked me in my shop."

"Okay, we're on Sixth Avenue, heading west toward Tropicana Field."

Sirens screamed blocks away, from the north, south, east, and west. All came toward Poynter Park, like needles pulled to a magnet.

"Come on, Rosie," Ted said.

"Let's do it," Rosie said. She ran with Ted, keeping up to him. "With any luck, the red lights might slow him down."

"Maybe," Ted said. "But listen to those sirens. He can figure he's being chased. He'll run red lights. He'd run over his own grandmother to get away."

"Let's take Fourth Street. It's not as busy as Third with all the Boat Parade traffic," Rosie said and opened the door to Ted's truck. Sliding onto the seat and buckling her seatbelt, she looked toward Bayboro Harbor. Paddlers were preparing for the next race. Everything had settled down, but the pounding of Rosie's heart, as fierce as the dragon drummer's beat, told her that time was running out, and maybe their luck was running out too.

"Hurry," she said as Ted turned the key in the ignition. The truck sputtered and jerked into the lane. Ted gripped the steering wheel, and Rosie prayed they would spot the black truck before it got away and disappeared from their sight. Maybe forever.

54

Ivy Chen

Saturday, February 25, 2012

It was one of those days I couldn't shake my unhappiness. It was the middle of the afternoon, but I wanted to go to bed, pull the covers over my head, and cry myself to sleep. The dragon boat stories I'd been telling Frank had made me so homesick, and I was losing hope of ever getting out of here. How naïve I was to think the stories could possibly save my life.

Oh no! The key rattled in the lock. I trembled with fear as Frank charged through the door into my apartment. His face was lava red with anger.

"Get out here," he said, jerking his head toward his quarters.

I couldn't seem to move.

Frank yanked me by the arm. I stumbled into his living room. He pushed me down on a chair. "I know more about the dragon than you do," he said and reached over his shoulder and patted himself on the back.

"I went to the dragon boat races at Bayboro Harbor today. They started out great. The teams got into their dragon boats with the big heads and curvy tails, and then, just because I tried to paint the dragon's eyes and splash the teams with water, people called me names. They told me to leave."

My stomach churned, and I felt sick. Frank's presence at the boat races was almost a blasphemy to the sacred spirit of the event, and now Frank had desecrated it.

Frank scowled. "Some of them tried to follow me. Police sirens blasted everywhere." His eyes opened wide, looking wild. "But I know shortcuts, back ways, alleys, and closed-off streets. I beat those nasty people and cops at their own game. As always, I win. They lose."

But maybe something good could come of this. Did anyone notice Frank's vehicle or his license plate? Unable to hide my enthusiasm, I asked him point blank, "Did they follow you here? Did they see where you lived?"

"Shut up. Don't think like that."

"But Frank—"

"Didn't you hear me?" He balled his hands into fists.

I turned away, but his fist crashed into my cheek, the very same spot where he had hit me yesterday. I reeled from the blow and fell to the floor.

"I outsmarted them," he said.

"Frank, please hear what I have to say." I pulled myself to my feet and shook away the dizziness. "It could save your life and keep us together." The words that tasted like bile held Frank's fist in mid-air and stopped the punch that would surely knock me out cold.

"Frank," I said in the sweetest voice I could muster, "the police will see your pickup truck and know you live here."

"No they won't. It's in the garage, and the door is shut," he said, but his voice wavered.

"That's just what they'll be looking for. A hiding place for a truck. Move it someplace they wouldn't think to look—a natural hiding place, maybe a park, some place with lots of trees. You need to move it now. You may not get a second chance."

While Frank paced the floor, I considered my options. If he locked me up and I couldn't escape, maybe the police would spot him and make him tell where I am. If he didn't lock me up, I would follow my plan and escape. This could be my last chance. I must make this work. I had to forget about the pain from Frank's punches. Escape, escape, escape, I told myself as if repeating the word could make it happen.

Frank stopped pacing. "I know a place. They'll never find it. It's a truck graveyard filled with abandoned broken-down trucks. It's ten minutes from here, and the road is open only to local traffic."

"Brilliant," I exclaimed. "Go! Don't wait another minute! Go now!"

He grabbed his keys and went to the kitchen door. He peeked out and closed the door quickly behind him. The brief blast of sunlight told me it was daytime. What a relief. That would make my escape easier and faster.

Noises, I heard wonderful noises. The garage door going up, the tires squealing down the driveway, and Frank's truck rattling as it sped away.

"Thank you," I whispered as I raced to my bedroom and opened the bottom drawer of my dresser, my escape drawer. I had timed this part of the escape many times and had it down to four minutes flat. I hurriedly slipped into warm-up pants and shirt, socks and sneakers, and an extra pair of socks for my hands, all so I wouldn't sustain injuries that would slow me down.

Speed was everything! I tied a scarf over my hair so it wouldn't get caught in the wire fence. I placed my erhu in my bed sheet and wrapped it up. I tied two pillowcases around the erhu, one near the top and one near the bottom, and knotted them. My hands were shaking. My pillowcase package was more haphazard than it was during my practice sessions. It wasn't secure. My erhu had been my life, my saving grace for three years and four months. I couldn't leave it behind, and I didn't have time to re-wrap it. I must get out of here!

I reached under the mattress.

Oh no!

The heavy black pan wasn't there. How could that be? How could Frank have found it and taken it away?

As tears rolled down my cheeks, I moved my hand back and forth in every direction.

There it was! It had been there all the time.

I grabbed the pan, my flashlight, and my pillowcase-package and hurried as best I could to the alcove door just outside my bedroom.

I didn't look back. I never wanted to see this place again. Exactly as I had done before, I did now, but quicker, much quicker.

Turn on the light. Crawl through the low-ceilinged part. Don't slow down because of dead rats. But I couldn't help myself. I hesitated and thought about what squished beneath my hands as I crawled.

Move on. Stand up at the high-ceilinged part. Grab the pan. Swing with all my might against the padlock.

I swung once.

The padlock held firm.

A second time.

It didn't budge.

A third time.

A grating noise burst forth.

I gathered all my strength and raised the pan as high as I could, slammed it down as hard as I could, and prayed fervently.

The padlock fell to the floor and shattered into pieces.

I cracked open the door. The bright afternoon light stung my eyes. There were no steps from the floor to the ground, but I remembered that from when I'd been outdoors. In one smooth, fast movement, I plunked down on the floor, edged forward with my pillowcase pack, and jumped down, landing squarely on my feet. I teetered but kept my balance.

Short of breath, not used to such sudden moves, I willed myself to cross the yard. I zigzagged past cans, bottles, and bags of trash. Tripped over a clump of weeds, a few feet from the hole in the fence. Pushed myself up and took several steps. Flattened myself and went through. Scrambled to my feet, but something was wrong. I looked over my shoulder.

The pillowcase pack had snagged on the fence. My erhu was trapped!

"Come on!" I cried and tugged hard, but it was stuck. "Come on!" I cried again and tugged even harder. I reached back and un-snagged it. Free!

The head of the erhu's carved dragon poked through the torn section of the bed sheet. I wanted to stop, to check my erhu, but I must keep going. I had to get away. Now!

55
Rosie and Ted

Saturday, February 25, 2012

Rosie and Ted raced to Fourth Street and turned right. Whoa! They came to a screeching halt, nearly plowing into the van in front of them. Vehicles were all over the place in both lanes, and traffic wasn't moving.

"What rotten luck!" Ted said through tight lips.

"We're stuck, and he'll get away!" Rosie exclaimed.

"Maybe not. He might have gotten caught in this mess too." Ted got out of his truck and climbed onto the hood. Shielding his eyes from the sun, he peered at the vehicles.

"Do you see his truck?" Rosie called up to him.

"No. Several cars and trucks are jammed up, but not his. People are out of their cars. Two men are shouting at each other and waving their fists. It must be a fender bender. Cars are trying to get past, but it's not working."

Ted got back into his truck. "Our guy got away. He has a head start. I didn't see any detectives, so they got past the mess. Maybe they've caught up to him by now."

"I'll call Detective DeLuca and see what he can tell us." She got right through to him.

"We lost him because of that traffic jam," DeLuca said, "but we've put out a BOLO for a black truck, male driver in work clothes. A few other details too. We'll get him."

Ted and Rosie sat in the truck complaining about losing time. Ted kept checking his watch. He peered at the traffic jam and reported to Rosie about the progress of the tow trucks at the scene and the police officers who had arrived to direct traffic.

Finally, after a half-hour, the jam broke up and traffic ran smoothly. "Do you think we might get lucky and spot his truck?" Rosie asked as they drove north on Fourth Street.

"Let's give it a try," Ted said and continued north, discouraged about the odds of finding the truck. After a while, they entered an industrial area of auto shops and storage areas and eventually came to a run-down section of warehouses, scrap metal piles, and vacant lots.

"This looks like an area our guy might be attracted to," Rosie said. "There aren't many people here. It's a long shot, but let's drive around."

"I don't believe it." Ted nodded toward the road ahead. "I see a black pickup way up there. Darn! There's at least a dozen cars between him and us. He just eased into the turn lane. He's turning left."

"I'll let Detective DeLuca know." Rosie grabbed her phone.

"I'll try to keep the guy in sight," Ted said. He gripped the steering wheel, tapped the brakes and then the gas. Brakes and gas again and again, inching closer to the turn lane. "He turned. That cross street is nearly deserted. He's getting away!"

"Detective DeLuca, it's Rosie. We had Frank in our sights, but—"

"Tell me where you are and then get away from there," DeLuca said. "He's dangerous. We'll take it from here."

Rosie named the street. "But we just lost him. We'll get back to you." She set her phone aside.

"I don't see him," Ted said, driving down the street Frank had turned onto. "We were so close." He slammed his fist on the steering wheel. "Where the heck did he go? All I see up ahead are old warehouses and vacant lots."

"Keep going," Rosie said.

They drove for ten minutes. "Nothing," Ted exclaimed. "I'm guessing he came this way for a reason. He's here somewhere. I'm going to double back and try again."

Minutes passed as Ted retraced his route. "Still nothing," he said. "I'll go this way and hope for the best." He turned right. In the distance loomed barricades and signs that said Local Traffic Only.

Rosie gasped. "Our luck just changed." Her voice rose with enthusiasm. "Quick. Pull over and park. Look up there, a few blocks ahead of us. I don't know where it came from, but it's a black pickup! It's our guy!"

56
Ivy Chen

Saturday, February 25, 2012

Gripping my erhu, I peeked over my shoulder and caught a glimpse of my gray prison shaped like a Quonset hut. I turned back, facing the street. Where was Frank? Was Frank anywhere around here? I turned left and started to jog toward the buildings and the sound of traffic.

I passed by warehouses and storage units surrounded by wire fences. What a desolate sight. Keep Out signs, Beware of the Dog signs, No Loitering signs were posted everywhere. In between the buildings, nothing but barren lots. Not a single person anywhere. There was no one to help me.

My ragged breath caught in my throat. I was already exhausted after just one short block. These three years and four months of confinement left me weaker than I'd realized.

Frank could be returning this way on foot. He could run right into me. I wish I knew which way he had gone.

Willing myself onward, I picked up the pace, but two dogs chased after me. They growled and nipped at my heels. I slowed down and yelled, "Go away!" Fear gripped me, held me paralyzed to the spot. Other dogs barked in the distance behind me. The two dogs turned and raced off toward that direction. The sound of their sharp nails scratching on the pavement echoed along the deserted street.

I jogged onward, but it felt like shards of glass were cutting into my throat with every breath.

Ahead, I saw barricades and a sign that stated Road Closed. Local Traffic Only. That's why there was no traffic here. Frank mentioned barricades and a closed road. This has to be where Frank had come to hide his truck. I looked in all directions, but I didn't see him. I had to get away from this place before he came this way.

I tripped over a brick, got back up, and held the bed sheet and pillowcase tightly so they wouldn't drag on the ground. A truck went by, driving through puddles, and splashed dirty water all over me. I waved frantically to the driver to stop, hoping for a ride, but he kept going.

A bright blue car slowed to a crawl as it approached me. Thank God. The window on the passenger side rolled down.

"Help me, please help me," I cried.

A male voice called out, "Looking for a good time?"

I looked away, ducked my head, and kept walking. Someone in the car whistled several times. They moved on.

One more block. Another block. Finally, I passed by a high prickly hedge on the left. It went all the way to the corner. I kept going and approached the corner. Across the street to the right lay a long stretch of deserted fields, littered with papers. Deserted. That had to be the way Frank went.

In the distance to my right, I saw a man walking, heading in my direction. He plodded along just like Frank. Perspiration ran down my face. My hands trembled. I had to get off this street and out of sight. I couldn't yell for help. Frank would recognize my voice and come after me. If that happened, I couldn't outrun him. I would never get away from him.

To the left where the hedge ended stood a row of several shops, each bearing a hand-painted sign. I hurried toward them. The sign on the closest one said Minna's Café. Before I climbed the steps onto the porch of that café, I looked back. Frank was coming this way, but he wasn't running. He was still plodding along.

He hadn't seen me.

But something must have caught his eye. He stopped in his tracks, looked my way, and shielded his eyes from the sun. He shook his fist. He took off running awkwardly in my direction.

For a moment, I stood perfectly still, doubting this was actually happening. Then I snapped out of it. Frank had seen me. He was gaining speed. Here was my last chance. Sick with fear, I walked across the porch of Minna's Café. Black dots bobbed up and down before my eyes. I felt weak. Too weak to go any further.

57
Rosie and Ted

Saturday, February 25, 2012

"I'm calling Detective DeLuca," Rosie said and pulled out her phone.

"Good. Get right on it," Ted said. "We need the detectives. They're pros. We're amateurs. I'll follow the guy at a safe distance, and we'll see where he goes."

"All I'm getting on the phone is static," Rosie said.

"Give it a minute and try again." The tightness of his voice conveyed fear. "The barricades and traffic signs aren't holding our guy back. He knows this area."

They drove along slowly. The guy turned right at the next corner. "I'm pulling over here," Ted said. "We'll hang back so he doesn't get suspicious. He's slowing down and turning into some kind of abandoned car area. I can't see him now, but if I get any closer, I might spook him."

"That might be where he's keeping Ivy." Rosie tried Detective DeLuca's number again. This time, she got a busy signal.

"Ted, look across the street." She pointed at a long hedge that bordered that side of the street. "Do you see that woman walking along in front of the hedge?"

"Yeah, I see her."

"She's carrying something wrapped in sheets. She's heading toward the café on the corner. Oh, my! Something's poking out of those sheets. It looks like a wooden dragon head!" Rosie's eyes opened wide. "It must be Ivy Chen."

Ted looked over at the woman. "I can't see her face, but—"

"There's a man on foot heading this way toward the woman." She pointed toward the right. "It's our guy. I'm sure of it. Don't even think about taking him on. He'll kill you."

"Do you have a better idea?"

"Yes," Rosie said, frantically trying to come up with an option. "Pull across the street. Go through the break in the hedge, into the driveway behind that café." She squinted at the name on the sign. "Minna's Café. The high hedge is going to help. It will let us get inside the place without Frank seeing us."

58
Rosie and Ivy

Saturday, February 25, 2012

The front door of Minna's Café opened and banged shut, sounding like a clap of thunder. The customers at the counter of the dilapidated building, a man drinking coffee and a woman eating a hamburger, looked up at the sound.

"Lordy, I need to get that door fixed," said Minna, the scrawny woman with sinewy arms who was wiping down the counter.

Ivy Chen stepped inside the café. "Help me. Please call 9-1-1," she said in a raspy voice. "I was kidnapped. I just escaped." She choked on her sobs. "The man, his name is Frank Brandt, is coming after me. He lives near here. Don't let him take me back there. Please help me."

"I'm Minna, the owner. You're safe now," she said, embracing Ivy and peering at the large bruise on the young woman's face. "No one's going to hurt you. Not in my place."

The cook came rushing from the kitchen, wiping his hands on his apron. "What's going on? Who's blubbering?"

"He's going to kill me!" Ivy cried. "He's a monster. He's coming down the street right now."

The back door flew open. Rosie and Ted, their eyes taking in everything all at once, rushed into the café.

"Ivy? Oh, thank God, you're alive!" Rosie threw her arms around Ivy and hugged her.

"She just came in," Minna said. "The poor thing. Look at that bruise on her face. Who would do such a thing?"

"There's a madman chasing her. Lock the door. Pull down the blinds," Rosie yelled.

The customers and cook sprang to action. Ted barricaded the locked door with tables and chairs.

"I know you. You're Rosie Renard," Ivy said as tears streamed down her face. "I've been carrying your business card with me for two years. Frank took it from your shop. Your picture is on the card."

"Yes, I'm Rosie," she said, hardly believing Ivy was right here in front of her, beat up, but alive and talking. "You need to come with us right away."

Ted pushed aside the curtain on the back door and checked to make sure Frank wasn't coming that way.

Rosie turned to Minna. "You, your customers, and your cook don't know Ted and me, but you must trust us and do what we say. Go hide in the back room and bolt the door. Stay there until the police arrive. Go on now. Hurry."

Ivy reached out to Rosie and clung to her. "Please tell the police that Ali Kent is buried in the well on Frank's property. Frank's sister Marta disappeared. She may be in the well too. I don't know. Ali Kent and Marta. Please don't forget those names."

"We'll tell the detectives," Ted assured her.

Heavy footsteps sounded on the front porch. Fists pounded on the door.

"Please come with us, Ivy," Rosie said.

"I'm scared," Ivy said and stood rooted to the spot.

"Your mother is worried about you," Rosie said, desperate to get moving. "She's here in St. Petersburg."

"Mama is here?" Ivy asked. Her entire body trembled. She seemed disoriented.

Ted scooped up Ivy and her erhu and carried them outdoors to his truck while Rosie, who stayed close by his side, on the lookout for trouble, called Detective DeLuca. This time she got through. As fast as possible, she filled him in on everything including the kidnapper's name, Frank Brandt.

"We're just minutes away," DeLuca said. "Get out of there as fast as you can. Is Ivy okay?"

"Yes. She's weak and frail, and she's been beaten. She has bruises on her face and neck, probably many more hidden by her clothing, but she managed to get away from that vicious monster."

"Thank God. Do you need an ambulance?"

"No. We're already pulling away in Ted's truck. It's best we just keep going."

"Okay. I'll alert Officer Randall. She'll pick up Mrs. Chen and meet you at Bayfront Hospital."

"Hurry, Detective," Rosie said. "Minna, two customers, and the cook are hiding in the back room. Frank may break in there any minute now."

"We'll be right there," DeLuca said. He was already filling in Detective Hernandez on everything Rosie had told him when the phone went silent.

"I am sleepy," Ivy said weakly.

"Hush now. Go to sleep," Rosie said and held Ivy so close she felt her heart beating.

"My erhu," Ivy said dreamily.

"Your erhu is safe too, right here with us." Rosie hummed a lullaby she remembered from her childhood. Ivy soon fell into a deep sleep.

59
Detectives Tony DeLuca and Hank Hernandez

Saturday, February 25, 2012

"No sirens, Hank," Tony said. He gripped the wheel of the unmarked car and whipped around the corner. "There are four people inside. We can't afford to send Frank into a frenzy and risk their lives."

The detectives' car roared to a stop in front of Minna's Café.

"There he is, on the porch, banging on the door," Hank said.

Tony clenched his teeth. "He's mine. His reign of terror is coming to an end."

"Let's get him," Hank said.

The doors of their car slammed shut.

Frank turned toward the sound. His eyes filled with fear as he saw two men, guns drawn, wearing bullet-proof vests, rushing toward him.

"Go away," he hollered. "I want what's mine."

"Here's what's yours," Tony said and waved his Glock. "A bullet through the heart if you don't start talking. And another between the eyes if you give us any trouble. Where's the place you kept Ivy Chen?"

"My home. But she's not there. She's waiting inside this café." He smiled. "She's going to put on a farewell concert for me and her."

"Yeah," Hank said. "And my name's Beethoven."

"Tell us where you live," Tony said.

"You can't make me tell you anything."

"My little friend here will do that for me." Tony waved his Glock again. "Now cough up the address."

"Fat chance," Frank said and jumped off the porch. He took off lumbering toward the alley between the café and the neighboring building.

Everything seemed to happen at once. Four officers wearing bullet-proof vests arrived and jumped out of police cars, guns drawn. Two rushed into Minna's Café. Two sprinted toward Tony and Hank.

"Stop!" Tony called after Frank.

"Go to hell," Frank called over his shoulder.

"Stop, or I'll shoot!" Tony shouted.

"I double-dare you!" Frank hollered.

Tony lit down the alley after Frank. He caught up and tackled him, knocking him to the ground.

Hank rushed toward them and jammed his knee in Frank's back, pinning him to the spot. "Try these on for size, you piece of crap," Hank said and cuffed him.

"Don't hurt me," Frank whined.

Tony pulled Frank to his feet. "Give us your address, and don't even think about lying."

Fear darted from Frank's eyes as he rattled off numbers.

"Where exactly is this palace?" Hank asked.

"A few blocks that way." Frank nodded his head toward the warehouses.

"Hustle him into the police car," Tony said to the officers. "Get him out of here, and lock him up."

As the officers carted Frank away, Hank said to Tony, "Come on. Let's make sure everyone in the café is okay."

Ten minutes later, Tony and Hank left Minna's Café after thanking Minna, the cook, and the customers for their cooperation and taking their names and contact information since they were witnesses.

"I hope Ivy's going to make a speedy recovery," Hank said.

"She got away. She's a fighter. She's tough," Tony said with a catch in his throat. "But even so, this is one of those times we should pray."

"Yeah," Hank said. "And this is one of those times I'd like to get Frank alone and knock the crap out of him. Let's see how he likes being on the receiving end of a beating."

"He'll get what he deserves," Tony said.

"Okay, the reinforcements are here, and the SWAT Team's in place," Tony said. "Ambulances are waiting, just in case. Let's go."

The team broke down the front door with a battering ram and stormed into the place. Tony and Hank and several officers followed, charging in with their weapons drawn.

"What a rotten smell!" Hank said.

"Let's move fast," Tony said, grimacing.

"Clear," the team members shouted as they went from room to room, breaking down locked doors, searching everywhere.

The team captain said, "There's no one here. Let's check the back yard. Ivy told Rosie the missing woman, Ali Kent, might be in a well out there."

"Tony, put up with the smell for another minute and check out the paintings on the wall," Hank said. His eyes were filled with admiration. "Ali Kent painted them. They aren't signed, but remember how other artists talked about her love of nature and her talent? They are right there in front of us."

"So is her suffering," Tony said, noticing the stark contrast between the first delicate paintings and the strident, garish final paintings in the group. "There's something I'll never understand. Why does someone end up like Frank with no heart and no soul?"

"There but for the grace of God go you and I," Hank said.

Tony patted Hank on the shoulder. "Amen, partner," he said, and opened the door to the back yard.

In thoughtful silence, Tony and Hank headed into the desolate yard. A short distance away, they stood by the ordinary field stones that circled the well.

"Is it just me?" Tony asked, "Or do those stones look like a necklace?"

"Somebody placed them like that," Hank said. "Maybe someone who cared about her?"

Tony cocked an eyebrow. "Are you thinking Frank was caught up in some strange kind of love for Ali Kent?"

"Who knows? And honestly, who cares? He doesn't deserve our interest. He deserves the death penalty and a quick trip to Hell."

"You're right," Tony said. "He's a sick monster. We'll know soon enough how sick he is. As soon as we finish here, we'll have the pleasure of interrogating him."

"I'm looking forward," Hank said. "Let's put every detail in the right place and build an airtight case. What do you think? Our usual good-cop bad-cop routine?"

"For Frank Brandt, we can make an exception," Tony said. "This time, it's bad cop and really bad cop."

60
At the hospital

Saturday, February 25, 2012

Mrs. Chen fussed over Ivy as the team of doctors stood around Ivy's bedside and shared their opinions about her medical condition. "She will recover, but it's going to take time"..."She has several cracked ribs that we taped"..."She's dehydrated and malnourished"... "For now she should have as few visitors as possible"... "She needs to preserve what little strength she has"... "She's been through a traumatic ordeal. Don't expect her to be the same person she was when you last saw her."

As the doctors left, Ivy pulled herself up to a sitting position, looking very tired and pale. She breathed in the fresh air and peered at the vases of flowers that had already arrived from close friends and family.

"Here are the cards that came with the flowers," Mrs. Chen said and placed them on Ivy's night stand. "You can read them and think good thoughts about the people who love you. The florists said more flowers will be arriving soon because news about you has spread. So many people are happy for you, Ivy," Mrs. Chen smiled, "but especially me. You've been the light of my life since the day you were born."

Mrs. Chen fluffed Ivy's pillow and smoothed her hair. "I should let you rest now. You've been through so much. I'll go back to the waiting room and sit with Rosie while you sleep. She insisted on staying with me until your aunties arrive."

"Mama, before you go, I must ask you something," Ivy said shyly and cast her eyes downward. "Do you remember the violinist named Vince that I mentioned to you?"

"Of course. I talked to him on the phone when Detective DeLuca re-opened the investigation."

"Do you remember that I said we had seen each other several times?"

"Yes, I remember."

"I was just wondering if he shared any, you know, personal information with you. Like, did he marry while I was gone?"

"No. He's not married."

Ivy smiled. "I would like to see him."

"How about tomorrow?"

"Mama, why are you teasing me? I would like to see him today."

Mrs. Chen smiled at her only child. "He's in the waiting room with Rosie. I called him after I saw you with my own eyes and knew that our prayers had been answered. He is desperate to see you. I told him you were exhausted, but he said he had to see you. So I said to myself, 'let's see what Ivy has to say.' Now at the mention of his name, I see your beautiful smile, that smile I thought I might never see again. Shall I tell him to come see you?"

"Yes, Mama, please. Tell him to come here right now."

"He will be so happy," Mrs. Chen said and smiled.

Two minutes later Mrs. Chen returned. Vince followed her into the room holding a bouquet of red roses and walked quickly to Ivy's bed.

"I'll be back later," Mrs. Chen said and slipped out of the room with a wave of her hand to Ivy and Vince. Lost in each other's eyes, they hardly noticed.

"Ivy?" Vince asked. He set the flowers on the bedside table.

"Vince, is that really you?" Ivy sat up and tried to cover the bruises on her face.

"Just stay quiet," he said, reaching for her hand and kissing her tenderly on the cheek. "I know I should have waited until you were rested, but I just had to see you and tell you I've missed you. I thought about you every day."

"I feel the same way about you," Ivy said. "We had something so sweet, so special, but now everything has changed."

Vince sat down on the edge of the bed. His dark eyes shone like pools beneath a moonlit sky. "For me, nothing has changed. I loved you then. I love you now. I never stopped loving you and praying for your return. I wish I had told you back then how much I loved you. I always told myself I would tell you tomorrow, and then tomorrow came and you disappeared from my life, taken from me." His shoulders heaved as he took several deep calming breaths. "But here we are together. Everything I'd hoped for is coming true."

"I thought you might forget about me and marry that cellist," Ivy said.

He shook his head and gave her a bewildered look. "What cellist?"

"I forget her name."

"There's no one else for me, only you," Vince said. "I've been thinking about you and waiting for you for so long."

"I thought about you all the time too," Ivy said. "I closed my eyes, and I could see your face. I remembered your words. I could picture the café where we sat, the sidewalk along the docks of the marina where we walked in the moonlight. I missed you so much."

Vince laced his fingers through Ivy's. "I missed you more than I can say right now. I'm still too overwhelmed. All I can think about now is that we can pick up where we left off…and move forward. That's what I want more than anything in this world."

Ivy nodded her head. "I want that too."

Vince kissed her fingertips, one by one. "You have a wonderful life ahead of you. Many people care about you and are cheering you on."

"And you, Vince? Are you part of the wonderful life that is coming my way?"

He kissed her gently on the lips. "A big part, that's what I'm hoping for."

Ted had left the hospital and gone back to work, and Rosie stayed with Mrs. Chen in the waiting room. They talked and talked as they gave Ivy and Vince time alone together.

"I'm not so sure Ivy will be able to trust anyone again, except for family members and friends," Mrs. Chen said. "She'll be cautious and fearful around everyone else."

Her tears spilled onto her cheeks. "I'm worried she'll never be the joyful confident daughter I used to know. That monster Frank Brandt took all that away from her."

"Let's be optimistic," Rosie said. "Let's imagine her becoming more like her old self, growing stronger and more confident every day."

"That's what the doctors said too." Mrs. Chen sniffled. "I'll wait until later to tell Ivy that her beloved Baba passed away. It's too much for her to bear at this time. For now, let her have these moments of happiness with Vince. Later, I'll tell her what her father would have said if he were here. He would say, 'Frank Brandt is evil, but he is one person. There are many good people to make up for him.' He would talk about balance and harmony, and Ivy would take courage from him and come around quickly. He had ways of making things happen. Good things. Wonderful things."

"May I see her again?" Rosie asked. "I feel so close to her even though she never saw me until today. I was amazed Ivy knew who I was from the old photo on my business card. I would stay a few minutes, just to wish her the very best."

"Of course you can see her. She wants to talk to you. She knows, of course, that you and Ted came to the café and got her away from Frank. I've told her you're the one who called in the police when you found her belongings in a footlocker."

"That seems like a hundred years ago," Rosie said, "and at the time that footlocker seemed so ordinary. I never could have guessed what treasures were inside it or what a tale those treasures would tell."

Mrs. Chen patted Rosie's arm. "Let's go peek in on Ivy and Vince." The corners of her mouth turned up in a slight smile. "Love is shining in their eyes."

"I'm so happy for them," Rosie said.

♫♫

"Here we are," Mrs. Chen said and gently cracked open the door.

Rosie looked past Mrs. Chen and saw Ivy wearing a hospital gown, lying in bed. Ivy was sound asleep beneath a sheet and blanket that covered her frail body. She was facing the window where the sun streamed into the room and brightened the dozens of vases of colorful flowers. Vince was lying next to Ivy, on top of the blanket, his tie loosened, his jacket hanging over the back of the chair where Ivy's erhu rested. He was sound asleep too. His arm was draped across Ivy's shoulder. His fingers were laced through hers.

"They missed each other," Mrs. Chen said. "I have a feeling Vince may be better for her than any medicine the doctors prescribe."

"This is so sweet," Rosie said, choking up. Ivy and Vince would share a happy future. She was sure of it.

"They look like angels," Mrs. Chen said, and tears of joy rolled down her cheeks. She inched the door shut.

In the hallway, she turned to Rosie, "Detectives DeLuca and Hernandez called me earlier. They wished Ivy a speedy recovery and a wonderful life. I thanked them for never giving up on my Ivy. I want to thank you too, Rosie. As the detectives said, you got the ball rolling, but you did more than that. You kept it rolling right up until Ivy was out of that horrible prison where he kept her. You wouldn't give up. You brought my Rosie back to me. My arms have ached to hold her for these three long years. Thank you, Rosie. You are the answer to this mother's prayers."

"You give me too much credit," Rosie said. "Ivy is a very courageous young woman. She set herself free."

"Well, regardless of who did what, we have a happy ending."

"Yes," Rosie said. "Everybody loves a happy ending, and today that's what all of us are enjoying."

Rosie and Mrs. Chen walked arm in arm down the hallway to the front door of the hospital. Mrs. Chen said, "When we first met, I asked you why you were doing so much to help my Ivy since you had never met her. You said there was a reason, and you would tell me at another time. Why not now?"

"It's a story about my cousin Tess, but it can wait," Rosie said. "I have a feeling we'll be seeing each other from time to time, maybe even in my apartment. A pot of tea, some treats, and a good heart-to-heart."

"I'd like that," Mrs. Chen said and hugged Rosie.

As Rosie stepped outside into the sunlight, she pulled out her phone and called Jack. Pick up, pick up, she told herself. Finally, he came on the line. "Jack, it's Rosie." She couldn't stop her tears. "I just wanted to let you know Ivy is safe. She got away from Frank and made it to a café. Ted and I got her away from there and drove her to the hospital. I've seen her. She'll need time to recover, but she'll be okay."

"This is great news," Jack said. "You helped save her. You can take consolation in that."

"You helped too, insisting from the very beginning that we get involved, that it would enable us to come to grips with our past and what happened to Tess. You were absolutely right. So let me give you your words right back. You can take consolation in that."

"Thanks, Rosie." His words caught in his throat. "I'm going to the hospital to see if I can meet Ivy. We'll talk later. I'm sure there will be lots to say."

"I'm looking forward to that," she said. Maybe they could put the past to rest and work on the future. Guilt was a tough nut to crack, but it could be done. If escaping from a flesh-and-blood monster could happen, maybe guilt could be conquered too.

The world looks brighter already, she told herself. The sun beat down on the sidewalk. The sky seemed so blue, the clouds so puffy, the day so beautiful.

61
Rosie Renard

Saturday, February 25, 2012

Rosie gave the taxi driver directions to her shop and climbed into the back seat. She sighed her relief that Ivy was recovering and would one day be facing a future she wanted. It might be marriage to Vince, a concert career, or even anonymity. The choice was hers. Being imprisoned for more than three years might change her hopes and dreams, at least until she had time to process everything that had happened to her. But Ivy had taken her erhu with her during her difficult escape. That hinted at her return to the world of classical music. And with Vince, a celebrated classical musician in his own right, by her side, well, that was up to them. Rosie closed her eyes and let the day's events roll over her like the waves in the harbor.

She pulled out her phone and called Ted.

"Can we get together this evening?" she asked before he even said hello. "There's something I want to tell you."

"Give me a hint," Ted said.

"I don't want to ruin the surprise."

"I'll pick you up at seven. How does that sound?"

"Wonderful."

"Where are you?" he asked.

"I just left the hospital. I'm on my way home."

"How's Ivy?"

"Weak, but from what Mrs. Chen told me, I predict a speedy recovery, at least physically. Her emotional recovery could take much longer. Vince is with her now. What a sweet reunion they're having. It's a happy ending for them."

"I'm glad," Ted said, "and I'm pretty sure I know what's been going through your mind. I wish your cousin Tess had survived her abduction. I wish your family and Jack's family had enjoyed a happy ending, but don't forget what Detective DeLuca said. You owe it to Tess to make a good life for yourself, to grab happiness when you can."

"Well, you just spoiled my surprise. That's what I wanted to tell you. I want to give us a chance. Ivy came through this, and she didn't give up on her love for Vince, so I asked myself why should I shut you out? I'm learning a thing or two from their sweet love."

"I like the sound of what I'm hearing," Ted said.

"I love you, Ted."

"I love you too, Rosie."

"See you tonight."

Rosie leaned back in the seat and felt the tension leave her neck and shoulders. Years of carrying the guilt and blame of Tess's abduction and death had worn down her emotions, but she could change. She wanted to change.

She pulled out her phone to check in with Rocco and Alonso, her father-and-son helpers. They had gone to an estate sale in the Old Southeast area of St. Pete on her behalf because she wanted to be at the hospital with Mrs. Chen. There was a message from Rocco: "There was a lot to choose from. I grabbed what I know you like. Alonso added things. Everything's at your shop. Jane helped us decide what to put in the holding area and what to set aside in the workroom. She's like you, bossing us around, but she still has a long way to go. Ha-ha."

"Here you are," the taxi driver said, pulling up to her shop. He turned to face her. "I know who you are. You're Rosie Renard. Your face is all over the news. Good work, young lady."

"Thank you," Rosie said. "Make sure you thank the detectives and officers who worked the investigation. They are amazing."

Rosie paid the taxi driver and walked toward her shop. She was glad to be home. Once inside, she opened the doors to her workroom and holding area. Truckloads of treasures were waiting for her. It was like a child's Christmas morning with all the presents spread beneath the tree. She went straight to the workroom where a very unusual item—a black lacquer daily-life trunk—caught her eye. That Rocco. What a sweetheart. He'd left the trunk right in the middle of the room where she couldn't miss it. Jane had probably told him to put it there.

Rosie dropped to her knees and rested her hands on the lid of this extremely rare find. She had never come across one until now. A key was taped to the lid. She ran her fingertips across the lid, feeling the warmth of the wood, and peeled off the key. Holding it in the palm of her hand, she studied its long blade and the bow with an intricate etched design of an unfamiliar creature. Maybe a sea creature? Possibly from mythology? Or a pirate legend? She couldn't wait to dive into the research, but that would have to wait.

She rubbed the key between her hands and let her mind wander. What treasure would she discover today in this trunk? What story would it reveal? Would it be a happy story? And what was the significance of the design on the key? Those questions rolled through her mind as she inserted the key into the keyway.

"Life is full of surprises," she said aloud. Without waiting a minute more, she turned the key.

About the Author

Diane Sawyer grew up in Greenport, Long Island. She graduated from SUNY at Albany, Seton Hall University, and Fordham University, where she received a Ph.D. She now resides in St. Petersburg, Florida, with her husband, Robert. Her short stories have won awards. Her novels have been published internationally. She is a frequent guest speaker at writing groups and workshops.

The Tell-Tale Treasure is Diane's first novel for SYP, Southern Yellow Pine Publishing. Others will soon follow. Her five previous novels—*The Montauk Mystery*, *The Montauk Steps*, *The Tomoka Mystery*, *The Cinderella Murders*, and *The Treasures of Montauk Cove*—were published originally in hardcover by Avalon, then in paperback by World Wide Mysteries, and recently in hardcover, paperback, and e-book by Thomas & Mercer, the mystery division of Amazon.

When not writing, Diane volunteers as a docent at the Dalí Museum. She also serves as Secretary of the Friends of the South Community Library in St. Petersburg. Diane loves fitness, adventure traveling, meeting people, and spending time with her family.

www.ingramcontent.com/pod-product-compliance
Lightning Source LLC
Chambersburg PA
CBHW020935260626
47169CB00006B/1738